Praise for *John Satur*

'A fascinating crash course in seventeenth-century cookery' Justine Jordan, *Guardian* Books of the Year

'This is perhaps the most visceral, the most claustrophobic, the most intensely sensuous kitchen since that of Mervyn Peake's *Gormenghast*. We enjoy the romance and intrigue, but we read on for the cooking' *Times Literary Supplement*

'Scrumptious foodie tale of a low-born master cook and his survival' Boyd Tonkin, *Independent* Books of the Year

'There's a mythic quality to Lawrence Norfolk's fourth historical novel … it skillfully entangles folklore and foodlore' *Observer*

'This book is a feast, a groaning table laden with delicious and carefully made sweets' *Independent*

'I was salivating at the descriptions of the food … It's a wonderful book' Mariella Frostrup, BBC Radio 4 'Open Book'

'An enthralling tale of an orphan kitchen boy turned master of culinary arts, with sumptuous recipes and intoxicatingly gorgeous illustrations' *Vanity Fair*

'A fabulous novel. It does what he has always done, which is wrap you totally into a world; utterly convincingly into that world … extremely, extremely moving' Alex Preston, BBC Radio 4 'Saturday Review'

'As vivid as it is mouth-watering … This glorious, multilayered banquet of a book is clever and finely wrought, and the prose, steeped in the arcane language of seventeenth-century cuisine, brings it vividly and sensually to life' *Metro*

'Norfolk is more than just an author of page-turners ... He mixes a fast-moving plot and rich characters with deeper themes' *Sydney Morning Herald*

'Shimmering with wonder, suffused with an intense and infectious appreciation for the gifts of bountiful nature, *John Saturnall's Feast* is a banquet for the senses and a treat for anyone who relishes masterful storytelling' *Washington Post*

'Norfolk is an intriguing storyteller. And if only one word could be used to describe his tale it would be intense. Norfolk's skill with words puts the reader on his protagonist's shoulder to experience the joys and pains he experiences; to taste the mouth-watering delicacies he creates; to ache for the love he loses, the enemies he bests, and the friends he carries with him throughout his life' *New York Journal of Books*

'Start with a love story, add a measure of seventeenth-century history, a dollop of ancient myth and religion, a dash of civil war, a pinch of arrogant aristocracy and a cornucopia of recipes. The result is a cookbook of sorts, one that exudes atmosphere from every page. The food – the outrageous, astonishing recipes – is authentic and captivating and the kitchen is alive in every pot and bowl. Delicious' *Herald Sun*

'All the ingredients are here to delight the taste-buds and pleasure the senses of the reader' *Die Welt*

'A masterful portrait of the time' Margarete von Scharzkopf, *Norddeutscher Rundfunk*

'A literary delicacy' *Madame*

'A book, and a banquet for the senses' *Bunte*

LAWRENCE NORFOLK is the bestselling author of *Lemprière's Dictionary*, *The Pope's Rhinoceros* and *In the Shape of a Boar*, three literary historical novels which have been translated into twenty-four languages. He is the winner of the Somerset Maugham Award and the Budapest Festival Prize for Literature, and his work has been short-listed for the IMPAC Prize, the James Tait Black Memorial Award and the Wingate/Jewish Quarterly Prize for Literature. He lives in London with his wife and two sons.

John Saturnall's Feast

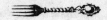

LAWRENCE NORFOLK

B L O O M S B U R Y
LONDON · NEW DELHI · NEW YORK · SYDNEY

First published in Great Britain 2012
This paperback edition published 2013

Copyright © 2012 by Lawrence Norfolk

The moral right of the author has been asserted

Bloomsbury Publishing, London, New Delhi, New York and Sydney

50 Bedford Square, London WC1B 3DP

A CIP catalogue record for this book is available from the British Library

ISBN 978 1 4088 3116 8
10 9 8 7 6 5 4 3

Typeset by Hewer Text UK Ltd, Edinburgh
Printed in Great Britain by CPI Group (UK) Ltd, Croydon CR0 4YY

www.bloomsbury.com/lawrencenorfolk

For Lucas and Joseph

From *The Book of John Saturnall*, with the *Particulars* of that famous *Cook's* most *Privy Arts*, including the *Receipts* for his notorious *Feast*. Printed in the Year of Our Lord, Sixteen Hundred and Eighty-one

ow Saturnus created the first Garden and when, this humble Cook does not pretend to know. Nor the Name writ over its Gates, be it Paradise or Eden. But every green Thing grew in that ancient Plantation. Palm Trees gave Dates and Honey flowed from the Hives. Grapes swelled on the Vine and every Creature thrived. There the first Men and Women sat together in Amity and no Man was Master or Slave. At Saturnus's Table did every Adam serve his Eve and in his Garden they did exchange their Affections. For there they kept the Saturnall Feast.

Now Saturnus's Gardens are overgrown. Our brokeback Age has forgotten the Dishes that graced the old God's chestnut-wood Tables. In these new-restored Times, Inkhorn Cooks prate of their Inventions and Alchemical Cooks turn Cod Roes into Peas. My own rude Dishes stumble after such Dainties like the Mule that limps behind the Packhorse Train, braying at his Betters. Yet as one who marched through the late Wars falls exhausted into the succeeding Peace, I set my last Table here.

For this late-born Adam would plant a new Garden in these Pages and serve up Words for Fruits. Here would he offer Receipts for his Dishes, enough to make the old God's Boards groan again. Now let my own Feast begin as that Original did when the first Men and Women did fill their Cups. Let the Saturnall Feast begin with Spiced wine.

To prepare that ancient *Hippocras* which is vulgarly known as *Spiced Wine*

From the first Garden's Fruits was this ancient Cup prepared, Dates and Honey and Grapes and more, as I shall tell. In a great Cauldron pour a Quart of White Wine and set it over a low fire until the Wine shivers. Add to it eight Quarts of Virgin Honey, not pressed from the Comb but sieved. If the Decoction boils, settle it with cold Wine. Leave to cool then heat again and skim. This will be done a Second Time and a Third until the King's Face on a Penny Coin may be seen plain on the Bottom.

Shuck the Flesh of Dates and soften them to a Paste with Wine. Roast the Stones before a Fire and give them to the Mixture. Add to it the Sweet Leaf called Folium, Ground Pepper as much as a Woman at Prayer might hold between her Palms and a Pinch of Saffron from the Crocus Flowers. Pour on these just above two Gallons of Wine or until the Liquor's Thickness will bear an Egg that you might see its Shell swimming above to the size of a Hazelnut Shell. Next tie up Cloves and Mace in a Lawn-bag or a Hippocras Sack, as more learned Cooks do term it. Let it steep in the Liquor . . .

THE PACKHORSES CREPT DOWN the valley. Swept by waves of fine grey rain, the distant beasts lurched under pack-chests and sacks. At their head, a tall figure leaned into the drizzle as if pulling them away from the dark village above. Standing beside the wooden bridge at the bottom, a long-faced young man peered out from under his hat's dripping brim and grinned.

Water seeped through the seams in Benjamin Martin's boots. Rain soaked his cloak. In the pack at his feet sat the load which he had contracted to deliver to the Manor. He had been on the road for almost a week. This morning the whole Vale had still lain ahead of his blistered feet. Then he had spied the packhorse train.

Ben's grin stretched his face like the yawn of a surly horse. He flexed his aching shoulders.

Behind the driver came a piebald, then a bay, then two dark brown ponies. But Ben's gaze was fixed on the rear. A mule trailed behind the others. A mule that appeared to carry nothing more than a pile of rain-soaked rags. Even an unladen beast had to eat, Ben told himself. The driver would be glad of his business. He glanced up the slope again to the village.

No lights showed among the cottages. No smoke rose from the chimneys. Nothing moved on the slopes that climbed to the dark trees far above. No one knew what had happened, the Flitwick men had said the previous night at the inn. Not a soul had been up to Buckland all winter.

It was none of his business, he told himself. When the packhorses got down he would make his bargain with the driver. The mysterious parcel could share a ride with the wet rags on the mule. It could get to the Manor without him. To this 'Master Scovell', whoever he was. The village, the Vale, the Manor at the far end: all shared the name of Buckland. Like a common curse, Ben thought. His eyes scanned the soot-streaked church then rose to the wood. He nudged the hated pack with his foot.

The beasts passed a row of split-oak palings. The cold rain seeped up his boots to his breeches. Ben's thoughts turned to Soughton and the warm back room at the Dog at Night. Tonight he would be on his way back. Master Fessler would take him, he was sure. He would never set eyes on this place again.

Three long loping strides took the driver down the last steep bank. The piebald mare teetered after, the two pack-chests swaying on her back. Joshua Palewick, they had called the lean grey-haired man at the Flitwick inn. Next came the bay horse, laden the same. The two ponies were loaded with panniers and sacks. Last of all the mule which carried only a bundle of rags and limped. Ben drew himself up. The only thing a packhorse man drove harder than his horses was a bargain, he reminded himself. A penny a mile was fair for a limping mule. The animals splashed through the puddles and mud. He raised a hand in greeting. Then, on the mule's back, the bundle of rags stirred.

A gust of wind, Ben told himself. Or a freak of the failing light. But the next moment showed him it was not so. Out of the rags rose a head. Out of the head stared a pair of eyes. The rags contained a boy.

Sharp cheekbones jutted from his face. His hair was a mat of soaked black curls. A sodden blue coat was draped over the rest of him. Hunched awkwardly over the back of the mule, the young rider

4

slipped and slid as if he were about to fall. But there was no danger of that, Ben saw as the mule drew closer. Thick cords encircled his wrists. The boy was tied to the saddle.

The driver stopped.

'Ben Martin,' Ben said in a casual tone. 'Got a load going to Buckland Manor. For a man by the name of Scovell.'

'I know Richard Scovell,' Joshua Palewick said. His eyes narrowed. 'And I know you. You were at the inn back in Flitwick.'

Ben nodded. Behind the driver, the boy watched from the mule, the rain dripping from his dark eyebrows and into his eyes. Unable to wipe the drops away, he grimaced and blinked. His gaze seemed to look through the two men.

'Put it on with him,' Ben suggested. 'Penny a mile's fair. The road's not so bad . . .'

'Ain't it now?' Josh raised an eyebrow. 'S'pose I must've imagined it. These last thirty years.'

Ben forced a grin. 'Penny and a half,' he offered.

Joshua Palewick shook his head. 'The boy gets the ride to himself. Agreed it with the priest.'

A sinking feeling grew in Ben's gut. 'I'll pay more,' he blurted out. But Josh's expression hardened.

'Not to me,' the driver said shortly. 'I shook on it.'

He pulled on the rein and the horses set off. The boy's thin body jolted this way and that. Hooves clopped over the bridge as the beasts ambled away.

Ben's spirits tumbled. He would throw the parcel in the stream, he resolved. Say he'd never seen it. No one would know except Palewick. And the boy, whoever he was. And this Scovell, if Palewick told him. And the dark-faced man who had hired him back in Soughton. The Moor or Jew or whatever he was. Almery . . .

The Dog's warm back room was disappearing with Josh's horses. He should never have left Soughton. Never have found himself soaked, with blistered feet on a rainswept bridge at the head of the Vale of Buckland. Suddenly Ben snatched up the straps of the pack and slung its bulk over his shoulder.

'Wait!' he shouted through the rain. He stumbled over the planks. Joshua Palewick turned, his face closed.

'I don't know the road,' Ben confessed.

'I figured.'

'I never set foot here before.'

The older man looked Ben over. Then it was as if some baleful influence lifted. As if the dark village with its soot-streaked church were already distant and Buckland Manor were close. As if the length of the Vale were a mere stroll. The ghost of a smile flickered over the driver's face.

'I saw you from up there in the village,' Josh said. 'Thought you was waiting for a ride in one of them Soughton chairs. You from up that way, ain't you?'

Ben admitted that he was.

'We'll walk aways if you like,' said the driver. 'See if we can stand each other.'

Ben nodded eagerly then the older man glanced back to the boy. 'That one's going to the Manor, same as that parcel of yours. You keep an eye on him for me. All right?'

Both men looked back. Balanced on the mule, the boy had twisted about. Ben Martin followed his gaze, past the village and up the overgrown slopes, all the way to the dark wall of trees at the top.

'That's where they caught him,' Josh said. 'Buccla's Wood.'

6

They were running as hard as they could, out of the hut and across the dark meadow, John's heart thudding in his chest, fear churning his guts. Beside him, his mother's hand gripped the heavy bag in one hand and his wrist in the other, the long grass whipping their legs as they scrambled for the safety of the slopes. Behind them, the mob's chant grew more strident.

> *Honey from the Hive! Grapes from the Vine!*
> *Come out, our Witch! Come drink your Wine!*

Oily-smelling tallow-smoke laced the warm night air. The banging of pots and pans mixed with the villagers' shouts. John felt his mother's hand tighten, pulling him along. He heard the bag knock awkwardly against her legs, the breath rasp in her throat. His own heart pounded. Reaching the edge of the meadow they clawed their way up the first bank.

Terraces cut long shallow steps in the slope. They climbed then ran then climbed again. The noise of the mob pursued them in waves, rising and falling. With each step, John's fear abated a little. Soon ghostly banks of furze and scrub rose around them, the night air heavy with grassy scents. John looked up. The trees of Buccla's Wood loomed.

The villagers never came up here. Old Buccla had witched the whole Vale with her Feast, they said. Until Saint Clodock came and chopped up her chestnut-wood tables. Ever since, once a year, they served her a feast in return. To keep her off.

That was tonight.

His mother climbed on, striding confidently through the narrow gaps and breaks. John hurried behind. The bag clutched in her hand held the book she had snatched from the lintel over the fireplace in the moments before their flight. He slipped past the thorny fronds,

7

edging through the thicket. Soon the path narrowed then came to an end, the bramble thickets forming an impenetrable barrier. Before an old wooden paling with a cross carved upon it, his mother halted.

He had never climbed this high before. Beyond the thicket of thorns loomed the trees of Buccla's Wood. He heard the heavy crowns of the chestnuts shifting, the leaves rustling in a thousand dry whispers. Far below, the mob's chant drifted up.

> *A Pigeon from the Perch and a Blackbird by,*
> *Come out, our Witch! Come eat your Pie!*

'It's just the Ale,' his mother said. She looked down into his worried face. 'When they've drained the barrel they look for their sport.'

John remembered the other times: red yelling faces, half-drunk men and their barking dogs. Himself clinging to his mother's skirts. She had always faced them down before. But tonight the chant had gained a new harshness.

'They came up from Marpot's house,' he told his mother.

'Did they?'

He stared at her. She knew it as well as he did. They had gathered to pray for little Mary Starling's soul. Then they had marched up to the meadow. Now they surrounded the hut and chanted.

> *Fish from the Canal! Eels from the Jub!*
> *Come out, our Witch . . .*

Out of the sea of flame-red faces, a black-suited figure climbed onto the thatch. John heard his mother's breath catch in her throat as if her cough were about to return. A burning torch was clutched in the man's hand. He waved it and the crowd roared louder. John saw his mother's hands fly to her mouth.

'No,' she murmured. 'They wouldn't dare.'

Every wave of the torch brought it nearer the thatch. Everything they owned was in the hut, John thought. The straw mattress, the chest, his mother's pots and bottles and jars . . . But then a shock of white hair appeared at the edge of the mob. John pulled at his mother's skirt.

'Look, Ma! It's Old Holy.'

Relief flooded through him as the priest strode into the midst of the villagers. From high above, John watched the man's arms wave, his hands cuffing at the nearest heads. The torch-bearer jumped down off the roof. The chanters fell back. The torches began to drift away.

'That'll teach 'em,' John declared.

'Will it?' his mother murmured.

She lowered the bag with the book to the ground. John felt her hand stroke his hair, her fingers untangling the thick black locks. He looked up at the dark line of trees and breathed in slowly, smelling wild garlic, mulched leaves, a fox den somewhere and a sweeter scent. Fruit blossom, he thought. Then that small mystery was eclipsed by a larger one. A stranger scent hid among the blossom, sweet and resinous at once. Lilies, John thought, drawing the scent deeper. Lilies mixed with pitch.

'What're you sniffing at now?' his mother asked with a smile.

He smiled back. He had a demon in his throat, she said. A demon who knew every smell in Creation. Breathing in the sharp saps and sweet blossoms, he felt them anchor themselves within him, their invisible trails fanning out around him. But here was a smell his demon had never met before. He looked up at the trees of Buccla's Wood.

'I don't know,' he confessed at last. His mother swept her long dark hair back from her face.

'Don't tell them you came up here, John. Understand?'

9

He nodded. Of course he understood. Saint Clodock had sworn an oath to God, so the old story went. He had marched out of Zoyland and come up here to chop up the witch's tables. He had taken the fires from her hearths and torn up her gardens. He had taken back the Vale for God.

But Buccla was still up there, the villagers said. Her and her Witch's Feast. And she was still hungry . . .

It was just an old story, John believed. The villagers' chanting was just their sport. Then Warden Marpot had come, waving torches and goading them on. Now Father Hole had seen them off. The thought of the old priest cuffing their heads made him grin. Below, the last torch-bearers were trudging away. When none remained, his mother turned to him.

'We'll go to church every week,' she said. 'I'll wear a bonnet like the rest of the women.' She attempted a smile. 'You can play with the other children.'

John, John, the Witch's Son!
Duck him and prick him and make him run!

It was their sport after the Sunday lesson. The moment Old Holy's last 'Amen' sounded, John was out and through the door, scrambling over the wall of Saint Clodock's churchyard then running as fast as his legs would carry him.

John, John, the Blackamoor's Son!
Paint his Face and pull out his Tongue!

Two summers had passed since the flight up the slope. He was taller and stronger than the child who had scrambled up the terraces to Buccla's Wood. But so were his pursuers.

Ephraim Clough led the pack as usual. Dando Candling and Tobit Drury followed close behind with Abel Starling and Seth Dare. The girls skipped along at the back and shrieked. John sprinted past the old well, over the bare patches of Saint Clod's Tears then around the pond, scattering ducks and setting the Fentons' geese honking. The villagers drawing water glanced up then shook their heads in disapproval. Susan Sandall's boy was causing trouble again.

He sped across the green, arms pumping, heart pounding. As he passed the Chaffinges' orchard, Tom Hob yelled at John's pursuers. But no one listened to Tom. Past the fruit trees, the back lane yawned, a high-hedged tunnel of shade. As John sprinted for the mouth, something cracked against his skull. Hot pain billowed from the back of his head. A missile from Abel, he thought. Buckland's champion stone-thrower.

He stumbled and a cheer rose behind. But a moment later he regained his stride. His feet hammered the ground. His pursuers began to fall back.

The first time he had tried to play they had lured him down to the Huxtables' barn where the muck heap was waiting. How had he been so foolish as to tumble in, his mother had asked? The week after that Ephraim and Tobit tried to throw him into the brambles. Witches didn't bleed, Ephraim had declared. Their sons were made of the same stuff. He had scrambled free that time but the next Sunday they had dangled him over the old well and Ephraim had raised a bucket of the water, threatening to pour the dark red liquid down his throat. The sour smell wrapped itself around his face like a wet winding sheet. *You fancy a cup of witch's blood, John?* The witch had poisoned the ground under the green, so Warden Marpot preached. That was why the water stank. Tobit and Ephraim had tried to prise open his mouth. Only Tom Hob had saved him that day, striding forward with his wooden mug raised and driving them off with a volley of curses. Every Sunday after that, John ran.

Now his head throbbed. He felt the swelling rise as he climbed the stile into Two-acre Field. A dead rook usually hung on the scarecrow but today the gibbet was bare. He smelt freshly turned earth in the warm spring air. The lane was silent. His pursuers appeared to have given up.

The girls were always the first to abandon the chase: Meg and Maggie Riverett, the Clough sisters, Peggy Rawley, Abel Starling's sister Cassie. The boys kept going for longer, Ephraim dividing them into packs to cut him off from the safety of his mother's hut.

John trotted around the edge of the field. On the far side, he heard spring-water splash into the old stone trough. He had a secret way through the hedge. Soon he would be up the bank, in the meadow and home. Safe for another week. He looked around once more then pushed through the bushes.

'Took your time, John.'

They were waiting for him on the other side. Ephraim Clough eyed him from the centre of the path, heavy-browed and half a head taller than John. White-haired Dando Candling and Tobit Drury flanked him. Seth Dare and Abel Starling stood back. John looked from one broad face to the next.

'How's your ma, Witch-boy?' Ephraim demanded. 'Still dancing around her pot?'

Ephraim was the worst. The one who led the others in the chants of 'Witch-boy' and chased hardest when John fled. The one who John, in his angry fantasies, found himself punching, over and over. Now the usual sick feeling churned John's stomach. His limbs felt heavy. Ephraim swaggered closer and pushed his thick-browed face into John's. It always began like this.

'You don't belong here,' Ephraim told him. 'You and your ma.'

John willed himself not to flinch. 'Don't we?'

'My pa says. You shouldn't never have come back.'

Puzzlement joined his fear. Come back? He had never been further than the village. Ephraim eyed him, waiting. John smelt sweat rising out of the boy's dark clothes. But a fouler smell hung in the warm air. Behind him, Tobit held a sack. Ephraim's arm flashed up. The boy's knuckles smacked the side of John's face, the sting of the blow spreading over his cheek. He felt his head jolt back and tried to throw a punch back. Ephraim swatted it aside and laughed. He was grabbed from behind and then he was fighting them all, struggling hopelessly. Just like all the other times. They wrestled him down. Ephraim gripped his wrists while Tobit forced the sack over his head.

'New test for you, John,' announced Ephraim.

'Old test, more like!' exclaimed Tobit.

He heard them laugh again. It was hot in the sack, the coarse cloth itchy on his face.

'Go on,' urged Ephraim. 'Give him his Witch's Feast.'

The string was loosened. John felt something being shoved inside. Suddenly the stench of rotting meat filled his nose. Feathers rubbed against his face. The rook from the scarecrow, John realised. He gagged and tried to twist away. But they had him fast. He felt something soft smear his face.

'Good and ripe, that one!' he heard Seth shout. A hand pressed the carcass closer.

'A Witch's Feast'll give you a fever,' Ephraim declared. 'You got a fever yet, John?'

John bucked and struggled. But there was no escape.

'Next it makes you puke,' Ephraim went on. 'You puke till you bring up your soul.'

'He don't like it,' Seth called out.

'He ain't got nothing to wash it down with,' answered Tobit.

' "Honey from the Hives, Grapes from the Vine," ' Ephraim sang out. 'Here it comes, Witch-boy, my special spiced wine . . .'

'You look where you aim,' John heard Tobit warn. An instant later the first hot splash hit.

John struggled harder but Tobit only pulled the sack tighter. Suddenly John got a hand free and lashed out blindly. His fist hit flesh and Tobit's grip loosened. John pulled off the bag.

Ephraim stood with his black breeches half down, his Sunday shirt pulled up, an arc of urine shooting out of him. Tobit rubbed his cheek, a scowl on his face. Abel was backing away. Run, John thought. But as he turned to rise, a dark shape filled his vision. An instant later, Dando's boot caught him under the chin.

He felt a gristly crunch. A clot seemed to swell and plug his windpipe. John dropped to his knees and clutched his neck, choking. He retched and a gout of blood spilled from his mouth. The boys fell silent.

'I told you we shouldn't do it,' hissed Abel. 'Now you've killed him.'

'You did it too,' retorted Dando.

'Sir William'll hang us.' Tobit sounded scared.

'He won't know,' Ephraim told the others. 'Grab the bag, Abe. Come on. Run!'

Their footsteps thudded down the path. John lay on the ground, hot shame coursing through him. Ephraim was right, he told himself. Or his grim-faced father. They didn't belong. They should never have come back . . . He would not go to church next week, he told himself. No matter what his mother said. He would run away. Run to wherever they had come back from.

Blood trickled down his throat, tasting metallic and hot. He swallowed hard and felt the air flow thickly into his lungs. He crawled to the long stone trough and looked in.

His skin was darker than the other boys'. His hair was black and curly where theirs was red or brown or fair. His eyes were as dark as his mother's. Or his father's, he reminded himself. Whoever that was. He splashed cold water over his head and scrubbed. He spat and watched the long red filaments drip from his mouth. As he felt inside his mouth, a high clear voice sounded above.

'Witches don't bleed.'

A girl looked down from the top of the bank, her freckled face framed by a white cotton bonnet. Startled, John looked up into the blue eyes of Abel Starling's sister Cassie.

'I'm not a witch,' he managed.

'I know that.'

She was a year older than him. She sang loudly in church in a high clear voice. She attended Warden Marpot's Sunday lessons. That was all he knew. But now Cassie Starling was talking to him. To his horror, John found himself blinking back tears.

'Come up here,' the girl commanded.

John climbed. At the top, the meadow's rank grass stretched away. To the right a stand of beeches grew. Ahead, the terraces rose in great blunt steps. Tall weeds and bushes choked the lower slopes. Dense scrub and furze barricaded those above. At the top, bramble thickets formed a thick cordon before Buccla's Wood. The girl regarded John.

'Grass is how the wicked spring up. Old Holy said, remember?'

John nodded. It was one of the priest's favourite texts. The girl pursed her lips and regarded John. A strand of her hair had come loose.

'Can you count?'

She wound the stray blonde strand around her finger. John nodded again.

'Good,' the girl said and pointed to a tussock. 'Sit there.'

A minute later, John reached out a tentative hand to Cassie's face. 'One,' he said.

'Go on.'

'Two, three, four . . .'

He could smell Cassie's hair and the wool of her dress. Her breath smelt of strawberries. His heart thudded as the girl wound and unwound the long blonde strand. The nail was bruised black, he saw.

'. . . twenty-nine, thirty . . .'

He was counting her freckles. He worked up one cheek, across her forehead and down the other. Cassie giggled then blinked as he dabbed around her eyes. The scents from the meadow-grasses laced the air between them. When he reached her white cotton bonnet, she pulled out the long pin and shook out her hair. He continued around her mouth.

'. . . forty-eight, forty-nine . . .'

As he approached her lips, she caught hold of his finger, her hand quicker than he would have guessed. Her grip stronger. The bruise under her fingernail darkened.

'You know what freckles are?'

He shook his head.

'They're sins.'

Cassie was half-touched, Abel said once. Had been ever since their little sister died. That was Mary Starling. Above the trees, a curl of

16

smoke rose into the cloudless sky. His mother would be waiting, he remembered.

'The first witch was Eve,' Cassie said. 'God sent her to test Adam. When she gave him the apple. He sent us a witch too.'

John thought of the wood, the air drifting out smelling of fruit blossom. 'But there ain't no witch, is there?' he said. 'Saint Clod saw to her, didn't he?'

'A witch don't look any different from you or me,' Cassie answered. 'Not on the outside.'

'Then how d'you see her?'

'God'll open your eyes. If you're chosen. The witch can't fool God. Don't matter where she hides.' Suddenly she leaned closer. He felt her warm breath in his ear. 'You go up there, don't you?'

She glanced up and John followed her gaze. Together they looked up the slope, all the way to the dark line of trees at the top.

'You can't,' he said. 'It's all brambles.'

'Thorns don't bother a witch,' Cassie answered. 'They don't bleed, remember?'

This was Marpot's preaching, he knew. When she wasn't singing psalms, Cassie knelt in the Warden's house with the Lessoners.

'I was praying up here,' she said. She looked over at the beech trees then smiled at John. 'I knew you'd come.'

John stared back. 'Me? How?'

'God told me.'

Cassie smiled then rose to her feet and hitched up her dress, poised for the run down the bank. John looked up at her bruised knees and bare white legs.

'You're staring.'

He felt his cheeks redden.

'You want to know?' she asked. 'Want to know what God said?'

He looked up hopefully.

'Next week,' Cassie told him. 'You wait for me after church.'

The scents of wilting leaves drifted in the hut's warm fug. John's mother looked up as he slipped through the doorway, her face red in the glow from the smouldering fire. Hung on its chain in the hearth, the blackened cauldron steamed.

'Took the long way home, did you?' she asked.

John nodded and scurried past. The bump on his head had not hurt while he sat before Cassie. Now it throbbed painfully and his throat felt raw. He took his place across from the fire and gazed about the hut. In the far corner their chest sat beside the straw palliasse where they slept. On the other side his mother's bottles were arrayed. Pots and pans hung around the hearth. On the shelf above, a large leather-bound book was propped open.

John knew the pages from stolen glimpses: the drawings of fruits, trees, flowers, roots and leaves, the blocks of forbidding-looking writing. That was as close as he was permitted. She put it away when the women came calling. Now, at John's glance, she reached to close the covers.

She had been up the slope, he knew. Her bulging collecting bag leaned against the wall. He breathed in carefully and smelled the fruits of her latest labours: fresh elder, henbane, dead-nettle and redwort . . . All familiar. But another smell filtered through the coarse mesh of the sacking, teasing him with a flowery scent. Absent-mindedly, he reached back to touch the bump on his head.

'They beat you again, didn't they?'

She always knew. He looked up to find her staring then shook his head mutely, bracing himself for the interrogation. But as he squirmed under her gaze, a fat plume of smoke billowed up and his mother began to cough. She covered her mouth to protect the liquor in the cauldron and leaned with one arm braced against the hearth while the spasms racked her frame. John snatched up the jug and hurried outside.

She was past thirty years. 'Mother Susan' was how the night-time callers at the hut called her. Or 'Goodwoman Susan' when the rear-pew women roused her from sleep. They had used to call in the daytime, handing over their penny loaves for her remedies, offering measures of barley if she would dispense her advice or a grimy coin if she threw on her cloak and followed them. She took promises if they had nothing better. Now they crept up the path after dusk with their offerings and tapped softly on the door. He watched the anxious faces enter. Then the hushed talk began: of aches and bleedings and crampings, waters breaking or not, babies turning or twisting, cauls too thin or too thick, or torn, or lost in the women's labyrinthine bodies.

They blessed her when her potions eased their labour-pangs. Or when her hands held up a wailing infant. They sent her back with collops of dried bacon or lengths of dimity from which his mother made his clothes. But they crossed themselves too, John knew. Behind her back they called her different names. She roamed the village at night with her covered basket, they told their children. She'd tie a noose round their guts with her stringy black hair. Mother Susan brought them into life, they said. But Ridder Sue could make them disappear. Like a witch.

John dipped the jug in the trough behind the hut and hurried back. His mother drank. When the coughing fit calmed, she reached for her bag. John watched her pull out a handful of thick green stems and snap them with a twist of her wrists. The tang of fresh elder sap cut through the smoke.

19

Newly cut branches kept away flies, John knew. Boiled, their liquor loosened the bowels. Judas hanged himself from an elder, Old Holy had told them in one of his lessons. And the sticks made blow-guns. You had to poke out the pith.

John's mother dropped shoots into the kettle set within the cauldron, took a ladle and stirred, her ladle drawing slow figure-of-eights in the steaming liquid. A measure of water followed and a little of the liquor from one of her jars.

It took the blink of an eye to taint a liquor, she had taught him. Snapping a root too short or boiling it too long; a pinch too little or a peck too much; gathering bulbs beneath a waning moon or on the wrong days in the year. The liquid in her kettle would be strained and cooled then mixed or left pure. Then she would pour it off to join the stoppered jars which stood in neat rows beside the chest: her decoctions, simples, liquors and potions.

Moonlight was glowing through the window-cloths by the time his mother shook the drips off her ladle and reached for their supper-pan. From the Starling cottage below, Jake and Mercy's arguing voices drifted up. The back log shifted and sparks flew up the chimney. Sitting against the wall, John waited for the waft of smells to curl from the pot. As his mother lifted the lid, a puff of steam rolled up and broke against the rough underside of the thatch. She looked over with a smile. It was their game.

'Mutton,' he said. 'Barley. An apple. Some lemon thyme. Bay . . .'

He had only to breathe in to know the names. When he had finished, she leaned across to ruffle his hair. As her fingers brushed the bruise, he winced. She frowned then drew him close, her fingers feeling gently around the swelling.

'John,' she soothed him. 'My boy. It's just their sport.'

They were the words she always spoke, cradling his head or

combing his hair with her fingers. Her whispers curled about his ears like riddles. Like the wisps of steam from her kettle that twisted up, stretching and dissipating into nothing. But John remembered the stink in the sack. Dando's kick. Abel Starling could bounce rocks off his head till his hair turned grey, his mother would still be murmuring in his ear. Suddenly his impatience flashed into anger. He pulled away.

'We don't belong here,' he said.

'Belong?'

'We should never have come back.'

His mother's eyes narrowed. 'Who told you that?'

'Ephraim Clough.'

'What does he know?' his mother retorted. 'This is our home. Everything we have is here.'

'And what's that?' he demanded, looking around the hut's narrow walls. 'What do we have?'

A reproachful look from his mother. Silence would follow, he knew. That was how all their disputes ended. They turned to nothing like the steam from her kettle . . . But now he saw her brow furrow.

'More than you know,' she said. To his surprise, she got to her feet, walked to the hearth and reached up. When she turned, she had the book in her hands. She set it on the chest and eyed him across the heavy slab. 'Open it.'

Was it a trick, he wondered? Some new riddle to bewilder him? As he lifted the leather-bound cover, the musty smell of paper rose up. He turned the first mottled leaf and looked down at an elaborately drawn image. A brimming goblet was decorated with curling vines and bunches of grapes. But instead of wine or water, the cup was filled with words.

John stared at the alien symbols. He could not read. Around the goblet a strange garden grew. Honeycombs dripped and flowers like crocuses sprouted among thick-trunked trees. Vines draped themselves about their branches which bristled with leaves and bent under heavy bunches of fruit. In the far background John spied a roof with a tall chimney. His mother settled beside him.

'Palm trees,' she said. 'These are dates. Honey came from the hives and saffron from these flowers. Grapes swelled on the vine . . .'

She spoke half to herself as if she were reciting words learnt long ago, her fingers skipping from the faded symbols to the images of plants and fruits. Then she turned the page.

It might have been a different book. The ink was bolder and the paper less mottled. Here were the palm trees again, and the crocuses and vines, but with all their cousins too. Flowers that John knew from the meadow sprang up beside bushes whose fruit he had never seen before. Creeping plants coiled like serpents amid monstrosities which surely had never existed in nature. Yet every vein of every leaf or petal was picked out as if drawn from life. Every stem was labelled with tiny spiky letters. More such pages followed. Then the ancient book returned with its faded ink. This time a forest of birds rose from the mottled paper.

'These pages were written long ago,' his mother said, looking down at the trunks and branches. 'Written and rewritten. Long before you and me.'

'What are they?' John asked, looking among the trees.

'Each page was a garden. Every fruit grew there.'

Kettle-steam, he thought again as his mother fell silent. But then the images drew him in. Birds flew or roosted amid the branches: plovers, larks and doves together with others that John could not name. They carried words in their beaks, fluttering up out of their treetop garden. The building featured again, larger now but obscured by the trunks of the trees. The chimney peeked over the top. His mother turned and the bolder pages resumed. They seemed to have been added later to illustrate the ancient ones, for these showed birds from great eagles to fig-peckers. John turned to a river with fishes jumping in and out of the water. Each scale held a word, the lines leaping from body to body. The building rose on the far bank. The next was a seashore teeming with tiny scuttling crabs. Now he could see that the building was grander: a hall with high arched windows. The chimney was a great tower. Orchards of cherries, apples and pears followed, the trees all laid out in a criss-cross pattern. There were the high arched windows and chimney again. Almost a palace, John thought. Who lived there?

A strange plantation passed before John's eyes. At the back of his throat his demon stirred as if he might smell the scents of the blossom or taste the fruits. Every plant and creature imaginable was here, he thought, the real and fanciful crowded together. But the wisps of steam still rose from her kettle. The strange gardens no more told him why he and his mother belonged in Buckland than the grass in the meadow outside. John felt his defiance evaporate, replaced by bafflement.

'I don't understand,' he confessed at last.

His mother smiled.

'I'll teach you.'

It was all but dark when the driver turned the piebald mare off the road. Josh and Ben tramped through a meadow to a broken-down barn. A ramp of earth led into the croft. Joshua hitched up the horses. Then he came to the mule. On its back, the boy lolled to one side.

'I told you to keep an eye on him,' the driver told Ben sharply. 'Now look.'

The boy was shivering. Joshua untied the bindings about his wrists and ankles then eased him off the animal's back. He collapsed on the floor.

'I thought you meant he'd run away,' Ben Martin offered awkwardly.

'How's he going to do that?' Josh snapped, chafing warmth into the boy's hands. 'Ain't got nowhere to run, has he? Come on, get hold of his feet.'

The boy struggled weakly as Josh stripped off the sodden coat. They worked on his shivering limbs then pulled a wool coverlet from one of the sacks. The boy seemed indifferent to these attentions, neither helping nor hindering. He was thinner even than he had appeared on the mule, his ribs and collarbone jutting out. His face betrayed no reaction as Josh wrapped him in the blanket.

While the driver brushed down the horses, Ben Martin foraged for wood. The parcel's strange odour wafted up. Out of the corner of his eye he saw the boy's head turn.

'You know this smell?' Ben asked.

The strange odour had hung about him since the back room of the Dog at Night the week before. Like pitch but sweet, even wrapped in oilcloth and sealed with wax. Almery had heaved the parcel onto the table.

Buckland Manor, the dark-faced man had told him in his strange accent. Carriage to Richard Scovell. Master Cook to Sir William Fremantle himself, the man had added with a grin. Nine shillings had seemed a good price at the time.

Before that night he had carried nothing heavier than the ledger-books of Master Samuel Fessler, wool-factor, who was Ben's late employer. He had never set foot in the Vale of Buckland. He had never been so far as the Levels. But Ben had nodded to the dark-skinned man in the warm back room. The next morning he had shouldered the strange-smelling pack and set out for the Vale.

The boy looked away. The fire crackled and Josh cut a loaf into three. The men watched the boy rip hunks off his share and cram them into his mouth, chewing and gulping with a grim determination.

'Where's his folks?' Ben Martin asked.

'Ain't got none.'

Josh recalled the trudge through the silent village, Father Hole's six half-flagon bottles clanking dully in their straw-lined panniers.

'They don't dare show their faces,' the priest had growled as he limped up the green from the smoke-stained church. A long rip in his cassock had been stitched with wool. A scar above his eye pulsed an angry red. They walked up the back lane where the priest called a wild-eyed man out of a white-painted cottage. Jake Starling led the priest, the driver and the mule up to the roofless hut. There the boy squatted in a sea of mud and filth.

Jake waded in then tied him to the mule. The blue coat was draped over his back. Father Hole had given his instructions then pulled a thin packet from his tattered robe and handed it to Josh.

'The priest wrote a letter,' the driver told Ben Martin now. 'Left it open too. Not that it'd do the likes of me any good.'

Ben Martin looked at the letter. He thought of the dark village with its deserted green, the silence in the Flitwick inn when he had mentioned Buckland. His world was the back room of the Dog at Night. Not this Vale of Buckland. Not the village, or a boy tied to the back of a mule. None of this was his business. He was a fool.

'I can read,' he told Joshua Palewick.

'*Annunciation Day, the Year of Our Lord Sixteen Hundred and Thirty-two*

'*To Sir William Fremantle, Lord of the Vale of Buckland, from his Servant the Reverend Christopher Hole, Vicar of the Church of Saint Clodock in the Village of Buckland*

'*My lord, the Wicked spring up like Grass and the Virtuous man stands like a Palm Tree. Just so have we in the Village of Buckland served as a Garrison of the Faithful since Saint Clodock swore his Oath and marched on the Witch with his Torch and Axe. Now I write to beg your lordship to stand Guard over one of our own, a Boy christened here John Sandall.*'

The firelight flickered. The letter was written in a loose running hand and it had been some time since Benjamin Martin had read so many words in a row. Josh listened and nodded from time to time but the boy only stared into the flames. The letter might have described people who were unknown to him, or a distant country that he had quit long ago.

'*Sire, I beg your lordship to take in this Boy. None here will care for him and the People here shun him, being fearful of their own past Acts. For an evil Presence moved among us here at Buckland this Summer past. Then many young Souls were struck down, enduring great Sufferings before the Lord would receive them. Neither did that Evil neglect their Elders, who descended into Division, nor their Priest who committed two Sins of Omission. For he did not see the wicked Blades of Grass spring up, nor did he recognise the Viper which slithered in Disguise through the Garden and infected all here with its Poison. Now the people will not look upon the Boy's Face for his very Features do reproach them for their Viciousness. Therefore I do consign him to your lordship's Care . . .*'

Ben's voice sounded unfamiliar to him in the dark barn. The animals shifted and snorted. Josh nodded to himself at Father Hole's account as if the boy's expulsion confirmed some long-held suspicion. The boy himself hugged his knees and watched the fire, his face betraying no expression. But as Ben settled himself on his blanket, he thought on Father Hole's words, wondering at the 'Viper' and the 'wicked Blades of Grass' and listening to the rain drip through the rotted thatch. At last he fell asleep.

The bang of the door awoke him. Josh was up. Outside the sun shone down and the wet grass steamed. The packhorses ambled out of the croft and picked their way over the waterlogged turf. The limping mule followed. The boy emerged on shaky legs, his damp coat hanging from his shoulders. As Ben hauled his heavy pack across the ground, Josh looked over.

'You can put your gear on the horses,' the driver said gruffly. 'Bit here. Bit there. Won't hurt none.'

A surprised Ben pulled the bedroll out of his pack.

'And maybe you can do something for me,' added Josh.

Pack-men's bargains, thought Ben. 'What's that?' he asked.

'See him?' Josh pointed. 'Won't talk, will he?'

The boy stood beside the mule, raking his scalp with his nails. He was crawling with lice, Josh had noticed last night. Father Hole's letter was all very well but the boy's arrival would hardly set the chapel bells ringing at the Manor. Or Mister Pouncey clapping his hands for joy. A useless mouth was bad enough. A lousy useless mouth was worse. But a lousy, useless and mute mouth . . .

'Get his tongue wagging,' Josh told Ben. 'Get him talking, understand?'

Ben flexed his shoulders and felt the welts from the straps of his pack. How hard could talking be? He handed up his bedroll. The oilcloth parcel followed with its curious smell. Josh packed both then picked his way around the puddles to where the mule pulled up mouthfuls of grass. The boy watched him warily, rubbing his wrists where the cords had chafed. Josh looked at the sunken cheeks and thin limbs wrapped in the blue coat.

'You ain't going to run away, are you, John Sandall?'

The boy gave the merest shake of his head. *The wicked Blades of Grass*, thought Ben. What had the priest meant?

'We're going to Buckland Manor,' Josh continued. 'You know where that is? Sir William's going to take you in.'

The boy pulled the blue coat around him and looked back up the valley.

'You can't go back,' Josh said quietly. 'You can't do nothing about what happened.'

God had been missing for forty-three years. A little old man in a long blue smock bent double beneath an enormous sack, he had vanished in an explosion of glittering splinters. A moment later Saint Clodock had followed, sung to his destruction with a toneless psalm by the Geneva-cloaked ruffians who had marched into the church with their stones, their long poles, their whitewash and brooms. The windows of Saint Clodock's had been bare ever since.

That had been Father Hole's first Easter in the parish. Now, sweating, swaying, his white hair waving, the priest climbed the creaking steps to his pulpit and wondered why the crash of glass should resound in his memory on this unremarkable Sunday morning. Why, after the reigns of a queen, two kings and the seating of six Bishops of Carrboro, should God's disappearance trouble him now? Resting his hands on the smooth rail he surveyed his congregation, seeking an answer in the upturned faces. From the ancient pews below, his parishioners stared back.

The wealthiest yeomen sat at the front, the Cloughs, the Huxtables, the Sutons and the respectable side of the Chaffinge family. The pews behind them were reserved for the Parkisons and Fentons, then the Drurys, the other Chaffinges and the Riveretts. Behind them, in the free pews, sat everyone else. They wore their best bonnets and dresses, their cleanest boots, stockings and breeches. They gaped at him and breathed through their mouths against the faint smell of decay from underfoot. The Starlings and Dares were ignoring each other this morning, Father Hole noted. Tom Hob swayed a little, his mouth open wide enough to catch flies. In front of him sat Maddy Oddbone, newly dismissed from her place in service, her swollen belly brazenly on display. Ginny Lambe had a fresh bruise on her face and Elijah Huxtable sported eyes even redder than his nose. In the corner, Susan Sandall sat upright in the back pew. Her boy, normally motionless and silent, seemed unable to stop fidgeting. At the back of the church stood his black-garbed warden, his heavy face surmounted by a full head of long blond hair and punctuated by two unblinking blue eyes.

That was it. That was why he remembered, realised Father Hole, swallowing the sprig of spearmint in his mouth. Timothy Marpot's eyes. It was their certainty. Their absolute absence of doubt. The black-cloaked window-breakers had possessed the same look.

But no zealot would wear his luxuriant blond hair so long, thought Father Hole. Nor work so selflessly for his parish. For Marpot would preach the sermon whenever Father Hole was indisposed, continuing long after the sands in the glass had run down, according to the reports of Gideon Stevens. He even led lessons in his cottage for the men and women of the parish, just as the Bishop had encouraged. No, Timothy Marpot's arrival in the parish was a boon. A godsend, he had told his new warden at their Audit Dinner. As he carved slices from the cheeks of the calf's head, a beatific smile had spread over the man's face as if some long-deferred prayer had been answered.

A loud cough from Gideon recalled him. Father Hole glanced at his chosen verse, turned his mottled face to his congregation and upended his hourglass.

'The wicked spring up like grass,' he announced to the parishioners of Saint Clodock's. 'But the virtuous man stands like a palm tree.'

The text was one of his favourites. Wickednesses were many, Father Hole explained. Happily the single trunk of virtue rose above, starving them of sunlight and rain. That was the palm tree. Evil withered, he remembered telling himself, hunched over the table in his parlour while the Zoyland zealots bellowed in his church. Untended, the grass of wickedness shrivelled and died. The chanting had stopped. It was over, he had told himself. Then the crash of the glass battered his ears. So he had sat with the long brown bottle, alone like the palm tree, waiting . . .

And he had been right. By the time the Constable and his men had been fetched from Carrboro, Brother Zoilus and his black-cloaked men had moved on. To the hamlets up on the Spines. Or out onto the marshes of the Levels. To the dank chapels of Zoyland. Brother Zoilus had made his last appearance bursting from the crowd after Mass in Carrboro Abbey. Bible raised in righteous anger, he had used it to break the Bishop's nose. In return, his lordship had cut off the man's hand.

'Thus the wicked decrease,' Father Hole told his congregation as the last grains of sand in his hourglass trickled down. 'They are turned to chaff. God blows them away. Such is the fate of the wicked.'

He led the prayers for the King, then Sir William at the Manor. He watched the men and women rise from their pews. His thoughts turned to the parlour and the bottle in the cupboard. He would wait until sunset, he resolved. This was the Lord's Day after all. A chorus of coughs, sniffs, mutterings and scrapings was rising in the nave.

At the door he offered blessings and examined his charges. The bruise on Ginny Lambe's face prompted a warning look to John Lambe. The bulge in Maddy Oddbone's belly provoked a glare and a shake of the head. Tom Hob was treated to a rap from his own wooden tankard, dangling from a string around his waist. The smell of stale cider from Elijah Huxtable prompted Father Hole to lay a hand on the man's arm.

'The new well's near two years old, Elijah. Have you tried its waters?'

'Well-water's for children and horses, Father,' the man muttered. Father Hole exchanged glances with Elijah's brother Leo as the others shuffled past. The older man shrugged.

He was their shepherd, thought Father Hole. They were his sheep. Like sheep, they mostly wandered where they wanted. At last only the children were left. Father Hole led them in and had them sit cross-legged on the floor. He held up a lump of chalk.

'Who will draw a palm tree?'

They looked at him open-mouthed: Tobit Drury and Seth Dare, Dando Candling whose hair was whiter than his own, Cassie and Abel Starling, the Chaffinge children, Peggy Rawley who always clutched a doll, the Fenton girls and all the others. He smiled down at them. He liked to ask them odd questions. Even startle them. God could disappear, he told them once. He could vanish like ice in a puddle. Like glass in a window.

'Come now,' he cajoled. 'Who will draw?'

Father Hole waved the chalk before the stolid faces. In his mind's eye, he saw the trunk rise, the great branches curving down like scythe-blades. Then, from the back, came a voice he could not recall hearing rise above a murmur before.

31

'I will.'

John rose to his feet, his heart thudding in his chest. He had barely heard a word of the sermon. He had fidgeted through the prayers. All week, Cassie's challenge had loomed in his thoughts. *You wait for me after church.* Now he edged past the other children. The cloying odour of decay hung in the air. One of the Huxtables had been buried the month before last in one of the lairstalls under the floor. The same smell had risen out of the old well, thought John. The wet winding-sheet smell. But why should a well smell of bodies? He took the chalk from Father Hole and drew the arc of the palm tree's trunk. He willed his hand not to shake as long-leaved branches sprayed out of the top and dropped to the ground.

'Yes,' Father Hole said when he had finished. 'That is how God fashioned the palm tree.'

John picked his way back through the cross-legged children. Ephraim was whispering to Tobit. Seth kept giving John looks. He glanced over at Cassie. He had been watching the white-bonneted girl all through the service, her words echoing in his head. *You want to know? You wait* . . . Father Hole was telling them how the palm tree's shade at once shielded the weak as well as starving the grass of sunlight. John waited for the lesson's end, part of him urging it on, another part hoping the priest would talk for ever.

At last they were dismissed. The children surged out, John at their head as always. But this time, at the gate, he stopped. At the sight of him, the little ones stared. Cassie emerged with Tobit, Seth and Abel. A scowling Ephraim followed with Dando. John stood his ground. Then he saw Tobit's heavy brow crease. Dando's eyes narrowed. He had been wrong, John thought suddenly. Cassie's challenge was a trick. He was a fool. They would fall upon him. But the boys looked at one another. Tobit stepped forward.

'We thought you were dead,' Tobit blurted out.

'There was blood all over,' added Seth.

'Cassie said you stopped breathing,' Dando told him. 'But she prayed and you came back.'

John stared, not trusting himself to glance at the girl. But as the children turned between himself and Cassie, a sceptical voice sounded.

'That so, Cassie?' Ephraim asked. 'You prayed him to life?'

Cassie turned a guileless gaze on the older boy. 'You doubting me, Ephraim?'

'You prayed for the son of a witch?'

Ephraim looked about at the other children, seeking their support.

'For Witch-boy?' He appealed.

But no one moved. No one raised a hand against John. A scowl darkened Ephraim's heavy-browed face.

'You take me for a fool,' he spat. 'But Ephraim Clough's no fool. Warden Marpot knows that.'

Cassie favoured Ephraim with her most radiant smile.

'God chooses his messenger,' she said. 'That's what Brother Timothy told me.'

The dark-suited boy shook his head but the little ones were already edging forward, crowding around John as if a fierce animal had wandered down from the hillside and begun tamely nibbling the grass on the green.

'Is it true your ma charms snakes?' Peggy Rawley asked, clutching her doll.

'Was your pa really a pirate?' demanded the youngest Riverett.

'Or a blackamoor?' added an undaunted Bab Fenton in her whiny voice.

Then they were all around him, jabbering and questioning. John stood in their midst, nodding or shaking his head, a bubble of happiness swelling inside him, growing and growing until he feared it might burst.

'So who turned the water in the old well sour?' asked one of the Suton girls.

'That was Marpot, moving in next door to it,' said Seth.

Cassie shook her head disapprovingly and Ephraim's scowl returned but the other children laughed. Then Seth took out his cap, threw it high in the air and looked across their heads.

'You playing then?'

It took a moment for John to understand. Then Abel added his voice.

'Well, John?'

He played drop-cap and catch on the green then fives with Seth's ball against the back of the church. He ran races around the pond and played hide-and-seek among the trees of the Chaffinge orchard. When the shadows from the well lengthened, he walked up the back lane with Cassie and Abel and it felt as if his feet barely brushed the ground. He floated over the stile and the clods of Two-acre Field. As they rounded the far corner, Cassie reached down and picked a pebble from the soil. She took out a purse embroidered with crosses and put the pebble inside.

'That was good what you said,' John said shyly.

'What was that?'

'About praying for me.'

'I did pray for you, John.' She gave him a smile. 'You want to know what God said?'

John nodded.

'He said you'd help me.'

'Help you how?'

'He said you'd help me find the witch,' said Cassie.

'What witch?'

'The witch that took our Mary. Up there.'

Cassie looked up, above the hedge that marked the edge of the field, all the way up the slope to the dark line of trees at the top. But before John could ask more, the clanging of Marpot's hand-bell came from the direction of the green. Abel trudged up, his boots crumbling the clods.

'Brother Timothy's calling,' he told his sister with a grin. 'Don't want to keep him waiting do you, Cass?'

Cassie gave her brother a pitying look then turned without another word. The boys watched her run off across the field, her brown wool dress flapping about her legs. Abel turned to John.

'She tell you she talks to God?'

'She said she prayed,' John said awkwardly.

Abel snorted then shucked off his blue coat. Picking up a stone, he weighed it in his hand.

'You know how to throw?'

John shook his head.

'Want to learn?'

'This was a garden once,' John's mother told him. 'A long time ago. Everything a body could need grew here.'

The dew soaked their legs, their limbs casting long shadows in the early morning sun. His mother carried the book in her arms. The promised lessons had begun.

'Whose garden?' John asked, looking up the slopes to the wood. 'Buccla's?'

His mother shook her head. 'There was no Buccla.'

'But the witch . . .'

35

'There was no witch.'

'But people say . . .'

'People say lots of things. I knew a man once, he could say what he wanted in every tongue under the sun. None of them were true. Come on.'

They climbed until the trees in Joan Chaffinge's orchard looked like sprigs of clover. Beside the stocks, the animal-pound seemed hardly big enough for an ant. Tiny cottages and houses fringed the wedge of the green where the old well stood like a thimble. Around it the bare patches of Saint Clodock's Tears pocked the grass. Across from Old Holy's house, people waited by the new well with their buckets and churns. Behind them, a row of beech trees screened Marpot's house and the Huxtable barn at the back. His mother opened the book.

'Look here. Foxglove.' Her finger circled a cluster of trumpet-like forms then pointed to a nearby stalk of purple bell-flowers. 'Foxglove's for the heart. This one beside it, that's lady's bedstraw. Good for cuts. Here's tansy, and juniper, and rue. There's meadow saffron. That's for gout. Self-heal flower soothes burns. Loose-strife calms oxen. You drape it on their horns, so people say. Do you believe that, John?'

He smiled and shook his head.

'That's right. Now look how it's written . . .'

They sat together high on the slopes, heads bent over the pages while her finger traced the alien shapes, her soft voice sounding them out and making him repeat them.

'See? It's not so hard.'

As their expeditions multiplied, his mother's herbal became his horn-book where he learned his letters, matching names to the pictures in its pages. His schoolroom was the overgrown slopes. There roots and stems hoisted their bright pennants while the book's black lines broke out in a hundred shades of green.

John scrambled up and down the terraces and banks, hunting out the secret breaks in the thickets or crawling through hollows woven from sharp-spined stems. Blackberries lured him into sun-pricked chambers. Old byways closed and new ones opened, drifts of nettles surging forward then dying back. The sun beat down until the grass on the green parched. But on the high slopes the rank stems sprang up as lush as ever. Springs ran beneath the turf, his mother told him. Enough water to fill a river.

Together they pulled peppery watercress from the edges of marshy puddles and grubbed up tiny sweet carrots, dark purple under the dusty earth. Clover petals yielded honey-beads and jellylike mallow seeds savoured of nuts. Tiny strawberries sheltered under ragged leaves and sweet blackberries swelled behind palisades of finger-pricking thorns. John licked the blood-red juice off his hands, his demon savouring the taste.

'The gum from these will take away any pain,' his mother told him in a high meadow of poppies. 'You mix it in a draught. Just a little, mind. People dream themselves mad.'

Cow parsley was just as dangerous. 'Tug any harder on that,' his mother told him, 'and one of us'll drop down dead.'

John snatched back his hand but his mother began laughing. 'Don't pull up any mandrakes either,' she wheezed. 'Or wish too hard on any four-leaved clovers. Don't believe every old story you hear.'

She meant the witch, he knew. But his mind went back to Ephraim Clough's claim and wherever they might have been before the village. For behind that question John sensed another mystery. A face whose features never resolved. He had asked her only once who his father was. Her reply had been given so bitterly he had never dared ask again. I never knew, she had told him. He couldn't speak his own name without lying . . .

Each day they climbed higher. The ridge of the Spines looped in from the west, the hillsides dotted with sheep. From the foot of the hills, the marshlands of the Levels stretched south and west. Zoyland Tor rose among distant peat-fire plumes and flat pastures cut by the long channels of the rhines.

Christ stopped at Zoyland, Father Hole had told them once. He planted a thorn with Joseph of Arimathea. Now herds of wild buffalo grazed the marshes. So Jasper Riverett said. The Romans had left them behind. To the south, the Vale of Buckland stretched away, dotted with villages which followed the meanders of the river. The higher John climbed, the further he saw until, reaching the banks of thorns, he and his mother looked out over the whole Vale.

John had never seen so far or imagined there was so far to see. His eye followed the river's wide meanders until they narrowed then thinned to a silver thread. In the furthest distance, a ridge rose and a tiny gatehouse broke the tree-line. Then, framed between the squat turrets, he spied a greater structure.

A great house seemed to break through the verdure and stretch two wings like a vast stone bird struggling free of the earth. Tiers of windows rose to a bristling plateau where domes and little towers jostled with cupolas and spires or dropped to invisible courtyards. Behind it rose a taller tower, its steeply raked roof pointing up like a blade. A church steeple, thought John. He turned to his mother.

'What's that?' he asked.

'Buckland Manor,' she said shortly.

'Where Sir William lives?'

'I reckon he must. No one's seen him outside it in eleven years.'

Eleven years, marvelled John. His entire life. 'Never?'

'Aren't many who've seen him inside either. He forbids his servants to look at him. So I heard.'

John looked out again at the house, his gaze fluttering over the ledges and eaves as if he might catch a glimpse of the elusive Sir William. But there were so many distant windows and tiny roofs. Another mystery, he thought. Like the book. Like the names of the plants. Like Cassie.

There she was, far below, her bright white bonnet in the meadow, crossing to disappear inside the beech copse. Then another movement caught his eye. In Two-acre Field, a tiny figure let fly invisible stones at the Huxtables' scarecrow. John grinned. The mysteries vanished. Buckland's Champion Stone-thrower was practising again.

They practised together now. Every Sunday after church he and Abel stood together beside the new well and aimed stones at the old one. They threw their missiles along fast flat arcs to hit the tumbledown walls with a crack or lobbed up pebbles, trying to land them in the old bucket.

'You keep your elbow high,' the blond-haired boy instructed John. 'Give your wrist a flick at the end. Like this.'

He held John's arm at the required angle. Sitting on the parched grass behind them, Cassie called the misses and hits, mocking or encouraging as the mood took her. 'You aiming at the church, John? Or was that one meant for Flitwick?'

John flushed under the girl's taunts and praise. Abel rolled his eyes. From the old well rose the wet winding-sheet smell he remembered, as if their assaults disturbed the dark water below. When the sun rose higher, they moved into the shade and took Saint Clodock's Tears for their targets, lobbing up missiles to land on the bare patches of earth. John gathered stones and stole glances at Cassie who pulled off her bonnet or flapped her brown dress to cool her legs.

They threw until their arms ached then joined Seth, Tobit and Dando. When the heat grew too fierce they walked together up the back lane, around Two-acre Field and through the hedge by John's secret way. They dashed water from the trough into their mouths or doused each other or sheltered in the shade of the beeches. John sat between Abel and Cassie, swapping secret looks with the girl while Abel and the others gossiped. The talk swirled about them as if the village would shroud them in a cloak of words: the brown bottles Old Holy bought from the packhorse driver after Lady Day, or what Maddy Oddbone had got up to with a man from Flitwick, or how John Lambe had made his latest peace with Ginny . . .

Only Ephraim's presence disturbed John's contentment. The older boy loomed over him, rolling his eyes if John chanced to speak and offering mocking looks. But the other children shrugged or pretended they had not seen. Cassie chewed at her blackened nail. Why, John wondered, did it never heal? So the afternoons passed. Then Marpot's hand-bell sounded, calling the faithful to prayer.

The Lessoners wore dark jackets or shawls, black skirts or breeches without buckles or buttons. Every Sunday afternoon at the clanging summons they gathered in the long low cottage at the bottom of the green: the Chaffinges, Jim, Eliza and Ephraim Clough's families, the Fisheroakes and most of the Fentons, Mercy Starling and Cassie and the others. Behind the dark wood shutters the devotees knelt to chant psalms, listen to Marpot preach and mete out punishments to the offenders among them.

'They strip them naked,' Abel told John one Sunday. 'Cassie told me.'

An unbidden image rose in John's mind; of Marpot peeling off Cassie's brown wool dress. Her pale freckled body.

'All they get is a sheet,' Abel went on. 'They didn't wear nothing in Eden, Marpot says. All they ate was what they picked from the trees. All they drank was water.'

Dando Candling nodded. 'Our pa says if Marpot loves Eden so much, why don't he go naked himself?'

'Maybe he does,' chipped in Seth.

The boys sniggered. From inside the cottage, Marpot's voice sounded.

'And the Lord spake unto Moses, saying: if a woman have an issue, and her issue in her flesh be blood, she shall be put apart seven days. And whosoever toucheth her shall be unclean until evening. And everything that she lieth upon in her separation shall be unclean: everything also that she sitteth upon shall be unclean . . .'

'Gideon didn't want to make him Warden,' Seth went on. 'The Cloughs argued him into it. Old Holy just went along.'

'He got the Ale banned too,' muttered Tobit. 'After what he did.'

John looked away, remembering the black-clad figure on the roof. The villagers' torchlit faces.

'Ain't banned this year,' Dando piped up. 'Gideon was telling my pa.'

Abel grinned. 'Marpot won't like that.'

Marpot's voice fell silent. In its place rose a toneless chant. But out of the drab recitation, a clearer melody rose high in the air. A girl's voice soared above the others: Cassie's voice.

She had been teasing him that first time, John thought now. There had been no more talk of witches since. Nor of John's help. The boys looked over at the shuttered and stone-tiled cottage, the sun beating down on its roof. It would be hot in there, John thought. He imagined them kneeling in rows, chanting psalms in the gloom. And Cassie singing to heaven.

It was late afternoon when he regained the hut. His mother nodded and smiled when he pulled open the door. No interrogations awaited him now. He no longer crept past her concealing the latest harvest of scratches and bruises. Every morning, they climbed the slopes together. Looking down, they watched the grass on the green parch until Saint Clodock's Tears disappeared in a desert of brown. But on the high slopes the summer heat seemed to draw deeper greens from the soil. John and his mother swished through carpets of vetches and fescues or pushed their way through the bushes, splashing through springs that broke through the turf and flowed through the grass in secret cascades.

In the afternoons his mother climbed towards the cordon of brambles. Then John took his own routes along ancient weed-ridden beds where he hunted out herbs or scavenged for strawberries. Rabbits scattered at his approach, their white tails flashing as they vanished into the brush. On the hottest days John sought the shade of elders and ashes until his mother reappeared, tramping breathless down the slope, her collecting bag bulging, back to the hut. There the book awaited him.

Every evening he pored over the pages, his tongue forming the unfamiliar words. Squinting down at the letters, John made his way among groves of date palms and meadows of crocuses. Eyes aching, he pushed his way through stands of medlars and plums then orchards of apples or cherries or pears. A flick of the page and fantastic creatures reared out of a sea: great finned fish, huge eels and long-tentacled monsters. A steep-sided island showed above the waves.

'That's Zoyland Tor,' he exclaimed, and saw his mother nod.

'All around there was a sea,' she said. 'All about Zoyland and Mere, the sea used to rush in every winter. But when the salt washed out, the grass grew even thicker. The brine floated, see? The sweet water sat underneath.'

The ancient pages rose among the others, palisaded with strange letters and words, the faint script hardly more readable than the footprints of birds. He read until his eyelids drooped. But as his head dropped, he fancied he caught the sharp savour of sap beneath the chalky dust of the pages, or the heavy perfumes of blossom from the orchards of plums and pears and apples.

The summer grew hotter. In church, the Lessoners sat together in a dark-suited clump. When a red-faced Father Hole announced the Ale and told the story of Saint Clodock, Marpot's faithful muttered among themselves. But the priest seemed not to notice when they tutted or Aaron Clough made the sign of the cross. The priest swayed slightly while the rest of the villagers fanned themselves against the heat and smiled when Old Holy stumbled over the words.

Each morning, louring clouds gathered above the Spines and advanced over the Levels. But as the sun climbed in the sky they burned to wisps that twisted and disappeared. The heat lodged itself in walls and settled into the ground. In Two-acre Field, the corn was hardly up to the scarecrow's knees. The water in the new well sank until a dropped stone hardly made a splash. The Lessoners' red faces scowled in the hot church. Seated beside his mother, John glanced behind at Marpot. But the man ignored him, seeming not to see John or his mother. He stood at the back as if he had never led the others up to the meadow, his blond hair bright against the plain black of his suit, his unblinking blue eyes watching over his followers. Leaving church on Rogationtide, John looked out to the west and saw a black line of thunderheads nudge the ridge of the Spines. He was about to tell his mother when Jasper Riverett's voice sounded.

'Looks like a flock of crows flew in,' the man remarked loudly as the Lessoners emerged.

'Zoyland crows,' added Dando Candling's father.

'Coming around the bounds with us, are you?' Meg Riverett invited the dark-suited group. 'Or the Ale?'

Marpot looked straight ahead as if he could not hear but, alongside him, Mercy Starling turned her pinched face to Meg.

'Ale? Is that how you call it? Hear its true name, Meg. It's a Witch's Feast.'

The Lessoners stopped. The Riveretts and Candlings gathered about Jasper. Mercy rounded on Meg.

'You wait till she comes,' Cassie's mother went on. 'I seen it, remember? I seen it with our Mary. First the fever grips you. Then you heave up your guts. You puke till you bring up your soul.'

The villagers gathered about the two women.

'Puking?' John saw Meg roll her eyes. 'Sounds like our Jasper last night.'

The village men laughed. But from the Lessoners, Lee Fisheroake pointed a finger.

'A witch ain't one of your jokes, Meg Riverett,' the man said. 'You mock God and He'll mock you back!'

'Mock us for what?' Rose Cullender challenged Lee. 'We ain't done nothing wrong.'

'Feeding a witch not wrong?' Lee retorted. 'Sounds like her imps been crawling in bed with you, Rose.'

'How dare you!' Rose shouted.

'Thou shalt not suffer a witch to live,' Aaron Clough declared. 'Moses said that.'

'Live, Brother Aaron?' Jasper Riverett countered. 'I don't know about Moses, begging your pardon, but our old witch ain't lived here in a while.'

Some among the parishioners chuckled. Mercy pushed her way forward again.

'Nor's our Mary!' she spat. 'You all served the witch a feast. You all mocked God. Just like Adam when he took the apple from Eve. You brought her down here. And she took my Mary.'

At Mercy's accusation, a low grumble started up among the villagers.

'Nonsense,' Eliza Fenton said. 'The Ale's for Saint Clod. And that's that.'

Then John heard a low voice behind him.

'That child was sick.' He turned to see old Connie Cullender. 'Mercy should have took her to your ma. She had them lot praying for her instead.' The woman nodded towards the Lessoners.

They were being jostled now. As John watched, Lee Fisheroake tried to shove Jasper Riverett. Jasper only laughed and Lee's face went even redder. Ephraim Clough scowled but kept close to his father. John searched for Cassie among the faces and found Abel instead. The boy looked unhappily between Jake and Mercy. As one of Clough's men barged into them both, it seemed that blows might be exchanged. Then Tom Hob ambled forward as though he had stumbled upon the gathering by accident.

'Buccla warn't no witch,' the big man said. 'She grew every green thing, my gramps used to say. All up and down the Vale.' The orchardman looked about affably. 'That's why it's called Buckland. Buccla's Land, see? And Saint Clod was Coldcloak. Shelter o' the Forest, that's a way of saying. He knew all the old stories, my gramps did. She didn't witch him neither. Our Saint Clod fell in love with her. That's why he cried them tears over there. There's other stories too . . .'

But before Tom could tell more, Marpot pushed his way to the front.

'That's enough of your nonsense! The only true story's in this book!' The man stood with his Bible raised. 'God's mockery is harsh,' he declared, his blue eyes challenging any to speak against him. 'Just like Brother Lee said. God sent witches into the world to tempt men with their wickedness. He sent one here.'

'That was an age ago . . .' began Jasper.

'A witch knows no age. She's as old as Eve.' Marpot brought his arm down as if his Bible were an axe and he was dealing a blow. 'That's how to deal with her. Like the good Saint did. With an axe and a torch.'

The Lessoners nodded behind him. The villagers stared back. Through the crowd, John glimpsed Cassie. She was gazing up at Marpot, her face rapt. At the same moment he felt his nose twitch. Wet hay, he thought. Or the mist that hung above the meadow in the morning. He felt a nudge. Abel stood beside him.

'Look.'

The boy gazed up and John followed suit. Faces upturned, they felt the villagers around them look up too, then all of them, abruptly united by the dark clouds sliding overhead.

'Thank the Lord,' Leo Huxtable declared. 'Rain.'

As he spoke, the first fat drops fell.

The rain fell for three days. Water flowed in sheets over the baked earth, encircled the church and jostled the skulls in the bone-hole behind it. A flood washed out the path below the Starlings' cottage and sped down the back lane in a shallow river. The old well filled with muddy water to the brim. The next day the new one suddenly did the same.

The hut smelt of damp wool, damp earth and smoke. John dodged the drips which fell through the thatch. He scurried out to gather logs from the pile at the back and stacked them by the fire to dry. John's mother coughed over her cauldron, her stirring arm revolving in a slow smooth action. When his chores were done, John hunched in the corner with the book.

Cold raindrops spattered his back. John squinted until the dim light filtering through the window-cloth faded, imagining trunks rising and green shoots springing up, hearing wings beat the air and feet rustle the grass. When he could read no more, he lay on the damp palliasse and stared up at the dripping thatch. Across the damp floor he heard his mother stir and cough.

She would teach him, she had promised. The plantations of the book would tell him why he belonged here . . . So she said. He had all but learned his letters and yet his ignorance remained as great as ever. It had even grown greater, swelling like the fruits on the strange trees. Who had once cultivated the slopes? There was no Buccla, his mother said. There was no witch. What, in all the book's mottled pages, gave John Sandall title to any more than the damp floor beneath him and the hut's narrow walls? He felt his impatience rise again, wondering anew at Ephraim's words. *You don't belong here. You shouldn't never have come back* . . . Outside, the rain drummed down.

The downpour stopped as suddenly as it had begun. The sun came out and the village steamed. Father Hole took his usual text after rain.

'And Noah removed the covering of the Ark,' announced the white-haired priest, upending his hourglass before a half-empty church. 'And behold the ground was dry.'

'About time too,' exclaimed a red-faced Tom Hob. Beside him, Jasper Riverett laughed. John looked among the congregation for Abel or Cassie but the boy and girl were absent. Their parents too. After the service, he waited by the well as usual. At last Dando and the others trotted over.

'Abel's sick,' the boy told John.

'Sick how?'

'Sick's all I heard,' Dando replied. 'He'll be better tomorrow, God willing.'

But the next morning Abel had a fever. The day after that he began to retch.

The stream swelled to a river whose meanders nudged the path then darted away through water-meadows and fields. To the west, Zoyland Tor rose out of the mists of the Levels then sank as the road descended. A cluster of ruins loomed before them.

'That's Old Toue,' said Josh. 'What's left of it.'

The broken walls were soon left behind. The river reappeared at Ruseley then came Middle Ock with its tumbledown chapel. Fainwick followed then the short climb to Rinton. After Lower Halling, Josh nodded back to the mule and the boy. 'Ain't you supposed to be getting him talking?'

Reluctantly, Ben Martin dropped back. The mule was limping on its left leg today, he noticed. The leg changed, Josh had told him, depending on the creature's inclination. 'We was talking about schooling,' the man resumed. 'You ever learned to tally, John Sandall? That was my first misfortune. That or the road that took me out of Soughton . . .'

The boy raked dirt-filled nails through his matted hair. His face betrayed neither interest nor surprise. His shirt and breeches were hardly better than rags, Ben thought. The blue coat might once have been smart, he supposed, before rain had leached out the colour and mud taken its place.

'You've heard of Soughton, ain't you?' Ben continued doggedly. 'See that place up ahead? Think of three of 'em nailed together.'

They were approaching Carrboro. The boy glanced up then dropped his head again. Soon the horses trudged between tall timbered buildings, their upper storeys overhanging the road. They crossed through the marketplace and passed the dark bulk of the cathedral. In the precinct behind it, a line of grey-faced youths dressed in faded smocks stood in a yard. A beadle waved a stick and bellowed orders. Like an ox stuck up an ash tree, thought Ben. Josh and Ben exchanged glances.

'That's the Poorhouse,' Josh threw over his shoulder. 'Don't want to end up in there, eh, Ben?'

'Certainly don't,' Ben replied. 'Wouldn't you say, John Sandall?'

The boy's gaze slid blankly over the ragged children.

The houses shrank to cottages then to huts. On the edge of town Ben Martin pointed out an inn but Josh shook his head. The horses ambled after their driver, loads swaying and leather straps creaking. At midday, Josh pulled off the road.

'Sir William holds all this,' the driver said, handing Ben a hunk of bread and throwing one back to the boy. 'He could walk from the Manor all the way to Soughton and never step off his own land. His man told me that.'

'Your friend Pouncey, was it?'

'He ain't exactly a friend.'

Ben looked back. The Spines were a smudge in the distance. The boy tore at his hunk of bread, hunched over it like an animal.

'He said anything yet?' asked Josh.

Ben shook his head. 'What if they don't take him?'

Josh shrugged. 'Then he'll be for the Poorhouse.'

They set off again, Josh loping at the head of his animals, the guide-rein of the piebald loose in his hand. Once more Ben took up position beside the mule.

'I was a bit older than you,' he resumed. 'Got myself apprenticed to a man called Fessler. Edging, fretting. Bit of bonelace. That was his tackle. He had me keeping the books for the piecework. But there was a fellow wanted my place. Nahum Broadwick he was called. A right black-hearted villain. Not that I realised . . .'

The road descended. The piebald picked up her pace, looking forward to the shade of Charlcombe Wood. Josh's heavy stick was wedged among the cases on the bay. The driver pulled it out and swung it over his head a few times.

'Now Fessler could tally better'n a Jew on Lammas,' Ben continued. 'But he couldn't have told Judas from Saint Peter. And that's all Nahum Broadwick was. A Judas, I mean. Not Saint Peter . . .'

The chestnut trees closed over their heads. Ben talked on. The boy wasn't going to speak. But that was no problem of his. And his silence made telling the story of Nahum Broadwick's treachery and his own dismissal easier.

'So Nahum lied his head off. But what could I say? Fessler'd no more believe me over him than King Charles'd marry the King of Spain's daughter. I was out the door with four shillings and ninepence. So I took myself down the Dog for a jug and that was when that fellow came in. Had a face that looked more like yours than mine. Touch of the Signor Hispaniolas, if you take my meaning. Anyhow, this Almery fellow had something he wanted taking to Buckland Manor, to a man called Scovell . . .'

The boy's silence was as stony as the road. This Pouncey fellow would run them off the Manor, Ben thought. He would throw John Sandall into the Poorhouse. And that would be that.

'Whoa!' Josh yelled. A rabbit had broken cover under the feet of the horse. The driver hurled his heavy stick and Ben heard a thud. He watched Josh pick up the carcass then noticed the boy.

John Sandall was gazing up into the trees. The thick trunks of the chestnuts spiralled out of the earth, their bark scored with deep lines and grooves. The highest branches quivered in the faint breeze. The boy's eyes followed their movements, darting from side to side.

'What you looking for up there?' Ben asked quietly. But the boy only gazed around the wood, following the chestnuts' branches and boughs as they touched and intertwined. At last he dropped his gaze.

'He's an odd one,' Ben told Josh.

'Still nothing?' the driver asked.

Ben shook his head and Josh sighed heavily. Then he dropped his voice and spoke in an undertone. Ben listened carefully as he outlined his course of action.

'Tonight,' whispered Josh. 'We'll never be rid of him otherwise.'

Both men glanced back at the boy.

'All right,' agreed Ben.

He dropped back and took up his tale with new energy, describing how he had tramped around the edge of the Levels and along the foot of the Spines.

'That's a dull bit of country, that is, John. Even that Zoyland Tor. They say Christ paid a visit with Joseph of Arimathea. All I'll say is, they didn't hurry back . . .'

The boy looked at him blankly. The packhorses snorted and shook their heads. As the sun dipped, Josh turned off down a path. Twigs crunched under the animals' hooves. Through the trees Ben glimpsed crumbling walls. Josh came up beside him.

'We can do it in there.'

Ben gazed at an ivy-covered pillar which lay in sections on the ground. Blocks of fallen masonry were scattered around the walls. Ben could hear water gurgling somewhere behind. Josh pointed past a broad flat stone in the centre to a deep fireplace, as high as himself and black with ancient soot.

'You light a fire,' Josh said. 'Then we'll see to him.'

The boy had dismounted the mule and now stood in the clearing. The animals were unloaded and hobbled. Josh led John into the courtyard. The boy sat on the stone without protest and let himself be positioned. Josh moved behind him and picked up his knife. He tested the edge then angled the boy's head. Then he brought the blade down.

When the task was done, Josh stepped back and puffed out his cheeks. 'Never thought something like that'd be so hard,' the driver declared.

'You did well,' Ben said solemnly.

'Better now, ain't it?' said Josh.

'Much better,' agreed Ben.

Hanks of matted black hair lay on the ground around the boy. Odd tufts still stuck out from his scalp.

'That's the lice,' Josh said with satisfaction. 'Let's hope he ain't got anything worse.'

'Worse?' Ben looked puzzled. 'Like what?'

'Whatever took off all them children.'

52

Flickering rushlights turned the church walls yellow. Oily smoke curled up into the roof. The last candles had been burnt on Holy Rood Day, Father Hole remembered, two weeks after Abel Starling fell sick. Now that seemed a lifetime ago. Bare and bonneted heads filled the pews of Saint Clodock's. At the front, on the floor, the penitents knelt.

More than a dozen were lined up tonight, men and women costumed alike in their thin white sheets. They held long wands of hazel and knelt bare-kneed on the hard flagstones. Father Hole watched them grimace and shift, clutching their sheets to their breasts. And in case they stirred from their places, Jim Clough's brother Aaron stood behind them with his stick.

After the first deaths, Father Hole had preached from Romans.

We glory in tribulations also: knowing that tribulation worketh patience.

A hard text. But the last grains in the glass had hardly fallen before Mercy Starling had risen from her pew.

'Patience, Father? It ain't want of patience making our children retch.' The woman had cast her eye about the church. 'Is it, Meg? You ain't laughing at me now, are you? Or you, Rose. Or you. . .'

Her finger had stabbed in accusation and the Lessoners had risen around her. Then a terrible clamour had filled the church, of accusing voices and fearful oaths. He should have descended, Father Hole knew. He should have stridden among them as he had on the night of the Ale, cuffing heads and scolding ears. But the noise had befuddled him, echoing back and forth in the nave until at last a voice had bellowed over the din.

'How dare we defile God's house with curses!'

Timothy Marpot had marched down the aisle.

'God tested Adam with Eve. His own wife. Now he tests us.'

'And how's he do that, Brother Tim?' a sullen voice had challenged from among the villagers. One or two chuckled. But Marpot raised his Bible.

'My name is Timothy,' he declared, his blue eyes raking their faces. 'Timothy means Fear-God. And I fear only God. He tests us as He did once before. With a witch.'

The church fell silent. In the pulpit, Father Hole looked on.

'We will let our faith guide us,' the warden had declared. 'If the witch walks among us, we will find her. We will examine consciences.' Then he had raised his eyes to the pulpit. 'That is, if Father Hole permits.'

So the hearings had begun.

'Keep silent there!' Aaron barked now as Connie Cullender shifted her weight and grunted. Marpot's instructions were precise, Father Hole knew. No idle speech. No raising of the eyes to heaven. For the defiant, the stocks beside the animal-pound. Tom Hob occupied them now. Or worse, thought Father Hole. At the end of the line of penitents, Jake Starling fixed his gaze on the floor, his lips moving in silent prayer. A livid bruise closed one eye.

Some examinees proved recalcitrant, Brother Timothy had explained. They might kneel before the table until nightfall while their neighbours bore witness to their deeds and misdeeds. They might resist until dawn, or even mid-morning. But at last their penance would be handed down and they would don the white sheet. Then the Lessoners would gather with their long switches and harsh laughter, ready for the run to church. They had mocked God, Marpot had declared. Now God mocked them back.

Father Hole dropped his own gaze to the floor. John Sandall had drawn the palm tree on these stones, the boy's hand shaking more than his own before the first drink of the morning. How long was it now since Susan Sandall's return to the village? Eleven years? He remembered her reappearance after Lady Anne's death, the church hung with black by Sir William's order and her belly bulging with the child who would take the chalk. A week ago they had watched him together from the door of the hut, picking his way through the meadow. What would become of him, she had demanded? She had exacted his reluctant promise. Now it weighed upon him. He felt weary. And thirsty.

Outside the air was damp. Tom Hob's snores resounded across the green. Lights burned in Marpot's house but the other cottages were dark. Some had hung buckthorn over their lintels until Brother Timothy's men had torn it down. The old ways, thought Father Hole. The old fears.

'Only the pure of spirit can see her,' the blue-eyed man had told him, flanked by Aaron Clough and his scowling boy Ephraim. 'That is why she attacks the innocent. To blind them to her true guise. For a child will know her, Father. Mark my words.'

But Father Hole remembered the bent old man in his blue smock. Would he have beaten simpletons? Or forced old women to kneel for hours? Would he have sent a witch to poison their children? From across four decades, the sound of breaking glass reached Father Hole's ears.

Absurd, he told himself sternly. His warden was no Zoyland zealot. The sickness would pass. His promise to Susan Sandall would lapse. He stood alone at the edge of the deserted green.

'The palm tree stands,' he murmured to himself. Then he turned and trudged back towards his house.

The sickness leapt from cottage to cottage, back and forth across the village. The children it touched burned with fever first. Then the retching began. Just as Mercy Starling had warned. At the end, John's mother told him, they writhed like worms on a pin.

After Mercy's outburst John's mother had banned him from the village. In the mornings he walked the slopes until the afternoon heat drove him down to the meadow and the stand of beech trees in the corner. There he waited and listened.

Sometimes he would sit in the shade all afternoon. On other days he would wait no more than a few minutes, listening and peering down the bank from time to time. Then the hedge would rustle. The bushes would part. One by one, the faces appeared.

Dando sneaked out whenever he could. Seth found it harder with his ma dragging him down to the church every day. Tobit came when he liked. The boys settled themselves about the gurgle of the water trough.

'My ma says Mercy Starling lost her wits years ago,' Dando declared.

'Mine says Jake ain't much better,' added Seth.

They looked up the path as if they could see through the elder and hawthorn to the white-fronted cottage.

'You hear about Maddy Oddbone?' Dando asked. 'Her waters broke in Marpot's lesson. They didn't let her out till evening.'

'What about old Connie Cullender,' Tobit said with a smirk. 'Aaron Clough promised they'd go easy on her. Then they stripped her naked and made her kneel half the day . . .'

'Naked?' asked Dando. 'Connie Cullender?'

John remembered the old woman murmuring to him outside church. It was hard to imagine her naked.

'Ephraim saw her,' Tobit added.

John and Seth exchanged glances. But before they could ask how come Tobit was talking with Ephraim, a soft high sound drifted down the path, growing in volume as they listened, the first note swelling and soaring. A high clear voice shaped the verses. John listened intently. Tobit rolled his eyes.

'There she goes.'

Cassie sang psalms every afternoon. Sometimes she sang in the evenings too. Then John walked the meadow above the Starling cottage, creeping closer and lying down in the grass so as not to be seen by Mercy.

'Singing's all she does,' said Seth.

'She's praying,' said John. 'For Abel.'

The boys stared at their feet, silenced by the mention of Abel. At last Cassie's voice fell silent.

'Ephraim asked me to come with him,' Seth said abruptly.

'You say yes?' Dando asked.

Seth shook his head. 'I ain't going around with them.'

'Nor me,' said Tobit.

'None of us are,' said Dando. 'Are we, John?'

John shook his head.

Tobit was the first to stop coming. Seth, Dando and John sat on the edge of the trough dangling their fingers in the cold water and discussing his treachery.

'I heard a thing about Marpot,' Dando offered as consolation. 'Meg Riverett was telling my ma. He's hiding.'

'Marpot?' asked John. 'How?' He remembered the man's baleful stare.

'The Bishop had him up in his court,' Dando continued. 'Marpot had a woman dancing around naked out Zoyland way. Then he beat her half to death.'

'What'd he do that for?' asked Seth.

'Don't know.'

They shook their heads at the incomprehensible ways of their elders.

'What if he's right though?' asked Dando. 'What if there is a witch?'

'How come they can't find her then?' asked Seth.

'They ain't examined everyone, have they?' said Dando. 'Ain't been down to the Huxtables'.'

'Marpot don't dare.'

'They ain't come up here neither,' Seth said with a glance at John. 'I ain't saying they'd find her or anything.'

John nodded and looked back at the meadow. Ephraim Clough's father and the others stamped about the village as they pleased, banging on doors. The thought of his mother being hauled out of the hut gave him a sick feeling. What would he do if they stripped her like Connie Cullender? Or made her run to the church?

Dando was the next to go. John and Seth passed awkward comments back and forth. But at last the desultory talk petered out. Cassie's singing came as a relief.

'Ephraim was boasting,' Seth said when she finished. 'Said his pa was going to examine your ma. Said he was going to test her.'

'Test her how?' He kept his voice casual.

'I don't know,' Seth said. He stared hard at the ground. 'It's just what I heard.' He rose to slip back through the hedge. 'Best get back.'

'See you tomorrow,' called John. But the bushes closed behind the boy. Seth did not answer. The next day John waited in vain.

He began to spend his days on the slopes. Tramping up and down the terraces, he heard Marpot's hand-bell and watched the dark-suited lines form outside the long cottage. When the latest white-sheeted figure stumbled out, he imagined the harsh shouts and mocking laughter as the hapless penitent scampered under the Lessoners' long switches.

When evening came he still wandered in the meadow, waiting

for Cassie to sing. But the Starling cottage was silent. When next he heard her song it was fainter, drifting up on the still night air. It came from the church.

The soft psalm stroked the bare ceiling and walls. It slid along the pews and curled around the pulpit's dark turret. The words settled on the hard stone floor. Cassie's heart swelled. She thought of the little stones in her purse, the ones she had collected. She knew each one, how it bit as she knelt her weight upon it. Now she heard them skitter on the hard floor.

Saint Clodock had carried an axe and torch against the witch. He had chopped up her chestnut tables. He had burnt her palace. Now the witch was back. But this time Brother Timothy was waiting. Together Cassie and he would finish Saint Clodock's work. They would set the witch a sharp trial.

Cassie understood sharp trials. She drew out the pin from her bonnet and put the tip to her blackened nail. She began slowly as she always did easing the point down its prickling groove. Witches did not feel pain, she reminded herself. They did not bleed. When the first drop fell, she began to pray.

She gave thanks for her life and the lives of her families, the old one in the cottage and the one to come, with Brother Timothy, the Cloughs and all the others. She prayed that Abel and her father would find their own way to the Garden. That everyone in the village should find their way there. Everyone in the Vale from Sir William all the way down to Tom Hob.

It was time. Brother Timothy had told her so.

She had asked God to take her after Mary died but God had refused. The witch had hidden herself among them, Brother Timothy said. Cassie's penance was to find her. Every Sunday, she had prayed in the corner of the meadow. She had all but given up hope before God had answered. But at last He had sent the one she needed.

She remembered his face, startled and bloody, looking up from the water trough.

The ache from her knees crept up through her bones. A second bead of blood trembled down the pin. She would count to a dozen tonight, she thought. From her corner of the meadow she had kept watch on John Sandall, a tiny moving speck high above. Then she had seen the woman weaving her way through the brambles. Disappearing into Buccla's Wood. At that moment all was clear. Rising to her feet and hitching up her skirts, she had felt God's purpose course through her veins. She had run to Brother Timothy.

A dark form loomed above. An instant later the man knelt beside her. She had thought she would expire of shame when he had stripped off her brown wool dress. She was a loosemouth, he had admonished her, to speak so promiscuously with the son of Susan Sandall. But she would have endured a thousand such penances. She was God's messenger, he had told her. Now the man's blue eyes found her own.

'Are you prepared, Sister Cassandra?'

A disturbance of the gloom, John thought first. His mother's worsening cough had driven him out. He stood in the meadow, the water jug clutched in his hands. High above something was moving on the slope. As he watched, a tattered white pennant seemed to flutter out of the dark brambles. Someone was descending. He stood before the door of the hut. Only when the figure reached the lowest terrace did John recognise the bonnet.

Cassie advanced through the long grass. But as she drew near he saw her halting gait. Her limbs moved with awkward jerks. Abruptly she stumbled and fell. John dropped the jug and ran forward, offering his hand to the girl. But then he recoiled.

There seemed no part of Cassie that had not been scratched. Long red lines ran over her limbs. Her woollen dress hung in tatters. Blood smeared her hands and forearms. She had used them, it seemed, to protect her face.

'Cassie?'

'I know the witch.'

Her blue eyes were almost black in the gloom.

'Come with me,' he told her. 'My ma will help you.'

But she shook her head, rising stiffly to her feet. 'I saw her go up there.' Cassie looked up the slope to the dark line of trees.

'But there's no way in,' John replied. 'It's all thorns, remember?'

'That don't make no difference.' The girl stood before him in her shredded dress. 'I told you, John. Witches don't bleed.'

A sinking feeling grew in John's stomach. He heard the hand-bell ring out from the green below. Faint shouts answered the clanging noise.

'God sent you to help me,' Cassie said, stumbling through the grass. 'You led me to her, John.'

'Cassie, wait,' he pleaded. But at the top of the bank the girl launched herself forward. Together they half ran, half fell down the bank. Picking himself up beside the trough, John heard a familiar voice.

'Took your time, John.'

Ephraim Clough stepped out of the hedge. John straightened and faced the older boy. Ephraim glanced at Cassie.

'What have you done to her, Witch-boy?' He turned towards Two-acre Field, and shouted, 'I've found her! Over here!'

A sick feeling gathered in John's stomach, familiar and unwanted.

But against it rose a new anger. He stared at the boy's heavy brow, his full cheeks and broad face. With a cry, John sprang, his first punch rapping the top of Ephraim's skull, stinging his knuckles and drawing nothing more than a surprised grunt from his opponent. But the second swing ended in a gristly crack as his fist found Ephraim's nose. Ephraim gave a cry and clutched his face. A giddy abandon took hold of John. He wrestled his enemy down then he and Ephraim were rolling about the path, grabbing and punching and kicking. Ephraim was bigger and stronger but John's anger seemed to lend him a new strength. Out of the corner of his eye he saw Cassie stumble away. He heard the hand-bell ringing. He hit out again and again, careless of the blows that Ephraim returned. At last he pinned his opponent, trapping the boy's arms. Blood streamed from Ephraim's nose.

'Go on, Witch-boy,' he dared John. 'We'll see how your ma sings.'

The words only enraged John more. He raised his arm. He would punch the boy's face as hard as he could. Keep punching until he was silent. But even as he shaped to deliver the first blow a hand gripped his shoulder. He was pulled backwards. A furious face glared into his own.

'Where have you been!' his mother hissed. 'Come, John! Hurry!'

They were running again, running as hard as they could, the long grass whipping their legs, across the dark meadow and towards the first bank. Once again, oily tallow-smoke laced the night air and the banging of pots and pans mixed with the villagers' shouts. Once again John heard his mother's breath rasp in her throat. Arms flailing, they hauled themselves up the first slope, the heavy bag bumping between them. Then the next and the next in a furious scramble. Only when the ghostly banks of furze and scrub rose around them did they look back.

Flickering lights ringed their hut with fire. The villagers were gathered all around. Then, as John and his mother watched, the first torch was thrown, tumbling end over end, drawing an arc of flame through the darkness to land on the roof of their hut. The pale yellow flames flickered, licking the thatch then spreading over the roof.

A tongue of red fire rose into the night. Around the hut the villagers were a dark mass, surging back and forth. He did not need to see their torchlit faces. Not only Marpot and his Lessoners but all the villagers were there: the Fentons and Chaffinges and Dares and Candlings, all the rear-pew women who had knocked on their door and their children too. As if Ephraim's thick-browed face were stamped on the faces of Seth and Dando and Tobit. Only Abel had stood by him, dying of fever in his bed. The fire took hold and it seemed to John that the flames ran through his own veins, their heat spreading through his frame. He had been right, he thought. He and Ephraim both. They did not belong here. They had never belonged.

He looked up at his mother. Her hands were pressed to her mouth, her eyes wide. Below, the hut blazed, the smell of smoke strong in the air. John reached up and took her hand.

'Ma?'

But she could only shake her head.

They resumed their climb. Soon the banks of brambles stretched out thick arms. The bag bumped between them as John and his mother edged their way into the thickets. When they reached the final bristling barricade, his mother wrapped her arms about him. A moment later she had plunged them both into the thorns.

The spines would tear his skin as they had Cassie's, thought John. He flinched as the first canes scraped his legs . . . But the stems and leaves rustled harmlessly. His mother seemed to part the brambles as easily as Moses did the sea. Emerging on the other side, he found himself unmarked. As he wondered at the miracle, his mother gripped a stem and ran her hand down its length, shucking the spines like peas from a pod.

'Fool's thorn,' she said.

John nodded and looked up. At the top of the bank, sheathed in deep-lined bark, the ancient trunks of Buccla's Wood leaned like pillars supporting a massive canopy. John scraped together a heap of dry leaves and lay down with his mother. Far below their hut smouldered, a red eye glaring out of the darkness. Deep inside him, John felt his anger glow like a hot coal.

A magpie cackled. Sunlight glittered. John opened his eyes and blinked in the glare. For one blissful moment, he wondered how he came to be lying on a bed of leaves at the edge of Buccla's Wood. Then his memory blew the hot ember into life: the shouts and cries, the flames, the familiar faces turned to a chanting mass. He felt the red coal lodge itself deeper inside him.

Beside him, his mother slept, her long black hair spread out over the ground. As John rose, she stirred. He looked down the slope to the roofless shell at the edge of the meadow. Smoke still rose from the blackened walls. His mother placed a hand on his shoulder.

'You said we belonged there,' he told her. 'You said we belonged more than any of them.'

'We do,' she answered.

But she paid no attention to the hut nor even the village. He followed her gaze down the Vale, leaping hedgerows and woods, tracking the river until it disappeared. There was the ridge and the gatehouse, the tower of the chapel and the great house beyond. Buckland Manor. That was it, he realised.

'You served there,' he said.

His mother rubbed her red eyes. 'Yes, John. I served there.'

'But you came back.'

'I had no choice.'

Another riddle, he thought. Even now.

'You said you'd teach me,' he said.

'I will,' she answered shortly. 'Come.'

She heaved the bag onto her shoulder and turned to the woods behind her. But as John turned to follow a flash of light caught his eye.

It came from the distant house. A second flash followed. Then more. A row of windows was being opened, John realised. Sunlight was glinting off the panes. He stood on the slope and watched the lights flash like signals sent the length of the Vale. Then he turned and followed his mother into Buccla's Wood.

From *The Book of John Saturnall*: For a *Dish* called a *Foam* of *Forcemeats* of *Fowls*

A true Feast has Mysteries for Parts, some clear to discern and others running deeper. Its Dishes speak in Tongues to baffle a Scholar yet a humble Cook must decipher them all. So the Air, being a Garden as Saturnus taught, a Cook must rename its Tree-tops as Beds and its Planters are Nests where Birds and Fowls fatten themselves and thrive in wondrous Variety. And to celebrate that Garden's Harvest he must exert his Art as I will tell you here.

Take your Birds and carve them each according to its Fashion. Unbrace the Mallard, rear the Goose, lift the Swan, dismember the Hern, unjoint the Bittern, display the Crane, allay the Pheasant, wing the Partridge, thigh one each of Pigeon and Woodcock and leave a Pair of Fig-peckers whole. Pluck them and draw them then roast them till the Skins are golden. Excepting the Fig-peckers, pick the cooled Meats in Strings no thicker than Packthread, chop them fine and season alternately with Cumin and Saffron. Take Whites of Eggs and beat them to the Airiness of Clouds. Fold each of the Meats in part of the Egg.

Fit a Pipkin close with a Cake-cage and steam it. Place the Pastes within, one inside the next divided by stiff Paper rubbed with clear Butter, the greater Birds outermost and the smaller within. At the Centre set the Fig-peckers. Let the Steam cook these Forcemeats and all the Time watch them, removing the Papers Layer by Layer. When all are risen and set, loosen the Cake-cage and lift out the set Foam of Forcemeats. Cut to show the Layers within, coloured red and yellow. Serve in Slices upon Sippets or fine Plates, as you please.

THE PROTOCOLS WERE SIMPLE, Lady Lucretia reminded herself. She had, after all, rehearsed them so many times.

In the presence chamber, noble ladies might approach Her Majesty. But they might not speak unless invited. In the privy chamber beyond, Her Majesty's Privy Ladies were permitted a salutation – but woe betide the courtier who presumed to direct remarks. Beyond that lay the withdrawing chamber where different rules applied. For there Her Majesty's most-beloved ladies might speak without her express leave, a privilege held by right, Lady Lucretia reminded herself, only by the wives and mistresses of visiting kings. The withdrawing chamber should be lively with whispers and shared confidences. Abuzz with snippets of gossip and advice. But that was not the innermost sanctum. Last of all, at the far end of the humming capsule, stood the door to the bedchamber proper.

None but the Ladies of the Queen's Closet were permitted to enter there and, among these, only one in particular might sit at Her Majesty's side, might treat with Her Majesty as intimately as she pleased and be cherished by Her Majesty above all others, namely the Lady of the Footstool.

That was Lady Lucretia.

So, after morning service in the chapel, it was Lady Lucretia who took Her Majesty's soft hand and, ignoring the familiar griping of her stomach, led her swiftly away.

'Come quickly,' she urged Her Majesty as the two of them slipped through the crush of worshippers. Urging was permissible from the Lady of the Footstool. And haste was devoutly to be wished when the first groups of servants were flooding into the passage and lining up for their own procession to the chapel. The pair glided through the far doorway and descended the stairs. Lady Lucretia felt her heart thud in her chest. With happiness, she told herself, taking Her Majesty's arm to guide her down the steps. Guiding was certainly permitted.

They crossed the servants' courtyard. Lady Lucretia's stomach clenched again. The mornings were always difficult, she reflected, passing the close-stools where Her Majesty and her Lady of the Footstool both wrinkled their noses at the stench. In the cobbled tunnel beyond, servants rushed about in the half-light and porters pushed handcarts. The kitchens belched their usual clatterings and smells. Lady Lucretia resisted the temptation to clutch her midriff and forced herself to think of the gallery, the hangings and carpets glowing with imagined colour, the succession of chambers through which they would pass. She glanced anxiously at Her Majesty but all was going to plan. Then, at the entrance to the kitchens, they encountered the boy.

Untidy brown hair flopped about an open face. His mouth appeared fixed in a permanent half-smile. He sat behind a large wicker basket half filled with feathers and held a half-plucked pheasant in his hand. A brief disdainful glance sufficed for Lady Lucretia. Grimy red livery identified him as a denizen of the smoky domain beyond the gaping entrance. In short, a kitchen boy.

Master Scovell's minions were beneath the notice of Her Majesty's companions, let alone Her Majesty. But the boy's eyes widened at the sight of Her Majesty. Dead birds lay in a heap on the bench beside him: ducks, two geese, a pheasant, little mounds of partridges and pigeons. Other feathery corpses lay in boxes beneath. Staring was insolence enough, in Lady Lucretia's opinion. But then, to her outrage, the boy winked.

'I will have that boy whipped,' she declared, glaring furiously. But Her Majesty raised a protest which could only be described as a wail.

'No, Lucy! You must not!'

Her Majesty's good nature was too good, thought Lucretia, gliding forward again. The pliant Queen needed her ladies to protect her. She needed Lady Lucretia, who propelled her forward then kicked a brisk diagonal path through the overgrown weeds in the knot-garden court-yard. On the far side, she pushed open a door to disclose stone steps rising in a spiral. Lady Lucretia listened to her own beating heart. The lodger in her stomach was quiescent now. The pair climbed. Before a locked oak door banded with iron, Lady Lucretia reached within her skirts and produced a heavy key. Beyond the door, she assured Her Majesty, in the bedchamber at the end of the next sunlit gallery, her ladies awaited her.

The sprung lock grated. The door creaked open. The promised sunlight indeed flooded in. The high ceiling soared. But there was no wood-panelled suite of rooms. The elm boards were bare, unadorned by carpets. No tapestries brightened the walls.

They would imagine the chambers, Lady Lucretia told herself. They had rehearsed it dozens of times. She patted her hair through her bonnet, plaited and wound in elaborate coils for the occasion. At the far end of the gallery stood the door of dark oak. Beyond it lay the bedchamber.

Her Majesty coughed in the parched stale air. Lady Lucretia hastened forward, lifting window-levers and hammering the long-stuck frames with her fists. One by one the stiff casements swung out. Sunlight flashed off the glass.

'People will see,' warned Her Majesty fearfully.

'Let them!' exclaimed Lady Lucretia gaily, throwing open the last and peering out.

Half the East Garden was a marvel of order. Lavender beds and little lawns were bordered by neatly clipped hedges and fruit trees pleached into fences. But part-way across the garden, that order was overthrown. A swathe of neglect extended. The lavender beds erupted in cow parsley and nettles. The hedges' geometric blocks bulged out of shape while the lawns threw up clumps of weeds. A long glass-house which formed the boundary at the back sagged part-way along its length, the frames bird-fouled and broken. Lady Lucretia touched the locket around her neck.

'Your Majesty might mention the poor husbandry of his gardens to Sir William,' she remarked. 'They do not befit a house befitting a queen.'

Her Majesty looked anxiously from the glinting windows to the closed door.

'We should not be here,' she said fearfully.

Lady Lucretia took her firmly by the arm. The Queen's anxieties were part of her privilege, the Lady of the Footstool told herself. Her timorous nature was to be expected. No one walked in that garden, she reassured Her Majesty. Not for years and years. Just as no one came here. The Solar Gallery had been closed in her first week of life.

She turned Her Majesty away from the rank beds and advanced over the dusty wooden floor. From behind a door disguised as a panel in the wall, the din from the kitchens sounded faintly, rising from the depths of the building. The insolent kitchen boy would be hauling the birds to his master, thought Lady Lucretia, listening to the dull clangour. No one climbed the steep steps behind the door now.

She heard Her Majesty's gait grow hesitant again. How fortunate that Lady Lucretia was there to propel her forward. The Lady of the Footstool sometimes administered mock-scoldings to Her Majesty, in which Her Majesty indulged her most beloved lady-in-waiting as a mother might indulge her child, submitting to playful hectorings and conferring by these allowances a signal of her love. Lucretia considered such a scolding now but decided instead to take the Queen by the wrist and pull her forward. This too, she decided, was permitted by the protocols.

Their dresses swished. Lady Lucretia wore her favourite green calico with a bright red hem. Heels clopped on the boards, raising small clouds of dust. Standing before the dark door at the end, Her Majesty questioned the propriety of a bedchamber before midday and remarked that this door, like the other, was locked.

Lady Lucretia smiled. She touched the tight coils of her hair. She felt her heart beat faster as she released Her Majesty's arm. The ache in her disobedient stomach was sharper now but no less familiar. Not a fist but a sharp-toothed mouth, gnawing inside her. Ignore it, she told herself. Deny it as she always did. Her hand reached inside her bodice and pulled out a bright green ribbon. On the end dangled a smaller key. The lock clicked. Lady Lucretia pushed open the door.

'Your Majesty's bedchamber.'

Her Majesty peered inside the dark chamber at the curtained windows and black damask-draped walls.

'Are our . . . companions here, Lady Lucretia?'

Lady Lucretia smiled. Her Majesty had remembered. For once.

'They are, Your Majesty.'

It had taken much planning to procure the key, and much effort to introduce the companions. Now, propped up on chairs around the canopied bed, lolled the Ladies of the Queen's Closet: Lady Pipkin,

Lady Whitelegs and Lady Silken-hair. Lady Pimpernel appeared to have fallen off her chair. She lay face down on the floor.

As Lady Lucretia skipped forward to lift her back, the Queen made mention of her own hunger pangs, unassuaged since breakfast when she had eaten a manchet roll with runny cheese and a bowl of broth. Could they not descend to the Hall?

The mention of sustenance had its usual effect. Lady Lucretia felt a faint nausea rise inside her and beneath it the usual insubordinate longing. That was her lodger. Her unwanted appetite. Her stomach clenched as the two impulses contended. Deny it, she told herself again. Starve it.

It was early, Lady Lucretia chided Her Majesty. Midday dinner would be served in a few short hours. But in that case there was no purpose in preparing for bed, protested Her Majesty. And the bed was extremely dusty.

'Let fatigue overtake you, Your Majesty,' Lady Lucretia urged, pushing the Queen down onto the bed and ignoring her playful struggles. She eased off Her Majesty's stockings and shoes, which disclosed a regrettable sin of omission.

'Your Majesty, when did you last wash your feet?'

'Last week!' Her Majesty replied indignantly.

She wanted to scold her but it was too late. Beside the bed, a crib with a chain of tarnished silver bells had been pushed against the wall. Lucretia pulled off her bonnet and knelt. She bowed her head and closed her eyes. Let Her Majesty remember, she pleaded. She listened to her Queen's soft breathing. They had rehearsed this part so many times.

A soft hand came to rest upon her head and Lucretia felt the touch like a balm. Deep inside her, the craving abated.

The appetite was not hers. It was a lodger that squatted inside her. A chancre. But as Her Majesty began to stroke her hair, Lucretia felt the ache begin to fade. The fingers glided gently over the coils, letting the thick black plaits loosen and unwind. Lucretia knelt between the crib and the bed, her welling eyes shut tight. The hand stroked and stroked.

But then Her Majesty giggled.

'I'm sorry, Lucy . . .' she spluttered.

Lucretia Fremantle opened her eyes. On the floor lay the long woollen stockings which earlier that morning she had persuaded 'Her Majesty' to wear. Her feet had not smelt so badly then. Perhaps the boots were to blame. The leather clod-hoppers which Gardiner decreed they must wear. At the thought of the housekeeper, she snatched up the nearest boot and threw it into the chairs. The Ladies of the Queen's Closet tumbled down, loose-limbed and beady-eyed. A little stuffing leaked from poor Pimpernel. The other dolls flopped and lolled. The girl on the bed stifled a snort of laughter.

'It isn't funny!' Lucretia scolded. 'You always spoil it, Gemma. And your feet stink too!'

The girl propped herself on her elbows, dark-haired like Lucretia but rounder in the face. Gradually her giggles subsided.

'Why must we play this game, Lucy?' she asked at last.

'I like it,' Lucretia answered shortly.

She placed a hand on the crib and rocked. The little bells tinkled.

'Well I hate this room,' Gemma complained, thumping the coverlet and sending up an explosion of dust. 'No wonder it was locked.'

Lucretia glanced around at the black drapes, the silver crucifix hung above the fireplace, the tiny book left on the mantelpiece. She had found the keys at the back of Mister Pouncey's drawer. Creeping up the staircase and pushing open the door for the first time, she had eyed the stain which spread from beneath the bed like a dark tongue lapping at the floor. She had thrown herself down and pressed her face into the pillow, breathing in deeply, hoping for a faint residual scent.

Dust. Musty feathers.

'Why is it so dark?' Gemma demanded. 'Why does no one ever come here?'

Lucretia thought of the face in the locket pressed against her breast-bone, the woman with dark hair and dark eyes, her hair dressed in plaits and coils. But as she contemplated her answer, a creak sounded from the gallery outside. Then another.

Someone was closing the casements. Gemma gave her a terror-stricken look. Footsteps approached.

'Lucy!'

The gait was too heavy for Mrs Pole. And Mrs Gardiner announced her presence by the jangling of her vast ring of keys. Lucretia knew these footfalls. They drew nearer and stopped. A moment later, the door was flung open.

A black silhouette filled the doorway. A broad-shouldered man stood on the threshold. Beneath a heavy coat he wore a black shirt and breeches. His eyes swept around the black-draped walls, paused at the dolls then came to rest on the two girls. Gemma looked up, wide-eyed with fright. Lucretia stared back.

She did not fear him. It was common knowledge among the serv-ants. The only living creature in the Vale of Buckland who dared defy Sir William was his daughter. She waited for the bellow the servants so feared. But her father eyed her in silence. He came here once a year, she knew, his heavy footsteps tramping down the gallery, waiting out the hours of night in a lonely vigil. Now his face looked about the chamber, the surfaces cluttered with combs, little bottles, pincush-ions, samplers, the little book on the mantelpiece, all covered in a layer of dust. His gaze came to rest again on Lucretia.

'Gemma was commanded by me,' Lucretia began. 'She had no will in this matter . . .'

'Be silent.'

Beside her, she felt Gemma quiver. She feared dismissal, she had confided to Lucretia. Where would she go? Lucretia's father's eyes roved about the room.

'You would play games in here?'

It was no game, she wanted to explain. Gemma was no queen. Only her maid and companion. But when her hand descended and her soft fingers stroked, Lucretia slipped from the body she tenanted. She escaped its rebellious appetites and aches. And the deepest ache of all.

Lady Anne had bled for three days, Mrs Gardiner had told Lucretia. Neither the prayers ordered by Sir William nor the wisest midwife in the Vale had arrested her decline. She had died here, in this bed, and after that the whole Manor had been closed up, entombed as if Buckland Manor itself had died with her.

But Lucretia had lived. That was the appetite in the depths of her belly. The craving that she denied and starved. As if she had sucked the life from her mother's veins.

Her father stared down. A new curiosity seemed to surface in his features. *What game is that, Lucretia?* What if he should ask her that? What if he should address her by name? What then would she do? She would answer him, she thought. She would go to him. She would. His mouth opened.

'What Providence was it that gave you breath?'

She looked back, silenced. The words dashed against her face. The man turned on his heel. Outside two familiar figures waited, one fat and one thin: Gardiner, the housekeeper, and Pole, Lucretia's governess. Both curtsied deeply to Sir William.

Lucretia rose and rounded the dusty bed. On the crowded mantelpiece, the book caught her eye. Before she knew it, she had plucked the volume from among the cloudy bottles and dust-furred combs. Gemma's mouth opened in a soundless exclamation but Lucretia merely clasped her hands and walked out, the leather-bound volume carried innocently before her.

'Ingrate!' exclaimed Pole.

'Why do you goad him?' demanded Gardiner.

'I have angered my father?' Lucretia enquired innocently. 'Then I will take up my fast again.'

'What, child?' exclaimed Gardiner. Pole only shook her head.

Some tedious penance would follow, she knew. Needlework, or learning verses by heart, or sitting on the stool in her chamber. She did not care. Behind her, Lucretia heard the heavy door bang shut. Suddenly her game with Gemma appeared childish. A silly charade.

She strode ahead, looking neither to left nor right, hot palms pressed against the tooled leather boards. Pole and Gardiner marched behind with Gemma. As her boots clopped down the Solar Gallery, the gnawing ache returned. Lucretia imagined the hands that last held the volume. Her mother's hands, clasping her own.

From *The Book of John Saturnall*: A *Broth* of *Lampreys* and all the *Fishes* that swam in the *Days* before *Eden*

ings raise their Statues and Churchmen build Cathedrals. A Cook leaves no Monument save Crumbs. His rareſt Creations are scraped by Scullions. His greateſt Dishes are deſtined for the Dung-heap. And as those Dishes care naught for their Origin, so None now, I aver, could name the Rivers that watered Saturnus's Gardens, nor number the Fishes that swam in those Quanats and Jubs. But swim they did, those Salmons, Sturgeons, Carps and Trouts. And Eels called Lampreys did nourish themselves upon those Fishes, which Beaſts I learned to dress from an Heretical Friend.

Heat water in a Kettle so that you may endure to dip your Hand in but not to let it ſtay. Put in your Lampreys fresh from the River for the Time it takes to say an *Ave Maria*. Hold the Head in a Napkin leſt it slip. With the Back of a Knife scrape off the Mud which rises in great Ruffs and Frills all along the Fish until the Skin will look clean and shining and blue. Open the Belly. Loosen the String found under the Gall (caſt that out and the Entrails) and pull it away. It will ſtretch much. Pick out the black Subſtance under the String, cutting towards the Back as much as is needful. Dry the Fish in Napkins. Now the Lamprey is dressed.

For the cooking, throw the Eels boldly in a great Pan foaming with Butter or slip them at your Ease in a simmering Kettle for no longer (as my Acquaintance put it) than a hurried *Miserere*. Add a Bay Leaf. Let your Fishes swim till the Waters be cold.

For the Broth take Mace, crushed Cumin, Coriander seeds, Marjoram and Rue, and at last (if you may find it) add that Root, famous in Antiquity for its healing Properties and its peculiar Scent, being at once bituminous and having the sweetness of flowers . . .

THE SMELL OF ROAST rabbit wafted up with the woodsmoke. A hazel-wood spit twisted over the fire. The three sat in silence, Josh leaning forward now and again to sink his knife into the haunch. The fire hissed as the blood dripped out. When the juices ran clear he lifted the spit and set to carving the meat. Ben's stomach growled in anticipation. The boy fell on his portion, blowing on his fingers when the hot juices scalded them.

'You can't eat like that at the Manor,' warned Josh. 'You have to cut your food first. Even the kitchen boys have knives there.' He turned to Ben. 'I heard some of 'em even have forks.'

The tuft-headed boy paid no attention, pecking at the meat like a ragged bird.

'Have to give that coat a brush,' Josh continued, looking him over.

'And the rest of him,' added Ben.

The three of them slept around the fire that night. In the morning, the broken walls glowed in the sun.

'That's Soughton stone,' Josh told Ben. 'Romans dragged it all this way. Now here it is and they're all gone.'

'Can't say I blame 'em,' declared Ben, looking gloomily around the woods. His belly gurgled. 'I think that rabbit's still kicking.'

The packhorses tramped back through the wood. Past a chapel, the road split. They took the ox-path around the hamlet of Fainloe.

Ahead, a cart piled high with firewood rocked from side to side as its wheels climbed in and out of the ruts.

'From Upchard,' called the driver when they overhauled his lumbering animals. 'Bound for the Manor. You?'

'Same.'

They passed a chapbook seller from Forham, a cooper's wagon with barrels from Appleby and another carrying sacks of charcoal. A man with bundles of withies on his back claimed to have walked through the marshes all the way from Zoyland. All were headed for Buckland Manor.

The mule limped on its left leg when descending, Ben noticed. It switched to the right for the climbs. His stomach churned as he strained to make conversation with the silent boy. Then, near the top of a rise, Ben clutched his midriff, hurried to the side of the road and scuttled down into the ditch.

Josh halted the piebald then glanced at the boy. By daylight his hair-cut didn't look so neat. More like he had been attacked. From the ditch, an effortful grunt reached his ears. The smell of Ben's success wafted up.

'We'll reach the Manor tomorrow,' Josh told the boy. 'Old Holy paid your way that far. After that it's down to you. Pouncey's not what you'd call the soft-hearted kind.' The boy seemed not to hear so Josh drew nearer. 'I can't feed you, lad. If that's what you're thinking. It's hard enough feeding the horses.'

In the ditch, Ben grunted again. Josh followed the boy's gaze across the hedges and fields.

'I know you can talk,' the grey-haired man said. 'You talk in your sleep.'

A flicker of expression passed across the boy's dark face.

'Spiced wine you were jabbering about,' Josh said. 'When'd you ever drink that?'

The boy only pulled the grimy blue coat tighter. Josh shook his head. His stubbornness would land him in the Carrboro Poorhouse, he thought. Not that he cared. The world was full of rag-headed urchins. If he didn't want to talk, that was his lookout. The boy was nothing to him, he told himself. Nothing at all.

'You keep your counsel then, John Sandall,' Josh said finally. But as he bent to tighten the piebald's belly-strap, a voice sounded behind him.

'John Sandall's not my name.'

Dry leaves and catkins rustled beneath their feet. The ancient trees wrapped John and his mother in shade. High above, a pigeon clattered. John looked up into the chestnuts' crowns. The great trunks grew thicker the deeper they moved into Buccla's Wood then split into copses with younger trees surrounding massive gnarled trunks. As John walked among them he saw that they formed an avenue.

He looked up at his mother but she strode forward as if nothing were amiss. Clearings opened on either side. Familiar smells drifted in the air: fennel, skirrets and alexanders, then wild garlic, radishes and broom. John looked about while his mother tramped ahead. Then a new scent rose from the wild harvest, strong in John's nostrils. He had smelt it the night the villagers had driven them up the slope. Now, as his mother pushed through a screen of undergrowth, he saw its origin.

Ranks of fruit trees rose before him, their trunks shaggy with lichen, their branches decked with pink and white blossom. John and his mother walked forward into an orchard. Soon apple trees surrounded them, the sweet scent heavy in the air. Pears succeeded them, then cherries, then apples again. But surely the blossom was too late, John thought. Only the trees' arrangement was familiar for the trunks were planted in diamonds, five to a side. He knew it from the book.

The heavy volume bumped against his mother's leg. He gave her a curious look but she seemed unsurprised by the orchards. As the scent of blossom faded, another teased his nostrils, remembered from the same night. Lilies and pitch. Looking ahead, John saw only a stand of chestnuts overwhelmed by ivy, the glossy leaves blurring the trunks and boughs into a screen. Then he looked up.

Above the tops of the trees, a narrow stone tower rose into the air. John gripped his mother by the arm.

'Look, Ma.'

The top pointed up like a jagged finger. The tower's sides were riven with cracks. But his mother merely nodded and pulled aside the curtain of ivy. John looked through an archway of crumbling stone to an overgrown courtyard.

Heavy stone slabs reared from the floor. Rough blocks lay where they had fallen. Walls smothered by ivy and creepers enclosed the long rectangle of a roofless hall. The tower was a chimney, he realised. Below, the hearth grinned a toothless welcome. Suddenly John knew where he was. He had seen this place a dozen times, growing grander with every page. He turned to his mother.

'This was Buccla's palace.'

She shook her head. 'I told you before. There was no Buccla.'

'But the witch . . .'

'There was no witch.'

He looked at her in exasperation. But before he could frame his retort, his mother spoke again.

'She was called Bellicca,' she said. 'She came here when the Romans went home. She grew every green thing. It was she who brought the

Feast to the Vale. Until Saint Clodock swore his oath and marched up here with his axe and torch.'

'So it was true . . .'

She looked down at John.

'It wasn't his true name. That was Coldcloak, just like Tom Hob said. Shelter of the Forest, that means. He came up here every year for Bellicca's Feast. He sat with her among her people. They were lovers, some say. But then he swore an oath to the priests of Zoyland. He came and chopped her tables to kindling. He stole the fire from that hearth. He tore up her gardens and fled . . .'

'Fled where?' John asked.

'Who knows?' his mother said with a shrug. 'He disappeared down the Vale.'

John thought of the bare patches on the green. 'But he cried for her.'

'What if he did? He betrayed her. The priests cursed Bellicca and condemned her for a witch. They took the Vale for Christ, and themselves. The people here forgot Saturnus. All but a few. Bellicca and her people were driven out of the Vale, all the way into these woods.'

'What happened to them?' asked John.

'They're still here.'

John stared, baffled, then looked around the ruins as if Bellicca's people might swing down out of the trees. 'Where?'

A faint smile passed across his mother's face. 'First they hid in these woods,' she said. 'They ground up chestnuts for their bread. They took apples from the orchards. They kept the Feast as best they could. Later they remembered Saturnus a different way. They still do.'

John's eyes scanned the cracked walls, the hearth, the thick undergrowth beyond. Were Saturnus's people watching them now? But as he stared, his mother chuckled.

'They took his name,' she told him. 'Saturnall.' She looked around the broken walls. 'That is our name, John. This was our home.'

The bag held a tinder box, his mother's cloak, a short-bladed knife, a cup and the book. They slept wrapped in the cloak, huddled together for warmth in the hearth. They drank from a spring which filled an ancient stone trough behind the ruin. Beyond it lay overgrown beds and plants John had never set eyes on before: tall resinous fronds, prickly shrubs, long grey-green leaves hot to the tongue. Nestling among them he found the root whose scent drifted among the trees like a ghost, sweet and tarry. He knelt and pressed it to his nose.

'That was called silphium.' His mother stood behind him. 'It grew in Saturnus's first garden.'

She showed him the most ancient trees in the orchards, their gnarled trunks cloaked in grey lichen. Palm trees had grown there too once, she claimed. Now even their stumps had gone.

Each day, John left the hearth to forage in the wreckage of Bellicca's gardens. His nose guided him through the woods. Beyond the chestnut avenue, the wild skirrets, alexanders and broom grew in drifts. John chased after rabbits or climbed trees in search of birds' eggs. He returned with mallow seeds or chestnuts that they pounded into meal then mixed with water and baked on sticks. The unseasonal orchards yielded tiny red and gold-streaked apples, hard green pears and sour yellow cherries. But each morning was colder. Each day, John had to venture further. Each night, he and his mother lay down with aching bellies.

When the first frost came, the ground froze. John's mother huddled and coughed in the corner of the hearth beside their flickering fire. Each morning John broke the ice in the trough with the cup. His damp clothes clung to his skin until the cold and fatigue melded to become one sensation.

The roads would reopen in spring, he told himself. He and his mother would go to Carrboro or Soughton. But returning one day he found her crouching outside the hearth, hunched like a beast over its prey, the ground before her spattered with blood. Staring down at the bright red flecks, he felt a new kind of cold, as if he were freezing from the inside.

'What will we do?' he asked her that night. In answer, once again, she took out the book. The volume shook as she struggled to lift it.

'I promised to teach you,' she said.

'You said we belonged here,' he reminded her.

'And we do.'

He watched her open the book. Once again he looked down at the goblet filled with words, the three scripts written over each other. His mother's fingers brushed the vines that curled about the cup.

'This was the first garden,' she said.

'That was Eden,' John told her.

'They called it that later.' She tapped the page. 'In the beginning every green thing grew here. Every creature thrived. The first men and women lived in amity together. They knew no hunger or pain. Saturnus's people kept the Feast.'

The other gardens, remembered John. Saturnus's long-dead people in their long-gone garden. But where was their own feast? His and his mother's?

'But their enemies came,' his mother continued. 'They worshipped a different god. A jealous god. His priests called him Jehovah. They condemned Saturnus as a false idol who had led his people into sin. Their amity was lust, the priests said. Their ease was sloth. The Feast was greed.'

He watched her hands, red from the cold, follow the lines of faded ink as if she could discern the alien words through her fingertips.

'This life was meant as a trial, Jehovah's priests claimed. In this world, men toiled in the fields for their bread. Women brought forth their children in pain and the strong had dominion over the weak. Only in Jehovah's kingdom would their tribulations end and only Jehovah's priests could guide them there because that place lay beyond death. So the priests told their people. But Saturnus's people knew different. They needed no priests, or guides. They knew there was no kingdom beyond death. Their heaven was here.'

'The garden,' said John, shifting on the cold hard ground.

'Yes,' his mother answered. 'And Jehovah's priests knew it too, and knowing it kindled a terrible anger in them. So they tore up the garden. They told their people that Jehovah had expelled them all for Eve's sin. Saturnus's people were scattered.'

John frowned. 'But Bellicca brought the garden here. She brought the Feast. How?'

'They wrote it down, those first men and women.' His mother laid her palm flat on the book. 'In here. And those that came after them wrote it anew, generation upon generation. They hid their garden in the Feast. Every green thing that grew. Every creature that thrived. They all had their place at Saturnus's Table.'

The fire glowed red between them. The broken walls and the heavy crowns of the trees loomed behind. Thin wisps of smoke rose from the embers and up the chimney. John watched his mother's fingers brush the trunks of the great palms with their bunches of dates. From the branches hung hives flowing with honey. Below, crocuses studded the ground. Then her fingers traced the strange symbols in the goblet and she began to recite.

'*Date Palms grew in the First Garden. Bees filled the Combs in the Hives and Crocuses offered their Saffron. Let the first Dish be great enough for All to dip their Cups. Let the Feast begin with Spiced Wine . . .*'

As she worked her way down the cup, John felt his demon creep forward. A new warmth crept through his limbs, not the anger he had felt at the villagers but a gentler heat as if the warm wine were filling his belly, soothing the scorching coal with its balm. The heady fumes wafted in his nostrils. The liquor steamed in its imagined urn, as vivid to John as if he had dipped his own cup beneath the glossy surface. This was what she had waited to teach him, he thought. This was why he had spent the long hours hunched over the book. As his hunger abated, so did his anger. The Feast was theirs, he thought. It would always be theirs. As his mother spoke, a strange contentment stole over him.

'*The second Garden was planted in the Air. Saturnus fattened Larks and Herns in the Treetops. Plovers and sharp-billed Snipes swayed on the high Boughs. All the Fowls increased in their Nests . . .*'

The villagers had chanted of blackbirds and pigeons, John remembered. Chicken-feet for candies, the women had said in the hut. Now strange birds fluttered up from treetops. Each garden yielded a surpassing dish. His stomach rumbled and growled. But beneath his hunger lay a new understanding, as if the dishes of Saturnus's Feast had always been waiting for them up here.

That night his mother's coughing seemed to abate. Even her shivering calmed. John slept soundly in the hearth.

After that, his mother took up the book every night. The third garden was the river where fishes jumped in and out of the water. The fourth was the sea with its scuttling crabs, then came the orchards. The 'cottage' he had spied grew with each appearance, becoming a great house then a palace with a towering chimney. By day, John's stomach ached as before. But when darkness fell, Saturnus's Feast filled Bellicca's ruined hall. Night after night the fruits of the old god's gardens entered on a procession of platters until John could lean back against the hearth's ancient stones, close his eyes and recite the words with his mother. When he asked his mother how she could voice the alien symbols, her expression darkened.

'A clever man told me their meaning,' she said shortly. 'A man who could speak any tongue under the sun.'

Couldn't tell the truth in any of them, John remembered. He leaned forward to ask more but at that moment his mother's cough returned. He bit his tongue.

As the winter deepened, she tired more quickly. Her arms sank under the weight of the volume. At last John took it from her hands and began to recite the words of the dishes himself. He saw his mother sink back gratefully against the wall of the hearth. His voice was enough to feed her, she said. When he spoke, she felt no hunger or cold. Every night, he ventured deeper into the book and its gardens. Every night the dishes of the Feast multiplied and his mother smiled as if she could taste the rich flavours and feel the warmth of the fires.

They made the chestnut bread. Loaves of Paradise, his mother called the charred twists of paste. Bellicca's people had fed themselves the same way. Saturnus's people had always lived in the Feast, she told him. Now she and John would do the same.

Of course they would, John thought as he foraged for scraps among the bare branches. The Feast was theirs. He scooped up the last wizened chestnuts from the frozen ground and searched the orchards for fruit. Each night, after he read, he pressed himself against his mother for warmth and felt her shiver through the hours of darkness until dawn came. Then it was time to forage again.

The bounty of Buccla's Wood thinned. The chestnuts gave out and the remaining apples were brown with rot. John's red fingers ached with cold but he did not care. They had only to get through until spring, he knew. His mother was only waiting for the roads to reopen. Then they could leave. They could take the Feast and leave . . .

So his days passed. Breaking the ice in the trough, a sudden clatter startled him. He looked up as a ragged shape fell through the frost-rimed branches, a wood pigeon, its slack wings spread by the fall. Above, a hawk circled.

John ran back to his mother with the prize still warm in his hands. He plucked the pigeon with cold-numbed fingers then took the knife and cleaned it as best he could. He set the bird over the fire. When it was done, he broke it in two. But his mother waved her share away.

'You eat.'

Her shelter was the book, she told him. Her sustenance was the words inside. He nodded, tearing the hot flesh off the bird. Afterwards he gripped the pages with greasy fingers, conjuring blazing fires against the cold and tables groaning with food. His mother corrected him when he erred, making him repeat the phrases until he was sure. Each morning the ice in the trough grew thicker. She took only water now. When she coughed she turned away so he would not see the blood. The Feast would carry them through the winter, John repeated to himself. The roads would reopen. To Carrboro or Soughton.

Every night John read further. Every night the banquet grew richer. His mother slept for most of the day now, saving her strength for when she roused herself to listen. At last he reached the final page. But as his fingers turned that leaf, his mother raised her hand.

'Wait.'

He looked up, puzzled. The flickering light from the fire threw their shadows onto the toppled stones. He saw his mother's arms redrawn in the firelight, closing about the dark slab of the book. He heard the thick paper crackle as she turned the last page. John looked down.

The palace had appeared in the pages before. But now he was inside its hall. A fire blazed in the great hearth and through the high arched windows the gardens of the book stretched away: the orchards, woods and rivers, even the shore of a sea . . .

It was the Vale, John realised. But the Vale long ago. Through the windows he saw the terraces he had scrambled up and down. At the bottom stood their hut and even its spring-water trough. No church rose but the long broad valley stretched away behind the green, the river's meanders leading John's eye past more orchards, gardens, ponds and fields. The marshlands of the Levels were a glittering shallow sea, just as his mother had said. Beside it, down the length of the valley, Bellicca's gardens covered the Vale. And inside the palace lay all their fruits.

The great chestnut-wood tables groaned under the weight of platters, trays, plates, dishes and bowls. The whole Feast was here, John saw. Every word in the book, every fruit in the gardens, every green thing that grew, every creature that ran or swam or flew. John felt his demon creep forward as a great wave of flavours and tastes washed through him, those his mother had shown him on the slopes joined with others he had never sensed before. He could smell the rich tang of the meats. His head swirled from the steaming fumes of the wine. His jaw ached from the sweets which rose in heaps on silver platters while honeyed syllabubs shivered in their cups. He felt the pastry crunch, shiny with beaten butter. He heard the sugar-pane crackle. The sweetmeats flooded his senses, banishing his hunger and cold. A great procession of dishes floated up out of the pages, all theirs.

'You can taste them, can't you?'

He nodded.

'I knew you would. From the day I bore you. We have always kept the Feast. Down all the generations.'

He thought of all the days spent tramping the slopes. All the nights spent bent over the book, his eyes aching, his head bursting with words.

'Now you will keep it, John. For us all.'

The word caught at him like the spine of a thorn.

'All?'

'I told you,' his mother said. 'The garden was for everyone. We were all Saturnus's people once. So we keep the Feast. We keep it for all of them . . .'

She looked down at the page and John followed her gaze. At first he did not understand. Then he saw the faces.

They filled the page behind the tables, the men and women dressed in smocks and skirts, their faces traced in faded ink: full-cheeked and heavy-browed. A great jostling crowd of revellers . . . John stared. The villagers stared back. At the sight of them, he felt the ember inside him glow.

She was playing a trick, he told himself. This was her final riddle. In a moment she would smile and explain. *Don't believe every old story you hear* . . . But she only watched him with sunken eyes.

'We keep it for them?' John echoed.

'For all of them.'

At those words, the ember glowed hotter.

'They've forgotten,' his mother went on. 'That is all. Forgotten the Feast. Forgotten how the first men and women lived. In contentment together. In amity . . .'

But John felt no contentment or amity. He saw the torch draw its burning arc through the darkness, the broad faces surging forward.

Ephraim Clough cringing beneath John's fist. In place of the spiced wine's balm, deep inside him he felt his anger flare into flame.

'But they drove us out,' he burst out. 'They burned our home. They called you a witch! They hate us! They've always hated us!'

He felt the hot tears prickle behind his eyes. But his mother was shaking her head.

'There is more to learn, John,' she said, her breath coming with effort. 'Beyond your anger. And others to beware. Ones who seek the Feast. Ones who would bend its nature to their purpose . . .'

'The Feast is ours!' he shouted. 'Not theirs! Ours!'

He jumped to his feet.

'John, wait, there is more to tell . . .'

But now the thatch was blazing again, the red flames licking up into the darkness.

'I wish you were a witch!' he threw at her. 'I wish you had poisoned them all!'

He turned and stumbled out of the hearth, her voice pursuing as he strode towards the archway. He pushed aside the leathery ivy. Then he was crashing forward into the wood, her voice growing fainter.

John, wait, there is more to tell . . .

He had learned enough, John told himself as he pushed through the low branches. All around him the outlines of the chestnuts rose up. The freezing air held the scents of the wood in layers. When he could no longer hear her voice, he sank down.

That night was colder than any before. Huddled in a hollow under a blanket of leaves, John drifted in a half-sleep, the torchlit faces of the villagers drifting before him, the flames galloping up into the night. When dawn came, his anger was buried deep inside him. Deep where no one would see. Not even his mother.

The smell of the fire guided him back. The chimney rose above the bare branches. But no smoke showed. The night's store of wood must have been exhausted, he supposed. His angry words returned to him, and his mother's answers. The answers he had shunned. There was more to know, she had claimed. More to tell. Now she would explain, he supposed. He would nod obediently. He pushed aside the ivy.

His mother lay in her usual place, wrapped in her cloak facing the back wall of the hearth, her long black hair hanging loose down her back. Her shivering had calmed, he saw.

'I came back,' John announced.

His voice sounded loud in the deserted place. But she made no reply. He rubbed his arms against the cold. The hearth's ancient soot smelled different, he thought.

'I said I came back,' he repeated.

Still his mother did not stir. A gust of wind raised a little blizzard of ashes from the fire. In its midst sat a black slab. John frowned, then walked forward.

The book's blackened pages still rested in their charred boards. As John stared, wondering at the volume's destruction, a different smell rose from under the soot. Not the charred pages. Something damp and clammy. A faint flutter started up in his stomach.

'Ma?'

He remembered her voice from the previous night. His own angry rejection . . . He would read her the whole book, he resolved. Cook her a sackful of Paradise Loaves. He would never utter an angry word again.

'We'll keep the Feast, Ma,' John promised. 'Just like you said.'

They could write the book again, he thought. He had every dish by heart. In a moment she would rise. She would shake her head at his temper. He would set off with the bag in search of that day's supper. His feet crunched on the frosty ground as he walked forward. He knelt down beside her. But as he lifted her hair out of the ash, his mother's head rolled back. Her sightless eyes stared into his own.

The breath caught in John's throat. Suddenly the wet winding-sheet smell was in his nostrils, the cloth wrapped around his face. The light in the wood seemed to alter as if a shadow had passed overhead.

We'll keep the Feast . . .

She must have waited here for him to come back. Lying here, coughing. He bent and touched her cold arm. He took her hand and remembered her stroking his head, combing his hair with his fingers. The moment the bump on his head had drawn a wince from him. He looked around at the silent trees and broken walls. A cold drift of air rolled forward through the dark trunks, its chill breaking over him. But the coal lodged inside him glowed with a steady heat. His anger would never leave him, he knew. Her lifeless fingers slid from his own.

Then his narrow chest heaved. No one would hear him, he knew, as the first bitter sob swelled inside him. No one would come. Alone in the depths of Buccla's Wood, John abandoned himself to grief.

———————————

'Saturnall?' Ben demanded. 'What kind of a name's that?'

'His,' Josh answered. 'That's what he said.' The driver could not remember seeing Ben Martin's long face look so lively as he glared indignantly at the boy.

'After all that jawing I did. Then he goes and tells you!'

John looked between the two men, one aggrieved, the other hiding a grin.

He had made no decision to be silent. He had made no resolution to speak either. When he opened his mouth, he recalled how Josh and Ben rubbed the warmth back into his limbs, the life creeping painfully back through his numb arms and legs. As if something frozen inside him was thawing.

It had taken three days to scrape a hole in the frosty ground. Another day to gather the stones. He could not bring himself to close her eyes so he had covered her with the cloak. After that the days of wandering began.

Hunger had driven him out of the wood. He was foraging on the slopes when Jake Starling had seized him and dragged him down. He was tied up in the roofless hut where Anne Chaffinge had thrust bread at him. Father Hole had come with Josh who led the mule on a halter.

'Buckland Manor,' the priest had growled. The scar on his face pulsed an angry red. 'It was her wish.'

Ben was still grumbling that night when they pitched camp behind a copse of trees. Josh spent the evening trying to clean John's coat. His filthy shirt and breeches could be hidden beneath it, the men decided. When darkness fell they lay down to sleep. The fire burned low. Somewhere beyond the circle of light John heard the mule stamp and snort. The trees of Buccla's Wood rose around him. If he closed his eyes he could see the tables bend under the weight of the dishes with their rich flavours and pungent smells. He remembered his own hesitant voice. He would keep the Feast, he had promised her. How would he do that now?

There was more to learn, she had told him. And she had warned him too. There were others who sought the Feast.

He tossed and turned on the hard ground, his thoughts veering from her last words to the day he had spied the gatehouse on the distant ridge. She had served there, she had said. She had chosen the Manor as his sanctuary.

'Remember, if they take you up before Sir William you keep your eyes down and you stand,' Josh explained the next morning. 'That's unless they tell you to kneel. He don't like being looked at, Sir William. That goes for his daughter too.'

'And your friend Mister Pouncey?' added Ben.

'Maybe him'n'all,' conceded Josh. 'Everybody else, you call 'em "Master", even if they ain't. And don't stare at 'em like you've been doing to Ben here . . .'

'Wasn't staring *at* me,' Ben corrected Josh. 'More like straight through.'

'Don't do that neither,' said Josh. 'No one likes being treated like a hole in a hedge.' He pulled John's coat straight and flattened tufts of hair. 'Understand?'

John nodded. His dull resignation had receded. Now, to his surprise, the first nerves fluttered in his stomach. As he helped lift the packs and chests onto the horses, he remembered his mother's dry comment on Sir William. *You aren't likely to catch sight of that one . . .*

The road dipped then rose again. A long descent brought them into Callock Marwood where they passed an ancient chapel built from undressed stone then a malthouse and mill. John walked beside the mule. Ahead, he heard men shouting and the rumble of heavy wheels. Around the next bend, their track joined a broader lane crowded with men, carts and animals. Ahead, the thoroughfare rose steeply.

The ridge, John remembered. It had seemed so tiny from the edge of Buccla's Wood. On the other side lay Buckland Manor.

A steady flow of wagons, carts and sweating porters was climbing the steep lane. To either side, beechwoods stretched away. At the top, two low towers flanked a pair of massive barred gates which bore a coat of arms. But heavy timbers obscured the design.

'Sir William nailed those gates shut himself,' Josh told John.

They reached the foot then began to climb. All around John drivers bellowed at straining horses or imperturbable oxen. Heavy wheels slipped in the gritty mud. From the towers, men dressed in green tunics looked down on the porters, carters and animals milling below, directing them to a narrower side-entrance. Josh led the piebald by the halter, following an ox-cart laden with timber. Soon the gatehouse turrets loomed over John. At the top of the ridge, he looked back.

The dark line of Buccla's Wood marked the far horizon. There was the chimney, barely visible above the trees, no thicker than one of the hairs from his head. His mother's last words came back to him, her sunken cheeks pocked with shadow. *There is more to tell* . . .

He would never hear those words now. Instead he would learn the rites of Buckland Manor. He turned and gazed down the broad drive, lined with beeches and flanked by lawns. At the end rose Buckland Manor. Once again, John's gaze fluttered about windows, doors, gates and roofs, searching for somewhere to alight. Above the massive stone walls, great chimneys belched thick white smoke. His mother had sent him here. His new life lay within . . .

'Oy, Addlewit! Get moving there or get out the way!'

Abruptly he was shoved from behind. A grumbling porter shunted him forward and, with a surprised grunt, John stumbled through the gate. He had entered Buckland Manor.

The carters' track ran behind a high brick wall which shielded the house from inquisitive gazes. Ben walked beside the mule. John followed, trudging down the muddy track towards a jumble of stables, outhouses and sheds which surrounded two great yards. Josh pointed to the outermost where carts and wagons, oxen and horses, drivers and porters formed long snaking lines.

'That's us,' the driver told John and Ben, pointing to the first of the two yards. At the gate before the second, men dressed in different-coloured tunics bent over papers laid out on trestle tables. 'Red livery's the Kitchen,' Josh explained. 'Green's the Household. Purple's the Estate. Not much love lost between them.'

They took their places at the end of a line, Josh craning his neck as if looking for someone. As Ben shuffled forward, a short greasy-haired man sidled up.

'King Charles himself,' the man muttered out of the side of his mouth. 'Progress with twenty ladies to Hampton Court Palace. His likeness. Like the sound of that?'

Ben stared. 'What?'

'Ocean of flies,' hissed the crooked-mouthed man. 'Dropping out of a cloud over Bodman. Very strange.'

Ben began to edge away. But the man followed.

'Terrible monster born near Hadensworth.' The man shook his head in sorrow. 'Tragic.' He thrust a pamphlet at Ben. 'Good picture though. Look. See the second head? That's how the little mite came out. You can read all about it inside, a clever fellow like you . . .'

'And it's all gospel truth, ain't it, Calybute?' Josh called over.

'Mister Palewick!' Calybute hailed the driver as if he had just noticed him. 'Of course it is. *Mercurius Bucklandicus*,' he waved more pamphlets, 'knows nothing but truth.'

'Is that truly the King?' asked Ben.

'A very close likeness,' confirmed Calybute. 'On his progress to Hampton Court Palace. With his ladies, as I said.'

At the mention of the King, several porters and carters shuffled over. John peered at a sad-eyed man with a drooping moustache and a pointed beard who looked out from under an elaborate hat.

'That really how he looks?' asked one of the porters.

'His hair's longer now,' Calybute confided. 'So my intelligencers tell me. That's the fashion at Court.' His crooked mouth arranged itself in a grin, disclosing several irregular brown teeth. 'Tuppence.'

'Done,' said Ben.

Calybute pocketed two of Ben's pennies then scurried towards another part of the crowded yard. Ben and the porters gazed down at the picture.

'He don't look no happier than me,' said Ben. Then the long-faced man gazed ahead to the official in green at the head of the line. 'We're not getting closer,' he declared to Josh. 'I thought you knew this Pouncey fellow?'

'Josh?' queried one of the men. 'Know the likes of Mister Pouncey?'

'That ain't Mister Pouncey,' Josh said quickly. 'You won't see him down on the gate. That's his chief clerk, Mister Fanshawe. That fellow beside him's Mister Wichett, Head Clerk of the Kitchens. He's Scovell's man in the yard. Jocelyn's the bailiff. Deals with the Estate. Nothing gets into the Manor but one of them checks it first. Those other fellows are under-clerks and this lad here, he's one of Master Scovell's kitchen boys. Good day, young sir!'

A boy wearing red was striding down the line. A year or two older than John with a broad flat face and thick black eyebrows that met in the middle, he looked them over disdainfully.

'Dole's already handed out,' he told them. 'No beggars in the line.'

'Beggars!' retorted Josh. 'We have goods for Master Scovell and papers for Sir William! And this boy is here to join the Household . . .'

Two porters sitting on their baskets looked up at John, impressed. But the kitchen boy took in his stained shirt and breeches, his filthy coat and hair and gave a burst of incredulous laughter.

'This little raghead? In the household . . . Ow!'

A short bald man in red kitchen livery had marched up behind the boy and slapped him on the side of the head. John tried and failed to suppress a grin.

'Mister Underley's already thrown you out of the jointing room, Coake! Now you're in the yard. When you're told to count heads, count heads! Understand?'

The boy glared up resentfully then nodded and backed away. The bald man turned to Josh, a long chain of keys jangling from his belt. Josh eyed him evenly.

'Good day, Master Josh.'

'Good day, Master Henry.'

'Good winter was it, Master Josh?'

'Adequate, Master Henry.'

Suddenly the pair laughed and embraced.

'This is Henry,' Josh announced. Ben and John looked in bafflement from the tall grey man to the short bald one. 'Henry Palewick. My brother. Henry's the cellarer here at Buckland Manor.'

Henry Palewick glanced around at the jostling horses, carts and pack-men. 'World and his wife pitched up for the dole this morning, Josh. Had to knock a few heads when we gave it out.' He sucked air through his teeth. 'Not sure I can push you up the line today.'

'Waiting's no problem,' Josh said airily.

'I'll have to choose the moment, see?'

'Don't want to cause no vexation, Hal.'

'Didn't say it'd be a vexation, did I now?'

'We'll wait, Hal,' Josh said firmly. 'Don't vex me none at all.'

'Did I utter any such word as vex?' Henry sounded irritated now. 'The only vexation here comes from your assuming. You follow me right now.'

With that, Henry Palewick took the bridle of the piebald and led the horses forward. Men and animals shifted aside in deference to the liveried man.

'This is more like it,' whispered Ben to John.

At the front, a man in the green of the Household scribbled in a large black ledger on a trestle table and barked answers to his clerks, who addressed him as Mister Fanshawe. He nodded to Henry Palewick.

'Now who's for what and what's for who?' Henry asked Josh.

'My lot's for Master Scovell,' replied Josh. 'Ben here's got a package too . . .'

'From a fellow in Soughton,' Ben interrupted. 'Master Scovell's been waiting for it since ages. So this fellow said.'

'Did he indeed?' Henry eyed Ben sternly.

The actual words spoken by the dark-faced man had been rather different, and delivered with a low chuckle. *He's been waiting for this since Eden* . . . But Ben thought it prudent merely to nod.

'Well, we can't have Master Scovell waiting,' Henry continued testily.

Mister Fanshawe shuffled papers and directed his scurrying clerks. Beside him, Mister Wichett in red did the same. Neither acknowledged the presence of the other. A team of clerks was moving up and down Josh's horses, opening panniers and chests. As Ben Martin's oilcloth package was pulled out and passed up, John was shoved from behind.

'Watch your step, Raghead,' hissed a voice. John turned in time to see the black-haired kitchen boy glide away. Then Josh took out the letter.

'Got a message,' the driver declared. 'It's for Sir William.'

At the words 'Sir William' a lull seemed to fall on the clerks. No one jumped or exclaimed. No one gasped. But the name seemed to thrum in the air. Mister Wichett looked up, as if evaluating the sunshine overhead. Mister Fanshawe rubbed the bridge of his nose. On ceasing these manoeuvres they exchanged the briefest of glances. The hint of a shrug from Mister Wichett was Mister Fanshawe's prompt.

'Anything for Sir William is Household business,' declared the Clerk of the Household. 'He'll have to see Mister Pouncey.'

'That's your friend, ain't it, Josh?' Ben piped up. Josh coughed and looked away. Mister Fanshawe cast an eye over his scurrying clerks, searching for one unoccupied. But all now were busy among the waiting porters and carters.

'Can I help, Master Fanshawe, sir?'

Coake stood eagerly at attention before the Clerk of the Household. A faint nod from Mister Wichett and a shrug from Henry Palewick served as consent to the kitchen boy's secondment. Josh handed over the papers, which were glanced at by Fanshawe then given to Coake. John watched the boy hurry off through the gate.

'Your horses will be groomed and watered,' Mister Wichett told Josh. 'Clerk of the Yard'll settle your accounts. Move on through . . .'

Bright sunlight shone through the mullioned windows. A lattice of shadows slanted over the floor. Rocking his heels on the boards, a sparsely haired man tapped a bony white digit against the papers in his hand. Mister Nathaniel Pouncey, Steward of the Manor of the Vale of Buckland, stood before a walnut table piled high with sheaves of papers, the topmost bound with white cloth tape. Everything was ready, Mister Pouncey noted with quiet satisfaction. Everything was in its place.

The steward wore a dark green tunic with a wide white collar around which hung the chain of his office. Seated behind the sheaves, dressed as always in black, Sir William Fremantle regarded his most senior servant. Only the slow tap of his thumb on the arm of the chair signalled his impatience. Mister Pouncey eyed the thumb, then the papers tied with tape, then his order of business, then Sir William himself. His lordship's most senior servant was no longer required to avert his gaze but he still stood in the Lord of Buckland's presence.

'The curacy of Middle Ock, my lord,' he announced.

The vacancy was the first item in their weekly meeting, the thirteenth meeting of the year, the fourteenth year of such meetings.

The curacy lay in the gift of the Vicar of Callock Marwood, the steward explained, that benefice being an advowson from the Manor of Old Toue. Old Toue itself was, of course, no more than three ruined sheds in a field but the old demesne took in the village of Sarwick whose copy-rents were collected through ancient custom by a family (the Bells of Lower Chalming, as Mister Pouncey recalled) who were liable in part for the upkeep of the Poorhouse at Carrboro and who collected tallage in return from the village of Wickenden and also the corpse-tolls levied in the parish of Saint Brice's in Masholt. Unfortunately, few corpses passed through Masholt these days, Mister Pouncey reported, and the Wickenden tallage had never amounted to a large sum . . .

He saw Sir William's attention drift. He had been steward since before her ladyship's death. A clerk before that. He had counted carp ponds in Copham and granted grazing rights in Grayschott. He had ranged through every hamlet, farm and manse of the Fremantle Estate, north as far as Soughton, south to Stollport, east as far as the plain of distant Elminster and west to the edge of the Levels. At the centre stood the Manor where gardeners tended beds that no gentleman saw and ostlers awaited the horses of visitors who never came, where three times daily the great horde of maids, coopers, blacksmiths, clerks and serving men and every other man, woman and child who wore Sir William's livery would cluster around the boards that filled the Great Hall and cram their mouths at his lordship's table. For the world of the Manor must continue unchanged, Sir William decreed.

Yet beyond the closed gates a thousand quarrels flourished, Mister Pouncey knew. In the Vale of Buckland every yard of crumbling wall was someone's to build, another's to repair and another's again to dispute until the stones tumbled like the ancient halls of Old Toue. Ever since the first of the Fremantle line had hacked his way through the wildwood and founded the Manor, Buckland's troubles had been making their way to his lordship's door. Once again, Mister Pouncey eyed the bundle in its white tape.

The Bishop's Court could settle the curacy of Middle Ock, Mister Pouncey suggested. Sir William nodded. Repairs to the stables came next then a dismissal among the clerks. A new tally man would have to be taken on in the counting house next door, if his lordship would permit it. Next, Mister Pouncey moved to the perennial matter of the Forham rents.

'Late again?' queried Sir William. 'Why this time?'

'Sir Hector's claim to the Lordship of Boughton was revoked at the last Visitation,' murmured Mister Pouncey. 'An expensive mistake. And the Countess is not received at Court. Another indiscretion, I hear.'

The Callocks were distant and troublesome kinsmen. Their quarrels and claims against the Fremantles littered the Manor records. Did the flicker of a smile pass across Sir William's hawkish face? There was a time he and Sir William had conversed at their ease. They had even played chequers to pass the hours during Lady Anne's confinements. Now the chequerboard lay in a drawer in the side-table, the pieces arrayed just as they had been when Mrs Gardiner's anxious face had appeared around the door. Lady Anne had requested his presence. She was bleeding . . .

The steward moved on. The pigs of Wittering had rooted up hurdle-fences belonging to the villagers of Selle and no one could agree on the fine. One of the Manor plough-horses was fit only for pasture and the next horse fair at Carrboro was three weeks off. And the one-horse trap, the steward mentioned casually, required repairs. At that, Sir William's expression darkened.

The vehicle had been a rare frivolity on her ladyship's part. Quite impractical on Buckland's muddy tracks, Mister Pouncey had argued at the time. But no expense had been spared when it came to Lady Anne: the new plantings, the East Garden glass-house, the windows in the chapel . . . Sir William had even refurbished the tower, repointing the brickwork and plastering over its ancient mosaics. Heathen views of the Vale, according to the foreman. Now the trap sat in the coach house behind the stables, no more likely to move from its station than the chequerboard from its drawer or the weeds from the East Garden. The glass-house would continue its slow collapse and the chapel tower would stand empty. The Solar Gallery would remain locked and the chamber at the end would keep its perpetual darkness. Perpetual, the steward reflected, but for Miss Lucretia's incursion last summer.

'Have it made good,' Sir William muttered.

Mister Pouncey nodded. Now only the sheaf tied with white tape remained. Mister Pouncey took a deep breath. Sir William observed impassively as the steward undid the papers and broke the wax.

'The Fremantle succession,' Mister Pouncey announced. 'As you know, my lord, I have pursued the task with which you charged me to the utmost of my diligence and abilities . . .'

He had pursued indeed. The evidence of Mister Pouncey's pursuit lay spread over the long table in his chambers: the rolls and folios of brittle vellum and parchment. In the drawers beneath rested sheaves of letters in Mister Pouncey's neat hand, the copies filed in order up to the letters from the Garter King of Arms himself who, as their correspondence multiplied, at last signed himself with weary familiarity, 'Segar'.

But none of Mister Pouncey's correspondents had furnished a solution. His own researches had taken him into the depths of the Manor Rolls where his eyes had strained to decipher the hands of his predecessors as they listed the possessions and privileges, ancient rights and obligations of the Lords of Buckland. They had held Buckland since Caesar's time, so the family story ran. From Sir William himself a line of ancestors marched back through the centuries, the figures growing ever more shadowy, back to that first Fremantle thane who had sworn an oath to God then hacked his way down the Vale to light his torch in a miraculous fire. There he had raised the tower where he would be entombed. Now his effigy kept watch from Buckland's ancient chapel and that miraculous fire still blazed in the torch of the Fremantle arms.

But that tale contained too the seeds of Mister Pouncey's present woes. For the oath sworn by that thane had been carved before his tomb as a Covenant to bind all future generations.

As God's Ministers directed me, and for the sake of his Son Jesus Christ, so I swear: that we and all our Descendants do keep these Lands and Hearths and hold them for our Sovereign King. Let no Woman take Fire to the Hearth, nor tend the Vale's Fires, nor give Nourishment save she be bid, nor rule in the Vale, nor hold Rights to a Virgate of Land, nor keep Retainers or Servants lest these Lands be surrendered again to the Enemies of Our Lord . . .

If Mister Pouncey closed his eyes he could see the ancient copy that rested among the Manor's records, every stain and mark on the vellum. Every faded letter.

Let no Woman . . . rule . . .

There was the nub. In the rite of the Fremantle succession, Lady Lucretia ranked no higher or lower than the daughter of a Wittering pig farmer.

'If it pleased God to take your lordship to his bosom today,' Mister Pouncey began carefully, 'I need hardly remind your lordship of the consequence. Lady Lucretia would be made a ward of court. That court's commissioners would hold the Estate, against whose chattels they might secure their debts as they did on the estate of the nephew of the Marchioness of Charnley. Or they might assign its rents to themselves as they did in the parish of Mere. Or they might seize it entire as they did at Old Toue . . .'

'I know the kind of men who populate the Commission of Wards,' Sir William retorted.

'Even if Lady Lucretia were to attain her majority,' Mister Pouncey continued implacably, 'without a male heir, Buckland would escheat. It would revert to the Crown, which is to say the King's creditors . . .'

On he went. Sir William shifted in his seat. But Mister Pouncey had spent many long hours poring over papers at his master's behest. Now his lordship could listen to his conclusions. Only when the black-clad man began to grimace did the steward fall silent. The shouts from the yard sounded faintly in the room.

'There must be another way,' Sir William said heavily.

Of course there was, Mister Pouncey thought. Ever since the death of Lady Anne there had been a simple solution. The words danced on the tip of his tongue. Now, he urged himself, and heard his own voice speak.

'My lord, there is a course of action.'

Sir William looked up.

'If your lordship were to marry again. If a son . . .'

'No!'

Sir William's voice boomed in the wood-panelled room. He glared at his steward. 'I will not take another. Not for the Vale. Not for all England.'

Mister Pouncey studied the floorboards. Sir William pushed back the heavy chair and stamped to the window. Mister Pouncey saw the broad shoulders slump within the heavy black coat. He would be toying with the heavy gold ring on his finger, the steward knew. Working it around and around.

'Find another way, Nathaniel,' Sir William said more quietly.

The steward nodded, shuffling sheaves, ordering them for their filing among the Manor Records. Perhaps when his own bones were dust, Mister Pouncey wondered, some later steward would peer at the neatly filed papers from this day: the costings for the stable roof, the horse and the carriage. He would find everything in its place, the steward thought with satisfaction . . . Then he noticed the three creased pages which lay on the table. A panting kitchen boy had handed them to his clerk moments before his lordship had arrived. Mister Pouncey cleared his throat.

'Forgive me, my lord. There is one other matter. A petition. It arrived at the gate this morning, my lord. From the parish of Buckland.'

The broad-shouldered man turned from the window. 'Buckland?'

'It lies at the head of the Vale. Above Flitwick.'

Sir William nodded, a curious look on his face. 'I know of Buckland.'

Mister Pouncey pursed his lips. He knew no more of the place than its location, and the contents of the pages before him. Odd that the whole Vale could be named for somewhere so obscure. 'The priest there styles himself the Reverend Christopher Hole. He asks your lordship a boon.'

'What boon?'

'A place, my lord. For a boy.'

Not for the first time, the steward shook his head at the fantastical ways of Sir William's petitioners. Since the closing of the Manor, the Household had little use for boys and Scovell in the kitchens made his own arrangements. He was about to drop the papers back on the pile when Sir William spoke.

'Read it, Nathaniel.'

'. . . *therefore I beg this Boon of your lordship. This Boy goes by the Name of John Sandall. He was born of a Family long of this Parish whose Mother made Potions against those Pangs which are the Legacy of Eve's ancient Foolishness. But this Summer we in the Village of Buckland fell Victim to a more grievous Affliction than Birth-pangs or the monthly Gripings of Women. A new-fashioned Viper crawled into our Garden to set the foolish Souls of this Parish against one another and against their Priest. Promising the Cures of our Children, this Pretender led the biddable Souls of the Parish against this Boy's Mother, condemning her as a Witch and driving her out to perish of the Cold.*

'But no Cure did this Hedge-priest effect. Instead, from Holy Rood Day till after Plough Monday, we were subject to the Rule of a Pharaoh. He calls himself Timothy Marpot and harks after that Zealot named Zoilus who long ago broke the Windows of our Church and the Nose of the

Bishop alike. But when this Marpot burned the Pulpit in our Church, the People of Buckland rose against him at last and that Pharaoh turned a false Moses, fleeing with his Followers from our Anger . . .

Mister Pouncey saw curiosity cloud his master's features. An uncharacteristic expression.

'A witch at Buckland?' Sir William asked.

'Shall I send a man to enquire?'

'No.'

A long silence fell. At last, Mister Pouncey rustled the grimy petition.

'My lord?'

Sir William's head rose. 'Yes?'

'What is your decision, sire?'

'Decision?'

'The boy.'

―――――――――

Livestock pens, a stables and a row of open-sided sheds enclosed the inner yard. Men and boys unloaded carts filled with firewood, straw and timber. Heavy sacks and barrels were hauled or rolled under cover while purple-liveried ostlers led strings of horses whose hooves clacked on the cobbles. The smells of hay and horse-dung mixed with harness-leather and the horses themselves. Behind the stables, dogs barked. While Josh and Ben settled their business with the clerk, John dodged rolling barrels, side-stepped swaying towers of crates, ducked under planks carried shoulder-high and skipped over low stacks of pallets being dragged back to the empty carts. Everywhere he stood, he seemed to be in someone's way. At last he wedged himself between a depot of barrels and a stall filled with straw.

The house loomed above, the walls of Soughton stone glowing in the morning sunlight. An elaborate stone staircase was sheltered by a portico, the torch and axe of the Fremantles rising from its corners. Beneath it, a pair of grand doors opened into a cavernous hall and behind the main house a long wing stretched back behind a high garden wall, its upper storey composed of high windows whose diamond-shaped panes glinted in the sunlight.

The flashes of light might have been sent from those, John thought. He sniffed the air as a smell floated down from a chimney, a smell at once familiar and strange which laced the fumes like a single dark strand in a head of fair hair. He had smelt it all the way down the Vale emanating from Ben's pack. John closed his eyes and tilted his head, tipping it back to breathe in deeply. The strange taste danced on his tongue. Silphium, his mother had called it . . .

When he opened his eyes he saw that he had been watched. Across the yard a boy with floppy brown hair dressed in red kitchen livery stood with his head tilted back and his eyes half closed. As John watched, the boy gave a loud exaggerated sniff.

John stared back stonily. Undeterred, the boy grinned then and beckoned. Keeping the scowl fixed on his face, John approached.

'Coake was meant to help,' the kitchen boy said, threading a thick wooden pole through the handles of a bulging basket beside him. 'Now he's run off. Sucking up to Pouncey most likely. I'm meant to be plucking birds, not hauling onions about.' The boy offered one end of the pole. 'You going to help me lug this thing or stand there sniffing all day?'

The chimneys of Buckland Manor tunnelled up from the depths of the kitchens, through the dark tonnage of stone and brick above. Sliding between walls and driving through floors, the hot channels funnelled heat, smoke and smells as they twisted past receiving rooms and jinked around chambers, wriggled past corridors and galleries, leaving enigmatic traces in the fabric of the house. Purposeless buttresses bulged from walls. Smoke percolated through cracks in the plaster. Certain corners of the house were inexplicably hot and chambers adjoining both the East and West Wings were infiltrated by the smells of roasting meat, or baking bread, or soup . . .

The whiffs and stinks came and went. Hotspots drifted, as if the flues of whirling fire and fumes writhed within the massive stonework, splitting and rejoining, rearing and rising until the thick brick fingers broke into the root stores and apple lofts under the eaves, driving through the attics where the maids huddled in the depths of winter, pressing themselves to the hot walls and waking to the morning tocsin of ladle on cauldron which resounded up from the kitchens below.

Now that din resounded in the crowded passage where two boys shuffled, wincing and grunting under the weight of a basket of onions.

'Philip,' the panting brown-haired boy introduced himself. 'Philip Elsterstreet.'

'John,' John gasped back. The pole dug into his bony shoulder.

'Just John?'

'John Saturnall.'

The passage led to a courtyard surrounded by high walls where liveried men rolled barrels, toted crates or trays or walked with braces of birds swinging from their hands. Others drew water from the well at the far end. Nearer, from a row of curtained stalls, rose the sharp reek of ordure. A sour-faced old man was scraping out the nearest bucket into a barrow. John set down the basket at Philip's signal. Beside a large basket of feathers lay a tray of part-plucked birds. The boy's faint smile appeared to be permanent. He eyed John's coat and filthy smock, his sunken cheeks and tufted scalp.

'Where are you from, John Saturnall?'

'Flitwick,' John answered carefully. 'Been riding with Josh Palewick.'

The boy's eyes widened. 'He goes all over. His brother's the Cellarer here.'

John nodded. 'I might be stopping here myself,' he offered casually. 'Joining the Household.'

Philip's eyebrows rose. 'The Household?'

'Josh can't keep me on for ever, can he? It's hard enough feeding the horses.'

The barrow and its stench approached. The scowling old man who pushed it was Barney Curle, Philip told John. But John was looking over his shoulder. A round-faced girl wearing a full grey skirt had slipped out from a doorway into the courtyard. She wafted a hand in front of her nose as she passed the old man and his barrow.

'Gemma!' called Philip as the girl approached. Two others followed in smocks and maid's caps.

'Lucy's disappeared,' Gemma told Philip, her brow furrowed. 'Lady Lucretia, I mean. I've been out for hours. Meg and Ginny here too.'

The maid called Ginny peered at John. Copper-red curls escaped from under her bonnet.

'Well, order her back,' Philip told the girl, grinning. 'You're her queen, ain't you?'

The red-haired girl giggled but Gemma glared.

'It isn't funny! Pole and Gardiner are looking all over.' She pointed down to the basket of feathers. 'You stick to your plucking, Philip Elsterstreet.'

'Just so long as she doesn't start another fast. Tell her the kitchen's had enough of cooking her gruel.'

Gemma ignored that, casting a curious look over John. 'Who's your friend?'

'Don't you recognise him?' Philip raised his eyebrows in disbelief. 'This is John Saturnall, come to call on Lady Lucy. He's a prince in disguise.'

The girl called Meg giggled. The other two looked John over who stood awkwardly before them, growing conscious of his roughly shorn scalp and the grime ingrained in his breeches and shirt. John drew his damp-smelling coat tighter. The red-haired one called Ginny smiled.

'Prince of where, John Saturnall?'

'Nowhere,' mumbled John, feeling his cheeks flush. Ginny's gaze swept over him then Gemma tugged her sleeve and led her escorts away. John scowled at Philip.

'That your idea of fun?'

'It was only to make them laugh.'

'At me?'

'I'm sorry,' Philip offered. He looked down at the basket. 'Come on. I can't lug this lot on my own. I'll show you the kitchens. You'll need to know your way around, won't you? If you're coming here . . .'

John looked at him suspiciously then bent and gripped the pole again. Both boys grunted and staggered across the crowded court-yard into the passageway opposite. After a turn they came to a high arched entrance from which cooking smells drifted. Philip led the way, lugging the basket into a vaulted room. The boys dumped the basket next to a table where a stout man with a round face was slicing onions, his knife a blur on the wood.

'Underneath the bench, Philip,' sniffed the man. He frowned at John. 'Who's the stranger?'

'Joining the Household, Mister Bunce,' explained Philip.

'Who says?'

'Sir William himself, I heard,' Philip answered without a pause.

'All right,' Mister Bunce muttered. Then he lifted his head and called, 'Stranger in!' With this salutation, Philip ushered John into the room.

The kitchen was not as large as John had imagined. A line of tables ran along one wall. At the end, three pots stood over a flickering fire tended by a ginger-haired boy. From a doorway opposite came the sound of water splashing and the banging of pots and pans. A man so expressionless he might have been any age looked out from that room.

'That's Mister Stone,' said Philip. 'Head of the Scullery. And that boy over there's Alf.'

'It's not so big,' John ventured. 'The kitchen,' he added when Philip looked puzzled. How could all the men in red livery work in here?

Philip grinned. 'Kitchen's not big enough,' he said to Alf who looked puzzled too for a moment. Then he smiled as well.

Philip led John across the flagstone floor and pulled aside a thick leather curtain. A deep hum reached John's ears. A short passage led to some steps and a set of heavy double doors. As he followed Philip, the din got louder. Then the boy heaved on a handle and the door swung open.

'This is the kitchen.'

A wave of noise broke over John, voices shouting, pots banging, pans clanging, knives and cleavers thudding on blocks. But he hardly heard the din. A great flood of aromas swamped the noise, thick as soup and foaming with flavours: powdery sugars and crystallised fruit, dank slabs of beef and boiling cabbage, sweating onions and steaming beets. Fronts of fresh-baked bread rolled forward then sweeter cakes. Behind the whiffs of roasting capons and braising bacon came the great smoke-blackened hams which hung in the hearth. Fish was poaching somewhere in a savoury liquor at once sweet and tart, its aromas braided in twirling spirals . . . The silphium, thought John. A moment later it was lost in the tangle of scents that rose from the other pots, pans and great steaming urns. The rich stew of smells and tastes reaching into his memory to haul up dishes and platters. For a moment he was back in the wood. His mother's voice was reciting the dishes and the spiced wine was settling like a balm in his stomach, banishing his cold and hunger, even his anger. He closed his eyes and breathed in the scents, drawing them deeper and deeper . . .

'Are you all right?'

'What?' John opened his eyes with a start. Philip Elsterstreet was peering anxiously at his face.

'You not going to be sick, are you?'

John managed a shake of his head.

'Good.' Philip pointed to a dark wooden board nailed above the door. 'Being sick's against the rules.'

Thick pillars supported a vaulted ceiling. Half-moon windows were set high in one wall. Heavy tables filled the middle of the kitchen where men wearing aprons and headscarves chopped, hacked, jointed and tied. Boys lurched between them, staggering under trays and pans towards the wide arches and passage on the far side. At a table near the centre, a circle of men whirled white cloth bundles about their heads as if performing a strange dance.

'Kitchen's older'n the house, Master Scovell says,' Philip went on. 'The fire's even older. If it goes out.' The boy drew a finger across his throat. 'That's it.'

At that moment the men whirling cloths all flung them down at once. Out tumbled a heap of bright green leaves.

'Sallet board,' Philip explained. 'Nothing but leaves allowed on that.'

Behind the sallet board, a cook was hauling down trays the size of small cartwheels from a heavy rack mounted beside a tall dresser. As John watched, he began rolling them over the floor with a call of 'Mind yer backs!' Men and boys swayed aside as the rumbling discs teetered across the room to topple into a pair of waiting hands. A stack of pewter bowls clattered onto each tray which was carried to the far side of the kitchen. There an enormous hearth stretched the full width of the room. At one end, a long-moustached man drew slow figure-of-eights in a pot with a stirring lathe while his stockier companion wielded a ladle. Fist-sized gobbets of steaming grey porridge slopped stickily into the bowls.

'End of breakfast service,' said Philip. 'For us, I mean. Them up there are still stuffing their faces.'

He gestured up at the ceiling with a dismissive look.

'Up there?'

'The Household. We don't have much to do with them down here. Except feeding them, of course.'

All around the kitchen, the cooks barked orders: 'Water here!' or 'Sharpener!' or 'Dressed and in!' Then an under-cook or a boy would run over to deliver something, or take it away, or lend a hand in another of the kitchen's inscrutable operations.

Beyond the tall dresser John glimpsed a passageway and the foot of a staircase. Across the kitchen, flanked by stacks of firewood, a great chimney breast rose above a gaping hearth. Then a new scent wafted past John's nostrils: sharp but rich. Nestled in straw in a wooden crate on the nearest bench lay a dozen or more fruits, bright yellow with waxy, finely mottled skins. He had seen them in the book. Now he stared.

'Ain't you never seen a lemon before?' Philip Elsterstreet asked.

'Course I have,' John muttered. 'I just didn't know.'

'Know what?'

John hesitated. 'I didn't know they were yellow.'

Philip gave him another odd look. At the far end of the hearth near the arches and the passage, a great cloud of steam billowed up.

The smell of fish soup wafted across the kitchen. John saw four men dressed in tunics and aprons step back from the scalding steam. One turned and caught sight of the boys.

'You two!' called the short bald man across the kitchen. 'Come here!'

'That's Master Henry,' whispered Philip. 'Josh's brother.'

'I know,' said John, trying to remember how exactly he was meant to address the man. Look at their faces, he thought. Or not look.

'The other three are the Heads of the Kitchen. Mind your tongue. Especially around Vanian.'

'Who's Vanian?'

'In the middle. Looks like a rat.'

The hearth yawned wider as they approached. John stared up at the wheels and chains of an enormous spit. Above a low fire, an array of simmering pots rose in size to a cauldron large enough to boil a pig.

'That's Master Scovell's copper,' Philip told him in an undertone. An under-cook was applying gentle blasts from a bellows to the glowing embers beneath. John caught the strange smell again. Lilies and pitch, thinner than he remembered.

'Where's Joshua?' Henry Palewick demanded as they approached. 'And that other fellow. Face like a horse.'

'Ben Martin,' said John. After a long pause he remembered to add, 'Master Henry.'

Henry Palewick began questioning Philip on what they were doing in the kitchen where, as Philip and everyone else knew, no one but kitchen staff were permitted unless by invitation. Not even Mister Pouncey could enter unbidden, as Philip well knew. Not even Sir William himself . . .

The rat-like Vanian flicked shrewd black eyes over John then returned to his discussion with the other two, which centred on a kettle suspended in the cauldron. The whiff of Ben's parcel hovered under the delicious aroma of fish. Suddenly John felt hungry. The men, he saw, were sipping from a ladle which they passed between them. The tallest of the three slurped and smiled.

'Whether or not Miss Lucretia consumes it, the kitchen has discharged its duty,' he declared cheerfully. He towered a whole head over the others. 'A simple broth is most apt for a young stomach, especially a stomach which chooses privation over nourishment. Lampreys. Crab shells ground fine. Stockfish and . . .' He sniffed then frowned.

'Simple, Mister Underley?' jibed Vanian in a nasal voice. 'If it is simple, then how is it spiced?'

'Came in a parcel this morning,' Henry Palewick offered. 'Down from Soughton. Master Scovell had it out in a moment. Smelled like flowers to me. Whatever it was.'

'Which flowers?' demanded the fourth man of the quartet, in a foreign accent. He pointed a large-nostrilled nose at Henry. 'Saffron, agrimony and comfrey bound the cool-humoured plants; mead-owsweet, celandine and wormwood the hot. Which did this smell resemble?'

'That's Master Roos,' whispered Philip to John. 'Spices and sauces.'

'What does it matter, Melichert?' answered Henry with a weary sigh. 'It is a broth of fish and lampreys.'

'Hardly a full description,' Vanian snapped disdainfully. 'One might as well ask a laundry maid how to weave a sheet. One may as well ask this boy!' he concluded contemptuously.

Heads turned. The other cooks peered down. John realised belatedly that Vanian was indicating himself. Before he could retreat, the rat-faced man had beckoned John forward and lifted the lid of the pot.

'Approach, boy,' he ordered, then turned to the others. 'Let us discover how well the untrained palate performs.' Vanian smirked. 'Or fails to perform.'

Beads of yellow oil trembled on the surface. A deep orange liquid shimmered beneath. A puff of pungent steam wafted up, carrying a rich salty smell. Lilies hung behind it, and the pitch. But they were blanched, or blended somehow. John sniffed and the aroma began to uncurl, the flavours separating on his palate, a strange sensation rasping the back of his throat. For the first time since Buckland, John's demon brought out his spoon.

'Observe,' began Vanian in a lofty tone, 'how the broth subsumes its parts into a single liquor, each one transformed. Let us begin with the spices.' He looked expectantly at John for a theatrical moment. 'No? Then allow me . . .'

'Mace,' said John.

Underley's head turned. Roos raised his eyebrows. Henry Palewick stared.

'Crushed cumin,' John continued. 'Coriander seeds, marjoram, rue. Vinegar. Some honey and . . .' His voice trailed off. All four Head Cooks were staring at him. Vanian's black eyes narrowed.

'And?'

He could smell the plant from the wood. But something in Vanian's look made him hold his tongue. Before the cook could ask again, a commotion sounded across the kitchen.

From the door, Mister Fanshawe and Mister Wichett approached like complementary red and green islands, surrounded by their clerks. At the rear trailed a stony-faced Josh Palewick. At the front, leading the little mob, was the black-haired kitchen boy. Coake's gleeful face found John.

'There he is!' the boy shouted.

'Hold him!' called Fanshawe. 'Take that boy!'

But none of the kitchen staff moved at the Household man's order. As Fanshawe's green-liveried clerks strode forward, John thrust his way between a startled Henry Palewick and Melichert Roos and ran.

The flight of steps rose before him. He passed it and fled down the passageway that led into the depths of the kitchen, the shouts of the clerks pursuing him as he wove his way between porters and cooks who toted baskets or trays, searching for a hiding place but finding only more kitchens where fires burned and aproned men worked at tables or store-rooms or larders from which a great jumble of tastes and smells gusted down the passage: hanging game, cheeses, yeast, warm bread . . .

He turned a corner, then another. Heart thudding, feet pounding, John ran as if every soul in Buckland were after him again. Behind him, angry voices called to each other. The kitchens seemed endless but at last the passage began to empty. At a final junction, John ran left and found himself in a dead end. A cobweb-shrouded doorway pierced the wall. He forced the rusted handle down and the heavy door swung back.

A cellar.

John gazed around the cavernous space. Light entered through a grate. A hearth broke the far wall, quite as great as the one in the kitchen. He edged along the wall, searching for a hiding place. Suddenly something knocked his elbow. A moment later a deafening clang sounded in his ears. A pan had fallen to the floor.

As John's eyes adjusted to the light, he saw benches and shelves stacked with pots, glass jars, kettles and pans. He was standing in a kitchen, he realised. But one abandoned with all its equipment. He looked around at the strange place. Then the clerks' shouts sounded, echoing down the passage outside.

He would be caught here, he thought. Then he would be thrown out. Why had he allowed himself to believe that he might find a place at Buckland Manor? What use had Sir William Fremantle, Lord of the Vale of Buckland, for the son of Susan Sandall? Fanshawe's clerks would find him and haul him out. He would be put in the Poorhouse in Carrboro. Or sent back to the parish.

The shouts drew nearer. But now the din from the kitchen rose too as if someone had opened a connecting door or this neglected place had come back to life. And through the faint clatter and roar he heard a different sound. A voice.

John cast about, his eyes probing the gloom. It came from inside the hearth, he realised. From an opening in the side-wall. A girl's voice.

Peering in, John saw a narrow staircase rise into darkness. The voice drifted down. Somewhere outside, he heard his pursuers draw closer. Quickly, John began to climb.

Spider webs brushed his face. Dust clogged his nostrils. He stifled a sneeze and felt his way up, the voice growing louder with every steep step. The girl seemed to be scolding someone. Rounding the last turn, he saw a crack of light. The outline of a door and a latch.

'Now sit up straight, Lady Pimpernel,' came the voice. 'A Lady of the Queen's closet should never slouch before Her Majesty, should she, Mama? No. Only the Lady of the Footstool may sit before Her Majesty. I beg your pardon, Mama. Did you speak?'

Mama made no answer. So the girl's voice continued.

'There now. Are we all in our places? You too, Lady Whitelegs? Good. Now listen.'

After a short pause, she began to recite in a sing-song voice.

> '*Come live with me, and be my love,*
> *And we will all the pleasures prove,*
> *That valleys, groves, hills and fields,*
> *Woods, or steepy mountain yields . . .*'

At the girl's recital, a strange hilarity gripped John. The shepherd would make his lover a bed of roses, she declared. He would clothe her in a cap of flowers, a mantle embroidered with leaves and a gown of lambswool. She was all but singing now.

> '*A belt of straw and ivy buds,*
> *With coral clasps and amber studs:*
> *And if these pleasures may thee move,*
> *Come live with me and be my love.*'

Then the voice dropped. John leaned closer, straining after the next words. Suddenly, he lost his balance. Grabbing at the door frame he caught the latch. The door swung open and he pitched forward, sprawling full-length on the floor. Behind him, he heard the door swing back. The latch clicked shut.

He was lying on the floor of a long high-ceilinged gallery. Sunlight flooded in through a row of tall windows. As his dazzled eyes adjusted to the brightness, he saw a girl of about his own age perched in a window seat and holding a small black book. She pointed a sharp nose at John.

'Those stairs go to the kitchens,' she declared. 'But you are not dressed like a kitchen boy. You are dressed more in the manner of a rogue. Or a thief.'

The girl wore a dark green dress with a bright red hem. A fine silver chain looped about her neck disappeared into her bodice. Her hair was plaited in elaborate coils but her feet were stockinged, dangling above the dusty floor. A pair of black boots with silver-tipped laces lay beside her. 'Which are you?' she demanded.

John looked around the gallery. 'I'm not a thief,' he said. 'Or a rogue.'

She smelt faintly of rose water. A smile hovered behind her features as if wary of showing itself. Her dark eyes examined him.

'You should kneel, you know,' the girl said. 'Or stand in my presence and avert your eyes. You do not recognise me, do you?'

Josh's instructions had not included what to do if faced with a girl. John got to his feet.

'I am Lady Lucretia Fremantle, daughter of Sir William and Lady Anne of the Vale of Buckland,' the girl announced. When John said nothing, she added, 'I have other titles as well.'

He stood before her in his blue damp-smelling coat, his stained shirt and mud-streaked breeches. Itchy tufts of hair stuck out of his scalp.

'Do you have a name?' she asked.

'John Saturnall.'

'John Saturnall, your ladyship,' the girl corrected him. 'What brings you here, Master Saturnall?'

'I came to join the Household.'

'But now you have run away.'

'They won't have me.'

She regarded him pertly from the window seat. He shifted from one foot to the other. In the alcove behind the girl, he saw a cloak laid out like a blanket. Some clothes had been rolled up to form a pillow. Four dolls watched him from the makeshift bed. Lady Pimpernel, he thought. Lady Whitelegs. Mama. He remembered the maids' chatter in the servants' yard.

'You've run away too,' he said.

'That is hardly possible, John Saturnall,' the girl said archly. 'I live here. What brings you to Buckland?'

She glanced about the dusty gallery. One of her plaits had come loose at the back, he noticed. And her hands were grimy.

'I heard you singing.'

'Singing? I think not.'

'Yes, you were.' John cleared his throat then attempted an imitation of the girl's sing-song voice. ' "Come live with me, and be my love . . ." '

There was more, about steep valleys and clothes. But he trailed off as Lucretia gave an unamused shake of her head.

'What place did you hope for?' she asked.

John thought of the great vaulted room below, the flood of tastes and smells that washed through it. 'In the kitchen,' he said.

'Cooking?' She spoke as if the notion repelled her.

'Can't eat otherwise,' John said. 'Your ladyship.'

'Eat?' She wrinkled her nose.

Her face looked like fine white china, he thought. Cold and perfect like one of her dolls. She regarded him in silence across the corridor. But then the silence was broken.

A gurgle sounded in the long gallery, a low liquid rumble that reverberated off the bare boards and rolled around the walls. The stertorous groan brought a frown of surprise to John's brow, a frown that soon turned to a grin. For a blush reddened the cheek of Lucretia Fremantle. The rumbling emanated from her stomach.

'Sounds like you ought to eat more,' John told her, still grinning. But the girl did not smile.

'Be quiet!' she hissed.

'Isn't me making a racket.'

'How dare you!'

He saw her whole face redden. Her eyes narrowed. She glared at him furiously. He stared back, puzzled.

'It's only your belly,' he said to mollify her. 'Calling for dinner.'

'How dare you!' she spat. Her loose plait swung as she got to her feet.

Before John could utter another word, voices sounded outside. He saw his own alarm mirrored in the girl's face. For an instant they stared at each other, united in the fear of discovery. Then Lucretia's eyes narrowed. Her mouth opened.

'Here!' she shouted down the gallery. 'He's in here!'

They dragged him down to the kitchens. Mister Fanshawe was waiting.

'Send word to the Constable,' the Clerk of the Household instructed two of his clerks. 'Then take him to the gate.'

'One moment, Mister Fanshawe, begging your pardon,' John heard Josh say. 'Let me explain it to him first . . .' Josh's face appeared in front of John. 'See, Sir William hasn't got a place here after all. You'll be going back Carrboro way . . .'

'To the Poorhouse,' clarified Coake. His flat face carried a broad smile.

'It's not so bad as I let on,' mumbled Josh.

'Not if you like picking rags,' Coake scoffed.

'That's enough, Coake,' Mister Fanshawe said. 'Take him out.'

John felt the hand on his neck force him forward. But he had not taken three steps when a deeper voice sounded.

'Let him up.'

John felt himself released. He straightened slowly. A tall grey-haired man with a close-cropped beard and grey-blue eyes stood beside the hearth. He wore the kitchen's red livery and a long white apron. A copper ladle swung from the cord tied about his waist. Mister Fanshawe, looking uncomfortable, offered a full bow.

'Master Scovell,' the Clerk of the Household addressed the man.

'Welcome, stranger,' Scovell replied and the red-liveried men smiled among themselves. 'Has the Household resolved to pay the Kitchen a visit?'

Fanshawe shifted uneasily. 'Your boy Coake led us here, Master Scovell. We were in pursuit.' The man sounded flustered.

'He was troubling Lady Lucretia,' Coake added.

'This boy's petition has been refused. Here it is.' Fanshawe opened his ledger and handed over the grimy pages. Scovell took them, glanced at the words then peered down. 'John Sandall?'

John hesitated.

'He says he's called John Saturnall,' Josh offered.

At that the Master Cook raised his eyebrows. As he peered over the priest's creased letter, John felt the man's gaze burrow under his skin. What had Josh said about looking people in the eye?

'Your mother is mentioned here,' the Master Cook said.

'Yes, Master Scovell.'

'She does not accompany you?'

'She . . . she died, Master Scovell.'

He had not said the words before. He saw the Master Cook's gaze slide away. For a moment he seemed lost in some private contemplation. Then he eyed John again.

'You wish to join the Kitchen, John Saturnall?'

'Master Scovell!' remonstrated Mister Fanshawe.

'Yes?'

'Mister Pouncey has given his answer! This boy is not of a character to join the Household. See here? His mother was accused of witchcraft.'

'Not by any here,' answered Scovell. 'Unless she was of your acquaintance, Mister Fanshawe?'

The men of the kitchen hid their smiles. The clerks with Fanshawe looked about uncomfortably.

'The boy absconded, Master Scovell!' Mister Fanshawe protested. 'He was found in the Solar Gallery . . .'

'Ah yes, those who stray where they should not.' Scovell turned on the man. 'Your own presence here, Mister Fanshawe, might be mistaken for trespass by uncharitable opinion. Unbidden strangers in the kitchen . . . But of course it is mere unfamiliarity. Wilful boys will run amok. We have our own penalties down here for such miscreant spirits. And those,' Scovell directed a stern look at Philip Elsterstreet, 'who admit such miscreants among us.'

The Master Cook turned again to John. Now his grey-blue eyes danced lightly.

'Do you wish to serve among us, John Saturnall?'

John stared back, silenced by this reversal in his fortunes. At last, he found his tongue.

'Yes,' he managed. 'Yes, Master Scovell.'

Scovell raised his ladle and swung and for one instant John thought the Master Cook intended to dash out his brains. But the heavy implement whistled over his head to strike the side of the cauldron. The deep clang drew a startled look from Fanshawe and his clerks, a scowl from Coake and a broad smile from Philip Elsterstreet. Josh nodded his satisfaction while Ben Martin looked almost pleased. All around the great room, every cook, under-cook and kitchen boy turned his gaze to John. Scovell held up his ladle for silence.

'John Saturnall,' the Master Cook announced. 'Welcome to the kitchens.'

––––––––––––––––––

'Etienne de Fremantle married Eleanor of the Catermole family, died without issue,' Mister Pouncey murmured to himself. 'Married again, Joan, Lady Apleby, two daughters and three sons, Rupert, Edward and Henry. Edward inherited. Married Lady Morsboro . . .'

Hunched over the table in his chamber, he lifted brass weights from his piles of papers, traced faded names beneath then replaced the discs of dull metal.

Find another way . . .

Sire a son, Mister Pouncey retorted gloomily to himself. The weights comprised a simple game, its only goal their alignment heaviest to lightest along the table. The two-pounder elicited a soft grunt from the steward. The single ounce he plucked up like a coin. Everything had its place. He weighed the two-ouncer in his hand, the little weight growing warm in his palm.

The order was not going to come out tonight, he suspected, rubbing his eyes before the neat piles in which the genealogies of cousins and kinsmen wove chaotic webs. As he lifted the next stack of papers onto the table, a tentative knock sounded at his door. Mister Fanshawe's cautious footsteps approached.

'A most unfortunate occurrence has occurred, Mister Pouncey. Among the kitchen boys . . .'

The clerk stood in Mister Pouncey's presence, looking agitated as he related the events in the kitchen. The boy in the priest's petition, Mister Pouncey remembered. The boy whose mother was called a witch.

'We were about to expel him when Master Scovell involved himself . . .'

Mister Pouncey frowned. The Charter of the Kitchen gave the cooks more rights than a king, he had once half joked with Sir William. And the Master Cooks of Buckland guarded their empire as fiercely as any Caesar. The privileges of Scovell's domain wove a web quite as fantastical as the liaisons of the ancient Fremantles, Mister Pouncey reflected. But why should the Master Cook meddle in this particular decision? Scovell did nothing without purpose, he knew. What was his purpose with this boy?

Another unanswerable question, he suspected. Unless it was intended as a slight against himself? It was hard to see it otherwise. Mister Pouncey sighed. It seemed that the ancient war between Kitchen and Household had resumed.

'Master Scovell is within his rights,' Mister Pouncey told his clerk. 'He may appoint whom he pleases down there.'

Bidding the man a curt goodnight, the steward considered his narrow bed. But now Scovell's affront revolved in his thoughts. He would not sleep, Mister Pouncey knew now. With an irritable shake of the head, he returned to his search.

Let no Woman take Fire to the Hearth, nor tend the Vale's Fires, nor give Nourishment save she be bid . . .

The Covenant was their curse, Sir William had told him once. Only his Lady Anne had lifted it. And now she was dead.

Mister Pouncey returned to the faded names under his line of brass weights. From Lady Morsboro's children, Guy Boviliers Fremantle had succeeded Edward. The younger siblings' lineages snaked away into the country, joining with the Rowles of Brodenham, the Charleses and the Suffords of Mere and the ill-fated Friels of Old Toue. And the ever-troublesome Callocks. It was the latter pedigree Mister Pouncey traced now. A Callock in the next generation had married one of the Sufford daughters. Their son had married into the Rowles . . . Mister Pouncey rubbed the bridge of his nose. He thought of Sir William's daughter, confined to her chamber again. Scovell's new kitchen boy had been discovered with her. Was that his significance? He rearranged the sheets before him, aligning the Callocks' pedigree with that of the Fremantles. Idly, he began to trace the accidental unions, the removes between cousins, how they branched to become the two separate clans, matching names. Two lines converged, he saw, one from the Callocks, another from the Fremantles.

An underground river, Mister Pouncey thought idly. The germ of an idea took hold in his mind. Could a line of succession run invisibly through the generations? Pulling out the Callock pedigrees, he cast a new eye over the old sheets.

The candle burned low. Mister Pouncey called for another. By the time that one began to gutter, the dawn light was streaming over Elminster Plain and poking in at Mister Pouncey's window. The steward rubbed his eyes. The Callocks were as ancient in the Vale as the Fremantles. Even more venerable, Sir Hector's father had contended. They, not the Fremantles, held the true right to the Vale . . . The steward eyed the two lines of succession. Might they, once again, be united? Might that satisfy the demands of the Covenant?

He would have to negotiate with Hector Callock, he realised. But the penniless Earl would leap at such an alliance. Then there was Lady Lucretia's part. The girl was as strong-willed as her father. She could be relied upon to resist. But the greatest obstacle lay far from Buckland. Any union would require the blessing of the Crown . . .

For that, Mister Pouncey knew, the gates of Buckland Manor would have to open again.

He sat back, remembering the night they had closed. The night of Lady Anne's death. A madness had seemed to descend upon Sir William as he drove out his gentleman servants then all those who had attended his wife. Mister Pouncey remembered the frenzied banging as his lordship hammered the nails into the Solar Gallery door. The next day the Manor had closed.

Buckland must reopen its gates, Mister Pouncey resolved. Resting on the piles of papers, his brass weights were almost in order. Almost in perfect alignment. A good evening . . . Only the Master Cook's petty defiance still niggled at the back of his mind. The vagabond youth. His name hummed in the steward's thoughts as if a fly had found its way into his quarters and now buzzed about the room unable to find a way out.

John Sandall.

Low fires bathed the ceiling in red. The pillars cast shadows over the floor.

'Where're you from, John Saturnall?' asked a voice.

'That's Adam Lockyer,' whispered Philip on the pallet beside John. 'Alf's cousin.'

'Up the Vale,' John answered. 'Flitwick way.'

'I'm from round there,' said a slow-sounding voice. 'Don't remember any Saturnalls.'

'You don't remember much past yesterday, Peter Pears,' someone else replied. John saw a bird-like face framed by curly hair. 'Jed Scantlebury,' he introduced himself. 'Is it true you found our Lady Lucy kipping down in the Solar Gallery?'

'She wasn't kipping,' said John. He remembered the girl's haughty face with its pointed nose. 'Worse luck.'

Jed laughed.

'Shut up there!' called Coake from the other side of the room.

'So you were riding with Josh Palewick?' Adam Lockyer ventured in a low voice. 'Must've seen a few things, up and down the Vale.'

'One or two,' John admitted cautiously.

'What about that parcel?' Jed said. 'Scovell couldn't hardly wait to open it. And how'd you know all what was in that broth?'

John heard the boys shift. One or two sat up.

'Just guessed,' he said carefully.

'You guessed right,' said Adam. 'Underley was saying to Roos. Colin Church heard 'em. He was in the still room. He told that squint-eyed fellow in Pastes, the one who used to be on the salting troughs . . .'

'Tam Yallop,' said a smaller boy.

'You sure, Phineas? Anyroad, he said he'd never seen the like of you, John Saturnall . . .'

He listened to the low murmurs of the kitchen boys. Josh had taken him aside before he slipped away. 'This lot's your family now,' the driver had told him gruffly. 'I'll be round next spring. Henry'll see you all right.'

The voices of the kitchen boys merged in a jumble of whispers. On the pallet next to him he felt Philip shift. This was where his mother wanted him, John told himself. This was his world. With Scovell and the cooks and the kitchen boys . . . But they had fallen silent, he realised. He looked up.

Three figures stood at the foot of the pallet. Coake was flanked by two boys with jowly faces. They folded their arms, looking down at him. He had been waiting for this, John realised. He felt the glowing coal lodged inside him.

'This him?' asked the bulkier of Coake's escorts.

'That's right,' Coake said. He paused for effect. 'See, it's his mother. She . . . she died!'

As Coake's smile became a sneer, the boy's thick features shifted in the firelight and it seemed to John that Ephraim Clough's heavy-browed face was staring down at him. A burning rose inside him. As his anger flared, John launched himself at Coake.

His first punch landed above the boy's eye. Coake clutched his face and John brought his knee up hard. A high squeal escaped his opponent's lips. Behind him, John felt knuckles rap the back of his head. Barlow or Stubbs, he supposed. But the blow only goaded

John on. Behind Coake's face cowered all the others. Ephraim Clough and Timothy Marpot. All the jeering faces. Coake was all the ones who had chased out his mother, who had driven her out to die in the wood. However many times he punched, it could never be enough . . .

Suddenly he was grasped from behind. Philip and Adam gripped his arms. As they pulled John back, he struggled to free himself and resume the assault. Then, from the doorway, a nasal voice sounded.

'What devilment is raised in here!'

'Stop,' hissed Philip in his ear. 'What's wrong with you, John? Fighting in the kitchen'll get you booted out.'

'New boy was disturbing us, Mister Vanian, sir,' Barlow called across the kitchen. 'Thought we'd quieten him down, sir.'

Stubbs was helping Coake to his feet. John heard a contemptuous snort as Vanian walked across with a candle. The man pointed his nose at John.

'I believe you were brawling.'

John eyed the man, struggling to control his breathing. He shook his head. Vanian looked about the room.

'Who was brawling here?'

No one spoke. The man's face twisted in a thin-lipped smile. Then he leaned closer to John.

'Save your performances for Master Scovell, boy. He appears to value them.'

Coake and his companions had shuffled back across the room. Vanian turned and stalked out. Adam and Philip looked at John with wary expressions.

'Thought you were going to kill him,' said Adam. Philip nodded. John looked between them. His anger had subsided. The hot coal had darkened. Now his head was throbbing and his knuckles stung.

'Lost my temper,' he mumbled. The other two were quiet.

'It's all Providence, my sis used to say,' Alf remarked. 'It's like ladders in an orchard. All you got to do is climb the right one . . .'

The quiet talk started up again. The boys lay on the pallets while John stared up at the vaulted ceiling. A lump on his brow began to rise. He listened to the boys' murmuring voices as they spoke of the still room, of Vanian in Pastes and Mister Bunce in Firsts, of Diggory's dovecote and the salting troughs . . . His new world.

One by one, the voices hushed. At last John's eyes closed.

He was back in the wood. He was shaking his mother's shoulder. She would wake up this time. If he only shook long enough she would rise from her place by the fire. She would chide him for running off. Welcome him back. But he shook until the church bell rang in the village below, until its noise roused the dead from their graves. Still his mother did not stir. Instead Peggy Rawley walked towards him, her white face caked with churchyard dirt, a doll dangling from her hand. Behind her came the Riverett girls, blue-lipped and waxen-faced. Then a boy wearing a shapeless hat. Abel pulled off his headgear.

'It was the well,' the dead boy said. 'When it flooded. The old one poisoned our Mary. Poisoned our Cassie's head too. But you knew all that, didn't you, John?'

'What do you want, Abe?' John asked.

'My coat.'

The dead boy gripped John by the shoulder and pulled. The bell rang on and on . . .

John woke with a start. Philip Elsterstreet was shaking him awake. The clanging was Scovell's ladle on the cauldron. John reached to pull the blue coat around him and his hands closed on his red doublet and shirt.

All around John, yawning kitchen boys were rising from their beds on the floor, stretching and rubbing their eyes. Rubbing his own, John winced.

Across the room Coake was rising, one eye purplish and almost closed. John saw Phineas look over and smirk. Then the doors swung open and through them hurried clerks, jointers, trussers, pastrymen, bakers, stokers and porters. Cooks and under-cooks jostled around Scovell who stood at his hearth, the ladle swinging from his hand. A final booming clang rang around the vaulted ceiling.

'Blow up the fires!'

In the hearth the cover was lifted. Bellows were pumped and embers flickered into flame.

'Stations!'

The men flew apart in a whirl of livery and aprons. John, standing next to Philip, looked about in bewilderment. Suddenly he felt a hard jab under his ribs.

'You caught me cold last night,' Coake hissed behind him. His bruised face scowled at John. 'But you wait. I'll be looking out for you, Raghead.'

Philip shrugged. 'Ignore him,' he said as Coake scuttled off towards the archway. All around John, men were readying themselves for the day's work.

'Where do I go?' he asked, looking around the bustling kitchen.

'Wherever you're put,' Philip answered. 'Maybe with Underley in the jointing room. That'd be all right. Or the cellars with Master Palewick. Or the spice room with Roos. I'm in with Mister Bunce . . .'

'Not now you ain't.'

Mister Stone loomed over the boys. The Head Scullion's lower half was wrapped in a leather scullery apron. His face looked down, blank as a pillar.

'You're in with me.'

'But I'm in Firsts,' Philip protested.

Mister Stone shook his head. 'Shouldn't've let this one in, should you?' The big man pointed up at the smoke-blackened board nailed above the door where words were cut in tiny dark letters. 'You know the rules. Go on.'

' "No blows will be struck," ' Philip read out reluctantly. ' "No vile oath will be heard. None shall bring in dung upon their boots" . . .'

'Not that.'

' "No fowl will be admitted uncaged" . . .'

'Not that either.'

' "No stranger shall enter the kitchens except by the order of an officer of the kitchens," ' Philip recited at last.

'That's right.' The man looked down severely at Philip and John. 'See Quiller and his serving men lining up there. Down here, they're strangers. That don't mean we don't know 'em. It means they ain't part of the kitchens. The King himself, if he came down them stairs. Stranger. Even Sir William. If you ain't part of the kitchens, you've no place down here. And an officer of the kitchens means Master Scovell or one of his heads or a full-made cook. It don't mean a kitchen boy who ain't been here barely a year.' The Head of the Scullery turned to John. 'Or one who ain't been here a full day. Understand? Now get in there.'

The scullery smelt of damp food. A row of small high windows admitted light. A long counter, a wooden bin and a series of troughs stretched down one wall. From the far end a lead pipe dripped into an ancient stone trough. A long wooden gutter was suspended from ropes. From Firsts came a clatter of knives as Mister Bunce and the others got to work.

'This here's the ash-bin,' Stone told them in his flat voice. 'Ash breaks up the grease. Counter's for the pile. Troughs are for cleaning.

Sand-box for polishing. Down there's the water-pipe. That's for water.' Stone turned his rounded head to the windows which looked out at ground level into a garden. 'There's some as think they can take our water. A gardener up there. Called Motte.' A hint of expression had entered Mister Stone's voice. 'He's wrong.' The Head Scullion slapped the nearest trough and handed each boy a spatula. 'That's for scraping.'

'How long are we in for, Mister Stone?' asked Philip.

'That's down to Master Scovell.'

The trough was as deep as John or Philip could reach, built of jointed elm planks and lined with thick yellow grease. Ribs of hard fat ran down the sides. Gobbets of food bobbled the bottom, embedded in the yellow-brown crust.

They had scooped out half a bucket of grease when the scullions filed in, grim-faced men in stained livery, each one as silent as Mister Stone. From Bunce's kitchen came shouts and bangs, the clatter of pots and pans. In the scullery, the wooden pipe swung over and water poured out. The scullions half filled the empty troughs and tipped a spade of ash into each. Then they stood at their posts as if gathering their energies. John looked out into Firsts and saw Alf heaving up a kettle of water. Behind him, Mister Bunce diced turnips, his knife whirling over the chopping block. A serving man holding a large wooden tray entered by the archway. Three wobbling towers of dull grey bowls approached.

'Right,' muttered Philip behind John. 'Here we go.'

They took up their spatulas.

'Come on!' yelled one of the scullions at the trough. 'Get on or we'll fall behind!'

Quiller's servers came in a stream, each one with his tray, each tray with its bowls, each bowl smeared with part-dried porridge. The men tipped their trays onto the counter where Philip and John fell upon them with their spatulas, scooping and scraping the gluey strands until the gobbet-free bowls could be shunted along to the scullions at the first trough. Alf staggered in with kettles of hot water but after the first salute neither Philip nor John had either the time to turn around or the breath to do more than grunt. The scullions plunged their arms into the troughs, scrubbing and splashing, only pausing to yell 'Washing out!' before pulling the plugs. Then ash and grease-thickened water poured onto the floor, washing about the boys' ankles before swirling down the drain in the corner. The big wooden pipe swung over and clean water filled the trough in a torrent. Then Philip and John shook the sour-smelling cold grey water from their feet and threw themselves upon the soiled bowls again, beating down the piles with their spatulas and shunting them down to the troughs.

But the faster they laboured the faster the porridge-slimed bowls arrived. For all their scraping, sweating and shoving, the pile only rose higher. Soon it teetered above them, a looming overhang of smeared pewter and tin which seemed to swell and rise no matter how fast they worked. At last only a narrow ledge remained where both boys snatched, scraped and toppled the bowls into the grey scum-flecked water. Every moment, the teetering heap threatened to crash down on top of them. So long as they toiled, John told himself, they could keep the porridge-slimed pewter at bay . . . Then the first pots arrived.

They had given up, John conceded afterwards. He and Philip still scraped but the battle was lost. The pots had overwhelmed them. Then Mister Stone had joined the fray.

'Falling behind,' he had muttered disapprovingly, taking John's spatula from his hand. 'You straighten up that pile.'

Mister Stone went to work. His large stiff body swivelled from pile to trough. He scraped and flicked in a steady fashion. He did not seem to move quickly. But the pile began to descend. At last, when only a token stack of plates remained along with a ten-gallon sauce-pot with a light ring of grime, Mister Stone stood aside. Philip and John finished up then staggered out into Firsts to eat their own breakfasts.

'We've got to get out,' Philip said, spooning cold porridge into his mouth.

'It'll get better,' said John.

It got worse.

Supper was a steamy chaos in which the piles of plates, dishes and bowls mounted ever higher. This time Mister Stone did not step in. The other scullions washed and scrubbed in silence, saying nothing to the boys. 'They know we won't be here long,' Philip explained hopefully as they tramped back into the kitchen that night.

'That's right. You'll be in the Carrboro Poorhouse.'

Coake stood with Barlow and Stubbs. The boy sneered as John and Philip trudged past the trio but they were too weary to answer. They pulled their pallet out from under a table. But it seemed their heads had barely touched the coarse calico before Scovell's ladle rang out again.

The days passed in flurries of crashing plates, gouts of water and scraping. Philip reorganised the pair. 'We're spending half our time dodging around each other. You scrape here, I'll shift the plates around like this . . .'

To John's surprise, the arrangement worked. They still bolted down their food in Firsts then collapsed on the floor of the scullery but they waited for the next onslaught in simple exhaustion rather than dread. Nothing happened in the scullery but dirty water and scrubbing. No words were spoken but the cry of 'Washing out!' and, when the pipe dried up, a loud shout from Mister Stone of 'Motte!' Then with the pots and plates piling up in the troughs, the Head Scullion strode out in pursuit of the gardener. Through the window, John and Philip saw his boots stamp over the gravel and grass of the Rose Garden. Words were exchanged and the flow resumed.

At midday, the tolling of the chapel bell called the boys to dinner. Another in the late afternoon heralded supper. John drank small beer from the butt, swilling down the thin, bitter liquor. He tore his bread into pieces and crammed them into his mouth, chewing furiously. Looking up he saw the other boys stare.

'It's how you eat,' Philip told him later.

'How's that?'

'Like a starving wolf.'

He chewed more slowly. The work grew no easier but when Philip complained of the filthy water that soaked them or the bowls and plates that threatened to engulf them, John remembered how the cold in Buccla's Wood had pinched his bones in its fingers, how his belly had ached and his scalp crawled with lice. How his mother's voice had pursued him through the dark trees.

We keep the Feast. We keep it for all of them . . .

By day, the clatter of bowls drowned out her words but every night, after he settled himself on the pallet with Philip, he returned to the silent trees. There his mother awaited him.

She had sent him to the Manor, he told himself. Why did she draw him back nightly to Buccla's Wood? Still he heard her voice calling after him. What more had she meant to tell him that night? Waking, the question goaded him, turning his thoughts to Scovell. How the man's gaze had slid away when he had told of her death.

But Scovell was another enigma. He had not addressed a word to John since his first day in the kitchen. Sometimes the Master Cook seemed to fill the room with his presence. At others he drifted through like a ghost. His chambers stretched under the whole house, the other boys said. He cooked strange-smelling dishes down there. He spoke languages that no one understood.

'Like Roos then,' offered Phineas Campin one night.

'That's Flemish,' said Adam Lockyer dismissively. 'Scovell's not Flemish . . .'

'What is he then?' asked John.

But none of the kitchen boys knew quite what the Master Cook was.

'I saw him watching you,' Phineas confided later to John. 'The first day you came here. When you told Vanian what was in that broth. I came in from Firsts and he was watching you. Just hanging back in the shadows.'

John's hair grew, black and curly as before. His ribs gained flesh. The bruises from his encounter with Coake faded. He no longer shivered his way through the nights or woke to the old gnawing hunger. He no longer gulped his food like a wolf. The work in the scullery settled into a routine.

Sunday afforded a longer respite when breakfasts and suppers were taken on trenchers, the rounds of hard bread disappearing either into hungry mouths or the dole-box. Then the boys were drawn up in lines, caps were jammed on their heads and they were led out of the kitchens. Philip and John walked with the others in single file through the passage and out into the bright sunlight.

'That's Roderick Tichborn,' Philip pointed out. 'He's in with Henry Palewick. And that's Morris Appleton. Same. Those two with the white hair, they're Jim and Jem Gingell. Don't do nothing but moan. The little'un with them, that's Wendell Turpin. He's out in the dovecote with Diggory Wing. Gervase next to him, he works in the dairy. Those two over there, they're Philpot and Dymion. Adam Lockyer and Alf you know. And Peter Pears and Phineas Campin. Look, that's Meg and Ginny up ahead. Ginny's waving at you . . .'

John nodded. The other boys were his family now, he told himself. But lost among the welter of names and faces, he looked back past the drive and the flanking lawns. Beyond the neat grass, rough pasture led down to a wicket gate and the meadows beyond where sunlight glittered off a series of ponds set about a massive oak. There an odd figure stood.

A tall boy with hair like a hayrick and dressed in rags was picking his way around the largest pond, raising and lowering his feet with odd pauses between steps. As John watched, he stopped altogether and spread his arms, extending two long poles hung with sacks which he flapped like a pair of enormous tattered wings. An approaching pigeon veered away.

'Who's that?'

'The Heron Boy,' Philip said behind him. 'He doesn't talk.'

The figure lowered his wings again, John thought of his own silence as he was carried down the Vale. He stared at the ragged figure but at that moment the line of kitchen boys moved off. The Heron Boy resumed his circuit around the pond.

They walked past the steps to the Great Hall, beneath the portico with its carved stone torches then up the path. Beside the wall of the East Garden, John glanced up at the high windows of the Solar Gallery, glinting in the morning sunlight. The image of Lucretia hovered in his memory, then the raucous rumble of her belly . . .

'What's funny?' Philip asked.

'Funny?'

'You're grinning.'

John shook his head. 'Nothing.'

The shallow slope carried them up towards the edge of the chestnut woods where the chapel emerged like a ship from fog, its nave a hull of weathered grey stone and the tall tower a swollen mast built of ancient granite. At the top John glimpsed openings like high arched windows and remembered his first distant glimpse from high on the slope. He smelt the chestnut sap from the trees behind then a sweeter scent, drifting in the air. Fruit blossom, he realised. The same as in Buccla's Wood . . . How could that be? But before he could wonder more, the path grew crowded. Men in purple livery blocked the way. A voice from the chapel shouted, 'All stand! All stand! Eyes down for Sir William!'

Around John, men and boys were pulling off headgear. The boys in front spilled back onto those behind. Within a few seconds, the orderly lines had become scrums. John found himself pushed aside by the milling men and boys.

'Out the way! Clear the way for his lordship! Eyes down!'

A flustered-looking Mister Fanshawe strode out of the chapel. Two household grooms followed. Suddenly the jostling bodies ceased jostling. Silence fell. Out of the door stepped Sir William.

John glimpsed a tall, broad-shouldered man with thick black hair and a hawkish face. Dressed in black from head to toe, he was accompanied by a smaller man who wore a chain about his neck. Sir William appeared unaware of the silent throng. As the mass of men began to bow, the two men proceeded down a corridor that opened before them. John bent his head like the others, barely glimpsing two women, one tall and thin, the other short and fat, both clutching small black books. Then he stared. Behind them walked a slighter figure. Lady Lucretia.

She wore an elaborate silk bonnet and the same dark green dress as before. John craned his neck to look at her face. The same sharp nose and dark eyes. But a moment later a hard hand rapped the side of John's head. Vanian's face loomed before his own.

'Eyes down!' the man hissed. A bony hand pushed John's head forward.

The little party passed. The men and boys filed in. John and Philip knelt with the other kitchen boys beneath a row of faded banners at the back. A stained-glass window showed a knight kneeling before a fire. The flames glowed brightly among the darkened wood and stone.

'Here's Father Yapp,' whispered Philip.

A pink-cheeked young man wearing a white surplice climbed the stairs of the pulpit. Light from the window bathed his head in purple. John settled himself, ready for the inevitable sermon. But the priest had barely gabbled the Lord's Prayer and a homily before Philip was pulling John to his feet.

'The liveries have to take it in turns,' the boy told him as they turned to leave. 'Not room for everyone.'

'What about up there?' John asked, pointing to a gallery with a heavy door set in its back wall.

Philip shook his head. 'That was Lady Anne's place. That door behind goes to the tower. No one's allowed up there now. Except Sir William.'

A long line of men wearing green livery filed in. The Kitchen exchanged glares with the Household. Among the Household men, John spotted a familiar face.

'Ben!'

Ben Martin looked almost pleased.

'They took me on doing tallies,' he told John. 'Can't hardly count, most of this lot. You?'

'In the scullery.'

The boys behind were pushing to get out. The clerks were pressing to get in. Ben stepped out of the line and leaned closer.

'There was a fellow here from Buckland. Said the whole place went to the Devil.'

'Who?'

'Didn't catch his name. He was in the old orchards. Grafting fruit trees.' Ben nodded towards the chestnut woods.

'Orchards?' queried John. 'In there?'

'Right ragged lot,' Ben said. 'All fruiting the wrong time of year. They don't give apples much bigger'n cherries. Root 'em out, I said. Sir William won't have it. Been here as long as the Manor, the orchard-man told me . . .'

Philip was quiet as they walked back to the kitchen. Entering the scullery, he turned to John.

'That Ben Martin fellow said Buckland.'

'So?'

'I thought you said you were from Flitwick?'

'Buckland's near enough Flitwick,' John replied. He upended a pot resting on the bench and inspected it for grime.

'What did he mean it went to the Devil?' persisted Philip.

'It just did,' John answered.

Philip considered this. 'You weren't riding with Josh Palewick, were you?'

John looked up. 'What?' Why should Philip care how he got here? But the boy's normally cheerful face now wore a dark frown.

'You lied to me,' Philip said.

'Lied?'

'Who showed you the kitchens?' Philip demanded.

'I never asked you to show me,' John retorted.

'They might be taking me on. That's what you said. John Saturnall with his famous nose. That wasn't true either, was it?'

John felt his temper rise.

'They chased us out, all right?' he retorted. 'They called my mother a witch. They burned our home. The priest paid Josh to take me. Satisfied?'

John felt his face flush. But Philip shook his head.

'What's that? Another story?'

'Believe what you like,' John shot back. 'I don't care.'

'Of course you don't.' Philip glared. 'You don't need Philip Elsterstreet now, do you? You don't need anyone.'

John clenched his fists. Suddenly he no longer cared what Philip thought of him.

'That's right,' he threw back. 'I don't.'

They scraped platters and scrubbed pots. They hauled porridge bowls from the trays into the trough and out again. They ate at the same table and washed from the same bucket in the servants' yard. They slept on the pallet among the other kitchen boys. But they did all this in a silence as heavy as the leather curtain hanging above the door to the kitchen. Since the afternoon of their quarrel, the two boys had not exchanged a word.

John swapped greetings with Alf and Adam Lockyer. He made pleasantries with Phineas Campin and Jed Scantlebury. He grunted morning greetings to the Gingell twins and Peter Pears. Coake and his minions sneered as they passed. But Philip remained as silent as the Heron Boy and when, on Sunday afternoons, they were confined together in the quiet scullery the seconds passed like clods of porridge dropping off Phelps's ladle. Philip sat on the floor. John leaned against the sink, tapping his fingers against the side and studying the ceiling. Through the window, he smelt the different scents from the Rose Garden. An obdurate and uncomfortable silence was broken only by the distant shouts of the other boys running in the fields below. But on the third dull Sabbath, the clip-clop of footsteps sounded on the paving-stones. Looking up through the window, John saw a pair of brown ladies' boots. Above them appeared a brown skirt. A moment later the brown boots were joined by a pair of shinier black ones. A dark green skirt with a red embroidered hem topped the dainty footwear.

'. . . but he may be handsome,' a girl's voice was saying. 'He may be charming.'

That was Gemma, thought John. And the other one . . .

But it was all too clear who the other one was.

'A cowherd may be handsome, Gemma,' answered a haughty voice. 'More likely he has dung on his boots and a straw in his mouth.'

'Piers Callock is no cowherd,' Gemma answered. 'He is the son of an earl. Sir Hector of Forham and Artois. Ginny heard Mister Pouncey telling Mrs Pole. Piers will be of age next year. He has been to Court.'

'To Court?' A curious note entered Lucretia's voice.

'And he rides very well,' Gemma continued. 'As well as any on his father's estate, Mister Pouncey said.'

'Then one might almost say,' Lucretia rocked back and forth on her heels, 'that he is a man?'

At shoe level, John felt a bubble of laughter try to force its way up. He choked it back.

'Almost,' Gemma agreed. 'It is only that . . .'

But the boys never heard Gemma's reservation for at that moment Lucretia rocked forwards more vigorously. John heard a sharp rip.

'Oh, by the Cross!'

'Lucy!' admonished a scandalised Gemma.

In the scullery, John stifled a snort. Behind him, he heard Philip do the same. Above, Lucretia Fremantle's boots shuffled back and forth as she tried to free herself. At last Gemma knelt to unhook the snagged calico. Her face appeared, framed upside down in the window. At the sight of John and Philip she frowned. Abruptly Lucretia's hem came free. Her skirt jerked up. John found himself looking at the whitest ankle he had ever seen.

A moment later the red hem dropped. The black boots stomped off and the brown boots followed, leaving nothing but the scent of rose water. John looked down again at Philip.

'I didn't mean to lie to you,' he said.

Philip looked up. 'About what?'

'My ma,' he said awkwardly. 'About what happened. It wasn't like I said . . .'

'And how was it?'

He told Philip everything: how his mother had served at the Manor then returned to the village with John in her belly, how she had gathered plants and given him lessons on the slopes, how Ephraim Clough and the others chased him. He described Cassie and Abel Starling. Once he began he could not stop.

The words spilled from his lips as he told how the sickness spread, how Marpot's examinations began. Then their expulsion, Buccla's Wood and the ruined palace. Last of all he told the story he had heard in its broken walls. Of Saturnus's garden and Jehovah's priests. Of Bellicca and Coldcloak. Of the Feast.

'I thought my ma had kept the Feast for me,' John said. 'She had taught it to me. When she said it was for everyone, I ran. And when I came back . . .'

John fell silent.

'But she sent you here,' Philip said. 'It wasn't to wash dishes, was it?'

John shook his head. 'She served here before,' he said. 'But something happened. Something made her leave.' He remembered his mother's bitter voice telling him of the man who could speak any tongue. Warning of those who bent the Feast to their purpose. She had wanted to tell him more. But he had run from her . . .

'Scovell knew her,' John continued. 'That's why he took me in, I reckon.' He looked at Philip. 'It wasn't for John Saturnall's famous nose.'

He chanced a smile but Philip dropped his gaze.

'I'm not like you, John,' he said in a low voice. 'You find it easy. But I can't stick my nose in a pot and tell you everything in it. No one banged a ladle when Philip Elsterstreet joined the kitchens. My first winter here I was in the yard plucking birds. It took me half a year just to get into Firsts. These kitchens are all I've got. And now we're stuck in the scullery . . .'

His voice trailed off but the complaint sank into John's thoughts. Philip had helped him when no one else had. The boy had risked his place. And this was his reward. He looked at his friend.

'I'm sorry,' John said. 'We'll get out of here. I promise.'

An awkward silence fell. Both boys looked at their feet. At last John glanced away, craning his neck to peer out of the scullery window where sunlight glowed off the deserted paths. The Rose Garden was empty. Gemma and Lucretia were gone. He looked this way and that to make sure.

'I thought you weren't so fond of our Lady Lucy?'

Philip's half-smile had returned.

'I'm not,' John retorted.

'You were staring at her.'

'I was staring at her *foot*,' John corrected him. 'I hope I never see the rest of her as long as I live.'

Lucretia slid the fine linen drawers up her bare white legs, pulled them over her hips and tied the drawstring about her waist. Pointing a toe, she slipped the first stocking over her foot, smoothed the fine silk over her calf then reached for a garter and tied it below her knee. The other stocking and garter followed. Half-clothed, she contemplated herself in the pier glass.

Pale blue veins showed faintly through her white skin. Her hipbones jutted. Her mouth was too wide and her lips too thin while the hair falling over her shoulders better belonged in a horse's tail. The finer down on her arms had darkened that summer along with some sparse wisps at the base of her belly. Gemma had more, she knew. A dark smudge she glimpsed when they undressed together. And her maid had breasts. Small but plump, while her own remained flat as a pair of plates. She stared in the glass. At the sight, verses from the book she had taken popped into her head.

> *Have ye beheld, with much delight,*
> *A red rose peeping through a white?*
> *Or else a cherry, double-graced,*
> *Within a lily's centre placed?*
> *Or ever marked the pretty beam*
> *A strawberry shows half-drowned in cream?*

No cherries 'double-graced' adorned Lucretia's chest. Her dark brown nipples more resembled bullets. She made a face at the girl in the mirror then glanced at the blanket chest where the volume lay concealed.

A prayer book, she had thought, marching back to her room. Or a manual of devotions. Mrs Gardiner never tired of telling her how devout her mother had been. In truth, she did not care what the little volume contained. Her mother's hands had held it. That was enough.

The spine had crackled as she opened the covers. The chamber's musty odour rose from the page. A commonplace book, she thought, seeing handwriting. Pole had one in which she copied out parts of Father Yapp's sermons after chapel, making a great show of her labours and comparing them with Mister Fanshawe's notes.

Sure enough, passages from the Bible filled the first leaves. Notes from homilies and sermons followed. Passages from Bishop Jewel. Her mother had added her own comments. *This way I too am convinced.* Or, *So the Virtuous also must guard against Temptation.*

Her mother's words, thought Lucretia. But as the passages multiplied she began to skip. Then she turned a page and looked down at a different hand. These letters were bolder than her mother's rounded script.

> *Come live with me, and be my love,*
> *And we will all the pleasures prove,*
> *That valleys, groves, hills and fields,*
> *Woods, or steepy mountain yields . . .*

Lucretia's brow furrowed. She was no innocent. She knew as well as the maids why the last tally man had been dismissed when he was caught with a woman from Callock Marwood. And only that spring she had crept into the stables with Gemma when the stallion brought over from Carrboro was put to the mares, staring wide-eyed from behind a bale of hay. Now she gazed again at the words before her.

Such devotions as these, she knew, had no place in church. Eagerly she read on.

> *A belt of straw and ivy buds,*
> *With coral clasps and amber studs:*
> *And if these pleasures may thee move,*
> *Come live with me and be my love.*

Little hearts decorated the margins. Romantic curls and swags hung from the verses that followed. The shepherd would make his lover a bed of roses. He would clothe her in a cap of flowers, a mantle embroidered with leaves and a gown of lambswool. Lucretia imagined her own waist, cinched with woven straw and adorned with studs. Despite herself, she felt her cheeks begin to burn.

'Gemma!' she had called from her bed. 'Come here!'

She hid the book in her blanket-chest, burying it among the folds of lavender-scented wool where Pimpernel, Lady Whitelegs and the others were consigned. Every night, when the last maid retired, the two girls wedged Lucretia's chair against the door and huddled together on the bed.

> *Let me feed thee such Honey-sugared Creams*
> *As cool the Quodling's 'scaping Steam*
> *That thy hottest Tempers doth oft-times bake*
> *Then let my cool Words thy Thirst to slake . . .*

'That's just baked apples in sweet milk dressed up in fancy words,' Gemma declared. 'My ma used to feed us them when we were babes.'

They read on. Her father had written out these lines, she knew. Her mother had read them and written more back. Lucretia knew what lay beyond the lovers' breathless exhalations. But how could such lofty exchanges portend that act she had seen in the stables?

Reign in my thoughts, fair hand, sweet eye, rare voice . . .

She and Gemma examined their eyes for sweetness in the pier glass. They compared the fairness of their hands. They debated the rarity of their voices. They read until the candle guttered then yawned before Pole the next day. Sitting in the stuffy nursery schoolroom, they copied out passages dictated by the governess from *The Offices of Christian Children*. When Pole raised her hand in a furtive wave to Mister Fanshawe below, Lucretia thought of her shepherds and nymphs. The girls exchanged looks and stifled their sniggers. Pole rapped the desk with her rod.

'Perhaps you wish to make a copy in Latin?'

The shepherds were princes in disguise, Lucretia told herself. The lovers were knights. Lying on her lumpy mattress, she thought of beds of roses. Pulling on her dark green dress, she imagined gowns of fine wool. That winter, shadowy suitors stalked the dusk beyond her ice-rimed window. Alone in bed, she pressed her palms to her cheeks, pretending her hands belonged to another. When Gemma tugged her laces before supper, Lucretia fancied a belt with coral clasps and amber studs was being tightened about her waist.

But the shadowy suitors remained shadows. When Gemma finished dressing her, she descended only to the winter parlour behind the Great Hall. There the usual tray awaited. No honeyed words, only Pole's frozen frown. No Ladies of the Queen's Closet, only Pimpernel, Whitelegs and the others. She had lain all night in the Solar Gallery, dreaming of passionate shepherds or princes in disguise, courtiers who would usher her away from Buckland . . .

Instead a ragged boy had burst in.

She recalled his tufted scalp and filthy blue coat, drawn about him to hide the foul state of his breeches. But he was well made beneath the dirt, she conceded. His dark eyes had watched her carefully. Strong cheekbones lent his face an almost noble cast. A prince in disguise might disguise himself thus, she had fancied for an instant. She might have excused his untutored manners, sprawled on the floor instead of standing before her. She might have overlooked his rudeness after she had condescended to conversation. But then her belly had asserted its dominion, trumpeting its hunger. And instead of pretending an unbroken silence or owning to the eruption himself, John Saturnall had laughed at her.

The memory still brought a flush of anger to her cheeks. Half-dressed before the pier glass, she looked down at her traitorous belly and recalled the ruffian's succeeding smirk. Of course she had called out to the servants. She should have screamed the instant he sprawled before her on the floor . . .

But now he was of no account. Gemma's revelation in the Rose Garden had banished him from her thoughts. Not a prince in disguise but a real earl's son was coming to Buckland. And a courtier! One who had actually been to Court.

'Lucy?' Gemma stood in the doorway, part-dressed as Lucretia was. 'Hurry or we'll be late.'

Lucretia picked at a strand of hair. She and Gemma were to show themselves to Mrs Gardiner in rehearsal for Lucretia's presentation to the Callocks. The two girls wriggled into cambric shifts then reached for their stays. Enclosed in the tight-sleeved tunic, Lucretia sucked in her stomach. Gemma slid the stiff plate of the busk into its pouch. She turned to be laced, giving a quick gasp as Gemma pulled on the strings. Their bodices went over the top. Next came skirts, Gemma wrapping the heavy cambric about her mistress's waist, fastening laces to eyelets.

She would powder her face tomorrow, Lucretia decided. She would have Gemma dress her hair as the verses described. She would discipline her stomach with gruel until it submitted to silence. She imagined the youth dismounting his horse, herself in the doorway of the Great Hall, awaiting discovery . . .

Now she was the one in disguise, sewn into her costume and pushed onto Buckland's drab stage to play the part Mrs Gardiner demanded. And behind the housekeeper, Mister Pouncey. And behind the steward, her father. But whatever his purpose, she glimpsed beyond it the glittering world the verses described, where grand ladies glided and maidens were courted. The world her mother had meant for Lucretia herself.

That night she took up the book again, leafing idly through the pages. The boards were loose with handling now. The papers glued inside the stiff covers were coming away at the back. Then she noticed that they were padded somehow. Something lay beneath. A loose page, she saw as she picked at the paper. A letter folded in four. She pulled it open and stared.

Her mother's words covered the sheet, the hand no longer neat but running on as if she could not confine her thoughts. Lucretia read in a greedy rush, picking out words and snatching up phrases: *my Love, now our Joy is truly complete . . . in my Confinement know our Love will be unconfined . . . my Increase is an Increase of happiness for you and me . . .*

My increase. That was herself, Lucretia realised. Her mother was writing of her. She read on avidly, her eyes wide as her mother recorded her joy at the child swelling within her. Lucretia's breast swelled too and she wondered if, through her own pleasure, her mother's joy somehow grew again. Then her eyes reached the last lines.

Let all Buckland rejoice, my lord, for my greatest Joy is to come. The Vale will be made secure again. In our great good Fortune shall the dead Hand of past Oaths be set aside. Let that ancient Covenant be replaced by mine. You shall have an Heir, my William. I feel it within myself. You shall have a Son.

The words swam before her eyes. The paper fell from Lucretia's hands, tumbling end over end to lie on the floor.

'The feast of Saint Joseph?' queried Peter Pears. 'I ain't never heard of it.'

'Ain't none of your business to,' Mister Bunce declared robustly from down the table. 'If Sir William goes eleven years without receiving a single soul then wakes up one day and decides different, it ain't for us to question it. And if he chooses Hector Callock who he loathes like Satan so I heard and invites him over for a saint's day I ain't never heard of, then it ain't for the likes of us to wonder why, now is it?'

A gang of Master Jocelyn's men ventured up the drive and levered off the timbers barring the gates. In the house, rumours took wing. The Earl was bringing the Bishop of Carrboro. Then it was the King's Master-at-Arms. Then the King himself.

A new hum emanated from the kitchen, like the thundering of a distant cart drawing nearer. Baskets and sacks piled up in the passage. Splashing about in the filth of the scullery, John heard barrels being rolled over the cobbles and the jangle of Henry Palewick's keys. But four days before Saint Joseph's Day, Alf pushed his red hair back from his forehead.

'I don't reckon no one's coming. I reckon it's Pouncey's way of getting at us.'

'Maybe there ain't no Earl of Forham,' offered Peter Pears.

'Oh, there's an Earl of Forham, sure enough.'

A greasy-haired man in a mustard-coloured coat leaned against the entrance to Firsts. 'He's here,' continued the man. 'Sir Hector, Lady Caroline and their beloved son Piers. And the Household, obviously.'

'What household?' asked Alf, looking around.

The shabby figure placed a stool in a corner by the entrance, sat down and grinned through a set of crooked yellow teeth.

'Pandar Crockett at your service. His lordship's cook. There's me, a maid, and some fellows been scraped off the floor of an inn and kicked through Sir Hector's livery room. Footmen, he calls them.'

Sides of meat were toted in on poles. Trays of loaves passed back and forth in the passageway. Vanian's ovens glowed. Great oak-sided butts were manhandled up from the cellar and cartloads of firewood piled up in the yard. Only Philip and John in the scullery remained untouched, scraping under the unblinking eye of Mister Stone. John cleared the drain in the floor and Philip scraped out the troughs. A sack of clean sand was the scullery's concession to Sir William's guests. On the morning of the feast a strange calm emanated from the kitchen as the kitchen boys gathered for breakfast. Then Scovell's ladle sounded from the kitchen.

'Stations!'

'Here we go,' said Alf.

John saw Colin and Luke tie back the leather curtain and open the double doors. The roar of the kitchen rushed into Firsts: the crackle of the fires, the clang of pans and clatter of pots, the thud of knives on blocks. Cooks called to the boys who advanced to their stations then were directed to their tasks, swerving around each other and whirling between the fires where great kettles of water boiled and the roasting spit creaked.

'At least we're out of all that,' Philip managed half-heartedly, rising from the table in Firsts.

'Thank God,' John agreed without conviction.

'You thanking God?' Coake smirked across the table. 'Forgetting your mother already?' The older kitchen boy had maintained a wary distance since their first encounter but now he was flanked by Barlow and Stubbs. As Barlow sniggered, John started forward. But an older voice sounded from the far side of the room.

'Now, now, now!' Pandar Crockett levered his head off the wall. 'No sense pounding each other like so many collops of bacon. You need to save your efforts.' He rested his head against the panelling again. 'Like me.'

Coake stalked out. Pandar's yellow teeth showed in a grin. 'The ones you want gone, they never goes,' the cook told John as he and Philip trudged across to the scullery. 'It's the ones you don't as do.'

In the doorway Mister Stone awaited them, spatulas in hand. But as John reached for the nearest, the big man shook his head.

'You ain't scraping today.'

'We're on the troughs?' asked Philip.

Mister Stone shook his head.

'Polishing?' queried John.

'Not that neither.'

A smile flickered on Mister Stone's face. He pointed to the room beyond where the noise had gained a deeper note, a low rumble, as if a great beast were stirring after long inactivity.

'Ask Master Scovell,' he told the boys. 'You're in the kitchen now.'

From *The Book of John Saturnall*: A Feast for the Day of Saint Joseph

Capon is fit for the Table when the Smoke waves like a Rag in a Gale. Pheasants, Geese and Ducks must wait until the Juices run clear. A Pig is cooked when its Eyes pop out. But when a Kitchen Boy is ready for the Kitchen is a Question for subtler Doctors than I.

It is a rare Feast, I own, that celebrates the Day of Saint Joseph and yet that Festival was my Entrance when the Kitchen's Music greeted me with the Crackle of Fires and the Splash of Wine, with the Creak of the Spit and the Knacker of Knives, the Panting of the Bellows and the Cracking of Bones.

The Feast is a Song of many Parts, I learned that Night. Below the Stairs, its Musicians grate and grind and hammer and rasp. Above sits the lusty Choir whose Choristers hymn one another with the guggling of Wine and the jawing of Forcemeats until the Sweets are sent up, the Trays returned Bare and the last Creations reduced to Crumbs.

A Hall of Feasters will eat until the good Earth's Fruits are exhausted and drink until the Oceans run dry. But only when the last Trumpets sound may those below pause and quench their Thirsts, from the Master Cook down to the Boy who enters the Kitchen with eager Eyes and twitching Nose, thinking on Saint Joseph and his silver Cruets but is furnished instead with the Handle of a Spit. For howsoever we imagine our Feasts, and hope our Desires will be assuaged, yet our true Wants and Lacks remain . . .

LUCRETIA HAD NOT EXPECTED a golden coach pulled by a team of six white horses. But perhaps a better pair than the tubby pony and gaunt roan gelding which appeared between the turrets of the gatehouse. And perhaps a grander carriage than the cart which rumbled down the drive, and smarter footmen than the small troop in grubby blue livery who broke into a run as the vehicle gathered speed. She stood beside her silent father on the steps, her face itching beneath its coat of powder. Her hair, dressed 'more freely' that morning at her insistence, had drawn a horrified gasp from Mrs Pole who advanced armed with combs and pins, scraping back her tresses and curling her fringe. Now annoying ringlets dangled in front of her eyes while beneath her bonnet the rest of her hair felt as if someone were pulling it out by the roots. She watched through the jiggling screen as the carriage veered to left then right, sweeping its tail of footmen from side to side. Somewhere behind Lucretia, one of the servants sniggered.

'Be upstanding the Household!' she heard Mister Fanshawe call out. 'For the Earl of Forham. And Artois!'

The wheels of the Callocks' strange coach creaked to a halt. A panting mud-spattered footman took his position at the door.

'The Earl,' he announced between gulps. 'And Lady. Of Forham. And Artois.'

The door opened. A large man with a mottled complexion and dressed in a dark brown travelling cloak emerged, glared up at the coachman then reached back to someone inside. A tall woman climbed out, her face hidden beneath a delicate broad-brimmed hat. A pale powdered face peered out from underneath. Lady Caroline raised a limp gloved hand as Sir Hector and Sir William made a show of greeting one another.

'Eleven years, Cousin William!'

'Indeed, Cousin Hector.'

But Lucretia's gaze was fixed on the youth who followed the Earl and Lady Forham. Piers Callock appeared two or three years older than herself, angular rather than tall. He picked his way up the steps dressed in a dark red coat slightly too small for him and matching breeches. Two flaps of fair hair framed a narrow face and high forehead.

'Come here, boy!' commanded the Earl. 'Introduce yourself.'

'Lord Piers Callock,' the boy said, his mouth twitching slightly. 'At your service.'

'Lady Lucretia Fremantle,' answered Lucretia. The boy's long pale face bore a very slight resemblance to a water parsnip. But as Piers made a low bow and offered his hand, Lucretia banished the mutinous thought.

By day, the Earl closeted himself with her father and Mister Pouncey. Lady Forham kept to her room. The boy spent his time with a tutor whom Lucretia, watching from her window, first mistook for one of the footmen. The man conducted his charge on long walks around the lawns while reading from a small black book. At dinner Piers Callock faced her across the table in the summer parlour where he cultivated a brooding silence whenever Lucretia peered at him over the dishes, putting her in mind of her knights, struck dumb before their ladies. The Callocks were almost as penniless as shepherds, she knew. Even if they were her father's kinsmen. Only Sir Hector's rebukes broke the long silences. 'Sit up, boy!' or 'Offer the jug!' or 'Don't wipe your mouth on your sleeves!' Lucretia offered sympathetic glances across the table at which Piers's mouth twitched as it had on his arrival.

She had put her mother's letter from her thoughts, carefully folding it and replacing it in the book. Piers would escort her in the feast, she told herself. His shy tongue would unbind itself then. Lying in her bed, Lucretia pulled her sheets tight about her as if lambswool dresses and caps of flowers already clothed her. Cinching her waist with her hands, she imagined the belt with its amber studs.

On the night of the feast, Lucretia watched her father take the hand of Lady Caroline and escort her silently through the ranks of the Household to her place at the table on the dais. Hector Callock, for want of any other partner, followed with Mrs Pole. Piers Callock extended his hand.

'Lady Lucretia.'

His fingers were cold. That was the chill in the Great Hall. The servants stood beneath the vaulted roof, Gemma grinning between Meg and Ginny as Piers led her to her place. The high table was crowded with unfamiliar silver plates and bowls, heavy cloth napkins, an ornate clock and a salt-cellar fashioned like a sailing ship. The Fremantle tapestry had been unearthed and hung on the far wall. Reaching her place, Piers Callock released her hand without a word. Still shy in such grand surroundings, decided Lucretia. As a shepherd would be, wandering in from the slopes. Seated, the youth dipped his hands in the finger bowl then wiped them on his velvet breeches.

His was an untutored spirit, she reflected. Piers's courtliness was learned at Nature's breast. As Father Yapp stood to say Grace, the boy chewed his tongue. Across the table, Lady Caroline offered a wan smile. She had suffered a disgrace, Gemma had said. One of Sir Hector's footmen had told one of the laundry maids. The woman's watery blue eyes drifted over the company.

Below the high table, the servants gabbled among themselves. Down the length of the hall, in the arched entranceway between the buttery and pantry, four serving men led by Mister Quiller struggled under the weight of a vast silver tureen. A heady smell of wine rose from the steaming vessel. Goblets were passed up and down the high table. Sir Hector toasted the King, then Sir William, then Saint Joseph, then held up his cup for more.

'This is a fine liquor!' the man exclaimed. 'I will have my cook prepare it, if the rascal can stir himself to learn . . .'

Mister Pouncey leaned forward. 'It is an old hippocras, Sir Hector.' He pointed to the tapestry. 'It is said the first Lord of Buckland warmed his holy wine on a fire he discovered in the wildwood here. When he found it miraculously spiced, he built a tower on the spot. Now his tomb looks out over the Vale . . .'

'First Lord, eh?' Sir Hector's voice had gained a new abrasive note. Lucretia saw Lady Caroline dart an anxious glance up the table. Mister Pouncey looked baffled. Sir Hector stabbed a finger across the table. 'Every old story can be told another way, Master Steward. We Callocks have our own tale . . .'

But before he could begin whatever recitation he planned, Lucretia's father spoke.

'We Fremantles have heard that tale before.'

The black-clad man drew himself up in his chair. Sir William's gravelly voice was neither loud nor sharp but the rebuke rang out as if he had bellowed it from the chapel tower. Along the table, conversations died. The servants hung back. Sir William's eyes sought out Sir

Hector Callock and held him with a cold stare. As silence fell in the Great Hall, Lucretia watched the stony face she had defied so many times and wondered at her own daring. Hector Callock's jaw worked. His red face grew redder as if the Lord of Buckland had forced a choke-pear into his mouth.

'We all cherish our old stories,' Sir William pronounced. 'But now our stories may become one.'

He eyed Sir Hector who forced himself to nod.

'Of course, Sir William,' the man offered in a strained voice. Lucretia's father watched the man then nodded. Lucretia felt a current of relief run around the table as the black-clad man gestured to the empty cups. Sir Hector nodded gratefully as his goblet was filled.

'We will drink a toast to our unity,' Sir William ordered. 'Let us taste this hippocras.'

Lucretia and Piers were served the same liquor with water. Lucretia sipped cautiously. It was love, she recalled, on which her shepherds grew drunk. But she felt her stomach grow warm all the same. She regarded Piers from behind her goblet. His hair had a certain shine, she decided. His chin was not so weak, concealed in shadow. Piers drank quickly and signalled for his cup to be refilled. Then Hector Callock's voice boomed again over the servants' chatter.

'It's a prettier devil than Buckingham who has the King's ear,' the man declared. But now his voice had gained a wary note. He glanced to Sir William. 'The Bourbon's at his side when he rises. She's with him when he sleeps. She's there when His Majesty takes the air and there at his table. Holds him when he makes water too, I shouldn't doubt. She has him like this.'

Mrs Pole looked alarmed but Sir Hector only raised a hand and tugged the fat red lobe of his ear. Lucretia directed a smile at Piers. But the boy seemed to find his cup more amusing. He gulped and waved again at the nearest serving man. Lucretia felt a twinge in her stomach. Not the usual ache. A sharper pinch. The aromas from the wine twisted up from the silver tureen, curling and coiling about the shadowy rafters. She sipped again.

'A King has his passions as God has his reasons,' Sir Hector declared to Sir William. 'We can change neither. If the King should wed a Turk, I would attend her. But a Papist . . . The Bishops do not trust her. Nor the Lords. The Commons hear Masses sung in Whitehall Palace . . .'

With a shock, Lucretia realised that by 'Papist' and 'the Bourbon', Sir Hector meant the Queen. She leaned closer to hear more but at that moment Lady Caroline murmured something to her son. Piers leaned forward.

'Lady Lucretia,' he said in an odd drawl. 'Let me offer my compliments upon your table.'

She stared back, baffled. 'My table, Lord Piers?'

'Yes, your table.' The youth gestured to the silverware. Lady Caroline murmured again. 'And upon your person,' added Piers.

The drawl more resembled a slur. Perhaps he always spoke thus, she wondered. But his eyes appeared to wander. Reaching again for his cup, he fumbled, spilling the dark liquor over the white cloth.

So much for the table, thought Lucretia. Suddenly she felt a bubble of mirth gurgle up from her wine-warmed stomach. Once again she regarded Piers's sloping chin and high domed forehead. His narrow, long-nosed face and close-set eyes. Water parsnip, she thought again and this time the mutinous notion would not be dispelled. A hiccup of laughter escaped her lips. Across the table, Piers frowned.

'Forgive me, Lord Piers,' Lucretia managed. 'I believe I have swallowed too quickly. It is but a passing indisposition.'

But another splutter followed.

'Do you mock me?' Piers's voice was thick. His eyes narrowed then drifted around the table. Lucretia watched Lady Caroline place his cup beyond reach.

'It is myself I mock,' she managed between eruptions. 'I assure you.'

How foolish she had been. How silly to imagine that Piers Callock might accompany her into that world she had imagined in her childish games. That he might disguise himself as the shepherds did in her book. He was as he appeared. And the Vale of Buckland the same. Her mother had given her life for a boy. Not her.

The candlelight thickened, the glossy flames burning a deeper yellow. Across the table, Piers's water-parsnip face sagged and drooped. She was drunk, she realised. Down the table, Mrs Pole glared. A new fusillade of giggles escaped her mouth. But they were mirthless now. As Piers eyed her suspiciously, a commotion stirred at the far end of the hall. In the arched doorway at the end, the serving men were mustering.

They had been working like slaves in the kitchen, Gemma had complained. She had hardly set eyes on her kitchen boy. Now Mister Quiller led in a green-liveried line bearing heavy trays, each one loaded with platters of food.

The bank of heat advanced from the hearth and pushed out into the kitchen. Philip and John ran back and forth from the courtyard carrying armfuls of logs. Shouldering aside the leather curtain, they edged their way between benches and tables where plucked birds rose in heaps, joints of meat hung from hooks and jacks, pots and bowls stood filled with fine-ground sugar, chopped pot-herbs, lemons, curdled cream . . . A swollen river of smells swirled about John: roasting meat, bubbling soups and sauces, the tangs of vinegar and verjuice. The boys manoeuvred their loads around the chafing dishes and stacked them next to the firedogs. In the hearth's cavernous mouth rose the wheels, handles and poles of the spit. There Colin Church and Luke Hobhouse were securing the plucked carcasses of capons, pheasants, geese, ducks and smaller birds that John could not identify.

'You two'll be turning,' Underley told them, gripping the two-handled metal wheel. 'Reckon you can do that?'

From the counters and benches behind rose a thudding, chopping, clattering and clanging that rolled beneath the vaulted ceiling until the air throbbed with the noise. To this din, the spit added its creak.

They counted rounds of twenty then paused in their labours for Colin or Luke to dress the sides of crackling flesh. The fat dripped onto skewers of smaller birds beneath then down into the bubbling juice pans below. Colin poured in half a jack of water then began to baste.

John and Philip strained at the wheel while Quiller and his green-liveried men jostled and elbowed on the stairs. On the other side of the hearth, Scovell stirred his cauldron, pulling out ladles of dark red liquor and pouring it back in long thin streams. So far, he had not glanced in their direction. Hands clamped to the crank of the spit, John smelt cloves, mace and honey under the wine. Pepper too. A familiar sensation tickled the back of John's throat; he knew this smell.

'Pour it through the hippocras,' commanded Scovell. The Master Cook beckoned to three men who manoeuvred a pot crane. Beneath it hung an enormous tureen. The cauldron was manhandled onto a bench and the gleaming pot set below it.

A large muslin bag was set within the tureen. The cauldron was tipped. The spiced wine gushed out in a steaming torrent, the rich fumes quelling every other scent in the room.

'Strangers in!' called Scovell.

The green-tunicked men rushed forward, grasped the tureen and staggered up the steps. The feast of Saint Joseph was under way. Master Scovell stood in the archway, pointing with the handle of his ladle or dipping its bowl into the passing pots and pans. John and Philip began to sweat. Soon their palms grew sore. Beside them, Luke Hobhouse and Colin Church reached over and around each other for knives or whisks or spatulas. Roasted by the fire on one side and chilled by the draught on the other, the two boys worked the wheel. Philip grimaced. John grinned.

'Here we are. Just like I promised.'

As the heat rose, the boys stripped to the waist and strained at the wheel, their hands slippery with sweat. John felt the blisters rise on his palms. Master Roos and Mister Underley barked flustered orders at the cooks and boys while Vanian harangued the men in Pastes, goading them on with his sharp tongue.

Only Scovell kept his cool. The Master Cook took up position by the archway, tasting dishes and calling out orders with a faint smile on his face as if the kitchen's frenzy were only an elaborate drama, a performance put on by actors. But out of the smoke and noise emerged platters of meat surrounded by jellies and garnishes, pies with glazed crusts, great silver fish decorated with slices of fruit. The birds from the spit were taken away for carving and returned arranged in an elaborate pyramid. The serving men swung the platters about and bore them away, glistening and steaming, up the winding stairs to the Great Hall above.

Bright red from the heat, arms aching, palms stinging, John and Philip laboured before the fire. The feasters upstairs would eat for ever, John thought. Until Creation itself was exhausted. The trumpets would sound and he and Philip would still be here, roasted on one side and blasted by draughts on the other. But at last the final platter of sweets passed through the archway. Then Scovell's ladle rang out over the din and the Master Cook's voice reached out to the men and boys slumped at their stations who wiped the sweat from their eyes and blew on their hot hands, who pulled off their headscarves and mopped their faces, some already sinking to the muck-spattered floor.

'Stand down!'

They slept like dead men. Rising bleary-eyed the next morning, John and Philip sat down to bowls of porridge in Firsts. Their blistered hands had hardly touched their spoons before Mister Bunce beckoned.

'This way.'

John and Philip exchanged glances as they followed the Head of Firsts through the kitchen. John had not ventured deeper into the kitchens since his first day's flight. Now the doorways that had flashed past disclosed salting troughs or larders, smokeries or cellars. Through a haze of flour in the bakehouse, John glimpsed men slapping balls of pale dough and labouring over the kneading troughs. The mouths of the bread ovens pocked the far wall. In the paste room, men wielded rolling pins, jiggers and cutters. A complex wave of smells drifted from Master Roos's spice room. Reaching the final junction, John looked down the passage to the deserted kitchen. Planks had been nailed over the door of his refuge. But Mister Bunce turned the other way. At the far end of the passage, a doorway broke the wall. Mister Bunce knocked. After a long pause, the Master Cook's voice sounded.

'Who is there?'

'Mister Bunce, Master Scovell. I've brought the boys you wanted.'

Another pause followed in which John and Philip exchanged looks.

'Send in Mister Elsterstreet.'

Mister Bunce beckoned to Philip. John waited with Mister Bunce in the gloomy passageway. After a short while the door opened again. Philip emerged and flashed John a look. Then Scovell's voice called once more.

'Enter, Mister Saturnall.'

A long vaulted chamber reached back to a hearth where a low fire burned. To either side, pots and pans hung from hooks. The Master Cook's quarters smelt of spices and woodsmoke. From the end of a workbench cluttered with little dishes, plates and bowls dangled a horsehair sieve, some long spoons and a stirring lathe. A chafing dish still filled with ashes stood beside it. On one side of the room, tall shelves were crowded with bottles, corked gallipots and papers. Tied in rolls, stacked in piles, bound up in bundles or thrown in heaps and weighted down with pots, the papers threatened to spill down onto the books shelved below. A row of small windows set high in the far wall looked up into a courtyard. A candle flickered above an open book. Standing over the table, Richard Scovell looked up.

'Come closer.'

John did as he was ordered.

'I asked myself if you would flag, scraping pots at the trough. Mister Stone tells me no. I wondered if you would wilt before the heat of the fire. Yet it seems not. But you have a gift beyond such qualities. You are not like the others, are you, John Saturnall?'

Scovell eyed him, his face half in shadow. John stared back. 'They work as hard as I,' he answered. 'And as well.'

Scovell smiled. 'Of course they do. But they are not guided as you are. Tell me, what do you call him? Imp?'

176

John looked across, baffled. 'Forgive me, Master Scovell . . .'

'Sprite? Sayer? The creature that lives on the back of your tongue. That steered your palate through the broth in my copper, naming its parts. There are not a dozen cooks alive who could perform such a feat. Your guide. How do you name him?'

'My demon, Master Scovell.'

The man nodded approvingly. 'A cook needs his familiar.' Scovell glanced at the shelves and compartments stuffed with papers and books. 'The earth's fruits are without number. No cook could master them alone.' The man turned back to John. 'Even Susan Sandall's son.'

John felt his heart quicken. He had been waiting for this moment, he realised. All through the monotony of their toil in the scullery, it had hung at the back of his thoughts. Ever since the Master Cook had looked up from Father Hole's tattered pages.

'You knew my mother, Master Scovell?'

'How could I not when she worked but ten paces from here?'

'My mother was a cook?'

Scovell shook his head.

'Had she been so minded, no doubt she would have gained that place. But no.' The man glanced across at the shadowy wall which divided the chamber from the deserted kitchen. Set within the stones, a dark alcove framed a low door.

'She was hidden away down here. Few knew of her presence. Fewer yet learned her name. No doubt her arts alarmed some pious souls up there. But Sir William would deny nothing to Lady Anne.'

'Lady Anne?' John looked at Scovell, puzzled.

'Of course. Who else would bring your mother here? Her ladyship had never brought a child to term. When she fell pregnant, your mother was summoned here by Sir William. Your mother attended her in her confinement. All was well until the birth. Then Lady Anne began to weaken. Your mother applied every art she knew. To no avail. Lady Anne died. The child alone was saved.'

A moment passed before John understood.

'Lady Lucretia?' he exclaimed. 'My mother delivered her?'

'She did. But beside the death of Lady Anne, the child's life meant nothing to Sir William. His grief knew no bounds. His gentleman-servants were driven out that night and all those who attended Lady Anne. Even your mother . . .'

A troubled expression clouded Scovell's features. The man glanced up at a high shelf where, half-hidden in the shadows, John recognised a row of galliot pots.

'I saved what I could from her kitchen; the rarest among her decoctions. Then Sir William nailed shut the gates. The Manor closed.'

So she had been driven out, thought John. But why had his mother refused to return? Why was her resolve so adamant?

'She disappeared into the Vale,' the Master Cook continued. 'She had never mentioned the village of her birth. For a time I believed she might return. But she did not.' The man looked up. 'Then you came.'

'She sent me here,' John said simply.

'You have a great gift,' Scovell said. 'Your mother was too wise not to recognise it. But your talent is untutored. Now you must bend your gift to its purpose.'

'What purpose, Master Scovell?'

'A kitchen demands many talents,' the Master Cook said. 'Some are common enough. Mister Elsterstreet and his fellows could master them. Others are rare beyond imagination. A true cook learns them all.'

The man held his gaze a moment longer, his eyes probing as before. There was more, John felt with sudden conviction. More that Scovell might tell. Or more that he might ask. But instead of any revelation, the Master Cook plucked a knife from the cluttered table. The blade was a slender crescent of steel, the wooden handle worn to a shine.

'Let the kitchen guide you,' Scovell said. He pressed the handle into John's hand. 'You will begin in Firsts.'

'Is it true he's got a woman's hand in a jar?' Wendell Turpin demanded that evening.

'I heard it was snakes,' Phineas Campin offered from across the darkened kitchen.

'I didn't see any snakes,' John answered truthfully.

'What about lizards?'

'None of those either.'

The questions petered out slowly. John lay back on the pallet, waiting, listening to the straw crunch as Philip shifted restlessly. At last, when all the kitchen boys slept, he whispered the substance of the encounter to Philip.

'Your mother delivered our Lucy?' Philip sounded incredulous.

'Shush,' John hissed. 'Or everyone'll hear.'

'And she worked next door to Scovell,' Philip said in a curious tone of voice. 'You don't think, him and your ma . . . ?'

'No,' John said flatly. The thought had flashed across his mind but something in the Master Cook's bearing told him it was not so. 'He said Sir William had summoned her. But how would Sir William know my ma?'

Philip thought. 'Maybe it was Pouncey. There ain't much in the Vale he doesn't know. What else?'

'He said I had a purpose.'

'What purpose?'

'I don't know,' John told Philip. 'He said the kitchen would guide me.' He remembered Scovell's disparaging words about the other boys. 'Guide both of us,' he amended hastily.

'Us?' Philip's face assumed a hopeful look.

'I promised you, didn't I?' John grinned back. 'We start tomorrow. In Firsts.'

'It ain't only sallets as get trimmed into shape in here,' Mister Bunce told John and Philip the next morning, hoisting a basket onto the bench. 'It's the likes of you too. Understand?'

They nodded.

'Good. Get to work.'

They washed and peeled and scraped and sliced. They cut stalks and pared roots. John's knife skidded on slippery-skinned onions and hacked at beets, their dull leathery hides toughened by months in the root lofts. Leeks followed turnips. Alf scooped the results of their labours into baskets and hauled them through to the kitchen.

'Most dangerous part of a knife's the handle,' Mister Bunce told them both. 'Know why?'

They shook their heads.

'That's the part that joins the blade to the kitchen boy.'

The Head of Firsts kept the knives wrapped in linen cloths and the linens wrapped in sacking inside a drawer which he locked each night. They were sharpened every Thursday on a saddle-backed whetstone and polished every other week by Mister Bunce using a cloth and a secret white paste made of goat's urine and chalk, according to Alf. When Mister Bunce chopped, the blade seemed to blur. Wafer-like slices flew across the board, each precisely as thick or thin as required. John's fingers might tire or turn to thumbs, but the man's thick digits worked on effortlessly.

'Look here,' he called to John as his knife darted in and out of a dice of turnip. 'We used to call these kickshaws. That's French, that is. Means what-you-like or somesuch. I don't remember exactly.'

Transparent slivers fell to the table. The man's blunt fingers turned the object with surprising delicacy.

'There's all kinds of kickshaws. Pastries, sweets. You can make 'em from anything. Even this turnip.'

The knife pricked and prised. At last the man held up a tiny cockerel complete with cock's comb.

'Used to do a lot of this work back in Lady Anne's day. You try.'

John poked and prodded, the turnip growing warm and slippery. At last he held up a creature that resembled a lopsided pig. Mister Bunce pursed his lips doubtfully.

'Needs a bit of work, that one.'

As summer approached, maunds piled high with drop-apples were dragged into the vaulted room. John eyed the red and gold-streaked fruits, most hardly bigger than gull's eggs, remembering the sour apples from Bellicca's ancient trees and the scent of blossom from outside the chapel.

'Fruit ain't like the roots you've been hacking,' Mister Bunce announced. 'It don't forget an insult. You have to be careful. You have to roll the blade down or the flesh'll bruise. Watch.'

Mister Bunce rested his knife point-first on the board and wedged an apple beneath the broad blade. John saw light catch the edge, a curved sliver of silver, then heard a wet crunch. The two halves rolled apart. Another crunch and the two were four.

'Think you can do that?'

John regarded the small bitter fruit. He took his own knife and held it poised over the remaining half-apple.

'No, no, no!' barked Bunce.

John adjusted. And readjusted. It took four attempts before Mister Bunce let him bring the knife down. When he split the apple, Bunce threw up his hands.

'You felling trees, John? Killing a pig? If you don't cut your own hand off it'll be young Elsterstreet's here . . .'

It didn't take an axe to cut an apple, the Head of Firsts told them. The flesh would brown or turn to mush. It was almost dinner when John took up the knife for what seemed the thousandth time and felt his hand follow the line of the cut, felt the blade split the waxen skin and slice through the flesh. The edge rolled down onto the board. Two clean-cut halves tumbled apart. He turned to Mister Bunce.

'I've seen hedges cut better,' the round-faced man declared flatly. He regarded the halves, still rocking gently on the board. 'Mind, I've seen worse too.'

The drop-apples were replaced by golden-skinned Pearmains, then damsons that arrived in bracken-lined baskets. Gooseberries and raspberries came from Motte's fruit cages. Mazzards and bigaroons followed. John and Philip pitted the fat cherries, peeled apricots and eased the stones out of plums. They tweaked the tiny stalks from strawberries, chopped last season's dried quinces for soaking and sliced greengages into translucent panes.

Working together at the benches, John and Philip eased the stones from peaches, cupping the soft fruit in their palms and sliding the knife between their fingers as Mister Bunce showed them. They stoned damsons ready for pickling. Midsummer was celebrated by Mister Bunce professing them not entirely useless. On Saint Meg's Day, the Head of Firsts summoned them.

'Let the kitchen guide you. That what Master Scovell ordered?'

They nodded.

'I reckon it's time for you to move on.'

At the benches and tables, before the hearth and over the glowing coals of the chafing dishes, on wooden blocks and marble slabs, John's hands shaped, gripped, chopped and pinched. At the kneading trough in the bakehouse, he and Philip pummelled maslin dough until the dull-skinned clods stretched and sprang. A scowling Vanian showed them how to make the airy-light manchet bread that the upper servants ate, then the pastes for meat-coffins and pie crusts. They baked flaking florentine rounds and set them with peaches in snow-cream or neats' tongues in jelly. They stood over the ovens to watch cat's tongue biscuits, waiting for the moment before they browned. John mixed the paste for dariole-cases, working the mixture with his fingertips, then filled them with sack creams and studded them with roasted pistachio nuts. In the fish house across the servants' yard, the two boys scaled and cleaned the yellow-green carp from the Heron Boy's ponds, unpacked barrels of herrings and hauled sides of yellow salt-fish onto the benches and beat them with the knotted end of a rope. On Sundays they filed into chapel, listened to Father Yapp announce the week's fast-days then shuffled out again. Lady Lucretia and the higher members of the Household were long gone by the time the kitchen boys emerged to run down into the fields. Now when John waved his arms at the Heron Boy, the ragged figure waved back, his looming movements mirroring John's own.

Winter approached. John and Philip manned the salting troughs, rubbing the coarse grey grains into collops of mutton, pork and beef and packing them into barrels. A week before All Hallows silence descended on the Manor. For Lady Anne, as Mister Bunce informed them sombrely. Upstairs, the Great Hall was hung with black velvet from floor to ceiling, Gemma reported to Philip. The Household servants wore mourning bands and walked the passageways in silence. Dinner was gruel and supper would be salt-fish. John and the others kicked their heels in boredom. Scovell, John noticed, was not seen all day.

The gatehouse closed on Old Saint Andrew's Day. The first snows fell, cutting the roads, and the yard emptied of all but those ragged men and women who struggled through the drifts for the weekly dole. In the kitchens, the smells of roasting meat and fowl mingled with the sweet scents of great fruit cakes and shivering blancmanges, quaking puddings and hot syllabubs. Mister Pouncey descended with a clinking satchel for Scovell who rang the great copper with his ladle. Once the men had been paid it was the turn of the boys.

'Phineas Campin!' the Master Cook called out. 'I hear your manchet loaves have grown so light, some were seen floating over the chapel.'

The kitchen boys laughed as a blushing Phineas collected his coins. Adam Lockyer followed whose knifework in Underley's jointing room was such a miracle he would soon be joining the King's Army in Bohemia. After him came Jed Scantlebury who must have stolen a pair of seven-league boots he had taken so many great steps forward, then Wendell Turpin, brushing feathers off his livery, Peter Pears ambled up then the Gingell brothers. Even Coake, Barlow and Stubbs received a few words of praise. When Philip had been congratulated on his escape from the scullery, John's name was called. Adam Lockyer gave him a playful push forward.

'Ah, Master Saturnall,' Master Scovell exclaimed. 'Tell me now, where has the kitchen guided you?'

John looked up. The Master Cook had barely addressed a word to him all year. He had set him on this course with no hint of his purpose. Yet now the man waited expectantly.

'I do not know, Master Scovell,' John mumbled, squirming under the eyes of the other boys.

'Then venture further,' Scovell said.

The man dropped the warm coins into John's hand.

Christmas came. On the Twelfth Night feast, the kitchen echoed with the horseplay in the Great Hall above. When the snows melted, the roads reopened. A week after Lady Day, Henry Palewick called John out to the yard where, at the back of a string of packhorses, a limping mule regarded John as if he had once done it a grave injustice. Beside the beast, a lean grey-haired man nodded a greeting.

'They're feeding you then,' Joshua Palewick greeted John, looking him over. John grinned. He had grown stronger working under the kitchen's regime, the long flat muscles rising in his arms and legs. The driver clapped him on the back. 'How's Ben?'

'The same. How's the village?'

'Old Holy's sick. The rest of 'em ain't much better.'

The driver looked unchanged by the intervening year, thought John, as if time outside the kitchen had remained frozen ever since he had entered the Manor.

'I hear John Saturnall's a name to reckon with,' Josh said with a wink to Henry.

'I'm just a kitchen boy,' John said, embarrassed.

'A kitchen boy with Master Scovell's favour.'

'He doesn't show it,' John retorted.

The packhorses were unloaded and watered. All around them, carters and porters raised their voices. Across the throng a red-faced Calybute Pardew cried the intelligences of *Mercurius Bucklandicus*.

'Monstrous birth in Southstoke!' the man bellowed. 'Shower of lizards at Tucking Mill! King's latest quarrel with Parliament! Fear-God and his naked prayer-meet . . .'

'What's that?' John swivelled about. Calybute thrust out a pamphlet.

The woodcut in the pamphlet was crude but 'Fear-God' stared out with familiar directness, his long hair hanging down on either side of his head. At the sight of Marpot, John felt a slow anger stir inside him.

'Inside's his wives,' Calybute said, turning the page. 'That's what he calls them.'

The women knelt in rows, their ballooning breasts and buttocks drawn in thick crude lines. Marpot stood before them, as naked as they, holding up his Bible. For an instant, Cassie flashed in John's memory. Her white legs as she pulled up her long brown dress to run down the bank.

'That Marpot?' Josh asked when Calybute moved on. 'The one who . . .'

John nodded mutely.

'They say he's preaching out around Zoyland. Him and a whole bunch of bodies. His family, he calls them. Adamites, that's the Bishop's term. His lordship'll have him in the pillory soon enough. Mark my words.' Josh nodded, turning the mule about. 'I'll see you next year, John.'

Marpot belonged to a country he had quit, John told himself walking back into the kitchen. Now it was Scovell's voice that reverberated in his head. *Where has the kitchen guided you?* . . . Instead of the shouts of the villagers, his ears rang with the clang and clatter of pots and pans. Instead of the chimney's old soot, thick fugs of cooking smells filled his nostrils and the wet winding-sheet smell was drawn away like the fat-flecked water that swirled down the scullery drain.

Now, instead of the hut and the meadow, he ran between Henry Palewick's root stores and apple lofts, or the cellars where barrels and tuns stretched away into the darkness. Where he once had fetched herbs from the slopes, now he carried cheeses wrapped in cloths or onions hung in nets from the larders. In Underley's jointing room, John and Philip scraped bristles and scooped guts into Barney Curle's barrow, stripped sinews and trimmed fat. In the main kitchen they minced the meat and in the spice room they watched Melichert Roos season it with ground fennel and mace.

Spring arrived. The feasts resumed. From the Great Hall above Mister Pouncey's nasal voice rang out again, the piercing tones finding their way down the stairs as he called out the places at the High Table.

'My Lord Hector and Lady Callock of Forham and Artois! Lord Piers Callock of Forham and Artois! My Lady Musselbrooke the Marchioness of Charnley! My Lord Fell, the Count of Byewater! My Lord Firbrough! The Marquis of Hertford!'

At Shrovetide, Sir Hector's threadbare retainers were joined by those of the Suffords of Mere and the Rowles of Brodenham. At Michaelmas, the Bishop of Carrboro and his retinue came. Processions of horses clopped down the drive. In the kitchen it seemed that each household vied to present more hungry mouths than the last. Midday dinner merged into supper and supper was hardly done before next morning's breakfast began. The days spilled into one another, overflowing at last into the final feast when everyone and everything in the kitchen clanged, shouted, crashed, swore, splashed, bellowed and roared.

'Just like the old days,' Mister Bunce observed with satisfaction. 'No one's got time to piss in a pot.'

Yet for all his industry, a frustration grew in John. The kitchen would guide him, Scovell had promised. But for every dish he mastered, a dozen others rose before his mind's eye. Each skill perfected by his fumbling fingers drew a score of new tasks. If the other boys came to him now when their sauces split, or their meats poached to shreds, or their creams thinned to water the more they beat them, it was only because they did not suspect the vistas of his ignorance. The kitchen knew no limit, he thought, watching Colin and Luke baste, or Vanian shape pastries. Falling asleep next to Philip on the pallet, John dreamed of processions of trays that advanced and rose up the stairs on the shoulders of Quiller's serving men then returned empty to be filled, over and over again . . .

He rose earlier than the other boys and was the last to fall back on his pallet. As the light from the hearth faded, the kitchen boys talked. Alf spoke of his sister while Adam and Peter debated the charms of Ginny and Meg. Adam had seen her naked, so he claimed. The boys rose on their elbows to listen. But John's thoughts drifted to the Rose Garden and the white ankle revealed beneath the dark green skirt. The sharp face in the Solar Gallery. Then a resentful confusion rose in him, a welter of feelings boring new channels through his body. His sweat smelt different, he fancied. Dark hairs marched up his belly. Why should Lucretia Fremantle invade his thoughts down here? His voice was changing too, adding its own odd lurches to the din of the kitchen. Then, with Melichert Roos's spice room awash with preserves and the first sides of pork arriving in the jointing room, the banging, clanging, crackling voices of the kitchen fell silent. Lady Anne's Day had come around again.

Once again gruel and salt-fish steamed in the hearth. Once again Scovell absented himself from the kitchens. The dull day wore on. Driven by boredom, John helped Luke and Colin beat the sides of yellow fish. As the wet salt caked the knotted rope,

Luke looked up. Mister Bunce stood in the doorway. His gaze found John.

'Master Scovell wants to see you.'

The long brown bottle. That was the smell. The same stale fumes had lurked under the mint on Father Hole's breath. Scovell sat in a chair by the fire, wearing a black armband.

'You summoned me, Master Scovell.'

The Master Cook stirred. 'Step into the light, John Saturnall.'

His voice was steady.

'You have combed every room, I hear,' the man said. 'Busied your-self in every corner. No kitchen boy was ever so hungry for knowledge, my Head Cooks tell me. What have you learned, John Saturnall?'

Firsts, thought John. The spice room, the bakehouse, the jointing room and the cellars. Each with its different arts to be mastered. But the vistas of his ignorance stretched before him.

'I know less than when I started, Master Scovell,' John blurted.

To his surprise, the Master Cook smiled. 'Then you have come far.' The man hauled himself from his chair and stood by his desk. 'I said you must bend your gift to its purpose. Do you recall?'

'Yes, Master Scovell.' But that purpose was a riddle, John thought. Another one to add to those left him by his mother. In his mind's eye, the steam twisted up from her kettle once more . . . The man beck-oned. The smell of drink grew stronger. Drawing near he saw that Scovell's grey-blue eyes were flecked with red.

'A true cook has one purpose. A purpose your mother understood as well as myself. A purpose of many parts. I think you know it, Master Saturnall.'

John looked back, feeling awkward under the man's gaze. What had his mother told the Master Cook? At the back of his mind he heard her voice. Her final riddle. *We keep it for all of them.* He shook his head.

'I do not know, Master Scovell.'

'The Feast.'

John stiffened, clenching his jaw to keep the shock from his face. In his memory he heard his mother's voice reciting the dishes, his own words returning across the fire. Slowly, he shook his head. Scovell's eyes narrowed. But then he gazed down into the fire.

'It was a mere story,' Scovell said, the flickering light playing over his face. 'So I believed at first. I was barely your age when I heard word of it. Fanciful tales were told in the kitchens where I spent my youth. Tales of a surpassing feast. Some said it was the one served in Eden. Others that it awaited us in Paradise. Its dishes took in every part of Creation and filled a table so great a man could not walk its length in a day. Tall tales. Yet some among the cooks believed an older truth lay behind them. Such a feast had once been served, they said. A feast so bountiful God himself had forbidden that it be kept. For men should earn their bread by labour in the fields, the Lord had decreed. Their wives should bring forth their children in pain. Such a feast would lead men and women into sloth and greed and lust.' Scovell gave a rueful smile. 'That feast led me too, but from kitchen to kitchen. Soon I learned that others believed as I did. Some were learned men. Others were fools. Some were honest. Others possessed no more scruples than a magpie. Only the Feast united them. To serve up the whole span of God's Creation . . . Such a cook might better call himself a priest. So I pursued my quarry through the great kitchens until I received word of a feast kept long ago at a place called Buckland. Here at the Manor I discovered old receipts handed down from the Master Cooks and beyond its walls lay the remains of ancient orchards and gardens . . .'

As Scovell spoke, John recalled the smell of the spiced wine from the Saint Joseph's Day feast. And the fruit blossom drifting through the chestnut woods above the chapel.

'But the receipts proved mere fragments,' Scovell confessed. 'The gardens were remnants. The Feast had vanished, I came to believe. Its dishes were lost. So I resigned myself to its disappearance. Then fate brought your mother.'

He glanced back at the low door then smiled to himself.

'There seemed no part of Creation she did not comprehend,' the man said quietly. 'Simple country woman though she was, she understood the Feast as though it were part of her own nature. I thought my search was at its end. We would keep the Feast again, I urged her. We would keep it together . . .'

Simple country woman, pondered John. How much had his mother revealed to Scovell? A new light had appeared in the Master Cook's eye. He began to speak of John's mother's knowledge, of the shared understanding that forged a bond between them. Then his shoulders slumped.

'But we argued. The Feast belonged to all, your mother maintained. When those who served and those who ate came together, only then could the Feast be kept.' Scovell shook his head, though whether in disagreement or regret, John could not tell. 'Were we only servants then, I challenged her? Kings built their castles. Bishops raised cathedrals. Yet there were cooks before either. What was their monument?' He looked up from the flames, his eyes bright. Suddenly part of John wanted to tell Scovell what he knew. Yet another part held him back.

'The Feast belongs to its cook,' Scovell declared. 'So I maintained. But Susan, your mother . . . She would never reveal her knowledge promiscuously.' A troubled look came over him. 'It was taken from her. Plucked from her by a magpie. But instead of bright trinkets, this magpie stole words. From a book.'

Magpie, thought John. That word again. His mother's book. As Scovell's eyes searched his face, John remembered the charred pages flaking in the fire.

'There is no book, Master Scovell.'

The Master Cook held his eye for a moment that seemed to John to last an hour. But at last he gave a nod.

'Not all books are written, are they, John?'

John remembered the Feast that he and his mother had conjured each night, the dishes rising into the cold air. 'I do not know, Master Scovell.'

'Then what does your demon advise?'

Was the Master Cook mocking him? A flicker of annoyance stirred in John. 'He keeps his counsel, Master Scovell.'

'He is wise. Would that I had kept my own counsel that night.'

John thought of the Master Cook's absences. Not for Lady Anne, he realised. They were for Susan Sandall. He imagined his mother standing in this room, keeping her counsel as Scovell sought to persuade her.

'The Feast belongs to its cook, I told your mother,' Scovell said. 'It was for all, she answered. Those were her last words to me. I understood her nature too late. But she understood mine better. When she left, I believed the Feast was lost for ever.' He looked up at John. 'Then you came.'

The Master Cook eyed the crowded shelves, the row of gallipots half-hidden in shadow then the low door that connected his chamber to the room beyond.

'She wrote her book,' Scovell murmured and it seemed to John that he spoke to the dead woman as much as to himself. 'But not on paper with ink. She wrote it in you. And she sent you here. She sent you to me.'

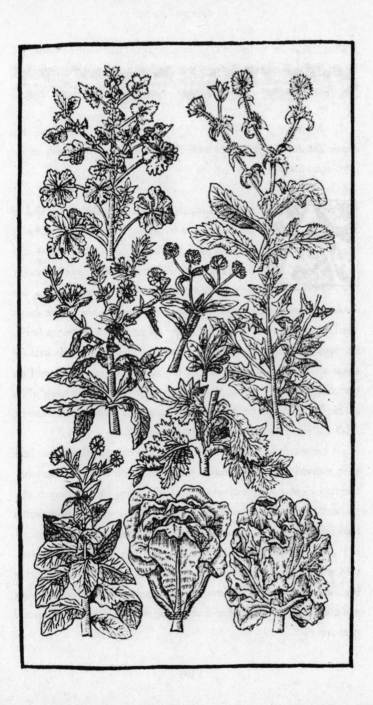

From *The Book of John Saturnall*: A *Dish* of Candied *Baubles* fit for
Two Late *Kings*

Receipt is but the Promise of a Dish but a Dish is
the Measure of its Cook. Know King Tantalus as
one who piled the Plate too high when he boiled his
Son Pelops and served him to Zeus. For that higher
King spat out his portion and chained Tantalus in a
Pool where his Circumstances did contrive to tease him; the Water shrank
when he stooped to drink and the Grapes sprang away when he reached to
eat. Some say King Tantalus's Fault was to steal Ambrosia for Mankind and
others aver it was Nectar. Whichever his Sin, that ancient Cook and I did
once conspire in a Dish that would have brought my Ruin as surely as his
did the Sire of Pelops. For if Hazard is the mightiest Demon in the Kitchen,
Malice is yet his worthy Rival, so I discovered.

First make a Paste short and rich with cold Butter and bake
it in a round Mould as great as you dare. While it cools manufacture
the Baubles of a King such as golden Coins baked hard in Biscuit, or a
jewelled Ring or a Crown of Sugar-candy. Let these Toys shine with a
hard Glaze. They will lie at the bottom of Tantalus's Pool.

Make its Water of amber Jelly set with Hartshorn and sweetened with Madeira Sugar and clarify that Jelly over a Chafing Dish of
low Coals. But now is the Time to guard against Hazard. Such a Liquor
will blacken in the Blink of an Eye if it be not watched and the Pan will
spoil too.

Next, the glaze. Some good Time before, set two Irons in the Fire till they glow near red-hot. Pass one slowly back and forth as many as a score of Times, replace it in the Flames and take up the next and so again until the Surface begins to ripple and melt and yet retains that Clarity that so tempted Tantalus. Leave these to set. But guard now against Malice, for he too will have his Way . . .

THE KITCHEN BOY PULLED a fistful of feathers from the bird, grunted and stuffed them into the sack at his feet. Turning on his stool, he glanced towards the hearth. Among the cob-irons and spit-poles, pot-hooks and pot cranes stood the chafing dish.

Charcoal glowed under a copper skillet. Within the pot, slow bubbles broke the trembling surface. He had been charged to watch it that morning. He gave the pan a hesitant shake and saw the grains lurch with the slow swirl of the liquor. Then he returned to his plucking.

The breast feathers came free in downy clumps but the tail feathers appeared to have been nailed in place. The kitchen boy grunted and tugged. The bird stretched and strained, its pale yellow skin tenting out from the flesh.

'Stop yanking!' called out an exasperated voice from down the bench. 'You'll break the skin.'

The cook glared then put down the knife he had been using to cut fine white sheets of pastry for the wooden paste-mould in front of him. A mere five years divided him from the kitchen boy but he shook his head now as if they were decades.

'In my day,' Philip Elsterstreet said in pained tones, picking up the carcass, 'pheasants were plucked in the yard no matter the weather. Now if you grip the bird like this and pull the quills like this,' he pulled, 'and stop grunting and sighing perhaps you'll find the work more to your liking.'

'Yes, Master Elsterstreet,' the boy answered and Philip sighed himself.

'It's Mister,' he said. 'Plain and simple.' Then he nodded and under-cook and kitchen boy both looked towards the hearth. 'And watch that pan like you were told.'

It was Simeon Parfitt's third day in the kitchen. Other cooks, the boy knew, would have given him the rough edge of their tongues. Coake would have hurled the pheasant at his head and had him scrubbing the floor where it landed. Mister Bunce's parting advice resounded in his head. 'Keep your eyes open, Simeon. Keep your mouth shut. Don't rush at things. Stop your sighing and don't daydream either. If you can do any task half as well as them in there, no one'll say I let you out of Firsts before time . . .'

So Simeon had paid close attention that morning. He had watched Philip Elsterstreet until he had been asked to direct his stare elsewhere. Then he had studied the under-cook who had taken up a station at the hearth and who seemed to see nothing but the chafing dish before him, arranging the charcoals then setting the skillet on top.

None of the cooks could teach him more than John Saturnall, Mister Bunce had told him. Not Adam Lockyer or Peter Pears, not Philip Elsterstreet or Phineas Campin. Certainly not Coake. So Simeon had watched closely that morning as John had stirred the skillet, brow furrowed in concentration under his thatch of curly black hair. Then Simeon's chance had come. Looking up, the under-cook had asked if the kitchen boy might do him a service?

'Watching's all it needs,' John had declared. 'If it darkens, lift it off. Keep an eye on it for me, will you, Simeon?'

The boy had blushed at the use of his name. John Saturnall knew more than most of the cooks put together, Mister Bunce had continued. All except Master Scovell, of course. The under-cook rarely looked up from his dishes, reaching blind for pinches of salt, or a spatula, or a jack of water. Yet he seemed never to hesitate or falter, moving about the kitchens as if he had been born there.

Simeon, by contrast, seemed always to be in somebody's way. The senior kitchen boys barged him. The under-cooks swerved. Those higher up seemed not to notice his existence. He had been nudged along the benches until Master Elsterstreet had found him a spot in the corner, plucking.

Around the kitchen, the other cooks and boys worked at tables and benches. Four more carcasses waited in the basket at Simeon's feet. How many feathers was that, he wondered, gripping the clammy skin and tugging at the quills.

He worked steadily as Mister Bunce had advised him, resisting the urge to rush or sigh. The sack soon swelled with feathers. Simeon's mind began to wander . . . He too would be a cook one day, he thought. He imagined himself wielding pots and pans between the bench and the fire as John Saturnall did. He plucked the last of the tail-quills and reached for the next carcass. Perhaps Master Scovell himself would request his opinions . . .

Simeon was imagining the first of those conversations when he smelt the smoke.

He spun about, a sinking feeling in the pit of his stomach. A black plume was rising from the chafing dish. As he watched, Master Elsterstreet hurried past to lift the pan off the trivet. His darkening expression and the acrid fumes told Simeon all he needed to know of the contents. *If it darkens, lift it off* . . . Hardly a difficult task, he berated himself. And here came the one who had entrusted it to him, striding across the kitchen as if the pan had called to him.

John's face turned this way and that as he walked between the tables and benches, wiping a spoon on his canvas apron, mottled with scorch-marks and faded stains. He ducked under a pot hanging from a hook. That year he had grown until he could reach the lintel above the kitchen door, half a head taller than Mister Bunce, and a head and a half over Simeon. The new kitchen boy watched him fearfully.

'Burnt again?' John asked.

'That's the third time,' confirmed Philip, fanning away smoke.

A flash of irritation passed through John. He pushed back his fringe of thick black curls and trapped it under his cap then peered down.

The bottom was as black as a well. The liquor burned itself in a layer that resisted everything (so Mister Stone had told him last time) but a full day's soaking and an hour of scraping with a metal spoon. John raised his head, imagining the conversation with the Head of the Scullery. How difficult was it to watch a pan? His irritation rose again. But then he glanced at the new kitchen boy.

Simeon Parfitt's shoulders were hunched. The boy hung his head as if he wished the kitchen floor would open and swallow him whole. 'Not as witless as some' was how Mister Bunce had described him to John at the beginning of the week. High praise from the Head of Firsts. He had asked John to look out for the boy. Now Simeon's lower lip was quivering.

'Master Saturnall, I . . . I was watching it. I just . . .'

'*Mister* Saturnall,' John corrected him, banishing his annoyance. 'Calm yourself, Simeon. It is a simple liquor. An easy matter to boil up another . . .'

The lip stopped quivering. John picked up the pan and carried it, still trailing smoke, back towards the scullery. Around the kitchen, heads turned at the unexpected sight of John Saturnall in charge of a burning pan.

'Simple liquor?' Philip hissed beside him. 'Easy matter? Madeira's twenty shillings a pound. What's Mister Palewick going to say?'

John looked into the blackened skillet. Three days ago its contents had been a loaf of Madeira sugar, locked up, wrapped and stamped with the Cellarer's seal. Madeira sugar was the most costly, the Cellarer had reminded John as he picked out one of the light brown bricks. Placing the block in a muslin bag, John had chipped off shards with a wedge and mallet then ground them in a quern. Tipped into a pan of steaming water, stirred and whisked, the sugar had thrown up a bubbling foam which John had skimmed and skimmed again until the syrupy liquor was poured into a clean kettle and clarified with the white of an egg. The reduction had followed, the hot charcoal in the chafing dish reddening his face as he stirred, the colour deepening through pale yellow to the amber he sought . . .

Now it was soot.

'Well?' Philip demanded. 'And what will you tell our Cellarer?'

'The Feast belongs to its cook,' John said.

'What?' Philip demanded. 'What does that mean?' But before John could answer, a look of weary understanding came over him. 'Scovell.'

'You will work with me, John Saturnall,' the Master Cook had told John as he stood before him in his chamber. 'Every true cook carries a feast inside him. Your mother and I agreed on that. Why else would she send you to me? We will find your feast together.'

John had felt an excitement rise in him at Scovell's words. Why should the Feast not be for its cook? he asked himself, head bent over the pans and trays. Down here in the kitchens where the dishes reached their perfection. Here the kickshaws and confections that John prepared for the High Table appeared untouched and flawless. What returned were crumbs.

Now alongside Scovell, John eased preserved peaches out of galliot pots of syrup and picked husked walnuts from puncheons of salt. He clarified butter and poured it into rye-paste coffins. From the Master Cook, John learned to set creams with calves' feet, then isinglass, then hartshorn, pouring decoctions into egg-moulds to set and be placed in nests of shredded lemon peel. To make cabbage cream he let the thick liquid clot, lifted off the top layer, folded it then repeated the process until the cabbage was sprinkled with rose water and dusted with sugar, ginger and nutmeg. He carved apples into animals and birds. The birds themselves he roasted, minced and folded into beaten egg whites in a foaming forcemeat of fowls.

John boiled, coddled, simmered and warmed. He roasted, seared, fried and braised. He poached stock-fish and minced the meats of smoked herrings while Scovell's pans steamed with ancient sauces: black chawdron and bukkenade, sweet and sour egredouce, camelade and peppery gauncil. For the feasts above he cut castellations into pie-coffins and filled them with meats dyed in the colours of Sir William's titled guests. He fashioned palaces from wafers of spiced batter and paste royale, glazing their walls with panes of sugar. For the Bishop of Carrboro they concocted a cathedral.

'Sprinkle salt on the syrup,' Scovell told him, bent over the chafing dish in his chamber. A golden liquor swirled in the pan. 'Very slowly.'

'It will taint the sugar,' John objected.

But Scovell shook his head. A day later they lifted off the cold clear crust and John split off a sharp-edged shard. 'Salt,' he said as it slid over his tongue. But little by little the crisp flake sweetened on his tongue. Sugary juices trickled down his throat. He turned to the Master Cook with a puzzled look.

'Brine floats,' Scovell said. 'Syrup sinks.' The Master Cook smiled. 'Patience, remember? Now, to the glaze . . .'

The tasks multiplied. Tasks which seemed more like riddles. Riddles which seemed more like tests. But every day added to the store of his knowledge. Little by little the kitchen's chambers came to seem his domain. Scovell was right, he thought as his fifth year at the Manor approached. The Feast could indeed belong to its cook.

'Who was Tantalus?' the Master Cook asked John that spring. 'Was he a cook or a king? What dish would you cook for him?'

Another riddle, John thought. But now he knew the answer. 'None, Master Scovell. The Feast belongs . . .'

'To its cook. So it does,' Scovell said quickly. 'But think of this. Even King Tantalus had a master to serve, one whose appetite was his command.' The man flicked his eyes towards the vault of the roof. 'Just as we do, John.'

The riddle had twisted again, John realised. But who was their master? Sir William had never descended down here. Nor his daughter, of course.

He considered the King in his pool, a king's baubles floating about him: a glittering crown, a ruby ring, a handful of bright coins. Tantalus's inedible riches would prove toothsome sweetmeats: the crown a confection of pastry and piped creams. Or a harder candy, the ring formed of spun sugar set with a crystallised cherry; the coins minted from paste baked and rebaked to a golden glaze. All hanging in a pool of pale amber jelly. Tantalus would look down into the depths, so clear he could see all the way to the bottom . . .

That had been his intention as he set to work, as he laboured and at last entrusted his creation to the oversight of Simeon Parfitt . . .

Now he contemplated soot.

'Why couldn't Tantalus just eat boiled beef?' Philip asked, pulling back the leather curtain to Firsts. 'That's a meal. And it doesn't take a loaf of Madeira sugar . . .'

'Forgot how to cook?' a nasal voice broke in. Philip and John looked up.

A black helmet of hair framed a sallow face. A smudge of stubble approximated a moustache. Coake's smirk seemed to reach up to his thick black eyebrows.

'At least we knew to start with,' retorted Philip. But Coake kept his eyes on John.

'Off for another little prayer tryst with Scovell, are we?' His face glistened, reddening in the kitchen's heat. 'Stir your pots together, eh Witch-boy?'

John started forwards but Philip barged between them. With a sneer, Coake pushed past and walked into the kitchen. John weighed the pan in his hand and scowled.

'Forget him,' Philip urged then rapped the pot with his knuckle. 'Think about that. And what you're going to tell Mister Palewick . . .'

John nodded. Philip was right, he knew. In fact, since their quarrel and perhaps before, Philip was almost always right. A glacé, he thought as they walked into Firsts. Gelled with hartshorn. Or with calves' feet to make a crystal jelly. The edible riches in the depths . . .

He would perfect the dish, he knew. Just as Simeon Parfitt would learn to watch pans as he was told. He would coax his creation into existence even if it took a hundred blackened pots.

He clarified sugar and poured it between pans. He mixed pastes and baked them in Vanian's slowest oven. He boiled down calves' feet to jelly and concocted a glaze. At last he poured a clear mixture over the baubles which rested in the case. A day in Henry Palewick's coldest storeroom and the dish was ready for him to carry down the passage. In Scovell's chamber, the Master Cook held up a candle. Together they looked down.

Jewel-like candies glinted in the depths. A crown lay on its side amidst a scattering of coins. Scovell tapped a fingernail against the glaze then broke off a fragment of pastry and chewed.

'That is the pool, Master Scovell,' explained John. 'It has turned the King's riches into sweets. Now he can eat . . .'

'I understand,' Scovell interrupted. 'The water is very clear. This glaze too. How did you achieve that?'

John pursed his lips. In truth, he did not know how the Madeira sugar and its flavourings had finally dissolved and gelled, except that anything stronger than the slowest heat had clouded the dish, poisoning his pool with darkness. For the glaze he had held a hot iron over the surface, passing it slowly back and forth.

'I kept it high over the chafing dish and the coals very few.'

Scovell nodded approvingly.

'Patience,' he said. 'Perhaps that was the fault of Tantalus. And forgetting the nature of his master. But we will not make such a mistake, John.'

The riddle again. But who was Scovell's master?

'Carry this back to the cold store,' the Master Cook ordered him. 'Ask Mister Palewick to keep it safe. Sir William's guest will taste it. Sir Sacherevell Cornish serves Sir Philemon Armesley, Mister Pouncey tells me. And Sir Philemon serves no one but the King . . .'

John nodded, still puzzled. What did it matter who broke the glaze he had so carefully made? Or spooned up the jelly? Its perfection lay here in his own hands. His thoughts were already returning to his dish. Hartshorn gave a clearer jelly, he considered that Sunday. On the other hand, the shavings took longer to dissolve . . . Dawdling out into the sun after chapel, he found himself wandering down into the meadows. Suddenly a loud splash roused him.

On the far side of the ponds stood a familiar figure. Coake was weighing a clod of earth in his hand. Barlow and Stubbs did the same. Across the water stood the Heron Boy. But at the sight of his tormentors, a hopeless confusion seemed to settle over him. He took a hesitant step forward then another one back. His wings trailed on the ground. John shouted across the pond.

'Hey! Leave him be!'

The three clod-throwers turned to face him. Standing behind the trio, the Heron Boy only looked bewildered. John waved as if to shoo him clear but the Heron Boy echoed John's gesture. Across the pond's muddy brown water, a notion took root in John's mind.

'Back from another prayer tryst with Scovell?' Coake jibed.

'What do you care?'

John swept an arm at Coake. Across the pond, the Heron Boy did the same. Slowly, John raised both arms in the air. Behind the trio, the Heron Boy's wings rose too.

'Want to give up, do you, Raghead?' sneered Coake. 'You shouldn't have got in our way, should you? You shouldn't have . . .'

But John never learned what he shouldn't have done. Dropping his arms, he saw the Heron Boy's wings descend, the poles sweeping down to crack against the heads of Barlow and Stubbs. A spin of John's arms and the Heron Boy's wings spun too, fetching Coake a blow on the skull.

'Agh! Damn you!'

Coake clutched his head and stumbled. Across the pond, John windmilled, sending the Heron Boy into the fray. Wing-poles swinging, the ragged figure marched on his enemies, whacking and thwacking. The three youths cursed and yelped under the barrage of blows, pulling up clods and hurling them back. Then, abruptly, they gave up the fight. Stopping mid-throw, Barlow and Stubbs lumbered back towards the house while Coake scrambled towards the trees opposite. The two comrades stared after them. Hands propped on his knees, John heaved air into his lungs. Across the pond, the Heron Boy bent forward and did the same. Slowly, John raised an arm. The pair saluted each other.

'I know you can talk,' John panted over the water. 'You talk in your sleep.'

His fellow warrior grinned. Then his puzzled expression returned. John realised his fellow warrior was looking at something behind him.

'Congratulations.'

Startled, John turned. A young woman wearing a short-brimmed riding hat sat upright on the back of a large grey horse. A dark green riding-skirt draped over the animal's flank ended in a pair of black boots. A sharp straight nose pointed itself at him. Once again, John looked up into the face of Lucretia Fremantle.

'Your manners have not improved, John Saturnall,' the young woman said.

'Your ladyship?'

'You are bold to observe me so frankly.'

He dropped his gaze to the pond's rippling surface. Her voice had deepened a shade, he thought. Her lips were fuller too. He had not set eyes on her since the glimpse outside the chapel. Now her reflection shimmered, dissolving then magically restoring itself. But nothing would dissolve the nature of its owner, he reminded himself. He recalled her shrill shout in the Solar Gallery. *Here! He's in here!* No amount of sugar would sweeten Lady Lucy's sourness. Across the water the Heron Boy stared as if Lucretia had landed on the back of a giant bird.

'I see you have risen to the rank of kitchen boy,' the young woman continued drily. 'Just as you hoped.'

Her manner had not changed either, John thought.

'I am a cook, your ladyship,' he replied.

'Yet more good fortune. I congratulate you, Master Saturnall.'

'Mister,' he corrected her. 'A cook's title is Mister.' He waited a fraction of a second. 'Lady Lucretia.'

'Very well.' She added her own pause. '*Mister* Saturnall. Thank you for that invaluable correction.'

'I am glad to be of service to your ladyship.' He paused again. 'Your ladyship.'

'And I am pleased to hear it,' she replied icily. But in her reflected cheeks, John fancied he saw two points of red growing.

'Then I thank you for that opportunity, your ladyship,' John answered. Perhaps this was how they spoke to each other up there in the house. Like a game of fives, but with words not balls.

'And I congratulate you on your new-found manners,' Lucretia replied in a strained voice. 'Would that I might guide you further into civility. Alas I must complete my ride. Now good day to you, Mister Saturnall.'

'The regret is all mine, your ladyship. Good day to you too.'

A small part of John felt a twinge of disappointment as he stepped aside. The horse walked past. He watched Lucretia's hips sway in time with the animal's gait. Had they been so full in the Solar Gallery? Abruptly she halted. To turn and deliver another barbed comment, he presumed. But she was looking to the gatehouse where the great timbers were swinging open. A familiar contraption appeared at the top of the drive.

'Oh, by the Cross,' she muttered.

On the drive, two mismatched horses looked two different ways. A gaggle of attendants followed. The Callocks' coach veered to left and right as it trundled down the drive.

She was courted by Piers Callock, the boys joked in the kitchens. Everyone knew that. But now she seemed anything but pleased. The coach came to an unceremonious halt outside the stables where it disgorged a portly red-faced man then a willowy woman whose face was concealed by a broad-brimmed hat. A youth a little older than John followed. Catching sight of Lucretia, he waved and advanced.

'Lady Lucretia!'

So this was the famous Piers, thought John. A long pale face was topped by a large floppy cap of crimson velvet. Green silk lined the slashed sleeves of his doublet while matching stockings clung to his legs. A pair of shiny buckled shoes picked their way through the damp grass. Beneath the hat, the youth's nose seemed to drip down his face and gather in a knot above his lip. Piers came to a halt and cast a fastidious eye over John's doublet, the material faded and spattered with ancient stains.

'You may go.'

John offered a bow to Lucretia. Across the pond, the Heron Boy did the same. But as John turned to leave, Lucretia spoke sharply.

'I have not concluded my business with my servant, Lord Piers.'

John looked up once again. Piers's pallor was achieved with a dusting of powder, he saw. Beneath it, Piers's cheeks were sallow while a network of broken veins covered his nose. The youth's eyes narrowed.

'I have ordered him gone,' Piers said.

'But he is my servant,' Lucretia retorted. 'And I have not.'

John stood between them.

'Your servant?' Beneath the powder, Piers's cheeks were beginning to take on the ruddy glow of his nose. 'A kitchen boy?'

'In point of fact, Lord Piers,' Lucretia's voice had reverted to its icy tone, 'Mister Saturnall is a cook.'

'A cook?' Piers's eyebrows rose in mock-surprise as he took in John's dark face and thick black hair. His lips curled. 'But he appears more apelike than cooklike. Would you not say, my lady?'

John saw indecision furrow Lucretia's brow. Should she defend John or agree with Piers? Her frown deepened but before she could make either of the disagreeable choices, the men on the gate shouted out. Six liveried horsemen had entered and were trotting down the drive, the foremost rider carrying a blue pennant on which yellow lions had been embroidered. John saw Lucretia's eyes widen.

'Those colours,' she said. 'Are they the King's colours?'

'They are indeed, Lady Lucretia,' Piers declared.

'Here?'

'They are carried by Sir Sacherevell Cornish who is engaged upon the King's business,' Piers continued. 'Their arrival was my purpose in addressing you. In private.' He glared at John.

Lucretia did not take kindly to being corrected, John knew. He waited for the girl's retort. But instead her voice sounded a new eager note.

'The King's business?' she asked. 'What business is that?'

Her annoyance had vanished. Her eyes searched Piers's face.

'Sir Sacherevell Cornish is steward to Sir Philemon Armesley,' Piers announced in a lofty tone. That was Sir William's guest, remembered John. The would-be consumer of his dish. But a note of disappointment entered Lucretia's voice.

'Only a steward?'

Piers favoured her with a superior smile.

'Of course, you have not been to Court,' he told her. 'Sir Sacherevell is no common steward. Sir Philemon, his master, is not only a Gentleman of the King's Privy Chamber, he is also a Whitestave of the Board of Greencloth.'

'The Board of Greencloth?'

'Indeed. I have exchanged greetings with him several times, I may say. Upon Sir Philemon's word whole armies march.'

'Armies?' asked Lucretia. 'What armies?'

Piers's smile broadened. 'Armies of servants, my dear Lady Lucretia. Sir Philemon's musketeers are grooms. His pikemen are pages. And his trusted scout is Sir Sacherevell. Of course he is here to do a steward's work too. To count the spoons and measure the rooms. To sip from the barrels in the cellars and taste the dishes from the kitchens. Perhaps he will sample the wares of your cook here. Let us hope his skills suffice.'

They both looked down at John.

'Suffice for what?' demanded Lucretia.

She stared at John as if the answer were concealed in his person. John looked back coldly. Piers conferred a look of benign condescension upon Lucretia.

'I garnered certain intelligences when last I attended Court,' he declared airily. 'If Sir Sacherevell's report to his master is favourable, and if Sir Philemon's recommendation is wholehearted, then I believe Sir Sacherevell's appearance signals His Majesty's future visitation.'

Lucretia's brow creased. Then understanding dawned. Her mouth unpursed. Her frown disappeared and an artless excitement took its place. Perhaps, John thought, there was after all a kind of sugar that might sweeten Lady Lucy's sourness.

'The King?' she asked Piers. 'The King is coming here?'

_____

In the attics the intelligence set the maids' tongues whispering. In the back parlours, the Household men talked gravely of points of etiquette. The kitchen hummed with the news.

'My gramps saw the King once,' Phineas Campin told the others, reaching for the ale-balm that was kept above the hearth. 'It was in his carriage in Soughton. He was taking the waters and after that his ague vanished. My gramps's, that is. Just from looking at the King.'

'Different King though, weren't it?' said Adam Lockyer, beating collops of mutton with the flat of a cleaver. Simeon Parfitt's head turned this way and that, his hands working busily on the goose before him.

'Don't make no difference,' Alf offered from the door. 'The King's the King, my sis used to say. Don't matter who it is.'

'Might as well be you then, Alf,' said Luke Hobhouse, walking in.

'I heard of a cobbler in Elminster.' Colin spoke up from the table under the tray rack. 'A ragged fellow came in his shop one day. No hat. Holes in his soles. So the cobbler patched his boots for love and it turns out the fellow was the King in disguise. That cobbler never had to pick up his awl again.'

'Who told you that?' Luke challenged Colin. 'Calybute Pardew? For every one of them cobblers there's a hundred lords. And every one of 'em's got his hand in the King's pocket.'

Across the room, John remembered the picture in *Mercurius Bucklandicus* that Ben Martin had bought. The sad-eyed man in his magnificent hat. At that moment, Quiller appeared at the foot of the stairs.

'They're exchanging toasts,' the man reported. Across the kitchen, Master Scovell nodded and John looked about for the last dish: his shining transparent tart. As it disappeared upstairs he imagined Sir Sacherevell cracking the sugary glaze to dig within its depths. Lucretia watching, he supposed. And Piers.

'Fit for a King,' had been Sir Sacherevell's words, as Scovell told John later. The courtier had risen to signal his approval by dangling a tiny candy crown from the tine of his fork.

'So you have lured His Majesty,' the Master Cook said with a smile.

Carts loaded with beams and planks arrived in the outer yard. Gangs of workmen jostled. A long lizard of backs bristled with picks and spades as it crept down the slope from the spring in the High Meadow. A gurgling water-filled trench filled a newly dug slate-lined cistern. Master Jocelyn's men unloaded beams and planks of oak and ash, set them at angles and nailed them together. The skeleton of a barracks rose then extended along one side of the yard. Men climbed ladders and shinned along beams, hammering down overlapping boards of elm. A similar structure abutted the stables.

'What're they trying to do?' Adam marvelled. 'Build the whole Manor anew?'

'By the time the King gets here,' Phineas answered, 'it'll look more like Carrboro.'

In the gardens, old women from Callock Marwood bent to weed flowerbeds under the direction of Motte while under-gardeners pleached straggly hedges into order. In the house, workmen painted walls, threw up partitions and hung new doors. Only the Solar Gallery, the East Garden and the glass-house were exempt. Mrs Gardiner's maids stitched curtains, aired bedlinen and hung musty blankets on lines. Mister Pouncey strode up and down passageways followed by a string of green-liveried clerks who carried ledgers, pens and a small collapsible table which Mister Pouncey employed as a portable desk. When the first snows fell, the works came to a halt but by the time Josh Palewick paid his annual visit, a barracks was rising beyond the outer yard.

'So the King's coming to Buckland?' the man asked.

'So it appears,' said John.

'They're talking of it all down the Vale.' Behind Josh, the mule stamped a hoof. 'Her Majesty too. That true?'

John nodded. The commotion and excitement swirled about him. But even in the midst of its eddies and whirls he remembered Scovell's words and wondered why Josh Palewick should care. If the feast belonged to its cook, what did it matter who ate it? A King sat and chewed and swallowed like any other mortal, thought John. But Scovell too seemed caught up in the nervous excitement, spending long hours closeted with Vanian, Underley, Roos and Henry Palewick who discussed together the order of service.

Orders for beef were placed with stockmen as far away as Soughton and for barrels of conger and herring from Stollport. When Calybute's latest *Mercurius Bucklandicus* showed the King's household moving in procession out of London, a new urgency seemed to grip the Household. From his command post in the doorway of the Great Hall, Mister Pouncey pondered lists of secretaries and seal-keepers, council clerks and sergeants-at-arms. Was the Clerk of Petty Bag senior to a gentleman groom? he wondered. How important was the Keeper of the Hanaper, or the Chafe Wax? In Mister Pouncey's anxious imaginings, bishops were seated next to mistresses and dukes jammed in with the yeomen. What if the High Table collapsed? the steward wondered. What if the spring in the High Meadow ran dry? What if bed-less courtiers pursued him through the Manor waving their slashed silk sleeves . . .

'Some do not appear on my lists,' he complained to Sir Sacherevell, flattening a sheet of paper on the balustrade and peering at the names. In the Great Hall behind them men on ladders were taking down and polishing the swords on the wall. Beneath the dais, disgruntled carpenters were hammering in unnecessary struts. 'Others appear several times.'

Messengers flew up and down the road from Carrboro. A week before His Majesty was expected, when Mister Pouncey had begun to believe that he had matters under his control, a forest of pennants advanced on the Manor flown from wagons and carts which lumbered through the gatehouse. Their mounted escorts ambled alongside, forcing Buckland's own traffic off the track. The royal baggage train had begun to arrive.

In the field beside the new barracks, marquees rose with the King's colours fluttering above until it seemed a billowing fleet rode at anchor there. With their animals stabled, the horsemen swaggered about the yard while a guard of bored yeomen dawdled around the tents. Almost the last to arrive was a tall man with a tuft of dark hair at the front of his forehead and an elaborate moustache who squabbled with a dozen subordinates. All wore navy-blue doublets worked with silver thread.

'It is disgrace!' he exclaimed in a strong French accent while looking around the yard. 'It is dishonour! We are entitled to beds. And linen. Clean linen!' He looked across at the stables then shouted at a passing stable hand. 'Clean linen!'

Mister Pouncey watched in consternation.

'Those,' Sir Sacherevell informed him, 'are the Gentlemen of the Queen's Kitchen.'

'But we have a kitchen. We have cooks. Many cooks . . .'

'No, no, no.' Sir Sacherevell waved the suggestion away. 'These are not actual *cooks*. These are the gentlemen grooms of Her Majesty's kitchen. The one with the moustache is the Page of the Scalding Room. The fat one behind is the Gentleman Sayer. Not that he assays, any more than the other one scalds, or the rest of them cook.'

'Then what do they do?'

'They attend.'

Everyone attended, reflected Mister Pouncey. Their Majesties had left Elminster, the posts from Carrboro informed the steward.

They had decided to take the waters in Soughton, he learned the next day. They were on the road to Toue, one messenger informed Mister Pouncey. Another brought news that they were a day away. Then three. Standing at his post, the steward found his eyes drawn to the gatehouse as if watching it might draw Their Majesties through its turrets.

'It is our fate to wait.' A deep voice spoke over Mister Pouncey's shoulder. 'Even if only for God.'

A man wearing a rich cloak of blue-grey fur directed a strange crooked smile at Mister Pouncey. But his unblinking eyes stared coldly, making the steward feel uncomfortable. Sir Sacherevell bowed quickly.

'I present my master,' he told Mister Pouncey. 'Sir Philemon Armesley.'

The smile was a scar, the steward saw, looking closer. A puckered red line tugged at the corner of the man's mouth, running almost to his ear.

'Got it at Rochelle,' said Sir Philemon, touching the ragged mark. 'One of the Cardinal's chevaliers judged my mouth too narrow. Stitched it up myself. Never was much with a needle.' He looked around as a new volley of hammering broke out. 'The King is in Carrboro tonight. The vanguard will set out after Matins. He will be here by midday tomorrow if the roads hold up. Everything in hand?'

The servants' barracks needed bedding, Mister Pouncey remembered. And he still had to settle who sat where at the High Table . . . He looked out over the chaotic yard to the tents. But Sir Philemon appeared content.

'No doubt all will be ready,' he said briskly. 'Only Their Majesties matter, you understand? Only ensure that they are content. All they see. All they hear. All they touch. Everything they taste and smell. All perfect. Do you understand me?'

Sir Philemon's scarred smile looked more like a grimace. Mister Pouncey nodded quickly.

'No one knows an estate like its steward. Isn't that true, Sack?'

Sir Sacherevell nodded. Sir Philemon pulled back the lapels of his coat to reveal a chain much like Mister Pouncey's own. Pinned to the doublet was a badge which looked like two white sticks.

'We are all stewards of a kind. Except His Majesty.' Sir Philemon's affability had vanished. Looking into the man's cold eyes, Mister Pouncey felt glad the negotiations were over. 'In these times, His Majesty needs men he can trust,' Sir Philemon continued. 'Their very presence will dispel the mutterings of his enemies.'

He gave Mister Pouncey a look that the steward recognised from the conferences that Sir William held behind the closed doors of his receiving room. Only the steward had been permitted to enter as he discussed the iniquities and insolences of Parliament with Lord Fell or Lord Firbrough or the Marquis of Hertford.

'But the King will give his blessing?' the steward ventured.

'As we agreed.'

Mister Pouncey felt a surge of relief course through him. In his mind's eye, the brass weights on his papers made their final hops, the lightest to the left, the heaviest to the right. But as he turned to leave Sir Philemon's voice sounded again.

'There is one other matter. Her Majesty has expressed a wish.'

'What wish, Sir Philemon?'

'She wants to see the girl.'

It was as if a windlass tightened a cord within Lucretia. Every passing day gave the rope another turn until on the morning itself, when she stood with her father before the Household, she felt the taut cord must snap or her frame collapse from within. Hair dressed in a fringe, face scrubbed raw then powdered, she fixed her eyes on the gatehouse while behind her the ranks of Buckland's officers, servants and menials filled the inner yard all the way back to the steps before the Great Hall. Long lines of green marked out the men of the Household, then Master Jocelyn's Estate men in their purple livery, then the red of the Kitchen. Their mutterings hummed behind her now as Mister Pouncey and Sir Sacherevell patrolled the ranks.

'Quiet there!' the steward ordered, glaring down a long red line.

'How come the Estate's ahead of us?' hissed Adam Lockyer beside John when the man moved on.

'Don't know.'

The cooks had spent the morning brushing stains off their doublets. John's thoughts shuttled between the candy crown and jewels stored in Henry Palewick's driest larder and the biscuit-coins which rested in a barely warm oven in Vanian's room. As the sun rose higher, he rehearsed the tasks awaiting him in the kitchen while the others shuffled and scratched.

'Look there!' Jed Scantlebury exclaimed at last.

Blue and gold banners were rising over the ridge. As the first riders trotted down between the great beeches, John saw Mister Pouncey hurry forward. Sir Sacherevell caught his arm.

'Do not trouble yourself so, Master Steward. Those are merely Sergeants of the Ewery. And behind are Pages of the Chamber. Lesser men.' The riders approached and began to form up. 'Here are the holders of the greater offices,' Sir Sacherevell continued. 'These are the

Grooms of the Privy Chamber. Behind them come the Gentlemen Ushers. The man carrying a stave is the Master of the Horse.'

'Who is that gentleman beside him?'

Looking up the drive, John saw beside the stave-bearer a man fully a head taller than any around him.

'That is Sir Kenelm Digby,' answered Sir Sacherevell. 'He was a Gentleman of the Bedchamber when His Majesty was Prince. He is one of *the* Digbys.'

The man gave Mister Pouncey a significant look which prompted, however, an expression of blank incomprehension.

'His father,' explained Sir Sacherevell, 'tried to blow up the late King.'

'Ah.'

Behind Sir Sacherevell, John and Philip stared at Sir Kenelm who wore a breastplate over his doublet. The metal glinted as he rose up and down on the back of a chestnut horse. Behind him rode two men on matching white mounts.

'Escorts of the Groom of the Stole.' Sir Sacherevell nudged Mister Pouncey. 'The royal coach will not be long now. Come. Let us take our places.'

The pair scuttled sideways through the ranks of servants. Below the portico, the horsemen had formed up in a long curving line. The latest arrivals took their places, their robes draped with chains and studded with badges of office. Suddenly, a hush descended on the company. In the silence John heard wheels.

'All kneel for the King!'

In one motion, the horsemen swept off their hats and bowed their heads. A wave rippled back through the Buckland Household as its members sank to their knees. In the instant before he too knelt, John glimpsed a gilded coach with six white horses. At the front of the

Household, beside the black figure of Sir William, he saw a slight figure stand upright a moment longer than everybody else. Then she too sank to her knees.

The gliding horses with their bobbing head-plumes, the gleaming coach, the bright banners and outriders in their livery . . . It seemed to Lucretia that the tight coil within her was released in a rush. They were here, she told herself, hearing the wheels slow and stop. Their Majesties were here.

For a moment there was silence. Then a footman walked forward and the carriage door was opened. Steps were carried and set down. She heard her father offer the greetings of the Household. At those words, Lucretia looked up.

A flurry of bright rustling silks filled her eyes and ears. Dresses whirled about Lucretia. Her Majesty's ladies unfurled their mistress from within their fluttering phalanx. A woman with a long straight nose, a pretty oval face and lively eyes gazed down at her and smiled.

'Lady Lucretia?' The Queen addressed her in a light French accent, her voice sounding, to Lucretia's ears, like a silver bell. Lucretia nodded and the Queen smiled.

'You will attend me this afternoon, yes?'

She gazed up, unable to speak.

'Say that you will,' Her Majesty urged.

Lucretia nodded again.

She was brought to the Queen's privy chamber. The dull apartments had been transformed with bright swags and canopies. A tapestry showed men and women hunting deer together. The Queen smiled as Lucretia curtsied. Beside her, folds of silvery-blue silk were draped over a stand, the shining fabric spilling and tumbling down. A dress, Lucretia realised. The Queen smiled at her and gestured to the stand.

'For you.'

The Queen's ladies-in-waiting led her behind a screen. Practised fingers unlaced her and clothed her anew. The cool cloth slipped over her skin, finer than any she had touched before. But when she glanced sideways into the pier glass, her heart sank. The bodice hung like a sack draped over a stick. The silvery-blue silk sagged from her shoulders. She emerged, reluctantly. Her Majesty patted the padded stool at her feet.

'Come and sit with me.'

As Lucretia sank onto the stool, the Queen bent forward.

'I will have my seamstresses flogged,' she whispered. 'But see how slender you are? You are just the age when I first saw the King. Have your courses arrived?'

Lucretia blushed. The cramping and blood came irregularly, sometimes not for months on end. Her mother had been the same, Mrs Gardiner muttered darkly. But she had not starved herself for attention . . . She gave an embarrassed nod.

'That is good. You must eat as the apothecaries advise.' Her Majesty smoothed back an escaped strand of Lucretia's hair. 'I would like to call you Lucy. Will you permit it? Say that you will.'

Lucretia looked around at the ladies-in-waiting then back to the woman who regarded her with a kind expression.

'You will wear this dress when you come to Court, Lady Lucy.'

Lucretia looked up, a long-submerged joy rising inside her.

'They told me you could not be wooed,' said the Queen to smiles from her ladies. 'That you were unbiddable. But now that I have seen you I cannot believe them.'

Doubt crept over Lucretia's face like a shadow.

'Wooed?'

There were scuffles among the lower tables, the serving men reported. Some courtiers hung about by the arched entrance to snatch dishes from the trays. Others dared to venture down the stairs until Mister Underley set up a chopping block at the foot of the staircase where, wrapped in his bloodiest apron and wielding a cleaver, he greeted any hatted and ruffed wanderers who descended from the Great Hall above.

Displaced from their dormitory, John and the others slept in the kitchen with the boys. Scovell's ladle sounded before first light each morning, clanging and ringing against the great copper in the hearth. Then the Master Cook roamed between the tables and benches, tasting, nodding or shaking his head. Henry Palewick complained that such a mass of bodies raised the heat of his cellars. In Firsts, a reluctant Pandar Crockett was put to work by Mister Bunce trimming sallets with the kitchen boys while Mister Stone's scullions kept up a constant din of splashing, clattering and curses.

The kitchen would divide in three, Scovell announced, according to the tables above. The King and Queen, their closest courtiers and Sir William, Lady Lucretia and the Callocks would occupy the High Table. Below them, at the uppermost trestles on the floor of the Great Hall, would sit the other gentlemen of the King's Household with Father Yapp, Miss Pole and the other higher servants. Placed below them, crammed in at boards hammered together by the Estate's carpenters, was everyone else.

John's dish for Tantalus would be served to the King's gentlemen. For the King himself, Scovell and Vanian would concoct a great tiered edifice in which the order of creation rose from dumb animals sculpted from sallets to the King and Queen themselves, fashioned from marchpane and crystallised sugar.

In Scovell's chamber, John, Colin Church, Luke Hobhouse and Tam Yallop worked over chafing dishes while Mister Vanian oversaw the bench behind. From there, elaborate concoctions were carried out to banqueting pavilions set up on the lawns: pastries shaped as swans, a ship made of fruit, a sugar tiara set with icing-paste gemstones.

The frantic days succeeded one another. No sooner did John's head touch the pallet than it seemed to be rising again. He had baked two pastry cases for his dish for Tantalus. The sugar liquor stood in a pipkin in Henry Palewick's cellar. The candies were locked in beside them. The night before the feast, he decided to check the cases and liquor one last time.

Tam Yallop squinted across Vanian's paste room as John walked down the passage. Phineas looked up from sweeping the floor. In the cold cellar, safe on the highest shelf, sat the cases. He would bring them through himself, John thought. He and Philip had been assigned Simeon to fetch and carry, and Simeon did not possess the surest pair of hands . . . He dipped the spoon in the liquor. The sweetness was perfect. Satisfied, he walked down the deserted corridor. He could sleep secure now, he thought. His eyelids drooped. Then he heard voices.

The sound drifted from Melichert Roos's spice room but no one should be down there now, John knew.

'. . . with lampreys it is another matter,' one voice was saying. 'The trouble is skinning them. Use a clean napkin, that's my advice. And pull slowly. Poach slower yet. The time it takes to say a slow Hail Mary . . .'

'You h-heretic,' chuckled a second voice.

'The broth is everything,' continued the first, unperturbed, 'and everything should go into the broth . . .'

John pushed open the door.

At the far end of the room, two men stood before the high shelves of Master Roos's spice rack. One, dressed in a rich silk doublet and holding a candle, stood almost two heads higher than the other who was dressed in the livery of the Household. John recognised Sir Kenelm Digby.

'What are you doing here?' John demanded.

'Doing?' queried Sir Kenelm in an affronted tone. 'Know whom you address before you speak so boldly.'

'I know very well,' John retorted. 'You are Sir Kenelm Digby whose father tried to blow up the King.'

To John's annoyance, the man in livery began to chuckle. His melancholy features and neatly trimmed beard appeared vaguely familiar. From the chapel, John supposed.

'You have b-been found out, Sir Kenelm,' the man stammered. He walked across the room to John. 'But who has done the finding?'

'John Saturnall,' John replied, increasingly annoyed by the Household man's assurance. This was his domain. His and Scovell's and all the other cooks'. 'Cook to Master Scovell.'

'Scovell, eh?' Sir Kenelm queried.

'Master Scovell,' John corrected him. 'And these kitchens are forbidden to strangers.'

But the serving man remained unperturbed. 'Are you a good cook, Master Saturnall?'

'Good enough to cook for the King,' John answered shortly.

'What if you should err? What if your acts should d-displease His Majesty?'

'We do not err,' John retorted. 'Sir William himself praises our efforts.'

'Ah yes, praise. B-beware praise. D-dip your spoon d-deeper,' the serving man stammered, indicating the spoon in John's hand. 'You will find that sourness lies beneath the sweet crust of praise.'

'Ha! Very good!' Sir Kenelm exclaimed. 'That is true perspicacity.'

John scowled. What did the man mean? *Dip your spoon deeper.* He gestured to the passage. 'You are not permitted here,' he said curtly.

Sir Kenelm opened his mouth to argue. But the serving man spoke first.

'We shall leave you to your p-pots and pans, Master Saturnall. God forbid His Majesty should go hungry tomorrow.'

Breakfast the next morning was a bowl of pottage eaten standing. Boys ran through the kitchen carrying billets from the yard and stacking them beside the hearth. A great tray of pastries wobbled past carried by Coake. Moved from the yard back to the kitchen, he had grown strangely affable. Even helpful, John was forced to concede, when he lent his strength to Simeon struggling under a maund of apples. Now the kitchen boy plucked the last pin-feathers from a basket of ducks. Behind the three of them, Colin and Luke spitted pheasants. John loaded charcoal into a chafing dish, fetched his sugar-liquor and began to stir. Soon his face was red from the heat. The syrup began to thicken. The cases waited on the bench, the candied jewels, crown and coins arranged inside. He poured in the liquid then he and Philip carried the cases to the cold larder.

'Will it set in time?' Philip asked.

'Has to.'

The kitchen's pace quickened. Adam beat a bucket of cream with a birchwood whisk, trying to make it stand in the heat while watching a pan for Vanian. Philip shook a bag of hot almond paste, waiting to pipe the mixture into the cases of a tray of tiny darioles. Across the room, Adam whisked on to no avail while at the bench beyond him, Coake rubbed powdered bay salt into tiny birds arranged in a roasting dish. Vanian and Underley were inserting roasted and larded quails into the breast of a swan, wrapping each in a nest of woven spinach stems.

Scovell, juggling two pans at the hearth, issued orders over his shoulder. Then, to John and Philip's astonishment, Coake turned to Adam.

'Need a hand there, Lockyer?'

Adam stared.

'Too hot in here for that,' Coake said, nodding to the sloppy cream. 'Let me.'

An astonished Adam handed over the whisk and Coake carried the bucket down the passage towards the cold store. As Adam, John and Philip swapped looks, a serving man appeared at the foot of the stairs.

'They're in the Hall!'

'Stations!' Scovell called from the hearth. From around the kitchen, the Master Cook received nods or raised hands.

John directed Simeon to watch his liquor, took an iron and placed it in the fire. Then he hurried to the cold larder. At the door he came face to face with Coake. The youth was sweating, Adam's bucket of cream dangling from one arm, the yellow peaks standing up stiff. They eyed each other in the doorway.

'What are you doing here?' John said.

Coake's face was a picture of injured innocence. 'Is it not plain?' He glanced down at the cream.

'Hard work,' offered John, still suspicious.

'Oh, it was worth it,' Coake replied airily. 'Catch it cold. That's what I say. Remember?'

The older boy grinned and slid past him. *Catch it cold?* He did remember. But from where? When Coake had gone, John craned his neck up to the shelf and looked down into Tantalus's pool. The liquor had not set in either. But it would, John knew. The crown had toppled over for some reason. He reset it in place.

In the kitchen, tiny meat pies topped with spinach and walnuts were loaded onto trays. Platters of mutton balls spiced with saffron and garnished with carved lemons waited beside them. Quiller's serving men toted plates of thin-sliced beef filled with artichoke and pistachio paste, then hollowed manchet rolls filled with minced eggs, sweet herbs, cinnamon and salt . . .

The spiced wine had already gone up. The cooks whirled from task to task, handing dishes to the waiting serving men: musk melons in syrup, a pottage of capons, boiled pigeons in sauce, a hash of chicks with a sallet, roasted fawn with an Italian farce then a custard quivering on a green Pearmain tart . . .

When Master Scovell sent for the great tiered dessert John knew his own moment had come. John bade Simeon put a second iron in the fire then he and Philip hurried out to the cold larder. The liquor had set clear. Together, they peered into the depths of Tantalus's pool. The crown, coins and jewelled ring lay at the bottom.

Philip cleared a space for him on the bench beside the hearth. John took a cloth, gripped the iron and drew it from the fire.

A hand's breadth above, John told himself. He lowered the iron to the surface and began to pass it to and fro, watching for the moment when the surface quivered. From the corner of his eye, he saw four men inching forward, balancing Scovell and Vanian's creation on a stretcher. They crouched so that the topmost tier might clear the arched entrance.

'Steady,' warned Scovell.

Gripping the hot iron, John worked over his dishes. Pass by pass, the surfaces turned to glass. When the iron cooled, John looked for the second one. Scovell and Vanian were pouring possets into pastry cups set into the upper tiers of their creation, Luke Hobhouse and four others rotating it slowly. But the hearth was bare. The hot iron was nowhere in sight.

'Simeon,' John hissed. 'The iron.'

The kitchen boy's expression told him all he needed to know. 'Master Saturnall, I . . . I forgot.'

'Forgot? Find one!' John ordered. But Simeon stood frozen by his mistake. 'Hurry!' John barked.

Startled, Simeon turned and began to run, blind to the chafing dishes, the pot crane, the stacked billets of wood. Blind too to Scovell's dessert. John watched, horrified, as Simeon collided with the rearmost man. He saw the man stagger, the corner sliding from his grip. From the bench behind, Colin turned and lunged for the wavering base. John reached out too. But the great creation began to tilt, then slide, then topple and tumble, the pastry tiers crumbling and posset cups spilling, the creams and sacks slithering and slipping, the marchpane animals leaping down followed by the King and Queen to smash on the flagstone floor.

For an instant, the whole kitchen was silent. All looked at a dessert-spattered Simeon. All except Scovell. His gaze was fixed upon John.

'I made him run,' John said in a flat voice. He looked down at the smashed pastry and the cream that ran in rivulets over the floor.

'Patience,' murmured Scovell.

Among the horrified faces, only the Master Cook's was calm. He pointed his ladle at John's two dishes, waiting on the bench.

'Which of these is the better?'

In a daze, John pointed to the clearest amber jelly.

'Good enough for His Majesty, would you say?'

'But Master Scovell,' Vanian objected. 'Saturnall is barely a cook!'

'John is equal to the task,' Scovell said. 'Are you not, John?'

John made himself nod. Scovell rapped his ladle in his hand.

'Send it up.'

The serving men were waiting, the desserts laid out on every table and bench. As the last round of dishes went up, the noise from the

Great Hall sank to an appreciative murmur then gained in volume, becoming an excited buzz of chatter. Scovell gestured to the remaining dish, still sitting on the bench.

'Would you serve your master as well as the King, John Saturnall?'

John took a knife and broke the surface, felt the jelly drag on the blade. It had set perfectly. He scooped out a slice and presented it to Scovell. The Master Cook picked up a wobbling cube and chewed. A contented look came over him. But then Scovell's face changed. He grasped a spoon and drove it into another part of the dish. His expression turned to alarm. He spun on his heel and shouted up the stairs.

'Call it back!'

But the last serving man had gone. Scovell turned on John. The smile had vanished. In its place, the Master Cook wore a horrified look.

'What have you done?'

'Master Scovell?'

'Salt!' exclaimed Scovell. 'You have poisoned it with salt!'

John felt his stomach sink, a mixture of bewilderment and dread contending within him. The men and boys of the kitchen turned to him, their faces disbelieving or dismayed. All except one. As John looked about desperately, he caught sight of Coake. And as their eyes met, he understood. Coake sprinkling the birds with bay salt. His retreat to the larder with the bucket of cream. The look of injured innocence and his strange good cheer. *Oh, it was worth it. Catch it cold. That's what I say* . . . It had been Coake's promise on his first night in the kitchen. His pledge of revenge. Now he had taken that revenge. With a cry of fury, John hurled himself at the older boy. But his hands had barely closed about Coake's throat before he was pulled off.

'He has lost his senses!' exclaimed Coake as a shocked Mister Underley held John back.

'First you taint the King's dish. Now you fight in the kitchen?'

John turned to Scovell. But the Master Cook wore a face of stone.

'Master Scovell . . .' John began.

Before he could say more, Mister Pouncey appeared at the foot of the stairs. A richly dressed courtier stood behind him.

'His Majesty spat!' the steward exclaimed. 'His Majesty spat it out!'

Mister Pouncey glared at Scovell as if too furious to utter another word. Beside him, wearing a chain like the steward and a rich fur cloak, the King's man looked on grimly. John saw a long scar running from his mouth up the side of his face.

'His Majesty orders its author be brought before him,' said Sir Philemon.

Scovell eyed John, his expression stony. Suddenly John felt he did not know the man. He had never known him. The Master Cook nodded to Sir Philemon.

'Take him up.'

A screen of grey-blue fur filled John's vision. His heart thudded in his chest. The scarred man led the way up the stairs, Mister Pouncey's footsteps tapping lightly behind. At the top, Sir Philemon turned.

'You have displeased the King,' he said in a hard voice. 'And that displeasure redounds to me. You will not repeat that error. Do you understand, kitchen boy?'

John nodded.

'You will kneel before him. You will not look up unless he gives you leave. You will not speak unless he asks. You will address him as "Your Majesty". At the rightful moment you will beg forgiveness.'

The scar was an angry red line. John could feel the man's breath against his face. Then the courtier turned to Mister Pouncey.

'All would be well, you promised,' Sir Philemon hissed. 'The kitchens, the cellars, the King's rooms. If you could not offer a palace, you would at least scrape the muck out of the barn. You gave your word. And I, in turn, gave mine. Now this.'

Suddenly John felt the courtier's hard hand grasp his neck. He was pulled down the passageway towards the screen at the end. As the clatter of voices and plates grew louder, Sir Philemon confronted John again.

'See this smile, kitchen boy?' His free hand rose and for a moment John thought the man would strike him. But Sir Philemon stroked a fingertip along the red line of his scar. 'Disappoint me and I will give you one of your own.'

A push sent John stumbling forward. He rounded the screen and entered the Great Hall.

The long tables swayed like boats in a sea, crowded with faces which surged back and forth. A wall of gleaming swords and spears rose before him. The High Table ran across the far end of the Hall, raised on a dais. John snatched a glimpse of the lords and ladies.

'Eyes down!' hissed Sir Philemon. He marched John between the tables. When they reached the front of the dais there was silence. Then a voice spoke from the High Table. A voice John knew.

'B-bring him up, Sir Philemon.'

A melancholy face regarded John. A neatly shaped beard covered the man's chin. Of course the serving man's face had seemed familiar last night, John realised. He had seen it the first day he had arrived at the Manor, staring out of the news-sheet that Ben Martin had purchased. Now last night's stammering servant regarded him from the centre of the High Table wearing a hat of rich black velvet trimmed with two lolling feathers and a black doublet of shiny silk. One of the King's hands toyed with a spoon, the other tapped the side of a great round platter: the part-eaten dish for King Tantalus.

'Behold,' he said, 'the cook who could d-do no wrong.'

The courtiers tittered. As Sir Philemon led him up on the dais, John recalled his words from the previous night. Why had he not simply expelled the intruders? On one side of His Majesty a flushed Piers Callock rested an elbow amidst the glittering silver. On the other sat two women dressed in rich silks and glittering necklaces. One wore a jewelled tiara. The other more resembled a porcelain doll, her face masked with powder and her hair dressed in elaborate black ringlets. Two dark eyes peered out from the expanse of white, varied only by a black dot on her cheek. A dress of silvery blue silk billowed around her. Sinking to his knees, John saw with a shock that the doll was Lucretia.

'So, Master Saturnall, you would cook for the King?'

As His Majesty spoke, more titters ran up and down the table.

'Your Majesty, the mistake was my own . . .'

The King tapped the dish before him. 'Was it? Surely the error was mine? In eating this . . . this salt-mine.'

John heard the titters turn to laughter. Piers's hearty guffaws sounded loudly. Squinting through his lashes, he saw Sir William smile. Among the diners at the High Table only Lucretia appeared unmoved. John felt his cheeks redden.

'Well might you b-blush, Master Cook,' the King pressed on. 'But what d-do you suggest? Look up, Master Saturnall.'

The laughter turned uncertain then died away as the King leaned forward. Kneeling on the planks of the dais, John looked up.

'Are you too floundering in this sea of salt?'

Sea of salt, thought John. He searched for the memory. What had his mother said as they stood together overlooking the marshlands of the Levels? The brine floating harmlessly over the sweet water beneath . . .

'Nothing to say, Master Saturnall?' asked the King. He held up his hand for silence. In his memory, John heard the man's words. But it was his own voice that spoke them.

'Dip your spoon deeper, Your Majesty.'

The nearest courtiers gasped. Piers's eyebrows shot up. But the words were out. Succeeding them came a silence so complete John fancied every man and woman in the Hall could hear his heart thud. The King leaned forward, a frown gathering on his face.

'What?'

John tried to keep his voice steady.

'I mean only to ask, Your Majesty, what sweetness might lie beneath the sourness of the crust?'

The courtiers looked horrified. Piers watched eagerly. The Queen appeared mildly surprised. Lucretia watched too, John saw. But her expression was unreadable. The King's eyes narrowed. They were not truly sad, John saw, but shrewd. The man glanced down at the dish, a spoon abandoned in its midst.

'Dig deeper, you say?'

John watched him sink the implement into the dish then lift out a gobbet of translucent jelly. The King's mouth opened. He chewed, his jaw working the jelly around his mouth. His face betrayed no expression. At last he swallowed. John looked up, waiting. The King raised an eyebrow. He puckered his lips. Then a broad smile spread across his face.

'The depths are sweet indeed, Master Saturnall.'

He turned to the Queen who offered a smile. The courtiers raised their hands in pleasure. One or two clapped. Beside Piers, John fancied he saw a flicker of approval in Lucretia's face. Then the King turned to his host.

'Sir William. I wonder if I might have the loan of this cook? I have a task for which he is fitted.'

As Sir William gave his assent, the King beckoned.

'Here,' he commanded. 'Sit beside me, John Saturnall.'

John rose. The eyes of the King and Queen, their courtiers, Sir William and the officers of the Household followed him as he walked along the front of the dais. Sir Kenelm towered over the others.

'Hurry along, Master Saturnall. Before he forgets why he wanted you.'

The other courtiers tutted and frowned. Beside him, the Bishop of Carrboro lifted a fleshy hand bearing an amethyst ring and waved John on. A red-faced Sir Hector sat next to Lady Caroline. The Queen nodded vaguely to John but Lucretia stared straight ahead. Behind the King a serving man held up a stool.

'Move along, Lord Piers,' the King commanded the youth beside him. 'Let Master John take his place.' John saw Piers's face darken but the King ignored him. 'In my father's time, a Sayer's task was to taste the King's food and pass it fit. Tonight I have learned the value of such a servant.' The King pulled the part-eaten dish along the table. 'Take up your spoon, Master Sayer.'

John dug and tasted. Under a layer of salt, the jelly in the depths was sweet. He began to scoop and taste, pronouncing the parts of his jelly sweet or sour. No need for his demon as he chased out the quivering gobbets from the salty chunks. Coake must have poured in half a sack. The King tasted after him, enquiring now after the dish's preparation until only the baubles remained.

'They are biscuits, Your Majesty,' John explained as the King crunched one of his coins. 'They are made of a paste very heavy with sugar. It is twice baked . . .'

The King's eyes had their shrewd look again. 'Yours is a singular dish, Master Saturnall. But what if the b-burden of a feast were set upon your shoulders?'

'I would strive to fulfil my duty, Your Majesty.'

Sitting beside the King, he felt as he had the day Cassie had spoken up for him outside the church at Buckland. The courtiers leaned forward to peer at him. Piers still scowled but Sir Kenelm offered a wave. Then, standing behind the table, Sir Philemon rapped his spoon on a glass for silence.

'All feasts p-propose a p-purpose,' the King announced. 'Now we reach our own.'

John saw the Queen lean towards Lucretia and whisper something in her ear. But her features seemed frozen, unreadable and remote.

'How fortunate is that K-King,' the King declared, 'who has such men as Sir William and Sir Hector. The houses of Fremantle and Callock are among the most ancient and loyal past remembrance. A King's authority c-cannot be divided. Otherwise it dissolves like salt in water. Our w-word has ever been our pledge. Now w-we have come to the Vale of Buckland to give our blessing to a different pledge.'

The King rose. As one, the Great Hall rose with him. John stood back as the King stretched out one hand to Piers and then, reaching across the Queen, the other to Lucretia. Now John could watch the young woman at his leisure. But she looked ahead, her face a mask. Then, for a moment, the mask slipped and John glimpsed the expression he had seen in the Solar Gallery, as if she were trapped again, about to be discovered.

'Lucretia, Lady Fremantle and P-Piers, Lord of Forham and Artois,' the King declared. 'I, Charles, King of England, Scotland and Ireland, do give my blessing and p-permission for this union. Let it be solemnised with rejoicing in the Vale of Buckland and let all those who rejoice sit with us on their wedding day.' As the applause began to swell, the King turned to John. 'And let this young cook prepare the feast.'

From *The Book of John Saturnall*: For a *Dish* of baked *Quodling Apples* served with a sweet *Cream*

now the Quodling from its unruly Tree whose upper boughs ape a Stork's Nest or an ill-laid Fire. Pippins, Pearmains and Genets may be eaten rudely off the bough. Try a Quodling thus and it will prove as sour as an unwilling Bride. Yet bake such a Fruit slow and it will sweeten after a marvellous Fashion.

Take the best Fruit from free or Paradise Stocks when the Day is bright and cold. If to keep, wrap them in Ferns and pack them in a Maund. If to eat as I direct, place them in an Oven whose Sides your Hand may touch for an Instant. Leave the Quodling for a Night then slide a Peel beneath to lift it. Its Innards will be turned as soft and thick as Pea Soup. Prick it that the Steam may escape.

Next take cold Cream, warm Honey and a Ladder. Climb the Ladder. Pour the Honey and Cream at a Fall into a Pot of Gascon Wine and let it froth, the higher the better. Whisk the sweetened Cream until it stands in melting Peaks.

A baked Apple is no Kickshaw or any dainty Dish. Set this Quodling as best you may upon a Plate and pour on the Cream. Break the Two together so that the hot Temper of the Quodling meets the Cold. As the Poet wrote:

Let me feed thee such Honey-sugared Creams
As cool the Quodling's 'scaping Steam

This is a hearty Dish and is most fit for One whose Sourness wants Sweetness or One whose hot Humour wants Coolness. Or both.

THE COOKS, UNDER-COOKS AND kitchen boys crowded about him, laughing, cheering and slapping him on the back. Mister Bunce presented John with a mug of ale.

'Cook the wedding feast, John! We'll have to ask Master Palewick to lay in more salt!'

'As much salt as you want,' Henry pledged from the other side of the kitchen.

John glugged his ale in a blur of congratulations. Even Mister Vanian conceded that John had served the Kitchen well. Then Scovell made his way through the crush and called for silence.

'Well done, John Saturnall!' the man announced. 'The champion of our kitchen!' Then he turned to John. 'I doubted him when I should not. A true cook knows no doubt. So he has taught us tonight. And he has reaped the reward!'

As the cheers echoed in the vaulted roof, Scovell offered his hand. John hesitated for a moment but then he gripped and shook.

'To the Kitchen!' he called out. 'To Master Scovell! To all of us!'

Everyone drank. Colin and Luke rolled a second barrel forward. The cooks crowded around.

'Where's Coake?' John asked Philip in the midst of the crush.

'Gone,' Philip said. 'Scovell found the salt in a pocket-bag tied around his waist. The look on his face . . .'

The marquees deflated and sank to the ground. Ambling horses were harnessed and saddled. The royal exit was as piecemeal as the entrance had been grand. When the last squadron of royal servants had trotted up the drive and disappeared through the gatehouse, John was summoned by Scovell. Entering the chamber, he saw a stout woman who carried at her waist a heavy ring of keys. She turned with a jangle.

'Is that Susan Sandall's boy?'

John recognised Mrs Gardiner the housekeeper. He nodded.

'She sent him here, Mrs Gardiner,' Scovell said from the hearth.

John shifted awkwardly as the housekeeper's eyes swept over him.

'I can see her face in yours,' Mrs Gardiner said approvingly. 'A good woman. And now her boy will cook for her ladyship's wedding.'

'So we hope,' said Scovell. The woman looked around the chamber.

'I haven't set foot down here since that night. Do you recall it, Master Scovell, how we drove that thieving magpie out? How long has it been?'

Magpie. John's ears twitched.

'Eighteen years,' Scovell answered shortly. He turned to a pan dangling over the hearth.

'What a commotion!' Mrs Gardiner continued. 'The villain.' She eyed the connecting door as if she expected the villain, whoever he was, to burst through it. She seemed about to launch into another volley of exclamations when her gaze returned to John. Her shrewd eyes narrowed. 'Susan Sandall's son,' she said in a curious tone, examining John's face. 'Now you're almost grown.'

'I am seventeen years of age,' John said as the silence lengthened.

'And now you'll be cooking the feast for the one your ma delivered.' Mrs Gardiner paused and considered. 'Just as soon as her ladyship returns to her senses.'

John looked between the Master Cook and the housekeeper.

'Mrs Gardiner has a task for you,' said Scovell.

_____

'No!' shouted Lucretia.

'My lady, the Fremantle Covenant is no old wives' tale,' Mister Pouncey explained patiently. 'It was an oath sworn to God. Your own ancestor made the pact . . .'

'I know the story well enough.'

'Then your ladyship will appreciate the great peril into which she places Buckland by her current, uh, reluctance.'

'To join myself to Piers Callock? That is not reluctance. It is disgust!'

'Your union is His Majesty's wish.'

'It is my father's tyranny!'

'He wishes only that the succession continue.'

Sitting on the top step with a bowl of pottage beside her, Gemma listened through the closed door as Mister Pouncey's voice rose and fell. The patient mumble had continued for an hour now. Pole's voice followed, more strident. That was a mistake, thought Gemma. Sure enough, a loud thud interrupted the woman's voice. A moment later the door was flung open.

'Out!' shouted Lucretia. 'Out, both of you!'

A red-faced Mister Pouncey hurried down the passage followed by an affronted Pole. Gemma looked up hopefully. But the door slammed shut again.

She had helped her mistress scrub off the powder and rouge. She had peeled off the beauty spot on her cheek. As she had lifted off the heavy silk of the dress, her mistress had begun to cry, bitter sobs that came from deep inside her.

'I will not!' the young woman had burst out. 'Never!'

Gemma could not remember the last time she had seen Lucretia cry. Now, contemplating the lukewarm bowl, she heard a rending noise sound behind the closed door. Sheets? Visions of a knotted rope dangling down into the garden passed before Gemma's eyes. When the noise stopped, she rose and knocked softly.

'Lucy?'

'Go away.'

'Lucy, it's me. It's Gemma.'

She heard the scrape of a chair. The door opened.

A headless torso lay draped over the chest. A pair of legs hung beside it. Another ripped body was slumped against the chest. Lady Whitelegs had been torn in two. Half of Lady Pimpernel flopped below her. Of Lady Silken-hair there remained only tatters and of Lady Pipkin not even that. But worse lay scattered over the floor. Through a haze of sawdust Gemma looked down on torn and crumpled pages, each one covered with familiar handwriting.

'Oh, Lucy!'

Gemma put down the bowl and picked up a fragment.

> *Let me feed thee such Honey-sugared Creams*
> *As cool the Quodling's 'scaping Steam . . .*

She knelt and began to gather up the pages. Glancing at the opened clothes chest she saw the folds of silvery-blue silk. At least the dress was unscathed.

'Mrs Gardiner bade me bring pottage,' Gemma said when she was finished.

'Pour it in the chamber pot.'

'But, Lucy . . .'

'Tell them I have resumed my fast.'

'We only exchange our freedoms, Lady Lucy,' the Queen had murmured in her ear at the feast. 'We only exchange our desires.'

At the King's announcement, the woman's hand had found her own under the table and Lucretia had found she could not reply. The kitchen boy had stared at her. Hauled up from the kitchens to caper for the King. Or perhaps to witness her humiliation. Returned to her room she had imagined John Saturnall recounting her fate to the others in his subterranean domain. They mocked her down there, she knew. Pouncey and Pole's embassy had only compounded her fury.

A terrible pleasure had gripped her as she ripped apart the dolls, and a worse one when she tore the pages from the book. Lucretia had thrown open her clothes chest and pulled out the dress. Taking up the silvery-blue silk, she readied herself to tear the fine material . . .

'The Covenant ties all our hands,' Mister Pouncey had explained in the nasal mumble he reserved for the imparting of confidences. 'But Piers may inherit on your behalf, being a cousin but once removed . . .'

She had grown up with the story. The oath sworn by her ancestor. She had never imagined it might bind her so closely.

'You would need only to wed Lord Piers,' the steward had assured her. 'You would not be forced into . . . into intimacy.'

Until he had need of an heir, she thought grimly. Then the Queen's words returned to her. *We only exchange our desires* . . . Was Piers so terrible, she forced herself to ponder, with his lank hair and trembling chin? Could he be worse than Lady Caroline's rumoured lover, the cold-eyed Sir Philemon with his slashed and stitched face? She imagined Piers's limbs entwined with her own, his clammy skin pressed against her, his stale-wine breath in her nostrils . . .

The thought turned her stomach. She watched Gemma gather the pages and take the pottage away. Left alone, Lucretia sat on the chair before her dressing table and looked out of the casement to the little banqueting house. Above its pointed roof, a white cloud was stretching itself across the sky. She remembered these hours from her previous fasts. Whole days of light-headed tedium.

That night a jagged stone seemed to roll in her belly. She slept badly and woke as the chapel bell rang for breakfast. Through the day, the ache in the pit of her stomach sharpened. After supper, Gemma's voice sounded outside the door.

'Lucy!' she hissed. 'It's me again.'

'What is it?'

There was a rustle of skirts. A second later, a small grey-brown slab slid under the door.

Lucretia recognised it from its annual appearance on the table in the back parlour. On the day of her mother's death. Maslin bread.

The servants ate it all year round. She had always disdained it, of course. Now the dark slab felt invitingly solid. The yeasty tang teased her nostrils. Hot juices joined the churning rock in her belly.

'I could get no better,' Gemma continued through the door. 'Pole was watching me. They were talking about you. Gardiner says if you don't eat then your courses stop. You dry up inside and can't bear children . . . Lucy?'

'Mmmth.'

Lucretia's teeth mashed the fat grains. The coarse gluey mass rolled around on her tongue. She held a cloth to catch the crumbs and chewed as hard as she could. Lucretia thought it possible she had never tasted anything so delicious as maslin bread.

Gemma smuggled out another block the next day but as she sank her teeth into the second heavy slab, Gemma hissed a warning.

'Lucy! They're coming!'

Several sets of footsteps were advancing up the staircase. Then they resounded along the passage. Lucretia chewed quickly but the key was scraping in the lock. She wrapped the remaining hunk in the cloth, dropped it to the floor and nudged it under the bed. She wiped her mouth as the door swung open to reveal Mister Pouncey, Mrs Gardiner, Mister Fanshawe and Mrs Pole.

A new smell entered with them too. A rich mixture of braised meat and spices. The aroma curled about the door and wove its way through the stuffy air. Lucretia felt the rock of her hunger stir. Then the source appeared. A youth clad in red livery stepped out from behind Pole. Strange to see a denizen of the Kitchen in the House, thought Lucretia, eyeing the tray and the steaming bowl.

'Sir William has assigned you a cook,' Mister Pouncey informed Lucretia, 'in honour of your new vow. He will describe today's dish for you.'

Her gaze rose to the bearer's face.

John glanced down.

He had dreaded this moment since Scovell and Mrs Gardiner had informed him of the steward's order. He had been cheered out that morning by his fellow cooks, Peter Pears slapping him so hard on the back that he had almost spilt the broth.

'Go on, John!' Adam Lockyer had called after him. 'How could Lady Lucy resist you?'

Her face wore a look of scorn mixed with boredom. Mister Pouncey, Mister Fanshawe and Mrs Pole waited.

'This is a broth of lamb, your ladyship,' John began. 'It is made with fillets taken from the tenderest part of the neck. The joints are simmered on the bone until the marrow can be removed and chopped into the liquor . . .'

If he looked sideways a little, he could see her reflection in the pier glass at the far end of the chamber. Lucretia appeared unmoved.

'Thus the juices are reduced. Now, the seasonings . . .'

His description lurched on. He tried to imagine that he stood in the kitchen. He was explaining the dish to Simeon or Heskey, or another of the kitchen boys. Not mumbling before a contemptuous Lucretia Fremantle. Gardiner and Pole nodded at his halting performance. Then, to his surprise, Lucretia spoke.

'How fascinating.'

She did not sound fascinated. But neither did she seem to mock.

'After the final seasoning, the liquor is strained,' John continued.

'Really? How?'

This time, John glanced at her.

'A colander is too coarse,' he explained. 'A horsehair sieve will clog. We use a strainer fashioned from fine wires.'

Lucretia stood and peered into the bowl.

'You have spent the day making this broth?' she said.

'Yes, your ladyship.'

The young woman leaned into the rising steam and took an appreciative sniff. Then, to John's amazement, she took the bowl in her hands. She was going to drink, John realised, struggling to keep the exultation from his face. His task accomplished in a single day! He watched Lucretia turn then hook out something with her foot from under her bed, something that scraped the boards of the floor. A bowl.

A chamber pot.

In the next moment, John realised Lucretia's intention. He took

246

a step forward but she was too quick. With a single fluid gesture, the young woman upended the bowl, sending the broth falling in a dark brown arc. A dismayed John watched the steaming stream crash into the pot and splash the floor about. A moment's silence followed.

'Filthy girl!' exclaimed Pole.

'Miss Lucretia!' Mister Fanshawe spluttered. 'How could you!'

A shocked John regarded his creation. Lucretia's triumphant face turned to Mister Pouncey.

'Did you think I would change my mind for a bowl of soup? Not a drop will pass my lips. Tell my father that. Not a crumb.'

It was left to John to pick up the pot. As he knelt amidst the pools of broth, a scattering of crumbs led his gaze under the bed. There, among the shadows, he made out a shape. A small slab lay on the floor. A slab part-wrapped in a cloth. As John's eyes adjusted to the gloom, he smiled to himself. A half-eaten hunk of maslin bread. So Lady Lucy's fast had already ended. Had probably never begun. He rose to his feet.

'Not a crumb?' he murmured.

Lucretia stiffened. Two dots of colour grew in her cheeks.

'What's that?' asked Mister Pouncey's nasal voice.

He had only to announce his discovery. He had only to call out as she had done . . . But as he drew breath to speak, Lucretia's expression changed. Her haughty gaze faltered. A look John knew flashed across her face. For an instant he was back with her in the Solar Gallery, the two of them united in the fear of discovery.

'Well?' the steward demanded.

'Nothing, Mister Pouncey, sir,' John heard himself say. His exultant mood had evaporated, replaced by a baffling inhibition.

'Nothing?'

'I was thinking of another dish, sir. One more to her ladyship's taste.'

'Why?' demanded Philip. 'If she's eating, she's not fasting, is she? Why didn't you tell them?'

'Nothing in that for me,' John answered airily. 'Finding a bit of bread under a bed. Besides, they'd have known your Gemma brought it.'

He clapped Philip on the back in jocular fashion.

'If Lady Lucy's filling her belly,' Phineas said, 'she won't touch what you're cooking.'

'That depends what I cook,' John answered with a smile. 'Doesn't it?'

But Lucretia did not eat the comfits flavoured with sugared cream which he presented the next day, nor the lemon possets with straw-berries which he took after that. Each day at the door, Pole inspected the tray. Each day John stood before her in the room, his eyes averted, the silence growing more oppressive between himself, the governess, the clerk and Lucretia while, on the tray he held before him, that day's creation cooled or collapsed or congealed.

Lucretia herself gazed out of the window, or busied herself at her dressing table, or pretended enthusiasm for her sampler, working a jagged row of stitches. After an hour that felt like three, his arms aching and his stomach rumbling, the bell for the end of dinner released John to return to the kitchen.

'Gruels and pottages,' suggested Henry Palewick. 'Master Scovell used to prepare them for her when she was a child. Not that she ate a spoonful.'

'Frumenty,' Alf pronounced authoritatively. 'Or a sucket. Or broth. That's what my sis used to make.'

Poached collops of venison came and went untouched. A hash of fishes and a quaking pudding with raisins, honey and saffron were spurned. The days succeeded one another. When Mrs Gardiner escorted John, he remembered her scrutiny in Scovell's chamber, the talk of a 'magpie'. But the quiet of the unfamiliar passages silenced his questions and more often now it was Fanshawe and Pole who marched him through the Great Hall and up the stairs to Lucretia's chamber.

The governess and the clerk seemed fascinated by each other. While their greetings remained as formal as ever, John caught glances passing behind his back. He glimpsed little smiles out of the corner of his eye. He heard their asides grow more elaborate. On the day Mrs Pole allowed a diminutive fringe to escape the severe scrape of her hair, Mister Fanshawe cleared his throat.

'Mrs Pole. A word in private, if I may?'

The governess and the Clerk of the Household retreated a little way down the passage. There they conducted a whispered exchange. When it was over they returned and again took up their places to either side of John.

They retreated the next day too, venturing further out of earshot. Soon their assignations carried them all the way along the passage and halfway down the stairs. At last only flutters of half-stifled laughter reached into the room.

John was left to stand like a sentry in the chamber. His arms ached. His every breath seemed to amplify. He took up position with the tray at the door, counting the seconds to his release, while Lucretia sat before her pier glass, pretending to sew.

He should have told Pouncey just as Philip counselled, John berated himself as the days passed. He should have held up the bread like a trophy. Now the chance was gone. Why should he scruple to betray her when she had so willingly shouted out his presence? He had been a fool, or something even worse than a fool. Then, as he stood before her with his tray holding a dish of forcemeats and sallets, the greens cooling and drooping beneath his gaze, the sauce growing a thick dull skin, Lucretia broke the silence.

'You did not tell them.'

Her voice was so unexpected he jumped. Lucretia looked up from her needlework, her pale face visible in the mirror. She glanced down at the bed beneath which the hunk of maslin bread had lain.

'You might have told Mister Pouncey. You might have claimed your reward.'

John glanced over his shoulder and down the passage.

'They cannot hear,' Lucretia said.

'I was promised no reward,' said John.

She snorted. 'You are their creature.'

'I am a cook,' he answered. 'Your ladyship.'

'Are you?' Her voice was scornful.

'I am your cook.'

'I do not believe you.'

John felt himself flush. 'Then I will prove it,' he said, annoyed. 'Your ladyship.'

Lucretia gave a little snort then turned back to her sampler, stabbing the needle into the cloth.

The next day, Pole uncovered the tray and frowned.

'Is this dish not too plain for her ladyship?'

John adopted a puzzled look. 'I imagined her ladyship's appetite might be provoked by its plainness.'

'Or too coarse?' continued Pole.

'Its very robustness commends it, Mrs Pole. We have always found it most toothsome, down in the kitchen.'

A loaf of maslin bread sat on the tray. Mrs Pole looked doubtfully at the dark brown block. 'Very well.' The key grated. John, Pole and Fanshawe walked in. Lucretia sat at her table, ignoring them.

This time the governess and the clerk delayed barely a minute before Mister Fanshawe made his request for 'a word'. John listened until they were out of earshot.

'Maslin bread, your ladyship.' He waited. 'And a stew.'

Lucretia looked up. 'A stew?' She eyed the loaf.

'A stew of beef,' said John. 'With sweet herbs and dumplings.'

A flicker of curiosity disturbed Lucretia's lofty air.

'What . . . stew?'

Setting the tray on the table, John carefully broke open the crust to disclose a case of rye paste beneath. This he lifted out and cracked with the spoon. From the crack, a puff of fragrant steam rose up. Hot dark juices flooded out and swirled around crumbling hunks of dark red meat. The rich smell drifted in the room. Lucretia eyed the glossy gravy. Then she looked to John.

'What trick is this?'

Closing the coarse rye paste around the cold stew had been the most difficult task. Then crimping the edges and punching an airhole lest the parcel burst. In the oven, John had turned his creation every few minutes. Slowly the paste had baked. John had plugged the airhole then set to work on the loaf, cutting a disc from the base and digging out the insides. Simeon, at John's invitation, had quickly disposed of the evidence. Now John watched Lucretia's nostrils twitch. From the stairs, Pole and Fanshawe's voices sounded. Her suspicion gave way to puzzlement.

'They will know you brought it.'

He shrugged.

'That you tried to deceive them.'

He shrugged again.

'You will lose your place. They will dismiss you.'

He looked down at her.

'Not if you eat it.'

Lucretia looked down at the melting meat in its glistening sauce then eyed the dark-haired youth.

'Why?'

Instead of an answer, John held out a spoon.

Peter Pears, Adam, Alf and Jed Scantlebury laughed and clapped him on the back. Simeon shouted so loudly he had to be told to pipe down. The others crowded around and banged on the bench, setting the spatulas and pastry-jiggers rattling.

'She gulped it down!' John repeated.

Peter nodded admiringly. 'So when will you tell Pouncey?'

'Oh, soon enough,' he offered casually. 'I'll give her a few dinners before that.'

The others nodded. But Philip frowned.

'Unless they catch you first.'

John grinned. 'Not much chance of that.'

The next day, Mrs Pole looked down on a pie crust. After that came a bulging tart. Then John offered a topping of baked parsnips and on the next day a bread pudding. Lucretia's governess returned to find the crust unbroken, the tart untouched, the bread pudding's brown surface as pristine as when it had arrived.

'Perhaps this plainness may be alleviated,' Pole suggested in the corridor. John nodded solemnly.

The next day, Pearmain slices raised little sails of fruit from within a lattice of pastry, each one dabbed with a pennant of cinnamon and sugar. Pole surveyed the gaudy fleet approvingly. Behind her back, John saw Lucretia purse her lips.

She kept her wariness at first, accepting his offerings with a suspicious look. But as the days succeeded one another, she ate more readily.

He waited in silence as before. But now the tray no longer weighed on his arms. The silence did not oppress as it had. The minutes no longer dragged. More than once John was surprised by the bell that signalled the end of dinner.

'Not a crumb,' John murmured to himself as Lucretia's lips parted to admit the last of the tiny pastries that he had concealed that day. The young woman looked up.

'Do you find my hunger comical, John Saturnall?'

'No one's hunger is comical, your ladyship.'

Down the passage, Pole's faint giggles mingled with Fanshawe's deeper tones. Lucretia rolled a last flake of pastry into her mouth then contemplated him curiously.

'Why?' she asked. 'Why do you serve me so?'

'I told you. I am a cook, your ladyship. Your cook, according to Mister Pouncey.'

'You have a fellowship down there in the kitchens, do you not? Gemma speaks of it.'

'We do, Lady Lucretia.'

'You could be among your fellows again. You would only have to tell Mister Pouncey. You would not have to attend me.'

John shrugged as if the question were of no importance. But Lucretia eyed him steadily.

'Would you?' she persisted.

'No,' John conceded. 'I would not.'

'Yet you do.'

She looked up at John, the question written on her face. The dishes were proof of his art, Scovell would say. That was reason enough to cook them. They were for all, his mother would add. Even for the daughter of the Lord of the Vale of Buckland. The different answers contended inside John, and among them one other that he sensed like a scent drowned beneath a welter of coarser smells. An uncomfortable silence ballooned in the room.

'It is my choice,' he said at last.

'Just like the old days,' Mister Bunce told John when the Head of Firsts found him preparing the deceptive dishes. 'They used to dye fish eggs green and serve 'em as peas. Or chop raw liver into strings and throw it on a hot steak. Looked like worms wriggling out of the meat. Those old cooks could make anything look like anything.'

'Could they make themselves look like servants dismissed for deceit?' Philip asked, looking over at John. 'They'll kick you out just like they did Coake.'

'Coake ran,' replied John.

'You think Lady Lucy'll speak up for you?'

John shrugged. It was a game, he had told himself, walking back from her chamber the last time. It was a test of his art. The feast belonged to its cook after all . . . He reached for the fat trout he had poached. He had promised Lucretia fish.

'I fear the heat was too high,' he explained regretfully to Mrs Pole the next day. 'The jelly clouded. But I think today, Mrs Pole, her ladyship may be tempted. This, after all, was the dish enjoyed by the King himself.'

She and Fanshawe glanced at the dull mass. Their customary retreat followed. Alone with Lucretia a minute later, John peeled back the quivering slab of clouded jelly to reveal the trout, its sides rescaled in shaved almonds and tiny slices of lemon. Lucretia looked up at John.

'There is no need for you to stand in such a fashion,' she said.

'Then how should I stand, Lady Lucretia?'

She hesitated. 'If it pleased you, Master Saturnall, you might . . . sit.'

'Sit?'

'You might regard me more readily.'

'Regard you?'

'You might look at me. When we converse. You might sit here.' She spoke as if it were the most natural thing in the world for him to sit with her. She glanced down at the seat beside her own. 'After all, you have sat beside the King. So surely you might sit with me. That is, if you wished.'

'But what if Mrs Pole were to return, your ladyship?' asked John.

'Then she would learn that Lady Lucretia Fremantle has a greater appetite than she believed.' She touched the place next to her. 'Come. Then you will not loom over me.'

John felt his usual sure movements desert him as he reached down to lift the tray from her lap. As he gripped the smooth wooden handles, his hand brushed Lucretia's. The touch jolted him. His arm jerked back. The wooden board tipped. John grasped for the edge but it fell to the floor with a clatter, scattering fishbones and flakes of pale pink flesh. For a moment there was silence. Then Pole's voice called out.

'What was that?'

John and Lucretia stared at one another. Quickly John knelt. He was in the kitchen, he told himself. Master Scovell was calling. This was a simple task. The bones first. His hands worked precisely. Next the jelly. How to lift it whole? In the kitchen he had a dozen spatulas from which to choose. Here he had only his hands. And hers.

'Help me,' he hissed as Pole's footsteps reached the top of the stairs. Lucretia slid down to join him. 'Put your hand under here. Now, ready . . .'

Together they flipped the jelly back to cover the bones. Where was the spoon? John spied it behind a leg of the bed beside a scrap of paper. He grasped both. Spoon on the tray. Paper under the dish. A moment later, Pole entered the room.

'What was that noise?' the woman demanded.

'I . . .' began John and Lucretia together.

'Tell me.'

'I regret to say, Mrs Pole,' John said, 'that I slipped.'

Pole's eyes narrowed, scanning the tray. They came to rest on the spoon. Two bony fingers plucked it from the tray. The woman's narrow nostrils flared.

'This spoon smells of fish.'

'Does it?' Lucretia said innocently. But John saw her cheeks redden. He snatched the spoon from Mrs Pole's hand.

'You are right, Mrs Pole!' John exclaimed. 'It has been licked too! No wonder her ladyship will not eat!' Staring at the offending article, he mustered a tone of outrage which Mister Vanian would have envied. 'Have no fear, I will convey your displeasure to the scullery. Master Scovell himself will hear of this!'

Let me feed thee such Honey-sugared Creams
As cool the Quodling's 'scaping Steam
That thy hottest Tempers doth oft-times bake
Then let my cool words thy thirst to slake . . .

'What's that?' asked Philip, squinting at the words over John's shoulder. 'She writing you verses now?'

John shook his head. If Pole had only lifted the dish she would have discovered the scrap of paper. Instead Philip had done so, which was proving almost as uncomfortable.

'Pole nearly caught you, didn't she?'

'Pole couldn't catch a dead trout.'

He turned away but Philip gripped his shoulder. 'Listen. If you won't tell them she's eating then tell them she won't. Say she won't touch anything you serve.'

John busied himself rearranging the knives on the bench. Longest on the left. Paring knife on the right.

'What's wrong with you?' Philip demanded.

'Me?' John bridled. 'Nothing.'

The next day he handed back the paper.

'These are verses,' Lucretia told him as if he had never seen writing before. 'They were written for my mother.'

He watched her eyes flick over the words. Then her gaze turned to the chest under the window. The smells of lavender and old wool wafted up as she lifted out a mass of silver-blue silk. The dress from the feast, John realised. Beneath it lay a book, its pages taped and gummed. Lucretia carefully sheaved the torn leaf between the others then looked across the bed.

'I thought Pole had caught you.'

John grinned. 'Not me.'

But the young woman did not smile.

'You must not come again.'

John felt his stomach give a strange lurch. 'Not come?'

'It is as wrong to order a servant to err as to ask an equal to go against their conscience.'

'No one ordered me, your ladyship,' said John.

'Then I fear you have gone against your conscience.'

'What if my conscience led me?'

Lucretia shook her head. 'I will tell Mister Pouncey that your presence hardens my resolve. That your labours work against their purpose. I know how to treat with him. He will dismiss you without fault.'

'Then what will you eat, your ladyship? Gemma cannot . . .'

'I will eat that feast which the King commanded you to serve.'

She wore the same expression that he had seen in the Great Hall, remote and unreachable.

'That is your wedding feast,' John said.

'Yes.'

'You will marry Piers?'

'Yes.'

'But you do not care for him.'

'No,' she said sharply. 'Nor he for me.'

A vein beat at the side of her neck. A tiny tremor, measuring her heart. A wisp of black hair lay across the pulsing ridge.

'My mother died for Buckland,' she said. 'She died to give my father an heir. That the Vale might be kept safe. She died and I lived. This was her wish. That the succession be assured. That the Vale be secured.'

She looked up at him. What else had he expected? John wondered. That she spend the rest of her life in here? That he grow old concocting dishes to slip past Mrs Pole?

'If you are to give up your fast,' he said at last. 'Let it end with a worthy dish. There is one more I would serve you, Lady Lucretia.'

She gathered herself. 'What dish is that?'

'Let it be a mystery,' John answered. 'Let it tell you something you have not guessed. Something of myself.'

Mister Pouncey was climbing the stairs from the kitchen as John descended that afternoon. Usually, the steward would offer a curt nod as John removed his cap. But today, to John's surprise, Mister Pouncey gave John a searching look then nodded and smiled, as though some intelligence had passed between them. John continued down into the kitchen then through the doorway to Firsts.

'Mister Bunce?' he asked. 'Do you know of an apple called a quodling?'

Pole gave John a hard look the next day. But she nodded approvingly at the oversized dumplings which he presented for her inspection.

Lucretia had plaited her hair, he saw as he entered. And an unfamiliar scent drifted in the room.

'Are there flowers here, your ladyship?' he asked when Pole had gone.

'Flowers?' Lucretia touched a hand to her cheek. 'Surely you have smelt rose water before?'

In the Solar Gallery, remembered John. The scent teased his nostrils as he bent to prise open the first dumpling. The soft dough parted and a puff of steam carried a second sweet smell into the chamber. Lucretia peered at the glistening mass then looked up curiously. 'What dish is this?'

' "Let me feed thee Honey-sugared Creams," ' John recited. ' "As cool the Quodling's 'scaping Steam." '

She stared at him, amazed. 'The verses? You can read?'

'Is it so strange in a cook?'

'I . . . no.' Lucretia gathered herself. 'Of course you must read your receipts.'

'They are our verses, your ladyship. We give each other recitals down there in our kitchens.'

John brought a corked flask from inside his doublet and poured sweetened cream over the apple. He watched her dig into the apple's oozing flesh, swirl the thick cream then slip the marbled mixture into her mouth.

'Your honey-sugared cream is as sweet as the verses claim,' Lucretia told him, swallowing. 'It all but conquers the sourness of the quodling.'

'I am pleased that it is to your ladyship's taste.'

He watched her lick the last of the cream off her lips. Then the distant look was back. Lucretia rose.

'The Queen gave me a dress. A beautiful dress. I was to wear it at Court.' She opened the lid of the chest and reached within. The folds of silk unfurled with a rustle. Lucretia smoothed the shimmering cloth over herself. 'Do you think I shall?'

John stared at her body wrapped in silver-blue silk.

'I know,' Lucretia said when he made no answer. 'It does not fit me.' She reached behind herself to pull the fabric tighter. 'Is that better?'

'Yes,' John managed. 'That is better, Lady Lucretia.'

'Desires can be exchanged, so Her Majesty told me,' Lucretia said. 'Why not antipathies too?'

She meant Piers, John realised. She had made her decision. He gestured to the tray.

'Eat, your ladyship.'

'I shall, John Saturnall.' She tapped the second dumpling. 'Just as soon as you arrange the dish fittingly.'

The smells of apple and rose water mingled in his nostrils as John bent down. Leaning across her to prise the soft dough apart, he caught the faint warm scent of her skin. He felt something trail against his face. A loose strand of her hair had brushed against his cheek. Without thinking, he swept it back over her ear. As his fingers touched her cheek, he let them rest against the smooth curve of her skin. She looked up, her eyes wide.

'Is that your mystery, John Saturnall?'

The sweet smell of apples mixed with Lucretia's own scent. He could feel the warmth of her breath. Yes, he thought. A mystery, until now.

Her hand still held the forgotten spoon. He bent lower and saw her lips part. Suddenly everything was clear. In the next instant, their lips would touch. He would taste her mouth. He felt her warm breath mingle with his own. But a nasal voice sounded behind him.

'I see your fast is done, your ladyship.'

The spoon dropped from Lucretia's fingers. John jerked away. Mister Pouncey stood in the doorway. Pole and Fanshawe flanked him. The steward eyed John.

'It appears your efforts have pleased her ladyship.'

John saw his own bewilderment mirrored in Lucretia's face.

'Your task here is done, Mister Saturnall,' Mister Pouncey continued. 'You may return to the kitchen. Mister Fanshawe? Escort him out if you will.'

Once again, the kitchen's congratulations swirled about John. Once again, the hands of his fellow cooks clapped him on the back.

'Count yourself lucky,' Philip told him.

John nodded.

'You could have been found out and booted out like Coake. Wouldn't want that, eh?'

John shook his head.

How had the steward known? John wondered as their praise engulfed him. He had exchanged a single baffled glance with Lucretia before Fanshawe had led him from the room, a welter of sensations whirling inside him.

'Why trouble yourself?' Philip challenged him airily when he asked what Gemma knew of Lucretia. 'Let Piers worry about her, eh? All you need to think about now is the feast.'

Ox-carts piled high with firewood rumbled down the track and were unloaded into barrows in the outer yard. Billets and logs were stacked in an ever-lengthening pile behind the stables. Sacks of coke lined the west wall of the servants' yard and soon rose halfway up the window of the old buttery. A cage-spit from the Carrboro smithy arrived coated with pork fat. New fire tongs followed, then a set of pipkins and larger pots. Four new skillets arrived blue from the forge and were oiled and proved in Mister Vanian's oven before being hung with the others above the salt chest. On the bench below, Philip Elsterstreet compiled lists and tallies, calculating strikes and pecks of breadcorn to be sent from the granary to the Callock Marwood mill. Next to him, Colin and Luke bickered as usual.

'Viscount Saye's declared against the King? You've been reading Calybute's rag,' scoffed Colin.

'Him and the Earl of Essex too,' Luke continued doggedly. 'Hertford and Carbery won't sit at table with them. They were here to meet Sir William again.'

'The Marchioness of Charnley too,' added Tam Yallop.

The swirl of names washed over John: the Earls of Essex and Warwick, Lords Brooke and Bullenden. There were intrigues in Parliament, according to some of the men in the yard. The King should send them all home again, reckoned others. But at every mention of 'that Devil Pym' or 'the blackguard Hampden' or 'the dullard Cromwell' and 'insolent Haselrig', John's thoughts sank into his own reflections. The names rolled over him: 'young Edward Montagu' and 'old Manchester's lad' and someone called 'Mandeville' who were all, John realised belatedly, the same person. Master Jocelyn drilled the Estate men and some of the Household in the meadows below the ponds, drawing them up in ranks and files and marching them about. Ancient spears and pikes were disinterred from the lightless vault of the armoury and polished. But all these commotions held no more significance for John than the bakehouse's new boulting cloths held flour. The Estate carpenters had promised new kneading troughs too, that reminded him . . .

In the cellars, the hogsheads of that year's March beer were stacked beside the tuns of weaker ale. Cages of mallards, teals, larks and thrushes quacked, twittered and chirruped from the aviary behind Diggory Wing's dovecote. The kitchens grew crowded with sacks of flour, which would have to be moved. But where? Henry Palewick's stores were already filled with sugar-loaves, cheeses, bags of bay salt and gallipots filled with conserves and preserves, pickles and conserves.

By day, John buried himself in preparations. By night, processions of dishes once again marched through his mind: poached fish covered in cucumber scales and steaming pies filled with hashes of venison and beef and topped with golden pastry crusts. Quaking puddings and frosted cakes and cups brimming with syllabub. The dishes ascended the stairs to the Great Hall and floated forward to the High Table. There, accompanied by her groom and wrapped in shimmering silver-blue silk, waited Lucretia.

She enjoyed a new contentment, Philip relayed to John when he asked. She loved nothing more than extolling the qualities of her future husband. She had begun work on a sampler depicting him in wool.

Lucretia could no more draw a likeness with her needle than she could pass through its eye, John thought. Unbidden, the scents of rose water and sweet apple rose in his nostrils.

He drowned the smells among the aromas of the spice room. Standing before the hearth, he let the great blaze dispatch the warm scent of her skin, drawing it away like woodsmoke up the chimney. He had been seized by a madness, he told himself, remembering the moment in her chamber. Only Mister Pouncey's inexplicable arrival had saved him. He thought of the lips that had parted before his own. Another moment, he insisted to himself, and he would have been lost.

The first cattle were slaughtered and hung in Mister Underley's jointing room. The ponds were cleared of weed by the Heron Boy in readiness for netting. Fish wrapped in leathery kelp arrived in barrels from Stollport. He would prepare the dish he had served the King, John decided. This time love tokens would lie in the pool of crystal jelly: rings, an arrow, a red heart.

The last days passed in a near-sleepless blur. As the excitement rose in the kitchen, John felt a tightening in his stomach, familiar from other feasts. The King had left London and was marching to

Nottingham, reported *Mercurius Bucklandicus*. The Earl of Essex had stirred a rabble against him. Upstairs, the arriving guests talked of little else while their unruly servants threw the Household into uproar. It was a feast like any other, John told himself on the eve. All was as it should be. Tomorrow Lucretia would be powdered and rouged and sheathed in her silver-blue dress . . . Ready for Piers.

'She's in with Sir William,' Philip's voice said. 'He called on her in her chambers. Gemma's just told me.'

'Sir William?' Somehow John could not imagine the Lord of Buckland mounting the stairs. Or making the walk along the passage. Knocking on the door at the end.

'Some sort of commotion,' Philip answered. 'Sir Philemon's holding conferences in the winter parlour. A messenger was sent to Elminster.'

'Now?' queried John. It was late. The kitchen was quiet. Philip shrugged.

'Maybe the King's coming back.'

Together they walked through the passages, peering in at the jointing room and the spice room, Philip opening the doors to storerooms and the cellars. The chambers were deserted, the tired men and boys of the kitchen sleeping, but as they approached the stairs, a familiar figure stumbled down the steps.

'Ah, the kitchen boy,' Piers slurred at John. He waved a flask at them, the smell of liquor coming off him in a thick wave. The other hand held a wooden tankard.

'Cook, Lord Piers,' John corrected the youth. He and Philip exchanged glances. 'Let us help you up the stairs.'

'When I came down here to toast the bride? Let's raise a cup, eh? All those dishes you served her.'

Piers's head swayed but his eyes fixed themselves on John. What, John wondered, had she told him? As Piers attempted to pour liquor into the mug, his legs gave way. John and Philip caught an arm each. The dead weight lolled between them.

'Get your hands off me,' Piers mumbled. 'I can stand as well as you.' An eye opened and settled again on John. 'I'll serve Lady Lucy a hot dish.'

'No doubt you will, Master Piers.'

'All those sweetmeats. She told me all about them. Thought you'd take my place, didn't you?' Piers's other eye opened. 'Next to the King.'

John said nothing. Piers was heavier than he looked. He tried to manoeuvre his half up the stairs. Piers waved his flask again.

'Let's toast the bride,' he offered once more with a leer. 'Raise a cup, eh, kitchen boy? Since you can't raise her skirts . . .'

A cold anger washed over John. With an unhurried gesture, he reached over and gripped the youth by his lank hair. Piers's head felt heavy but unresistant. John knocked it against the wall then made to repeat the blow. Philip lunged for his arm. The trio swayed on the step, Philip pulling at John and John struggling with the drunken Piers who seemed barely aware of the assault.

'Stop it!' Philip hissed. 'John!'

John released the youth. At the top of the stairs Pandar Crockett appeared in an ancient yellow nightshirt and cap. A bucket dangled from his hand.

'Pandar,' Piers slurred. 'There you are, Pandar.'

'Now, now, now, Lord Piers. In our cups again, are we?'

Before Piers could answer, a deeper voice bellowed.

'Down there, is he?' Sir Hector Callock stamped down the stairs accompanied by two footmen. At the sight of his father, Piers offered a sickly grin. Sir Hector gripped his son by the collar. 'Drunk even tonight? Upstairs, you sot! Word has come from the King . . .' It seemed as if he might say more but the presence of John and Philip silenced him. He hauled Piers upright. The two footmen followed as the youth was dragged back up the stairs.

'What word?' wondered Philip aloud. But John could think only of those that had issued from Piers's slurring mouth. The dishes he could have learned of from Lucretia alone. She would be sleeping now, he thought. Lying in the bed where she had invited him to sit. His own sleepless brain whirled with thoughts that he could neither resolve nor banish. He walked quietly down the dark passage. As he reached the end a figure eased itself out of the shadows.

'John.'

Scovell wore a heavy cloak. A single rushlight flickered beside his face. Startled, John recoiled. But the Master Cook smiled.

'Are you ready for the feast?'

'I do not know, Master Scovell. I hope I am.'

'However we prepare, the day will demand more.' The man eyed John. 'Ask your demon.'

John eyed the man, not intrigued but vexed. Every cook carried a feast inside him. His own feast. But the Master Cook's mysteries no longer beguiled him.

'My demon asks who was the magpie.'

Scovell's gaze faltered.

'He is long gone,' the man said.

'But who was he?' John persisted.

'He was called Almery,' Scovell said at last. 'Charles Almery. He was a heretic and a thief, so he described himself. And he was my friend.'

'But you argued,' John pressed the man.

'Yes, we argued.'

'My mother too?'

The Master Cook shifted the load on his shoulder and began to walk down the passage.

'You will acquit yourself well tomorrow,' he said. 'And all the days after, I trust.'

'We all will,' John answered.

Scovell paused. But only the man's voice drifted back to John.

'A cook stands apart,' he said. 'Even in the feast he is alone.'

'Get up, John. Get up . . .'

He had barely touched his head to the mattress. Now Mister Bunce was shaking him awake.

'Come, John,' the man urged in an undertone.

'What is it?' His head rose blearily. But in the next instant he was wide awake as the man leaned close and whispered.

'It's Master Scovell. He's gone.'

John stumbled after the Head of Firsts. The door to Scovell's room stood open. Mister Underley, Mister Vanian and Henry Palewick were gathered about the hearth. But the fire was cold. Books were missing from the shelves.

'He may be taking the air,' offered Underley in a doubtful voice.

'He has gone,' said Vanian.

John looked above the hearth. The ladle hung from its hook. He lifted it off, weighing the metal in his hand. This was Scovell's last riddle, he thought. But there was no time to ponder its meaning now.

'I say we tell no one,' Henry Palewick said. 'Not till after the feast.'

The others nodded.

'There's commotion enough up there,' Henry Palewick said. 'Sir Philemon arrived last night with a squad of lifeguards. He's been in with Sir William ever since and now everything's late.'

'Makes no difference if Master Scovell's here or not,' Mister Bunce said stoutly. 'John's our Master Cook today.'

*　　*　　*

He swung the ladle and heard the copper ring out. He listened as his voice called the men and boys to their stations. He watched as the kitchen sprang into action. Simeon and Hesekey handed the capons and ducks to Luke and Colin for placement on the spit. Alf hauled in baskets of greens and pot-herbs from Firsts. Adam filled coffins with hashes of meat while Tam Yallop worked over the chafing dishes. At the hearth, Phelps hauled logs with a pair of long-handled tongs until flames roared up the chimney. Philip darted from bench to bench.

John stood in the midst of the whirl, Scovell's final words running through his head. *A cook stands apart . . .* In his mind's eye, the next hours were already arriving, the dishes ascending on the serving men's trays: pies and tarts, birds and fish, loaves, cakes, puddings and pastries. He saw the sea of faces swaying and rolling. At the high table beyond, Lucretia and Piers were seated together.

'John!' Philip gripped his shoulder. 'Did you hear me? The lower tables are seated.'

Across the kitchen, Mister Quiller's serving men jostled at the foot of the stairs. Luke had the first trays ready. Phineas hung in the doorway ready to signal to the bakehouse. In front of the fire, the spiced wine sent its heady fumes through the room. A hundred familiar smells swirled in the kitchen.

But the aromas in John's nostrils were not of spices or roasting meats. They were of apple and rose water. And his thoughts were not of the feast, or even Scovell, whatever had lured the Master Cook from Buckland. Instead John thought of his pool of crystal jelly lying in Henry Palewick's coldest larder, the love tokens suspended in its depths. A ring. An arrow. A red heart. There was the stair where Piers had slurred his taunt. *Raise a cup . . . Since you can't raise her skirts . . .* He had no cup, he thought. Only Scovell's ladle. He felt its curve, smooth as the bow of her cheek. He saw her lips parting before his own.

'What is it, John? What's wrong?' Philip loomed into view.

'Nothing is wrong,' he told Philip. 'Nothing.'

Without another moment's thought, he swung the ladle. The great copper rang out, the clang reverberating and rolling under the vaulted roof. As the echoes died, the room fell silent. All around the kitchen, faces turned to John.

Stand down!

They were his next words. He had the whole order of service in his head. Without him, there could be no feast. He opened his mouth. But before he could speak, Philip's hand gripped his shoulder.

'John, look.'

Across the kitchen the cooks, under-cooks, kitchen boys and scullions were murmuring and pointing, turning to look through the arch then pulling off their caps and dropping to their knees. A black-clad man stood at the foot of the stairs. His hawkish nose turned this way and that as his eyes took in the unfamiliar scene. Wearing a heavy cloak and black tunic, Sir William surveyed the vaulted room.

'John,' hissed Philip, and nudged him.

'Strangers in,' John managed.

Watched by the astonished cooks, the Lord of the Vale of Buckland stepped into the kitchen, his gaze reaching into the furthest corners of the room to take in the men and boys. At the great copper, he halted.

'Sir Philemon brings grave news,' the black-clad man declared. 'The King has raised his standard. There will be no wedding. We are at war.'

From *The Book of John Saturnall*: A *Dish* for those *Unfortunates* lost among the *Dead* upon *Naseby Field*

he Angels in Heaven eat Manna so our Churchmen tell us. The Gods on Olympus quaffed Ambrosia and Nectar. Hades took Kore down to his Palace in Tartarus and set a Feast before her to tempt her but what were its Dishes I do not know. The Dead complain little of their Appetites and so a Cook can only hazard their Hungers.

But a Soldier will eat what he may find. His Kitchen is the Corner of a Field and his safest Bed is a Thicket of Brambles. Gather therefore what you may from the Hedgerows and snare the Same in the Woods, and if Fortune smiles so broadly upon you that you do take a fat Rabbit, then follow these Instructions which an old Man upon the Road vouchsafed me many Years ago.

First skin the Beast and draw it then spit it upon a Hazel Twig that, twisting and turning in the Heat of the Fire according to that Wood's miraculous character, the Rabbit's scant Juices do baste the lean Meat that lies close upon its Frame. Take Sprigs of Rosemary too if you will and stitch these beneath the Flesh to sweeten it with the Oils of the Herb. When a Dagger pressed into the fat Part of the Thigh brings Juices running clear, then the Meat will be cooked . . .

THE SMOKE BILLOWED UP in a thick white trunk, its heavy crown spreading then toppling to engulf those below. Through streaming eyes, John saw ghostly figures stumbling blindly through the acrid cloud, coughing and choking as they breathed in the fumes. The clang of iron on iron beat against his ears. Suddenly a body reared before him. A pole of black iron loomed, its end spiked and hooked. As John scrambled aside, the metal thudded down and a fountain of sparks crackled into the air. An angry voice rose above the noise.

'Who was it?' demanded Philip. 'What pudding-head put green wood on the fire?'

The latest encampment of the Buckland Kitchen was a roofless barn on a rise overlooking the valley below. Spread out over the fields, the troops of the King's army gathered around their fires. The smells of woodsmoke and latrines drifted up the shallow slope. Rubbing his watering eyes, John watched Philip hook the smoking branch with his iron, pull it out of the blaze and drag it crackling over the mud floor. Adam Lockyer held the door open, his face streaked with soot and dirt.

The Lord of the Vale of Buckland had marched out of the Manor bearing the Fremantle standard, the torch and axe fluttering over his head.

'Supper back here in Buckland,' Mister Bunce had told John and Philip sternly before they left. 'Remember you're cooks. You follow your nose. That'll bring you back safe.'

At each village, the women and children hung out of windows or cheered from doorways. At each stop, the men had mustered, waving scythes and sticks. Now they wielded pikes and shot muskets.

They had all learned new skills, John reflected. Even the cooks. Scavenging meals from hedgerows, snaring rabbits, finding firewood and shelter in the midst of downpours. From one of Prince Maurice's dragoons, John and Philip had even learned to ride, bouncing around a field on the back of the man's cob. And the same dragoon had let them spy through a crack in a barn wall one night when a swaggering woman with a mane of black hair took a coin each from the group of men. Faces pressed to the wall, John and Philip had each heard the other gasp as she pulled off her smock and stood before the soldiers, naked but for her boots.

'Look at that,' murmured a breathless Philip, staring at the thick ruff of dark hair springing up between her legs. 'That's a sin, that is.'

'It surely is,' John murmured back, his eye glued to the hole.

But the next night found them in the same barn with the same woman whose breath smelt of onions as they took their turns, John unmanned by nerves until she took his hesitant hands and clamped them one on each buttock. Then a fierce pleasure took hold of him and at length she too began to pant, her heels drumming on his buttocks as she urged him on.

'That cooked your collops?' she demanded of them afterwards, her sharp teeth tearing at a chicken leg from the basket they had brought her. 'My oven hot enough for you two?'

Philip and John looked sheepishly at each other and grinned.

The first winter had been worse than any fighting. Mister Underley had caught a chill and John had boiled up meadowsweet and elder. But the chill turned to a fever and carried the man off. They had buried him on the side of a hill. The next day they had marched on.

How many camps had followed, John wondered now as Philip dragged his smoking bundle of hazel rods down the slope and dropped it in the wet grass where it hissed and steamed. To one side of this camp, a great herd of horses bent their heads. On the other, a troop of men formed into lines under the commands of a sergeant. From the roofless barn Phineas emerged bearing a tray with a cover.

'Dinner for the Lord of the Vale of Buckland and his esteemed staff,' announced Phineas. 'Freshly snared rabbit. Who's taking it down?'

'Your turn,' Philip told John.

He pulled John's collar into place and brushed at some dirt on his coat. 'Tell Master Palewick we have firewood for two more days and provisions for three. And no one is accepting our notes.'

John tramped down the hillside, his stomach growling at the smell of roasted meat. Around the camp, Sir William was said to eat better than anyone except His Majesty. But the King was at Oxford, not here where the stench of latrines grew stronger as John approached the dragoons enlisted with Prince Maurice then weaved his way between shelters and improvised huts before crossing to Sir William's camp. The familiar accents of the Vale greeted him.

'That mine, Master Cook!'

'What you got for us, John? Hedgehog again?'

'I'm still chewing the last lot of quills . . .'

John passed through the village militias, the men lying on lengths of blanchet or sacking or stretched out on their buff coats. Helmets and breastplates lay tossed in heaps. Pikes were stabbed point first into the ground. But the men reclined untroubled by sergeants.

'Course they stand their ground,' the same dragoon had confided to John. 'Most of 'em are too drunk to walk.'

Kept back with the baggage train, the Buckland Kitchen had seen no fighting. The closest John had come to the enemy was across the bare flat grassland of Elminster Plain where a dark line had smudged the eastern horizon. Word was passed down the column that it was Parliament's army. Fairfax was its commander and Waller and Cromwell were his generals. More names, thought John, watching the rippling smudge, the odd glint of sunlight flaring off a breastplate, and wondering whether, somewhere along its length, a cook looked back at himself.

The gateway to the farmhouse rose. Two pikemen wearing helmets, corselets, tassets and gorgets moved aside as John approached. In the yard, a group of young men gathered around one of their number who sported two pistols in holsters, a heavy carbine and a sword. Breastplate polished to a high shine, Piers Callock struck a pose for the benefit of his fellows.

'So I rode in at full gallop and I swear if it wasn't that traitor Waller himself then it was his brother. I reached for my pistol but the damned flint cracked. So I reached for the other and the damned powder was wet. I'd got the carbine off on the charge so that was gone. That left this.'

The others watched intently as Piers gripped the hilt of his sword. He had been mentioned in a dispatch to the King, John had heard, for the capture of seven dragoons and their mounts. He had gained a name for reckless courage, charging at the front of the line. John hurried across the yard. He had almost reached the doorway when Piers noticed him.

'Ah ha! The kitchen boy! Where's Pandar?'

'Back at the kitchen, Lord Piers,' John replied and hurried inside.

A group of officers turned from the hearth. Seeing a cook, they turned back again. From the back room, Hector Callock's voice sounded.

'Your Highness, I say we let the centre foot advance by file in the cover of the pikes, like this. Your lifeguards may make their charge from the left. Our own horse will follow close in a caracole. Thus.'

A dozen men stood about a table on which coloured wooden counters were arranged in ranks and files. Sir Hector waved his arm in an arc to indicate the caracole then moved a number of orange blocks. Across the field of battle, a red-faced man with a heavy grey moustache watched from a large chair.

'Ja, that's bold, Sir Hector,' said Prince Maurice in an accent that reminded John of Melichert Roos. 'Recalls me another soldier, the victor against the Swedes at Breitenfeld.' He slapped his chest. 'Me.'

John hovered behind the men, ignored as Prince Maurice reached across with a wheeze and flicked over a block of blue wood among the forces on the other side of the table. 'Only way to take a tercio. From the corner.' He flicked over more blocks then reached for the goblet beside him, took a swig and turned to a thin-faced and stern-looking man beside him. 'Ha, Zoet? Remember at Lech? That tercio. The horse?'

'Fell upon the first rank as they began their counter-march,' confirmed Zoet.

'Dropped dead on their corner!' Prince Maurice slapped the table. 'That was enough. We were among 'em. Ja.'

'A good day,' agreed Zoet.

'A bold day,' added Prince Maurice.

He and his men had sailed all the way from Bohemia to fight for the King, the troopers said. Gustavus Adolphus himself had learned his tactics from Prince Maurice. The men around the table watched him scratch his red nose. Holding the rabbit, John looked around for Sir William.

'Then Lutzen,' the Prince said, moving more orange blocks. 'Remember Lutzen, Zoet? In we came from the left. The caracole again. But . . .' He righted some blue blocks and knocked over the orange. 'This time the Swedes were waiting. Demi-hearse formation in close order. A salvay at half a length. I lost two horses.'

'And three regiments of men,' Zoet added.

'Ja.'

'John!' whispered a voice. Ben Martin stood at the outer door. 'Master Palewick wants you in the commissary.'

The commissary was three benches arranged side by side in the stables. Henry Palewick stood ticking items in his ledger as if he had never moved from the outer yard at Buckland.

'Sir William?' the Cellarer answered John. 'He is as far away from the Prince's courtiers as he can set himself. The posts got through from Elminster. A gang of footpads from Zoyland paid the Manor a visit. Knocked every piece of glass out of the chapel then hauled out the altar rail on the end of a rope. Their colonel would have done the same to Father Yapp if he hadn't been stopped.'

'He cut a man's hand off in Masham,' said Phelps, entering behind John. 'Rides with a baggage train of women and calls 'em his family. They're as bad as the men. Still, they didn't figure on Lady Lucretia.'

John put down the tray. The last he had seen of Lucretia, she was standing on the steps of Buckland Manor as the column moved off, waving a handkerchief at Piers. John had watched her from among the servants until Philip had nudged him in the ribs.

'What did she do?' he asked casually.

'She saw 'em off,' Phelps said emphatically.

No doubt she had, John thought. He was still smiling as he left the farmhouse. Suddenly a hand pushed him to one side.

'Something funny, kitchen boy?'

Piers stood before him, sabre in hand. The young cavalrymen clustered to watch his latest demonstration of swordsmanship. A red-haired youth called Montagu nodded appreciatively as Piers's exaggerated thrust jabbed towards John.

'Damn good, Callock,' the youth declared. 'Who's this?'

'Oh, just a kitchen boy.' A smile played about his lips. He jabbed again, closer. But before he could advance further, Pandar rounded the corner.

'Now, now, now, Lord Piers. What duels are you fighting when there's Waller and Cromwell to chase?'

'Cromwell?' echoed Montagu. His broad freckled face took on a puzzled expression. 'Where?'

'Heard it from His Highness not a minute ago. Overheard, I should say. He seemed mightily impressed with the new intelligence, did the Prince.'

'What new intelligence?' demanded Piers.

'You have not heard? Shame on the rascals that talk among themselves and keep such eager Hectors as yourselves kennelled up like hounds.'

'Does he call us hounds?' asked the redhead, looking even more puzzled.

'It is just his way, Montagu,' Piers answered. 'Which is to go from the church to the chapel by way of the next village. I warn you, Pandar . . .'

'Waller's army is marching on London,' Pandar said.

'London!' Montagu exclaimed. 'At last!'

'But London is held by the trained bands,' Piers said suspiciously.

'Perhaps it was Banbury,' Pandar conceded. 'Or Oxford.'

'The King is at Oxford,' said Montagu. 'God preserve him.'

'Is this the truth, Pandar?' Piers demanded. But at that moment the first horns sounded. The cries of the sergeants sounded among the men.

As John climbed the hill, he heard panting behind him. Pandar hurried up.

'How do you bear him, Pandar?'

'Piers? He is only a fool. Save your ire for our enemies.'

Below, the sergeants were moving through the camp. Inside the barn, Philip, Adam, Phineas, Alf and the others were dismantling the spit. The Buckland Kitchen was on the move again.

They marched with the baggage at the back of the column over roads churned to mud by those ahead. They tramped through hollow lanes bordered with high dense hedges, past water-meadows and pastures, along stony roads that climbed hillsides and dropped into steep-sided valleys. They jumped aside as squadrons of dragoons or cuirassiers thundered past. At each halt, John, Philip and the others unloaded pots and pans, spits and plate, skillets, trivets and roasting grates. Moving on they left nothing but a charred circle of ground, the latest of the Kitchen's sooty footprints.

Talk of skirmishes and battles swirled up from the camps like smoke from their cooking fires. But the great clashes and charges in which Piers and his fellows rejoiced were over when they unloaded their clanking wagon. Clutching pikes amidst the farriers and carters, John and Philip and the others were drilled by bored sergeants who bellowed at their untidy lines and wavering weapons.

'Don't trouble yourselves,' Pandar reassured them, dropping his pike. 'They'd as soon arm the whores before they put us in the line.'

In place of cannon, the ears of the Buckland cooks resounded with the clang of pots and pans. Instead of planting musket rests, John and the others assembled the spit. Their 'Twelve Apostles' were not the bandoliers of arquebusiers but the sets of Sir William's spoons that they kept locked in a case. Wherever the army pitched camp, there the Buckland Kitchen sprang into being. Outside Harborough the slow-moving mass of animals and men drifted to a halt between two villages.

'That one over there's called Sulby,' Henry Palewick told them.

'And what's that one?' asked Philip.

'Naseby.'

John and Philip sweated in the early summer heat and slept out under the stars. They were to relieve the King at Oxford, they heard. Or they were to march on London. Or they were to camp here until the King's enemies should give up and go home. John lay on the grass and looked up at the pinpricks of light.

Scovell would see the same stars, he thought, wherever he might be. And Almery. The friend who had proved a liar and a thief. Now John wished he had grasped Scovell's sleeve and demanded more answers. But he had thought only on the feast, he remembered. And Lucretia.

It had been a kind of madness, he had told himself. To think that Sir William's daughter might take a cook for her groom . . . But even as he cursed himself for his foolishness, she rose before him, the silver-blue dress wrapped about her limbs, or the green one with its bright red hem. He remembered the slight rip as it caught on the Rose Garden thorn. Her exasperated curse and his glimpse of her bare white ankle. Or he was in her chamber, bending over her, her hand touching his own . . .

'Up and out everyone! Up and out!'

A rude shout broke in on his thoughts. Henry Palewick's voice bellowed over the meadow. John groaned, rolled over and opened his eyes. Beside him Philip did the same.

'What's going on?'

'Come on, you two!' shouted Henry. 'Fairfax's for'ard guard ain't ten miles away! The scouts spied him past Harborough. Up and out!'

'Another alarm,' muttered Jim Gingell. Adam Lockyer and Phineas Campin yawned and stretched. Colin and Luke grumbled. All around John, the Buckland cooks rose and pulled on their coats.

On the hill's flat top, men ran hither and thither in the moonlight, looking for their standards. As the sergeants called their troops to order, Philip spotted the tattered flag with its torch and axe. Sir William rode beside his standard-bearer, Master Jocelyn. In front of them Piers Callock wheeled his horse back and forth, flintlocks jiggling in their holsters, sabre rattling and breastplate gleaming. A torch flamed in his hand.

'The word is God and Queen Mary!' Piers exhorted the sleep-bleared men. Pikes and muskets waved in the night air. 'Every able-bodied man is called to arms! For God and Queen Mary!'

A thin chorus answered his cry. Piers called again and this time more voices joined in. The youth persisted, leading the chant until the response spread and grew. John heard the rest of the Kitchen take it up, then the men beyond. Soon the words rang out over the hilltop.

'God and Queen Mary! God and Queen Mary!'

Flushed at his success, Piers waved his torch in the air. All around John the battle cry grew louder. The sergeants blew their horns and shouted commands. Slowly, the troops shuffled into ranks and files. With a clatter of weapons, the King's army began to form up.

The sun rose over a copse of trees to fall upon Naseby Field. Drawn up in ranks and files, the King's army waited. Helmets and spear-points glinted. Muskets and breastplates shone. But across the shallow valley, a shadow spread. Along the ridge opposite, a dark line thickened as the morning wore on. John, Adam and Philip watched the ranks of their enemies multiply. Near the end of their own line, Henry Palewick held a pike and stared out grimly. Phelps and Ben Martin stood next to him.

The cooks formed the rearmost rank. Lines of footsoldiers were arrayed ahead, pike-points bristling and glinting. Behind them lay the baggage train.

'John,' said Philip. 'I . . .'

But at that instant, John felt a nudge from Adam on the other side.

'Look there, John. Old friend of yours.'

A faint cheer was rising from the men ahead. A troop of cuirassiers in full armour was advancing at a walk along the front line. At their head rode a figure dressed in black armour and mounted on a massive white stallion. When the rider halted and removed his helmet, a cheer went up. The King rode slowly along the line followed by his guards. As John watched, Philip spoke again.

'John, it was me.'

'What?'

'It was me.'

'What was you?'

'It was me that told Pouncey. That you were taking her food. I said you'd sent me . . .'

John remembered the steward's confiding look on the stairs. He stared incredulously at Philip. 'Why?'

'You know why. If you had been caught . . .'

'We almost were caught!' he retorted, remembering the man's entrance the next day. Another minute and his lips would have touched Lucretia's. And in the one after that who knew what pleasures

282

might have been theirs? Instead all his affections amounted to was a breathless night in a barn . . . 'You said you were not like me,' he told Philip. 'God knows you spoke the truth that day.'

'You should thank me,' said Philip.

'Thank you? I've a mind to punch you!'

'What're you two jawing on?' asked Luke Hobhouse further down the line.

'Look,' Colin Church added. 'Up ahead.'

John pulled his angry gaze from Philip. Ahead pikes rose in a bristling palisade. From the other side of the valley, a faint fanfare sounded. Across the shallow dip, the first line of horses detached itself from the enemy ranks and began to advance. At the sight, John's anger dissolved.

'Supper in Buckland,' muttered Philip.

'Supper in Buckland,' John replied.

The mounted men crept slowly at first, as if they were performing an exhibition. It seemed to John that they took an age to descend. But they picked up speed over the valley floor and moved to a canter up the gentle incline. Then a gallop. Suddenly their hooves were thundering over the turf. As they reached the line, the armoured beasts formed a wall of tossing heads and weapons.

'God and Queen Mary!' bellowed the pikemen.

'God alone!' came the cry of the Roundhead riders. In the next instant, the men and horses drove into the front line like cannon-fire pounding a wall.

The shock of the clash rolled back through the ranks. The din of musket-fire crackled all about John's ears. In an instant the air filled with smoke. From either side, the sergeants shouted to hold the line. John felt himself begin to shake and gripped his pike harder. Another volley of musket-fire sounded. At the end of the rank, John saw Henry

Palewick shout something and look down the line. In the next instant the man's forehead seemed to burst from within. Blood and brains sprayed over Ben Martin who clutched his head as if he too had been shot. When he lowered his hands, his face was drenched in blood and flecked with slivers of white. John saw Ben open his mouth to cry out but then the next charge came.

The smoke thickened to a choking pall. John heard screams and shouts as men fell. The Buckland standard rose out of the smoke with Sir William beside it, rallying a troop of dragoons. Sir Hector Callock had hold of a horse next to his own and seemed to wrestle with its rider. Suddenly the other horseman broke free. Sir Hector lunged after the fugitive with his dagger but as he did so a Roundhead horseman rode in on his flank. John saw a sword flash then it was driven under Sir Hector's ribs. A single shriek burst from the man's lips and he fell.

Ahead of John, another charge came. The men staggered back, one stumbling and falling. A clangour of swords and pikes filled the air. John saw Phelps fall. Beside him, Luke Hobhouse fended off a slash from a passing horseman. The dragoons with Sir William cried 'For God and Queen Mary!' and started forward again. But John felt panic creep like a sickness through the ranks. He smelt it under their skin, cloying and metallic like blood.

The third charge broke them. A loose horse scythed through the ranks and rose before John and Philip, rearing and snorting, its huge hooves pawing the air above their heads. A pikeman drove his weapon into its flank but the beast knocked him down. All around John men were turning and running, melting before the onslaught. Then he was running too with Philip, Pandar and Phineas. Ahead, a horseless cuirassier was making his escape through a hedge towards the copse of trees beyond. They scrambled after the man, Phineas trying to drag his pike behind him. Pandar turned on him.

'Drop it, you fool!'

Phineas stared back, his face blank. Pandar shouted again, furious.

'He can't hear you!' shouted Philip. He took the boy's fingers off the shaft and threw it aside. They forced a way through the hedge and ran. The cuirassier was part-way across the next field, limping towards the stand of trees. As they reached the trunks, the cavalryman turned and pulled off his helmet.

'Back to the field! I order you!'

Piers Callock's lank hair was matted with sweat. He had discarded his armour, all save the breastplate and helmet. His unfired flintlocks sat in their holsters and a dark bloodstain ran down one of his legs. He stared wildly at the cooks. But Pandar's eyes followed the blood to its source, which was Piers's left buttock. The cook bared his yellow teeth in a grin.

'A knife in the arse? A telling wound, Lord Piers.'

Piers scowled and Pandar's grin broadened. An instant later Philip shouted 'Down!' as a volley of musket-fire sounded. John heard a bullet crack against the tree beside him. He pulled Phineas to the ground, the youth grunting with pain. Together they scrambled away through the trees.

They emerged in a field. A ditch ran along the side. Piers limped out behind them.

'Help me!' he gasped.

'Wound stiffening up?' asked Pandar. John and Philip exchanged glances. Each took an arm. John nodded to the ditch.

'Over there.'

They part slid, part rolled down the muddy slope and lay on their backs. Phineas clutched his groin, dark red blood welling up through his fingers. John prised the youth's hands away.

A thick flap of flesh hung open. The youth's intestines bulged out, glistening grey and pink. John remembered the pigs they had gutted in Underley's jointing room.

'Caught a good scratch there, Phin,' he said jovially.

'We'll bind it up,' Philip said quickly. He glanced anxiously back at the trees then pulled off his jacket and shirt and started tearing the latter into strips. John peeled back Phineas's hose.

'Doesn't hurt too bad,' Phineas said. 'Just my legs are cold.'

Across the field the musketeers emerged from the trees.

'We must fall back to a defensive position,' Piers said in a commanding tone.

'Phineas can't fall back anywhere,' Philip answered shortly.

'Leave him here. They will bring him to a surgeon,' Piers said.

'They'll slit his throat,' Pandar said bluntly.

The musketeers were walking across the field.

'Come, Pandar,' Piers urged. 'I need your help.' He clutched at his buttock. 'Think of my father's generosity.'

Your father is dead, thought John. Crouched down in the ditch, he rose to eye the gate across the field. 'Stay here,' he whispered to Philip. 'Don't move, you hear me?' Then he turned to Piers. 'To me, Lord Piers. I'll get you away.'

The youth did not hesitate. 'My father will reward you for your service,' Piers said breathlessly, taking his arm. 'For your courage, I should say. I will reward you myself . . .'

Ignoring the others, John got an arm under Piers. He cast an eye over the fine breastplate and the slashed silk sleeves of Piers's shirt. He glanced again at the flintlocks, primed in their finely worked leather holsters.

'What do you say to being Master Cook at Buckland?' Piers went on as they limped, crouching, along the ditch. 'When I marry Lucretia, naturally . . .'

They were almost at the gate. Suddenly John grasped Piers by the arm and hauled him up the side of the ditch. They arrived at the top in full view of the musketeers. An astonished Piers was too startled to resist as John pulled a flintlock from his holster. He pointed it towards the group and shouted at the top of his voice.

'For God and Queen Mary!'

John fired, the flintlock kicking high into the air.

'You madman!' gasped Piers.

Across the field, the musketeers swivelled and ran forwards. As John pulled Piers through the gate, a volley of shots crackled. Cursing and wincing, clutching his injured buttock, Piers limped after John.

'How dare you! To use me as a decoy . . .'

'Us,' grunted John. On the other side they faced a great wall of brambles. He pulled Piers to the side, his eyes probing the thicket. 'This way.'

They crawled in, Piers wincing.

'God curse you, kitchen boy.'

'Cook.'

John crawled forward, imagining musket balls piercing the protective thorns, piercing him like Phineas or Henry Palewick. But beneath his fear, a grim hilarity rippled. He was in a bramble bush again, except now he was with Lucretia's bridegroom. Wincing and hissing, Piers followed his wriggling progress. Soon they were deep in the thicket, the sunlight prickling through the thorns and glowing off the lush grass outside. Then a shadow fell. Abruptly, John clapped a hand over Piers's mouth. The outline of a musketeer was visible through the thorns. The two youths watched the soldier halt, his weapon swinging lazily. Another joined him. They began to circle the thicket.

'We'll die in here,' Piers whispered.

'Be quiet,' John whispered back.

The dragoons circled, three or four at least. Their dark outlines appeared and disappeared. Long minutes would pass then another shadow would reappear. But they did not fire their weapons as John had feared. At last they gave up the silent hunt.

'It's because of her.' Piers's voice startled John after the long silence. The youth eyed him resentfully. 'Isn't it? Dragging me in here. It's not for your little troop of kitchen boys. You courted her and you want me gone . . .'

'I cooked for her,' John interrupted. 'That's all.' But now he wondered if Piers spoke the truth. What if a musket ball had burst Piers's head as it had Henry Palewick's?

'You cooked and I courted,' Piers mused. 'And now we're here.'

'Think of all the Callocks will gain,' John said drily. 'The Manor. All the lands of the Vale. All those rents and deeds . . .'

'Better to think of what we lost,' Piers broke in bitterly. 'We were all Callocks once. Did you know that? Before half of us called themselves Fremantles like they were Normans. The whole Vale was Callock lands. We've been trying to get it back ever since.' Piers shifted his leg, prodding gingerly at his buttock. 'You know who gave me this wound?'

John shrugged, thinking of Philip and the others left behind in the field. He had heard no shots except distant reports.

'My father,' announced Piers. 'I could not hold the line. I turned my horse and he tried to hold me. He always said I would prove a coward.'

John remembered the struggling horseman glimpsed tussling with Sir Hector. 'But you captured seven dragoons,' he said, puzzled. 'You led a charge.'

'They surrendered,' Piers said. 'And I led no charge. I was drunk and my horse bolted. Montagu was too stupid to notice. But my father will trumpet my failings, as always . . .'

'He will trumpet nothing,' said John.

'You do not know him,' Piers muttered.

'I know he is dead.'

'Dead?' Piers looked incredulous. 'Truly dead? Are you sure?'

John nodded and a smile spread over Piers's face. 'He lived to regain the Vale. That and the King's favour.' Piers looked out of the thorns as if he could see the battlefield. 'Who'd give a farthing for it now?'

'The King will gather his forces,' said John. 'He will fight on.'

Piers gave a snort. 'The cause is lost.'

They lay down beneath the brambles and waited for darkness. Several times, groups of soldiers passed by. In the distance they heard musket-fire. John drank the last of his water and thought again of Phineas, Philip and Pandar, left behind in the field. What of the others? The last he had seen of Adam Lockyer the youth was running from the line. Ben Martin the same, and Peter Pears, and Colin and Luke . . . In his mind's eye, John summoned the Buckland Kitchen, not knowing if its members were among the living or the dead. Beside him, Piers shifted and groaned. Then, as the light began to fade, John heard a low snort.

'A horse!' Piers hissed beside him. 'Look!'

They could see its outline, saddled but riderless, head bent to the grass.

'Slowly,' said John as Piers wriggled out. 'Don't scare it off.'

'Scare it?' whispered Piers. 'He's our ride out of here, kitchen boy.'

The horse was a brown gelding, big enough for two. It looked up placidly as they emerged.

'Not even winded,' said Piers. 'There's room for a whole troop on that saddle.'

The animal bent its head, its reins trailing in the grass. This would be easy, John thought. But as he approached, the horse skipped away.

'Use a stick,' Piers urged. He handed one over. 'Hook the reins . . .'

The horse side-stepped again. John looked anxiously back towards the battlefield. Through the gate, the field stretched back to the stand of trees and the double hedge beyond. There was no sign of Philip and the others. As the horse bent its head, John reached out. A moment later the reins were in his hands.

'Careful,' Piers warned. 'Help me up.'

John put the youth's booted foot in a stirrup. Piers winced as he swung his leg over. At that moment John saw a movement in the distant hedge. Across the field, a soldier wearing a slouch hat emerged.

'Quick,' John urged, reaching up a hand.

'Let me settle the beast first.'

Piers sat gingerly in the saddle. Beyond the stand of trees, the man was joined by half a dozen others. These wore helmets. Piers took up the reins. As John reached up for the pommel of the saddle, Piers drew his remaining pistol.

'Cook for her, would you, kitchen boy?'

John stared up into the gun's black barrel. Piers filled his lungs.

'God and Queen Mary!'

His shout resounded over the field. John saw the musketeers raise their weapons. Then the youth dug his heels into the horse's sides. The animal started forward and Piers galloped away.

He was running again. Heart pumping, feet thudding, his lungs heaving in great burning breaths. Once the musketeers fell back, John crept along the lines of hedgerows and ditches. As darkness fell, he found shelter in the lee of a bank.

A bright moon rose, casting a wan light over the turf. Crouched beneath the hedge, John cursed Piers Callock for the hundredth time and tried to work out where he was. Sulby lay to one side of the battlefield. To the other was Naseby. He smelt woodsmoke but saw no fires. From time to time horses' hooves thundered somewhere ahead of him.

He could make ten miles before dawn, John told himself. Hide again at daybreak. Then another ten, and another. All the way back to the Vale.

A broken-down well stood on the far side of the field. John remembered how thirsty he was. But he had not taken a dozen paces towards it before a great crack seemed to split his head in two. He fell.

'Over here!' shouted a voice. He was lying on the ground. Two Roundhead troopers stood over him. A little way off, four others were hauling a two-wheel cart. The nearest one drew a flintlock. Two reddened eyes stared out of a mask of dirt. The cart, John saw now, was loaded with corpses.

'What's the word?'

'God alone,' said John.

'Papist liar.'

The man aimed his flintlock, bringing it closer until John felt the metal of the barrel touch his scalp. He saw the man's hand tighten. Then a soundless white flash exploded in his head. John smelt burning hair and felt something hot run down his cheek. He was falling.

But strange sensation overcame him. He fell slower and slower, as if unable to reach the ground, and when his eyes opened again, it seemed the moonlight had drained all colour from the scene. To his surprise, he felt no pain.

The dragoon with the pistol was staggering away. He must have missed, thought John. As he watched, a sharp clang rang out and the dragoon stumbled sideways. His comrades looked about, one pulling out his own flintlock. A moment later he clutched his face. Another reached for his sword then dropped it as if stung on the hand. John looked about for their attacker and saw the soldier in the slouch hat standing alone on the bank.

He wore a heavy leather coat and his face was hidden beneath the brim of his hat. Stones rattled in the bag slung over his shoulder and a short sword dangled in its scabbard. As John watched, he reached into the bag, weighed a stone and let fly. The trooper nearest John cried out and clutched his knee.

'Damn you,' he grunted.

'Too late for that,' said the lone figure. 'I was damned long ago.'

The accent was familiar. But the voice sounded strange, as if John were hearing it from the bottom of a well.

'Who're you with?' a dragoon demanded as the man jumped down from the bank.

'Me?' the soldier answered. 'I ain't with anyone.'

John felt blood from his head drip down his neck. The ball must have grazed his scalp. The dragoons began muttering.

'Throw him on the cart,' said one, sounding far away.

But there was no cart. And John could no longer see the soldiers. He tried to rise but a great weight pressed on his chest. The wet winding-sheet smell filled his nostrils and the ground seemed to harden beneath him . . . Suddenly the stone-thrower loomed over him.

'You run fast, John. Just like in the old days.'

Then John knew the voice. The slouch hat cast a shadow over the figure's face but its owner pulled off the headgear.

Abel Starling looked hardly changed from the boy John had last seen on the green at Buckland. Only the moonlight lent him an awful pallor.

'Thought the fever took me, did you?'

John nodded, too surprised to answer.

'Thought I was dead myself once or twice.' Abel reached down a hand. 'Come on.'

They began to walk.

'That fever burned hotter than fire,' Abel said. 'And the hotter I burned the higher I flew. Half of me was in that cot. The other half was up with the angels. Except there weren't no angels, John. There weren't nothing up there. When I came down again, you and your ma were gone. Cassie told me you'd run up into Buccla's Wood. Marpot took us off to find Eden. Marched us out on the Levels all the way to Zoyland. But it weren't no Eden . . .'

The moon rose higher. John's face felt wet. He wiped his forehead with his sleeve but the sensation persisted. The bleeding from his head, he supposed. He stumbled beside Abel who stared over the pasture, grey-faced in the bleaching light.

'Weren't even a church,' Abel resumed as John remembered the picture in Calybute's news-sheet. 'Just a barn. Marpot put the women in there and had 'em strip naked.'

'Not Cassie,' John said.

Abel grinned. 'You were sweet on her, weren't you?'

'Yes,' John said. It did not seem to matter what he admitted to Abel. 'I was. I thought she was sweet on me too.'

'Think of it,' Abel went on. 'Our Cass married to a cook at the Manor. Be better'n what she got.'

'How did you know I was a cook?' John asked.

'You ain't no soldier, are you?'

They tramped along the edges of moonlit fields, John unsure if they were prisoner and captor or two fugitives united in flight. For long minutes Abel would seem to forget John's presence. But whenever John was about to break the silence, Abel would speak again.

'Marpot hauled that priest out at Buckland,' he said abruptly.

'You were there?'

'Saw as much as I needed. If you lend the Devil a finger you owe God a hand. That's Marpot's way. He carries a block on the back of a cart. He would have had your Father Yapp if it weren't for Lady Lucy. She kicked up a right fuss. You can imagine.'

John grinned. He could.

From time to time, John heard faint cries. A noise like wheels creaking came and went. They rounded a copse of trees then climbed a stile and walked across a field.

'Abel, where are we going?'

'Look over there.'

In the corner stood the broken-down well. John stared, his head throbbing. They must have walked in a circle, he supposed. How long could this night last?

'Reckon you can hit it from here?' asked Abel, rattling his bag of stones. 'Keep your elbow high, remember? Give your wrist a flick at the end. Like this.'

He launched a pebble that flew flat and straight to crack against the well. Then John chose a pebble, the stone feeling oddly light. He threw and the well seemed to draw the stone to it.

'There you go,' said Abel encouragingly. 'That's it, John.'

John's head had begun to throb again but he no longer cared as Abel held his arm at the required angle. They were back in Buckland. It was just like the old days. But no children were sick. No torches surrounded their hut. No flames lit up the night. Abel took off his hat and jammed it on John's head.

'You're going to be all right, John,' Abel said. 'Like in Buccla's Wood when your ma wouldn't wake up. Or the Manor when Sir William came down those stairs. Same here.'

John's head was pounding now. How could Abel know what

happened in Buccla's Wood? Or the kitchen? He tried to frame the question but his fatigue rose in a black wave. He closed his eyes and found he could not open them again. It was too late to ask Abel now. Too late to ask anything. He was sinking deeper. Falling again. Then he felt himself land.

The ground was hard as a board, lurching and jolting against his back. A terrible stench filled his nostrils. The wet winding-sheet smell wrapped itself about him. His eyes opened.

A single eye stared into his own, dangling from a head slashed ear to jaw. Other corpses pressed down on his limbs. He was trapped beneath a jumble of arms, legs and heads, all mangled, cut, slashed or pierced. They were loaded together on a cart. The cart stopped and John began to struggle. He looked up through a gap in the limbs. A face swung into view.

'This one's alive.'

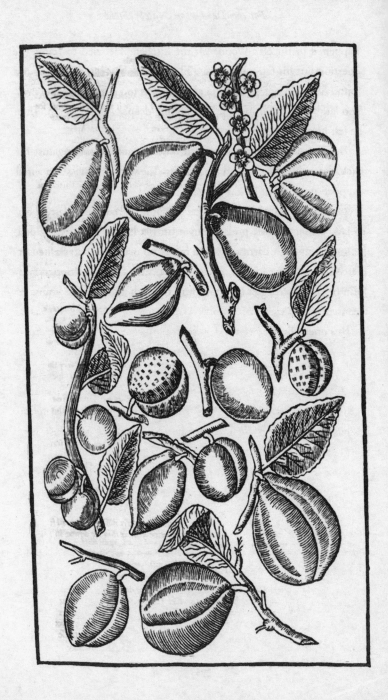

From *The Book of John Saturnall*: A *Feast* to commemorate the *Accession* of our late Lord High Protector, Oliver Cromwell, Gentleman

f those Multitudes who marched in the late Wars, the most Part were divided upon Naseby Field. For there did many fall, blown apart by Cannon or cut in twain by Swords, never to rise again except as Phantoms to guide the Living or as old Souls when the four Trumpets blow. Some were carried off in Tumbrels or Carts. Others limped or were borne away by their Comrades. Some rode from the blood-stained Sward upon a stolen Horse. Others marched as Victors.

But among all these One did rise higher than all the Rest, being our first Minister as it came to pass, who was christened plain Oliver Cromwell.

Armed with Flintlock and Bible, he did preach an unfamiliar Lesson to the Nation. That there was no Christmas, nor May-feast, nor Hocktide, nor Feast or Fast. Indeed he eschewed all such Luxuries. Then Oysters were mixed with Crumbs and Dukes did seek their Dinners in the Hedgerows or they fled to the Garrets of Paris.

Find here, therefore, a Feast for that One who would have None, calling it a Papist Invention, and remember in these Dishes those Times when a pickled Fish and a Bowl of Gruel was a Benison for a Lord and a Drop-apple was Supper enough for the fattest Bishop . . .

A GUST OF WIND blew up the slope, rustling the dark crowns of the trees. Standing watch on the gatehouse, Simeon Parfitt heard the charred stubs of the gates creak as they shifted in the breeze. The red-eyed youth yawned and glanced across at the opposite turret where Hesekey's thin body was silhouetted against the pre-dawn sky.

Another two hours to breakfast, thought Simeon shuffling his feet on the planks and shivering in the pre-dawn chill. His stomach grumbled in expectation of the bowl of thin porridge.

Lady Lucretia had insisted that the gatehouse stay manned. 'Lest our enemies mistake the Manor for one of their churches and sing their psalms on the lawn,' as she had put it. But when the Militia had arrived, Buckland's sentries had offered scant resistance.

Simeon remembered the black-cloaked ruffians running through the corridors, smashing glass and daubing crosses, hauling armfuls of papers from Mister Pouncey's rooms before dragging the steward outside. The hangings they could not hide had fed a bonfire whose black scar still marked the lawn. Then their women had tumbled the stained wooden block from its cart and their colonel had hauled Yapp from the chapel.

That scene glowed hotly in Simeon's thoughts. A manacle had been nailed into the bloodstained wood. Yapp had soiled himself as they clamped his hand in the metal, the dark stain spreading out from his crotch. Their colonel had denounced him, his blue eyes wild. The axe had risen. Then Lady Lucretia had forced her way to the front . . .

A sharp crack resounded out of the trees, rousing Simeon from his thoughts. Little enough traffic arrived at Buckland Manor by day, let alone before dawn. A fox, Simeon decided. Or a badger. He wrapped his thin cloak more tightly about him. But then, at the bottom of the hill, a figure stepped out from the trees.

On the east turret, Hesekey leaned out to stare.

'See that?' he hissed.

'I do,' Simeon replied with more assurance than he felt.

A lean man clad in a long coat stood in the road, a slouch hat pulled down over his face. As the youths watched, he began to walk up the track. With a nod to Hesekey, Simeon climbed down. They stood together beneath the smoke-blackened archway.

'What's he want?' whispered Hesekey.

'How should I know?' Simeon whispered back.

In the weeks after Naseby, bands of ragged soldiers had crept home along the drovers' tracks. But the last of those had passed by months ago. A few beggars still came in hope of the dole-boxes in the yard. But the dole-boxes had been empty since the first winter. Perhaps a fugitive from the Militia, wondered Simeon. But the dark figure walked with an air of greater purpose.

'He has no sword,' Hesekey offered hopefully. 'Can you see a sword?'

Simeon shook his head then looked back at the darkened hulk of the house. The remaining servants would be asleep inside, huddled on mattresses made of sacks stuffed with straw. No one slept in the outbuildings now, not Diggory in his dovecote or the maids in the dairy; not even Barney Curle in the servants' yard. Only the Heron Boy kept his place in the shed by the ponds, grinning a mute refusal when Mister Bunce had tried to order him up to the house.

The figure drew nearer, his long legs striding up the incline. Making the last yards, he came to a halt before them, his face shielded by the brim of his hat. Simeon summoned his deepest voice.

'Who comes to Buckland Manor?'

'That depends,' replied the man. 'Who's its master these days?'

'Sir William Fremantle,' Simeon declared. 'Same as any day.'

The man nodded then turned and gave a low whistle. Down the slope, men began to step out from the trees. Some limped. Others supported their fellows. A ragged column began to move slowly up the slope.

'Who comes here?' Simeon demanded again, alarmed now. 'What's your business?'

By way of an answer the figure pulled off his hat. Simeon's eyes widened.

'Master Saturnall!'

The ladle hung where John had left it. Lifting the handle off its hook, he touched the metal to the cauldron, the familiar tone chiming in his memory. The peal began softly, no louder than a skewer tapping the shoulder of a bottle. A faint red glow rose from the embers in the hearth. Soon the sound grew louder. Around the kitchen, heads rose from their ragged nests as the rest of the men followed John in. Then the door to Firsts swung open and a familiar stout figure entered with a rushlight.

'My eyes! Is that Philip?' exclaimed Mister Bunce. 'Pandar too? Are you all back?'

'Not all,' Pandar responded gruffly. But his answer was lost in the noise.

The Head of Firsts clapped Luke and Colin on the back then advanced on Jed Scantlebury. Mister Stone rubbed the heads of the Gingell twins then Adam Lockyer and Peter Pears while Tam Yallop stationed himself by the door to shake the hands of all who passed. Even Barney Curle offered a grin and Ben Martin smiled reluctantly in return. The survivors of the Buckland Kitchen walked or limped into the great vaulted room where they patted the benches or gazed around at the pots and pans hanging from their hooks or simply smelt the air. All the time, John hefted the ladle, drawing great clangs from the copper.

'Strangers in!' declared Mister Bunce, catching sight of Ben. 'And all the more welcome for that.'

Flanked by Simeon and Hesekey, John swung on, the metallic din rising up the hearth to resound in the flues and echo through the house. In the Great Hall, Diggory Wing and Motte uncurled and stretched. The serving men who slept in the old buttery roused themselves. Upstairs, Mrs Gardiner's head lifted from a straw-filled pillow. In chambers once swagged and draped the jangling tocsin rang brightly off the bare walls, waking the sleepers who rose and trudged in nightshirts and caps down the kitchen stairs.

'You too, Motte!' Mister Stone greeted the gardener. 'In you come! And you, Quiller. All strangers in!'

The serving man advanced and his men crowded in behind. As Wendell Turpin led the kitchen boys in a rowdy circuit of the benches, a bonneted figure descended the stairs. A sharp cry cut through the noise.

'You!' Gemma stood poised for a disbelieving instant then flung herself on a blushing Philip. 'You're back!'

As they embraced, Mrs Gardiner advanced to hug a reluctant Alf and Mrs Pole moved among the returned men, offering quick nods of greeting like a chicken pecking corn.

'Henry dead?' John heard Mister Bunce exclaim in dismay to Colin. 'We heard about Underley, but Henry? That can't be true . . .'

'A lot of things can't be true,' Pandar said, looking around the bare shelves. 'Don't mean they ain't happened.'

Their faces were thinner, John saw, and their livery was patched. But the ladle's metal shaft felt good in his hand, thrumming each time he beat the copper. Soon the kitchen heaved with bodies but he beat on, searching among the faces, letting the ladle's loud music roll beneath the vaulted roof. Meg approached then Ginny, her eyes widening as she caught sight of John. Then a third maid pushed her way through the throng.

She wore a faded dress and a thin cotton shawl. At her waist jangled a bunch of keys. Abruptly she snatched the ladle from his hand.

'What in the Lord's name possesses you to wake my household at such an hour?'

Only then did John recognise Lucretia.

He had not set eyes on her since they had marched out three winters ago, the young woman waving her farewells with a handkerchief. But hers was the face he had seen as he tramped through the hollow lanes or crept along the edges of fields. Hers was the memory that had drawn him back to Buckland. Now her face was thinner and her cheekbones jutted.

He stood before her in his filthy clothes, his hair cut short, smelling of woodsmoke and sweat. Just as he had the first time.

'We came back,' John said simply.

In the Great Hall, the trestles and boards had all gone along with the dais built for the King. In their place, pallets were scattered over the floor. The broken windows were boarded and in place of the tapestry on the south wall, a crude cross had been daubed in white paint. Lucretia and Gemma's skirts swished ahead as they led John through the Manor. In the presence chamber, Lucretia took her place behind her father's walnut table, a businesslike expression upon her face.

'Sir William is at Oxford and may not be moved,' she told him. 'You know of his injuries?'

John shook his head. Ben Martin had seen the man's horse fall beneath him in the final charge and Luke Hobhouse had heard from a sergeant that he had been injured. After that John knew only the rumours that had flown around the camp in Tuthill Fields.

'One leg was crushed,' Lucretia said. 'His surgeons will decide the fate of the other. Now he fights for Buckland from his sickbed. The Committee of Sequestrations will soon hear our case.'

'Sequestrations, your ladyship?'

'Our enemies were not idle while you sat in your field.'

He stood before her, blistered feet burning in his boots. Abruptly Lucretia rose.

'Come. I will show you their handiwork.'

He watched the quick sway of her hips, following the two young women through the quiet corridors. Even through his fatigue, he recalled her white ankles beneath the worn cloth of her dress. He felt the thin scar left by the musket ball tighten about his scalp. They came to a halt outside Mister Pouncey's door. Gemma knocked and entered.

A sour smell hung in the air. Grey light entered by the single window. Before a long bench covered with neat stacks of papers sat Mister Pouncey. His thin hair was long and unkempt. His face was gaunt. His silver chain still hung about his neck. As Lucretia, Gemma and John watched, the man lifted a weight on one of the heaps and examined the paper beneath it. But whatever he found there appeared not to satisfy him for he replaced the weight and reached for another.

'Mister Pouncey.' Gemma spoke gently. 'Her ladyship is here.'

The steward shook his head. 'Not ready,' he muttered.

'Colonel Marpot's men hauled him out,' Lucretia said. 'When he offered defiance . . .'

'They cut switches,' said John. 'They made him dance a jig.'

'Yes.' Lucretia gave him a curious look. But mention of Mister Pouncey's tormentor seemed to agitate the steward. He banged his weight on the table.

'That's it!' he shouted. 'Dance off your sins!'

'Enough, sir,' Gemma soothed the man, placing a hand on his arm. 'Take some rest.' She helped the steward rise from his chair and led him to the narrow bed. John and Lucretia retreated to the musty passage. It was the first time they had been alone since the steward had burst into her chamber.

'I saw your face when we marched.'

Her shoulders stiffened beneath the cotton of her shawl.

'You must banish such thoughts,' she answered.

'I cannot,' he said. 'No more can you.'

He remembered the sweet scent of apples drifting up in her chamber. Her lips parting before his. No steward would burst in on them now. But as he stepped towards her, she held up a hand.

'I am betrothed, Master Saturnall. Have you forgotten?'

'Betrothed to Piers,' John said dismissively.

Two dots of colour grew in her cheeks. 'Master Piers fought bravely,' she retorted.

'Bravely?'

'He was commended. The story was told in the news-sheets. How his horse was killed beneath him. How he captured another.'

'Captured?'

'I will have you know that Master Piers scaled a tree and dropped from its branches to overpower one of their cuirassiers. Callock's Leap they have dubbed it. And all this with a wound to the thigh . . .'

'Thigh?' John burst out. 'It was a knife in the arse! And his own father gave it him! Piers ran like a rabbit!'

Lucretia folded her arms, her face stony. 'I will not hear such insolence.'

John took a step towards her but Lucretia turned her head away. He stopped, baffled by her refusal.

'He does not care for you,' John said softly. 'Nor you for him.'

'We may exchange our desires,' Lucretia answered. 'I told you that once. We may exchange our antipathies too.'

'Marpot's footpads took what they wanted,' Mister Bunce told John. 'What they couldn't steal they spoiled. God's bounty, they called it.'

The dry larder held oats, four sacks of dried beans, strings of dried apples and a solitary half-loaf of Madeira sugar wrapped in sacking-cloth which had been hidden behind a rafter. In the pantry a few hard loaves sat on the shelves above three sacks of meal. Melichert Roos's spice room was deserted but for a few dusty jars set on top of the rack and nothing emanated from Underley's jointing room but a faint foul smell.

John, Philip, Mister Bunce and Mister Stone walked the passageways behind the main kitchen. Some splintered planks hanging from a hinge were all that remained of the door to Scovell's chamber. Inside, books and papers lay scattered over the floor. The table and chair had been overturned. John smelled soot, the musty smell of damp cloth and paper.

'They came down here first,' said Bunce. 'Then they went upstairs and got their hands on Pouncey. They'd hardly finished with him when they hauled Yapp out on a rope. Had him clamped to their block. Said he owed a hand to God for all his Papist preaching. They would've lopped him if it weren't for Lady Lucretia.'

'She stopped them?' John asked.

'Took Marpot off to the chapel. Was in there more'n an hour. Praying, one of their men said. Up there on the tower. She had the key fetched from Mister Pouncey's rooms. Anyroad, when she came out, they let Yapp go.'

Why, John wondered, would Lucretia take Marpot up the tower? But after their last encounter, none of her acts made sense to him.

'Melichert packed his chest the next day,' said Mister Stone. 'Took a berth from Stollport. At least he bade his farewells. Vanian just vanished.'

Like Scovell, thought John, looking around the wrecked chamber. The gallipots still sat on their shelf.

'Just Marpot's name was enough to empty the yard,' Bunce went on. 'He camped half his Militia in Callock Marwood. It got so as you couldn't wear livery in the village. After that the hands started leaving. Now they won't take our notes in Carrboro Market. People reckon we won't be here to pay 'em back.'

'No one's had a penny since last Michaelmas,' added Fanshawe. 'Mister Pouncey knew what was due. Wages, rents, levies. Every hide of land from Flitwick all the way down to Stollport. It was all in his head. Now he don't know what day it is.'

Through the gateway to the yard, the barracks built for the King's visit leaned drunkenly. In the stables, two palfreys snorted beside an elderly draught horse. In Motte's kitchen garden weeds flourished and bean frames sagged. Beyond its wall the choked drain-culvert led down to water-meadows rank with weeds. Across the river, Home Farm appeared to have cultivated no more than half a field of kale and the same of rye. Standing on the bank, John eyed the jetty and the glossy green waters. Now the planking was split. The banks were choked with crack willow and alder. Upstream, the blades of the mill-wheel scooped skeins of riverweed from the sluggish water.

Walking back up the meadows, the carp ponds alone appeared as they always had, cleared of weed and birds by the Heron Boy. John raised an arm and the ragged figure flapped his wings in greeting.

'Still talking in your sleep?'

The Heron Boy threw his head back in a silent laugh.

John and Mister Fanshawe continued up past the Rose Garden wall and the steps to the Great Hall. Beyond the East Garden wall, the chapel was locked.

'Marpot's pastor took the key,' Fanshawe told John with a grimace.

'Pastor?'

'Didn't her ladyship tell you?' Fanshawe said. 'Marpot left him behind. Pastor Ephraim Clough.' The clerk looked curiously at John. 'Master Saturnall? You look like you've seen a ghost.'

'You wrap these around your knees,' Mister Bunce told John that Sunday, handing him a pair of rags. 'Tie them like this and hide 'em under your breeches. That way our pastor reckons we're all in agonies, kneeling on that floor. Best to let folks believe what they will, I reckon.' The stout man grinned.

'And don't do nothing but kneel,' Tam Yallop warned. 'They beat one of the hands for fastening his button. Working on the Sabbath, Pastor Clough said.'

At Ephraim's name, John's dull foreboding returned. It had been growing all week. All around him, the others were binding up their knees and covering up the bandages. Soon a familiar ringing sounded. A hand-bell, John realised. Harsh shouts echoed in the servants' yard then the nearest cooks shuffled aside. A man garbed in black breeches, a plain black smock, black jacket and short black cloak entered. In one hand he carried a Bible. The other held the bell. The heavy-browed face looked about at the men of the Kitchen.

'So our congregation grows,' Ephraim Clough declared. Then his gaze found John. A flash of surprise showed in his face. Then a slow smile creased his heavy features.

'Let us give thanks to the Lord,' he declared. 'He has sent us another errant soul. Let us pray together for his correction.'

All that remained of the altar was a rectangular scar on the floor. The glass had been smashed from the windows and the bare walls whitewashed. The pulpit, the altar rail and the pews had gone along with Lady Anne's balcony. Its disappearance uncovered a rough wall broken by a small heavy-timbered door. Buckland's new pastor cast his eyes over the Household, threw his arms wide and sent his short cloak flapping like the wings of a monstrous crow.

'Kneel,' Ephraim ordered. 'We shall hearken unto the words of the Lord.'

All around John, the Household sank to the hard stone floor. At the front, flanked by Gardiner and Pole, John picked out the plain dress and bonnet worn by Lucretia. Gemma, Ginny and Meg knelt alongside her. Behind the congregation, lining the back wall of the chapel, a dozen Militiamen set down their muskets and swords. Two score of them were garrisoned in Callock Marwood, Mister Bunce had told John.

'The Lord spake unto Moses,' Ephraim recited. 'And Moses spake unto the people saying, Arm yourselves unto war and go against the

Midianites. So there were delivered out of Israel a thousand of every tribe and Moses sent them to war and they slew all the males. And they slew the kings of Midian, namely Zur and Hur . . .'

Even through the rags, the stone floor seemed to harden as Clough droned on. Along the row, John saw Philip then Alf, Adam, Colin and Luke. Jed Scantlebury was at the end. Clough paused and looked around the sea of heads.

'The Lord told Moses all that,' Ephraim declared to the silent faces. 'And Moses told the Children of Israel. The Midianites deserved no mercy. Eschew pity therefore . . .'

John remembered Father Hole's stories about date palms and fruits and deluges of rain. They seemed to belong to another world to this one. Ephraim's voice bored into his brain, describing God's vengeances and violences.

'Only for the Chosen does God reserve the fruits of his garden. The grapes from his vines and the honey from his hives. For them he loads the tables with sweetmeats and dainties. For those who follow the true path, he serves feasts as he did in Eden . . .'

It seemed an age before the droning voice fell silent.

'All rise!' the Captain commanded at last. Slowly, pulling each other up, the Household rose. Ephraim waited by the door, a self-satisfied smile upon his face. As John approached, he held up his hand.

'One moment, Master Saturnall.'

Philip paused beside him but a Militiaman pushed him forward. John eyed his former antagonist.

'Perhaps you imagine I seek revenge,' Ephraim said. 'Or that I harbour ill-will towards you for your offences against me. For your malice and violence. But I do not. I serve a higher Authority. Colonel Marpot purged me of such thoughts as keep me from God. Thus do I purge this household of its luxuries and vanities. The low and high alike.'

Ephraim glanced back. Alone in the chapel, Lucretia still knelt on the floor. A smirk creased Clough's features.

'Now we both serve Lady Lucretia. You in the kitchen. And I here, in God's house.'

With that, Paster Clough stepped back into the chapel and swung the door shut.

'What do they do?' John asked Philip.

'Gemma says they pray,' Philip told him.

'Is that all?'

'What else would they do?'

In the week she kept to the house. Without sight of the young woman, John could no more penetrate the sanctum of Lucretia's thoughts than his eyes could see through the thick oak planks of the chapel door. He buried himself in the kitchen where, at Mister Bunce's insistence, he swung the ladle each morning.

'Scovell left it for you, John,' the Head of Firsts told him as the others nodded their approval across the table in Firsts. 'Left you the whole kitchen, I reckon.'

Under John's instruction, the men and boys once again took up their proper stations for the preparation of breakfast while Quiller's serving men stood in line on the stair. Colin and Luke rolled the trays as they always had and Philip supervised from the hearth. Finding shovels in Motte's shed, John set a reluctant Jim and Jem Gingell to clearing the foul-smelling culvert below the Rose Garden. The stagnant pond around the kitchen drain disappeared leaving nothing but a scum-line on the flagstone floor. Simeon joined Tam Yallop in the bakehouse and once again the smell of baking bread drifted through the passages below Buckland Manor. Colin and Luke scoured the storerooms and larders, the beet lofts and old root clamps for scraps to enliven the evening pottage. Immersed in the kitchen's work, John kept his thoughts from the young woman above. Then Sunday came again.

'And the Children of Israel took all the women of Midian captive,' Clough intoned. 'They took their little ones, and took the spoil of all their cattle, and all their flocks, and all their goods. And they burnt all their cities, and all their goodly castles. And they took all the spoil and all the prey. And Moses said unto them, Have ye saved all the women alive? Behold, these caused the children of Israel to commit trespass. Now therefore kill every male among the little ones and kill every woman that hath known a man by lying with him. But all the women that have not known men, keep alive for yourselves . . .'

The words echoed in the bare interior. Kneeling on the bare stone floor, the Buckland Household wrapped rags around their knees and concealed them beneath their breeches. John knelt with the others under the eyes of the Militia while Clough's voice buzzed and whined like a wasp trapped in his ear. At the end of the service, Lucretia again remained behind. Once again Clough closed the door of the chapel.

John's blisters healed. He rose earlier than the other cooks and was the last to take to his bed, yawning and rubbing his eyes as he stumbled among the men and boys snoring in the kitchen and Firsts. Every Sunday, he wrapped his knees in rags like the others and knelt in the chapel. At the end of each tedious lesson, after the Household had shuffled out, the door closed on Ephraim and Lucretia.

John took to walking in the High Meadow, tramping through the long grass and looking down on the ancient nave. No lights showed within. No sound issued from the gloom beyond the glassless windows. But Lucretia's words resounded in his head, their meaning just out of reach. Like Tantalus in his pool.

We only exchange our desires . . .

What had she meant to tell him? He twisted and turned on the question's hook but he could not get free. He snapped at the boys in the kitchen and fell into long silences until Philip roused him. As winter approached, a cold wind blew in from Elminster Plain. The pottage thinned. The bread grew harder.

'Remember Phineas's loaves?' Philip reminded John as the latest batch was carried out like so many dark bricks.

'Even Phineas couldn't have got a loaf out of ground beans and rye,' John replied. 'We might as well sweep the dust out of the stables.'

'Some of the men are talking of leaving,' Philip said. He broke off a chunk of bread and chewed gloomily. 'Lady Lucy's fast. That's what they're calling it.'

'Who is?' John demanded. 'Where would they go? Zoyland?'

'Ben's ledger doesn't lie. We'll be eating our boots by Plough Monday.' Philip looked down at his own worn pair. 'If we still have boots.'

'Adam and Eve hid in the garden,' Ephraim Clough announced to the puzzled Household the next Sunday. For some reason he had stationed himself outside the chapel. He stood before the door, his eyes bulging strangely. 'But the Lord spied them in their finery. Now I learn their fallen descendants repeat that ancient error, wrapping their limbs for their comfort and ease.'

'What's he talking about?' Philip murmured to John. 'What are those doing here?'

Barrows were drawn up beside the chapel wall, each one filled with pebbles and stones. John shook his head.

'But the Lord's servants are not deceived.' Ephraim wagged an accusing finger as if the men and women of the Household were disobedient children. 'Bind the fig leaf about you and the Lord will strip it away. Paint your faces if you will. The Lord will scrub them clean. Mock God and He will mock you back.' His features twisted themselves into a grin. 'And his mockery is harsh.'

Ephraim pointed to Mrs Pole. Two of the Militiamen grasped the governess's angular frame. As the woman shrieked, a third soldier pulled up her skirts to expose the clouts bound about her knees.

'Strip them off!' cried Ephraim.

The Militiaman ripped the cloths free. A low mutter of protest rose from the Household but the other soldiers raised their muskets. Ephraim surveyed the men, women and boys.

'Who will be next?'

'Someone told him,' muttered Philip. 'Must've done.'

'But who?' asked John. Then a movement caught his eye. Lucretia strode forward, her face set.

'I will command my Household, Pastor Clough.'

As she pulled up her skirts to expose coarse woollen stockings, John saw a fascinated look pass across Ephraim's face. All around the assembly men and women were stripping off bandages and pads of rags. At a sign from Ephraim, a gang of Motte's gardeners were pushed forward by the Militiamen. Wheeling the barrows into the chapel, they began shovelling their contents onto the floor. Pebbles and stones skittered over the flagstones.

'The Lord shall smite thee in the knees and in the legs,' Ephraim declared. 'Now enter the Lord's house as you deserve. On your knees.'

They were forced inside. John felt the stones and pebbles bite into his knees. At the front he saw Lucretia's bonnet. The young woman knelt before her Household, motionless and unbending.

'How many Militiamen are there?' Adam Lockyer asked that night, still rubbing his knees. 'Two dozen? There's two score of us. Able-bodied, that is.'

'And one traitor,' Philip said, looking about him darkly. 'How did Clough know?'

'We could drive 'em all off,' Adam persisted. But Mister Bunce shook his head.

'They'd be back with Marpot and the rest of them. Lady Lucretia saw him off once.'

'So what if he comes?' Adam said defiantly. 'We'll throw him out too . . .'

But Bunce shook his head. 'Not them. When Marpot found the Bishop had got away he slit the noses of his men. Even the boys.'

'He cut a man's hands off at Masholt,' added Stone.

'Then what do we do?' demanded Adam. 'Nothing?'

At the other end of the table, John remembered Ephraim's heavy-browed face lying temptingly beneath his poised fist. But then he recalled Lucretia's pact with Marpot, whatever it had been. Her hours in the chapel with Clough. She had saved Yapp. Saved Buckland . . .

'We can do nothing,' he said.

The same ritual was repeated the next Sunday and the one after that. Ephraim Clough seemed to take a particular pleasure in his new regime, talking until the grunts and groans from the floor threatened to drown him out. He seemed to direct much of his harangue at Lucretia, John noticed. As he limped out with the others, he endured

Ephraim's lofty smile. Released from the cold bare chamber, he walked off the aches in his legs and knees, making long circuits of the house. But always he found himself tramping the rank grass in the High Meadow above the chapel. On Old Saint Andrew's Day, a cold wind blew but John did not feel it. He looked down on the chapel trying to imagine whatever might be taking place within its walls.

The windows remained dark. The chapel remained silent. Slowly the wind abated and the great tower loomed out of a darkening sky. A grey blanket of cloud thickened above. As John looked up, the first flakes of snow drifted down. Then he heard a cry.

This was not her face, Lucretia had thought, staring at herself in the pier glass on the night before her wedding. Not her arms and legs. Not her breasts or sex . . . She shuddered at the thought of what tomorrow would bring. The walk into the chapel with Piers's clammy hand draped over her own. All around her the Household hummed, from the maids' garret above to the kitchens far below where the cooks were working.

He was down there. Preparing the feast to celebrate her union. Tomorrow his dishes would practise a different deception. As would she. She had only to speak the words, she reminded herself. Gemma fussed about her, combing and curling her hair. Then heavy footfalls sounded, advancing down the passage. Her father's gait.

The broad-shouldered man stood in her doorway as he had in the Solar Gallery, a dark silhouette blotting out the light. At a gesture from Sir William, Gemma scurried out. Lucretia watched him turn the heavy gold ring on his finger. He had come to gloat, she thought. To affirm his victory over her. Then her father spoke.

'You have never feared me, have you? Even when I harangued you. You never flinched or bowed your head. When I demanded your obedience, you defied me. My daughter.'

She stared at him, too surprised to speak. He had never addressed her in such a manner before. Let alone called her 'my daughter'.

'I have paid you those respects which are your due, Father,' she managed. Her father nodded.

'This Vale of Buckland has always been our legacy,' he went on. 'Won for us by the first Fremantle. That is our Covenant, carved at the foot of his tomb. That we should keep the Vale, generation upon generation. But as the Lord gives, so he takes too, as the first of us learned. Up there in his tower, he still looks back whence he came.'

The ring turned on his finger, around and around.

'I too dared to look back. When I first set eyes on Lady Anne it was as if the Lord had gifted me that happiness which all mankind enjoyed in the first days. Adam and Eve were no more joyful than we.' He glanced down at the table where her sampler lay, the legend 'Piers' surmounting a lopsided image of a man. 'Now, on the eve of your nuptials, perhaps you too may gauge that happiness?'

He looked at her. But Lucretia's desires had fled the clumsy cross-stitched figure. Piers's whey-faced image sank to be replaced by a darker face, his red livery mottled with ancient stains. He had fed her. She had wrapped herself in the dress for him, imagining his hands drawing the silk tight about her.

'Yes,' her father said. 'I see the same happiness in your eyes.'

She bowed her head demurely.

'The Lord took back my joy,' he said. 'The same Providence that gave Lady Anne and me such pleasures offered such sorrow that I would have followed my love despite the Lord's prohibition on that act. Only a promise stayed my hand. A promise I made to your mother. She brought you forth out of love for me and to keep safe the Vale. I promised her that I would care for you.'

As he spoke, Lucretia saw his face take on an expression she remembered from the Solar Gallery. It was puzzlement, she saw now. As if he could not comprehend his fate. He approached her now, his heavy limbs seeming to fill the room. He took a seat before her. Then her surprise became amazement. Her father reached forward and took her hands in his own.

'I broke that promise,' the man said. 'I neglected you, Lucretia.' He paused. 'Forgive me.'

His hands pressed her own as if he were trying to draw strength from her. Lucretia remembered the moment in her mother's bedchamber when she had thought to go to him. 'If you ask it, then I forgive you,' she said awkwardly.

He released her but she still felt the press of his hands.

'I wish there to be no harshness between us,' her father said. 'For there is more to tell. News has come. I am called to the field and only Providence knows who will ride out again and who remain. Alas, my daughter, a new sadness must afflict you. I fear you must exchange your nuptial gown for armour.'

'Armour, Father?'

'There can be no wedding tomorrow, Lucretia.'

She felt her pulse begin to race. She never knew how she kept the jubilation from her face. His broad hands took her own again.

'The King has raised his standard,' he said. 'Now I must beg a promise of you, my daughter. That you will uphold your mother's will, and mine.'

Your mother's will . . . At that moment she would have promised him the earth and everything upon it.

'How, Father?'

'Promise you will keep Buckland safe . . .'

She had promised. She had watched him lead out the column. She had waved a handkerchief at Piers. But as the men marched away her eyes searched the back of the column and the men in red livery who marched behind a great wagon piled high with the supplies of the Buckland Kitchen. Among the youths at the rear she had spied him, his curly black hair escaping from under his cap. He had looked back at her, her face hidden behind the bunched handkerchief.

The war was her reprieve, she had told herself. The Household would be her Militia. Her apron and keys were her armour. But the Household had proved no match for Marpot and his ruffians. Let loose on the house, they had run through its passages and chambers, snatching what they could. They had dragged out Mister Pouncey by his heels and whipped him till he danced about a bonfire of his papers. From the chapel, the roars of the soldiers mingled with Father Yapp's cries. They hauled the priest towards the bloodstained block. Their blond-haired Colonel had sat motionless on his horse. Then Lucretia's mind had unfrozen. She had pushed her way forward.

'By what right do you handle my servant!'

The man's blue eyes stared down. She had believed he would swat her protest away. But at last he spoke.

'A witch hid here in the Vale once,' the man declared. 'She hid among Eve's daughters. She spread her wickedness like spittle from a drunk . . .'

These were the sermons preached by the Zoyland crows, she thought. Then her father's words returned to her. Their own legacy. She summoned her humblest tones.

'Colonel Marpot, we Fremantles have always known this.'

She must show no fear, she told herself as she led him into the chapel. He must see only humility and faith. That was her true armour. Not a chink must pierce it. Not a single weakness. Her boots crunched on the shards of smashed glass. She climbed the steps to the top of the tower.

The effigy of the first Fremantle sat looking out through the high arched openings, watching over the Vale. So this was the author of the Fremantle Covenant, she thought. He appeared as she had always imagined he would, his features worn by the wind and the rain. She pointed to the words carved on the flat stone plinth before him, rendering them for the blond-haired man.

'Let no Woman take Fire to the Hearth, nor tend the Vale's Fires, nor give Nourishment save she be bid, nor rule in the Vale, nor hold Rights to a Virgate of Land, nor keep Retainers or Servants . . .'

'It was our Covenant, Colonel Marpot,' she told him as his blue eyes jabbed at her. 'The first of us fought as God's champion.'

He leaned so close she felt his spittle fleck her face.

'You take me for a fool.'

'No, Colonel.'

It was an old story, she had always thought. But the man's blue eyes had narrowed, looking at the effigy as if he recognised something in the worn stone face. Then the man turned and looked out over the Vale. On the far horizon, Lucretia saw the dark line of a wood.

'Very well,' Marpot declared at last. 'You will learn the humility that Eve forgot. We will strip away luxury here at Buckland. Bare the skin to bare the soul just as the Lord stripped Adam and Eve. I will leave a pastor to guide you.'

Lucretia nodded dutifully. 'We at Buckland will embrace his correction.'

Marpot's thieving Militia had emptied her larders and driven off the horses in the stables. His wailing family of women had sung psalms on the lawn. Father Yapp had fled. In his place had come Ephraim Clough.

'Adam and Eve were naked,' the black-garbed youth breathed, his eyes bulging as they prayed together the first time. 'Naked as babies.'

She met his gaze coolly.

'But we are not babies. Are we, Pastor Clough?'

He circled her as she pretended to pray. She heard him panting behind her. Afterwards she imitated him for Gemma, both of them laughing on her bed. But he dared not touch her. Lucretia armoured herself in piety. She wrapped herself in the colours of penitence, burying her fears and desires deep inside herself where no one could see them. Not the Household. Not Marpot. Not Clough. No one, she told herself, would pierce her armour. Then John Saturnall had returned.

How typical that he should ring the copper to announce himself. As if the entrance of a cook merited fanfares and hosannas. As if his comfits and kickshaws, the steaming stews and poached fishes he had cooked to soften the ache in her belly, or the baked apple in its pool of sweet cool cream . . . As if such tit-bits signalled victories and conquests. Her heart thudded out of irritation alone as she stamped down to the kitchen. And in the passage outside Mister Pouncey's quarters, when he tried to embrace her, she rejected him.

Charnley Hall was burnt to ashes, she reminded herself as he turned from her. At Forham, not one stone still rested on another. But Buckland was safe.

Clough's doltish affections protected them. She knelt with him in the chapel. She listened to him stumble through his tracts. He would guide them all out of error, she told him. They would enter Marpot's new Eden together, he urged her eagerly, his fat grey tongue lolling in his mouth. But then the dolt had grown miraculously intelligent, pulling up Mrs Pole's skirts and tearing the clouts from her knees.

'You took me for a fool,' he hissed in her ear that Sunday as she knelt on the pebbles. 'But I'll teach you Ephraim Clough's no fool.'

His eyes bulged as they had the first time. But now the diffidence was gone.

'I'll send word to Colonel Marpot? Lady Lucretia is not the penitent soul he believed. Buckland Manor deserves no better than Charnley, or Forham.' He pushed his face close to hers. 'Shall I, Lady Lucy?'

Lucretia stiffened at the impertinence.

'No.'

'Then show your penitence.'

Lucretia gritted her teeth. 'I am penitent, Pastor Clough.'

But the black-clad man shook his head.

'Show me.'

She looked up, baffled.

'Strip to your shift.'

She held his gaze for a long moment. But Ephraim Clough's bulging eyes did not waver now. Bury your pride, she told herself as her reluctant hands reached behind her. Deny your fears and desires, as she made her fingers grip the laces of her bodice. She pulled the bows that Gemma had tied that morning. She forced her legs to step out of her skirts. The worn cotton of her shift was thin enough to show her flat breasts, the jutting bones of her hips. As his gaze fell upon her, she thought a vessel would burst in her head for shame.

'Good,' Clough breathed behind her. 'Very good.'

The pain in her knees was a welcome distraction. But as the minutes passed her legs slowly numbed. Her shame too would fade, she told herself. Eve had sinfully clothed herself. Now Lucretia would be virtuously unclothed. This was her Providence. This was her Eden.

But with every week that she shivered in her shift, her thoughts fled further from Clough and the chapel. Instead of the bare walls, her mind sought out the soft hills and sunlit fields where her shepherds and princes had wandered. Kneeling on the stones, she imagined their hands draping her in gowns of soft wool or fastening belts studded with amber about her waist. Instead of Clough's sour sweat, she smelt sweet creams and the heady scents of apples baked to sweetness. If she closed her eyes, she could almost taste the soft flesh marbled by the cold cream. She could all but feel the warmth of his breath. In the freezing chapel John Saturnall's face hovered before her own once again.

Afterwards she hobbled out. She no longer joked with Gemma as the young woman rubbed her reddened fingers and knees. On Old Saint Andrew's Day, Lucretia led her Household into the chapel under louring grey clouds, her breath steaming in the freezing air. The hateful voice droned through the verses. Then she was alone with Clough again. She heard his feet crunch the pebbles. She felt his breath.

'Soon I must leave for the winter, Lady Lucretia.' His voice grated on her ears. 'So I have thought further upon your penitence. Before I go. You must humble yourself further.'

'Further, Pastor Clough?'

His answer was a sharp tug at her shift.

'Take it off.'

For an instant her mind froze. He could not intend that. It was unthinkable. But he was waiting. It was indeed his intention. She could do it, she told herself. She could strip off the thin fabric and bare herself before him. Eve was naked in her garden. She would be so here. It would mean nothing. But as she reached for the cotton, the bare walls and floor seemed to harden against her. Clough's heavy-browed face leered into her own and a hot anger rose inside her, an outraged rebellion against her fruitless Eden and its clottish master.

'No!' she shouted and swung her fist. She felt her knuckles crack against his cheek.

'Touch me, would you?' she shouted as he staggered back. 'You stinking Zoyland crow!'

A wild pleasure gripped Lucretia. She swung again and felt her fist sink into his spongy flesh. Clough grunted. But the next time he caught her wrist.

'Whore.'

His voice was cold. And he was stronger than she had imagined. She kicked at his shins but it made no difference. One hand gripped her arm. The other reached between her legs.

'You would not dare,' she hissed.

They struggled, swaying back and forth. But he was too strong. He twisted her arm and forced her down. She was lost, she knew. The Manor was lost with her. Her promise broken and gone for nothing. *Let no woman . . . rule in the Vale . . .* There were no courtly shepherds or princes in disguise. Clammy-fingered Piers had run away. Her new groom was brutish Clough. He cuffed her hard about the head, dazing her. She fell face down to the floor, felt the stones graze her knees. He was behind her. His knees were forcing her legs apart. She heard the thin cloth rip. So this was her marriage bed, she thought. A cool stone floor.

Somewhere behind her a loud bang sounded. The door. Quick footsteps sounded, crunching over the stones. As Clough shifted to look, she tried to reach back to cover herself. Then she felt something thud into Clough, lifting his weight clear. A moment later an unearthly howl filled the chapel. Lucretia rolled over. Clough staggered back clutching his groin. John Saturnall stood before her.

'Up!' ordered John, hauling Clough to his feet.

He had kept the coal buried so long, hidden deep inside him. But he had felt it flare at the sound of Lucretia's voice. Now it blazed as brightly as it had in Buccla's Wood. He propelled Ephraim forward, half cuffing, half dragging him through the door.

Outside, the fat flakes tumbled down. A layer of snow already carpeted the ground. Ephraim twisted free and aimed a wild punch. John swatted the blow aside, a mixture of elation and rage rising inside him.

'Just us now, Ephraim,' he said. He took aim and hit Clough full in the face. Clough fell again, clutching his nose, the blood trickling between his fingers. John looked down at the thick brow and full cheeks. There was no-one to hold him back now. He raised his fist.

'Stop!'

Lucretia stood behind them, her dress clutched about her. A wild-eyed John stared at her.

'Leave him!' she ordered.

John looked down at Clough's battered face. Suddenly the sight disgusted him. He rose and the black-clad figure scrambled up still clutching his groin, blood flowing freely from his nose. Philip and Gemma were approaching with Adam.

'You fools,' he snarled, backing away. 'How dare you.'

A group of Quiller's serving men followed Adam, then others from the kitchen. They advanced in a silent mass to form a ring about Clough. Pandar stepped forward. In his hands, he held a shovel.

'The ones you want gone, they never go.' He eyed Clough. 'Do they?'

Clough's last defiance vanished. 'I never hurt anyone,' he whined to the surrounding faces. 'I never laid a finger on a soul, did I?'

Pandar raised his shovel. But as he advanced, Lucretia's voice sounded again.

'Let him go.'

She had pulled on her dress but her feet were still bare. The snow was falling faster. More and more of the Household were walking up the path. Looking from side to side, Clough began to back away. At Lucretia's command they parted before him, watching him in silence until he turned and ran up the drive. In a minute, Ephraim Clough had disappeared through the charred gates.

'Reckon we'll have Christmas after all!' Simeon declared then, scooping up a handful of snow.

The members of the Household turned to each other, breaking into smiles and clapping each other on the back. John looked about, searching for Lucretia.

'You going to boil the brawn then?' Meg challenged Simeon.

'I will if you'll nibble his ears . . .'

John edged away from the laughing men and women. Brushing the snow from his jacket, he walked through the servants' yard and into the darkened Manor. Across the deserted Great Hall, the East Wing passage beckoned. At the end rose the stairs to Lucretia's chamber. But no light showed there. In the knot-garden courtyard, snow already clung to the low hedges. He pulled open the heavy door opposite and stepped inside. His limbs felt light, climbing the stairs. His heart thudded as he pushed open the door to the Solar Gallery. Once again, he breathed the dusty air. Except now another scent hung in the long dark space, a scent he remembered. Lucretia stood by the window seat.

'He's gone,' John said.

He remembered her naked back as he burst into the chapel, its white length against the dark stone floor. He felt his heart thud harder, his footfalls resounding down the gallery. At his approach, she raised a hand. To touch his face, he supposed. Or stroke his hair. But as he drew close her arm swung quickly. Before John could duck, Lucretia's palm slapped him full in the face.

'I ordered you to stop!'

The report rang in his ears. John reeled back, clutching his stinging cheek.

'And let him take his pleasure with you?'

Her second blow caught the top of his head but at the third, he captured her wrist. They struggled briefly, the girl stronger than he imagined.

'Let me go!' she hissed.

John shook his head.

'He will be back. They all will.'

'Not tonight,' John said. He gestured behind her where moonlight reflected off the wreckage of the glass-house. The broken panes were already furred in snow. And beyond the high windows, the flakes were falling faster.

Her answer was to push him back. John felt his shoulders knock against the panelling. He could smell rose water and her fresh sweat. She made to strike him again. But his fingers grasped hers.

'Unhand me,' Lucretia demanded.

'No.'

'Then what will you do?'

Her head was thrown back, her black eyes watching him. He leaned forward until he felt her breath on his stinging cheek. Her free hand gripped his arm, to push him back or draw him closer he did not know. But he saw her lips part. Then he closed her mouth with his own. They hung there, joined by lips and fingers. As he reached to clasp her tighter, she twisted away. But it was to take his hand and draw him down the gallery. He followed her to the door at the end.

Inside the chamber they stared at each other, their breathing quick and shallow. A moment later her hands were pulling at his clothes. His own fumbled at her laces. For a few seconds they swayed, locked together. Then they tumbled down onto the bed.

From *The Book of John Saturnall*: A *Feast* for *Old Saint Andrew's Day*, being a *Bagatelle* and a *Cinglet* of *Sugar* for *One Beloved*

or the Love of Adam did Eve pluck an Apple and make of it a Dish. Solomon fed Sherbets and Rose Jellies to the Maids that warmed his Bed. Even now do we token our Affections with Dishes and Feasts.

No Snow fell in Eden, I believe. And Foxes, not Hedge-priests, did afflict the Garden of Solomon. Yet even in the Depths of Winter a Cook may serve his Mistress a Gift to match those Pleasures that Lovers afford one Another.

The Spanish in their Privacy, I have heard, do offer one another the Loin of a Piglet which has never yet stood, that tenderest Fillet being seared in Oil, rolled in Seasoning and diced. The French dangle above each other's dainty Maws those Birds we call Fig-peckers, roasted and dusted in Sugar, and oftentimes with the Feathers unplucked. The Amants of the Duchy of Bavaria eat sweet Pork Dumplings and those of Prussia crunch tiny Biscuits called Widewuta's Teats after their first Empress. The Romans eat much Garlic and the Hungarians more while in the Markets of Sidon lovelorn Men pay Ransoms for a Jelly dusted with Sugar from which the Scent of Roses does rise and which no veiled Maid can taste without yielding.

And on these far-flung Shores such amorous Sweets may be fashioned too, and given, and consumed even in the depths of Winter, as I shall now relate . . .

THE SNOW FELL FASTER, the heavy flakes cartwheeling down out of the sky, swirling and whirling in the gusts of wind, piling up in drifts. With the roads cut, Buckland Manor rose like a great dark ship riding at anchor in a sea of white. Within its walls, its crew hurried and scurried to prepare themselves for the voyage through winter.

Tramping into the woods, John led the Kitchen into the orchardmen's abandoned gardens from where they carried down baskets of skirrets and carrots, fat leeks and leathery green kale, pink-topped mangels and purple-bottomed turnips. From the clamps came baskets of tiny apples.

'Ha!' exclaimed Mister Bunce. 'Remember these, Master John?'

They scoured the woods for fallen timber and drove down the pigs and ewes from Home Farm. The pigs were housed in the stables while the sheep were penned in the sagging barracks whose roof groaned under the weight of the snow. There, amid squeals and bleats, Mrs Gardiner tutored Ginny, Meg and the maids in the art of milking. The farm's chickens joined Diggory Wing's doves.

John cleared Scovell's room and Mrs Gardiner sent down bedding for the cot. Every night, once the kitchen's work was done, John made his way back through the passages, rushlight in hand, towards the Master Cook's chamber.

But at the junction he turned away from Scovell's room. Taking the door at the far end and hurrying through the deserted kitchen, he climbed the narrow staircase to the Solar Gallery where the moon offered a ghostly light, scudding over the snow-bound lawns to shine through the high casements. When the moon sank the gallery was dark. But from under the door at the far end, a crack of light showed, glowing from the bedchamber. There Lucretia waited.

The first night she had trembled beneath him, her dark eyes staring up. He found himself frozen by her gaze, fearing to injure her or brush against her grazed knees. But at last Lucretia had pulled him to her and it seemed that a tight string within her was cut. Her arms and legs splayed. He heard her breathing grow hoarse and felt her arch to receive him. At last they fell back. John felt for her hand.

'I had not thought such pleasure might be mine,' Lucretia said.

'Nor I,' he said beside her. 'Yet it is.'

Their pleasures were repeated the next night, and the one after that. John recalled the woman in the barn. How his nerves had paralysed him at first. Now his tongue felt dry in his mouth and his heart thudded in his chest. But his desire for Lucretia increased.

She was not bold, she told him. She made him turn his back while she tugged at laces and stays or pulled off her shift then slipped unseen beneath the covers. But once they touched, she abandoned her reserve. She pulled him to her and ran her hands down the smooth slopes of his back. He buried his face in her hair or pressed his lips to hers. Soon she kicked off the covers, spreading her arms that he might have the pleasure of looking upon her.

He laid fires in the hearth and watched her stand before the flames, raising an eyebrow at his gaze or touching a finger to her lips as if to preserve the silence. She brought her book and held its torn and taped pages to the flickering light, the coverlet draped around her shoulders.

Come live with me, and be my love,
And we will all the pleasures prove,
That valleys, groves, hills and fields,
Woods, or steepy mountain yields . . .

A belt of straw and ivy buds,
With coral clasps and amber studs:
And if these pleasures may thee move,
Come live with me and be my love.

John let the words dress her, imagining the cap of flowers, the mantle embroidered with leaves, the gown of lambswool and the belt with its amber studs. Lucretia closed the book and smiled.

'Gemma and I used to pretend a shepherd would come and carry us off.'

'Instead you got a cook.'

'I am content with my cook.'

'And what of the valleys and groves?'

'Here is where I want to be,' she said. 'Here in this room.'

They pushed off the heavy blankets, revealing themselves to each other in the fire's flickering light. His gaze played over the curve of her back, down her thighs and slender legs. Her fingers combed his thick black hair, finding the scar left on his scalp by the musket ball. She brought a candle and held it over his body.

'You are very dark, Master Saturnall.'

'I'm told my father was a blackamoor.'

'And was he?' She passed the candle back and forth, her face so close he could feel her breath on his skin.

'Or a Barbary pirate.'

'And your mother?'

He regarded her across the pillow. 'You set eyes on her once. But I do not think you will recall.'

He told her how his mother had come to the Manor and how she had left. The mysterious argument between Almery and Scovell. 'Mrs Gardiner called him a magpie. He tried to steal from her.'

'Steal what?' she asked.

'A book. Or so I believe. Did you not wonder how a kitchen boy came to read?' He described the lessons his mother had taught on the slopes then his life in the village with Cassie and the others. He told her how the sickness gripped the village. Then their flight and the ruined palace in the woods. The anger that had burned inside him and how the sight of Clough had ignited it again. At last he spoke of Saturnus and the woman who had brought the Feast.

'She was called Bellicca,' John said. 'She came here when the Romans went home. She brought the Feast to the Vale. Every green thing grew in her garden, my ma said. Every creature that walked or crawled or flew or swam. The Feast was for all, she said. Back then, all men and women sat together as equals and exchanged their affections . . .'

'As we do,' Lucretia said. She smiled but John had not finished.

'Then Coldcloak came,' he told her, his expression darkening. 'Some say he loved her. Others that she was a witch who enchanted him. He sat at her table and took his place at the Feast. But he had sworn an oath to Jehovah's priests. Bellicca had witched the whole Vale with her Feast, they claimed. So Coldcloak vowed to take it back for Christ. He pulled up her gardens. He doused the fires in her hearths and chopped up her tables. He drove her people out and took every green thing. The Feast was lost, except for the book . . .'

He stopped. Lucretia's smile had faded and a strange look had taken its place. Suddenly she seemed remote from him.

'What is it?' he asked.

'Only that he betrayed her,' she said quickly. 'That he sat at her table then turned on her.' She shook her head as if to rid herself of the thought then gripped his arm. 'Promise you will never betray me.'

Before the gazes of the servants they were cool, addressing each other with a stiff formality. But Philip had to remind John of dishes he had set simmering or those left to cool. Ephraim Clough had made off with his head, he told John in exasperation.

Motte's men shovelled out the stones from the chapel and moved in a table. They gathered there on Sundays to sing a psalm and join in prayer. As Christmas approached, John and Philip scoured the larders and storehouses.

'We've as many apples as we could wish,' Philip reported. 'Bacon, hams, half a sack of dried fruits, some jars of conserves, that sugar-loaf in the larder. Two sacks of meal. The ewes are still giving milk. Mrs Gardiner has said she will make slip-cheese and whey. The carrots and turnips in the clamps are good. We can make frumenty, and a minced-meat cake. We can slaughter a pig. But we need more wood. The pile in the yard is almost gone . . . Are you listening, John?'

He celebrated the long nights with Lucretia, kept safe by the heavy dark curtains. She read the verses from her book to him, sitting by the fire then stepping carefully around the chair, the little table and cradle for fear of disturbing the dust. She dressed her hair in plaits so that he might have the pleasure of releasing the coils, winding the thick locks around his fingers then letting them fall over her face. Her dark eyes watched from behind the disorderly fringe.

'The first moment I saw you,' she murmured, 'I hated you.'

He nodded drowsily. 'I hated you too.'

They gazed at each other across the long bolster.

'What if they knew?' John said quietly. 'Piers. Sir William . . .'

'They are far away.'

'But when they return?'

'Then you will leave me,' Lucretia said. 'You will ride away down the Vale. You will forget me . . .'

'I will not,' John said. 'You will marry Piers.'

'Perhaps he will find another. One more to his taste. The women of Paris are most alluring, I hear. What is your opinion, Master Saturnall, on the women of Paris?'

But a darker mood had descended on John. 'You will marry him,' he persisted.

'Douse your anger, Master Saturnall.'

It seemed they might argue but before John could answer, from under the coverlet, a loud growl sounded. John laughed and Lucretia blushed.

'You are my cook, Master Saturnall,' Lucretia said, smiling. 'Feed me.'

'The first men and women drank spiced wine. They warmed it with honey and flavoured it with saffron, cinnamon and mace. They roasted dates and dissolved them . . .'

He knelt above her, his lips brushing the shallow valley formed beween her shoulder blades. The words of his mother's book rose easily in his memory as if Lucretia's hunger called them forth. Once again the heady fumes twisted up and the wine seemed to warm his belly. As he murmured the words, the imagined liquor soothed him as it had in the freezing wood. Now its balm worked upon them both. When he reached the nape of her neck, she twisted about.

'I should like to taste your spiced wine,' she demanded.

John rose and took the tall pitcher from the tray. He poured then watched Lucretia sip. Her throat bobbed as she swallowed. She gathered a droplet that ran down her chin on her finger and sucked. At last she turned to him with a doubtful expression.

'I am bound to say, Master Saturnall, that I cannot taste the dates.'

'Perhaps they were not sufficiently softened. Or perhaps some lazy cook neglected to roast the stones, or add the saffron, or the cloves and mace . . .'

'I fear, Master Saturnall, that your spiced wine tastes more akin to cold water.'

John raised his eyebrows in mock-surprise.

'Only the laziest cook blames his kitchen, your ladyship. But in this instance I must plead the paucity of our larders. Not to mention our cellars. And our storerooms. In point of fact, we have no wine.'

He saw her eyebrows rise in alarm. 'Then how will you feed me?'

Night by night, he led her through Saturnus's gardens, describing the dishes that might come from each one.

'Poached collops of venison,' he whispered in her ear. 'A quaking pudding with raisins, honey and saffron. Custards flavoured with conserve of roses and a paste of quinces. Beef wrapped about a mash of artichoke and pistachio, then hollowed manchet rolls filled with minced eggs, sweet herbs and cinnamon . . .'

He described the foaming forcemeat of fowls then set before her a dish. He watched her scoop up a little of the pale orange mash.

'I confess that to this poor palate your forcemeats taste strongly of turnips.'

'Ah, but I have not yet described the seasonings of cumin and saffron, the beaten egg whites and the folding of the forcemeats into the pipkin.' He scooped more of the turnip mash and held out the spoon. 'Taste again, your ladyship. Imagine the spices . . .'

He carried up the plain dishes and presented them to her with a joking flourish. She played along, looking up as if she still sat in her chamber with Pole and Fanshawe outside on the stair. Spoon poised over the dish, she looked up from the little table.

'Perhaps, Master Saturnall,' she asked, 'you might sit with me?'

'Sit, your ladyship?'

'Like those first men and women.'

They ate together. Afterwards they lay together. Sated and drowsy, John put his lips to her ear.

'Flaking florentine rounds,' he whispered. 'Peaches in snow-cream.'

'No,' she murmured. 'No more.'

'Meat pies. Mutton balls topped with spinach and walnuts and cumin ground fine . . .'

'You have no cumin. Mister Fanshawe told me this morning.'

'We have no mutton either,' he said. 'Nor walnuts until next autumn.'

The larders were less than half full, he knew. As Christmas drew near the stores sank lower. They would serve spiced cider in place of wine, John told the kitchen. Cold sallets of sorrel, tarragon and thyme would follow hot ones of skirrets, beets and onions. They would dress lettuce leaves with cider vinegar, salt and oil and dip the endives in oil, mustard and beaten yolks.

In the bakehouse, Tam Yallop and Simeon tried their hands at Vanian's darioles. Adam Lockyer pledged his dish of songbirds, boned, roasted and salted. Jed Scantlebury proposed himself for the sallets. Hesekey declared that he and Simeon should make honey cakes while Wendell Turpin and Alf assigned themselves baked apples. Philip and Mister Bunce took charge of the boar and supervised its transport across the yard, the massive carcass leaving a dark streak of blood in the snow.

'Should see us through,' remarked Philip two days later, surveying the carcass which hung from the beam in the jointing room. A basket heaped with apples stood beside it. John peered up at the roof.

'We'll give them a Twelfth Night feast to remember.'

Adam and his under-cooks scalded off the beast's hair and cleaned the carcass. In Firsts, Mister Bunce cored and peeled apples. Diggory brought in a basket of feathered corpses which Simeon began to draw and pluck. Sacks of skirrets and rampions were carried down from clamps in the woods. Barrels of cider were consigned to the darkest corner of the cellar to cool. Outside, beyond the west wall of Motte's garden, two of Motte's gardeners dug a roasting pit.

Bent over the cauldron with Scovell's ladle in his hand and the spiced cider sending up its heady fumes, John heard the hum of activity rise, the clatter of pots and pans, the thud of cleavers on boards and the voices of the cooks. Slowly the kitchen stirred into life. At midday he was met by Philip who wore a baffled expression.

'She wants us all up there.'

'Who does?'

'Lady Lucretia. Up there. In the Hall. She wants us to eat together.' Philip shook his head as if the ways of the Mistress of Buckland were quite beyond the pale of normal comprehension. 'The first men and women ate together, she told Gemma. Now we should too.'

As John turned away to hide a smile, a snow-dusted Adam Lockyer entered with Peter Pears.

'The Heron Boy won't move,' said Adam. 'Six inches of ice on his ponds and he still won't come in.' He handed back a bunch of keys to Philip. 'And some of that sugar-loaf's gone.'

The spiced cider was poured into a plain tureen. Philip marshalled the dishes and ordered the trays. Luke and Colin sweated over the chafing dishes. A grinning Simeon carried in the first tray of darioles and Alf began to pipe in a compote of apples and cherries. From the servants' yard, John heard Mister Bunce directing his porters – 'Left a little, Hesekey! Mind that cobble, Adam!' – then the leather curtain was thrown back. Borne shoulder-high on a litter of poles with Hesekey holding a drip-pan beneath, the boar entered the kitchen. The beast's back almost scraped the ceiling. His belly bulged with stuffing. From the wooden tusks attached to his snout hung two delicate cages woven from twigs. In each cage perched one of Diggory Wing's doves.

'Scovell would have been proud of him,' Philip told John, surveying the beast's glistening, golden-brown crackling. 'Now, how are we going to get him up there?'

It took Quiller, all his serving men, Colin, Luke, John and Philip to manoeuvre the boar up the stairs. In the buttery corridor, the buzz of voices from the Hall seemed to John almost as loud as when the King had come. Mister Bunce carried a carving knife the length of a cutlass. John steadied the beast on its tray then Mister Fanshawe's tones rang out, as nasal and penetrating as Mister Pouncey's had ever been, announcing each member of the kitchen.

'Mister Adam Lockyer of Buckland, Cook! Mister Hesekey Binyon of Buckland, Under-cook . . .'

At last John's name was called. He stepped out from behind the boar and stared.

Candlelight glinted off the polished platters, the little flames flickering throughout the Great Hall. A makeshift High Table ran the length of the room. Behind it stood Lucretia. John stared.

She wore the dress of silvery-blue silk, the cloth shimmering as the candlelight caught its folds. Beside her stood Mrs Gardiner. Next to her stood an empty chair. Lucretia beckoned.

'So the Buckland Kitchen has consented to join us, Master Saturnall,' the young woman declared. 'We of the Household count ourselves fortunate.'

Her face was flushed. John made little bows to Pole and Gardiner then took his place between them. From the High Table, he saw Philip and the rest of the Kitchen looking over at him, nudging each other and grinning. Down the table, Gemma leaned out from beside a quiet Mister Pouncey.

'A draught for Master Saturnall,' Lucretia commanded from the other side of Mrs Gardiner. One of Quiller's men poured poached cider into a goblet. In front of him rested the salt caddy in the shape of a ship.

Waving his cutlass, Mister Bunce attacked the flank of the boar. Wielding a knife as long as his forearm, Mister Quiller carved slices from the rear. Plates of pork larded with mutton and apple were handed up. A platter of golden-skinned birds joined it. Soon John's knife and spoon added their noise to the clatter of cutlery in the Hall. Beside him, Mrs Gardiner slurped heartily from her goblet. At length she stifled a belch and leaned back. John raised his cup.

'To your health, your ladyship.'

Lucretia acknowledged his salute.

Across the Hall, the serving men joined the Kitchen, Motte's gardeners, the Estate men and the maids, all of them busy lifting food off the platters. Down the table below, Philip was conducting an energetic conversation with Meg, watched by a frowning Gemma. Beside the maid, Ginny glanced up at John and smiled. Pandar leaned across the table, confiding something to a shocked-looking Hesekey and a laughing Simeon. Jed Scantlebury seemed to be choking but was still pushing hunks of pork into his mouth while Peter Pears slapped him on the back. As John watched the familiar faces, Lucretia spoke across a drowsy Mrs Gardiner.

'Do you remember when last you sat here, Master Saturnall?'

'I was the King's Sayer,' he said.

As Mrs Gardiner's eyes closed he leaned over.

'I would be alone with you now.'

She smiled. 'And why would that be, Master Saturnall?'

'I have a dish for you.'

'Turnips again? More melted snow?'

'A mystery,' he whispered back.

She eyed him across Mrs Gardiner's slumbering form. Suddenly a red-faced Jed Scantlebury got to his feet.

'Who says old Iron-arse banished Christmas!' the young man shouted. He raised his cup. 'To Christmas! To the King!'

The Great Hall raised their cups.

'Tonight,' whispered John under the din of the toast. 'Come as soon as you can.'

'Is this your mystery?'

She eyed the flat wooden box. But as she lifted the lid, a disbelieving smile spread over her face.

'Jewellery?'

' "A belt of straw and ivy buds," ' said John. ' "With coral clasps and amber studs." '

'The verses . . .'

' "And if these pleasures may thee move . . . Come live with me and be my love." '

There was a long silence in which Lucretia did nothing but wipe one eye, then the other.

'How did you make them?' she asked at last.

John recalled the twinge of shame as he had smuggled out the broken brick of Madeira. He had ground the sugar in his chamber then refined it and spun out its threads, weaving them as they hardened in the air. Now Lucretia looked down at the belt made of golden

341

hoops, a ring with its faceted jewel and a clasp woven from the finest gold wire. He shrugged.

'It was no great labour.'

'I fear they might be too sweet for my taste,' Lucretia said.

'They are not for your lips.'

She looked at him, puzzled.

'Then whose?'

Some minutes later, a strange duet disturbed the peace of the chamber.

' "Come live with me," ' said John. *Crunch*.

'Ow!' Lucretia exclaimed.

' "And be my love." ' *Crunch*.

'Stop, John . . .'

' "And we will all the pleasures prove." ' *Crunch, crack, crunch* . . .

Her yelps would wake the household, John chided her as he bent to bite another of the candy hoops. He had fastened the belt about her naked waist. But as he bent to nip again, hilarity overtook her.

'Stop!' gasped Lucretia. 'Please stop, John.'

' "That valleys, groves, hills and fields," ' *crack*, ' "woods," ' *snap*, ' "or steepy mountain yields . . ." '

At last she escaped.

'Now you wear it,' she commanded.

'Me? Where?'

She advanced upon him, dangling the chains.

'No!'

'Yes . . .'

Later, when the belt and clasps and studs had been crunched between their teeth, when their sticky lips had unpeeled themselves and they lay back panting among the disordered sheets, John felt

Lucretia's hand creep into his own. Together they looked up at the ceiling where the light from the fire cast flickering shadows.

'This is our garden,' Lucretia said. 'Here in this chamber.'

'Garden?'

'You said they served one another. The first men and women. They exchanged their affections and lived as equals.' She turned to him. 'This is our garden, John. This is our Feast.'

The last snow fell on Saint Agnes Eve. Weighing sunflower seeds in her palm, Lucretia prayed for their future then threw them over her shoulder. John heard them crackle and spit in the fire.

'Pull back the curtain,' Lucretia said.

John drew back the heavy fabric, dust cascading down the velvet. The light flooded in. Together they peered out of the window.

'The snow's melting,' said Lucretia, resting her chin on his shoulder.

'Winter's over,' said John.

The thaw uncovered the pastures. Tables of green began to rise through the slush. Soon the snow lay only in the deepest hollows and at last even the great white mound below the gatehouse disappeared. On Lady Day, the roads reopened. Then Marpot came.

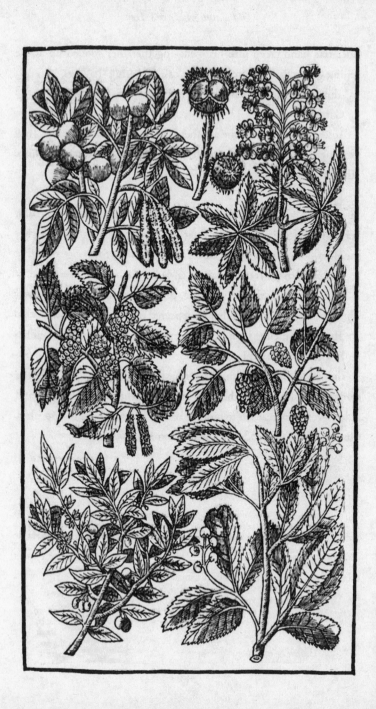

From *The Book of John Saturnall*: A *Bread* such as the first *Men* and *Women* did eat and their *Heirs*

hat loaves they baked in Paradise only a Master Baker may tell for none but he might master all the Grains that grew in those ancient Fields and that gave up their Awns without the Sweat of Man or Beast. Then fine feathery Wheat yielded an airy Manchet and coarser Rye gave Maslin. Spelts and dried Beans gave Horse Bread which crunched on the Teeth of Adam and Eve and growled in their Guts. Lower Meals too were made from Mast but how they were threshed without heavy Whips or Flails, or milled without Stones or Querns, or sifted without Sieves or Boulting Cloths, I do not know. Nor how such Dough raised itself without Balm and kneaded itself without a Trough and baked itself without an Oven. For in that first Garden, Adam never strained in gathering Billets.

Thus that effortless Bread was first prepared and never again until the denizens of a colder Eden scavenged Nuts for their Meal and eschewed Balm (having none) and gathered as little Fuel for their Ovens as Adam did. Their Paradise was a bare Garden compared to Eden and its Loaves were of a different Kind, being coarser, less toothsome, neither airy as Manchet nor as nourishing as Maslin nor hardly edible by Man or Beast. Those Loaves they called Paradise bread, which are made as I shall tell . . .

THE MAN'S COLD BLUE eyes stared out from under a heavy brow, his gaze scaling the walls and roving over the windows. He sat mounted on a dark horse. Beside the animal stood Ephraim Clough and before them both the host of his Militia gripped muskets or rested grimy hands on the pommels of their swords. Penned together in the inner yard and surrounded by the grim-faced men, the members of the Household watched the horseman sit up in his saddle and pull off his helmet to reveal a mane of lank blond hair.

Marpot wore his hair as long as before, John saw. He had known at the first clang of the copper, the ladle beating the side of the cauldron. Men and boys had run hither and thither. Then the Militiamen had broken in, clubbing and beating the Manor's would-be defenders before driving them out to the yard. Now Marpot eyed them from his horse.

'Who here dares raise a hand against my minister?'

Penned in with the others, John felt the Household shift around him. But no one spoke. A bleak smile appeared on Marpot's face. He twisted and gestured behind.

The ranks of the Militiamen parted. Through the gap, a small group of women clad in ragged dresses and plain cotton bonnets struggled forward pulling a two-wheeled cart. As it came to a halt, two men jumped up. A moment later a great block rolled off the back and thudded on the ground. Its surface was mottled with dark brown stains. A manacle was nailed to its centre.

At the sight of the block, a low murmur ran through the Household.

'They don't like it, Brother Ephraim,' Marpot said loudly. 'They resist their correction.'

But John's gaze was drawn from the sinister object to the women standing behind it. Some cast their eyes down. Others looked up wonderingly at the house. But one stared straight ahead as though she were looking through the mass of stone to something beyond it.

Cassie's blue eyes were the same as he remembered. And the freckles. For an instant her gaze met John's own. Then she dropped her head.

'I say who dares raise a hand against my minister?' Marpot repeated.

The mounted man gestured and John saw muskets rise, their barrels pointing at the men and women of the Household. A squat man with a bushy black beard pointed his barrel at John's midriff.

He had summoned them here, he knew. The moment he had aimed a blow at Clough. The moment he had pulled him off Lucretia. He had brought Marpot and his men to Buckland. With a sick feeling, he raised his arm.

'That hand is mine.'

Marpot's blue eyes looked down. If he recognised John, he gave no sign of it. John gazed up at the man who had goaded on the villagers, who had led them against himself and his mother, fear and anger contending within him as his memories battled with what would come next. John looked down at the block. But then a second voice sounded.

'My hand too.'

John looked about in surprise. Behind him, Simeon Parfitt had raised his arm.

'Simeon!' he hissed, gesturing furiously. But Simeon nudged Hesekey beside him. Slowly, Hesekey too raised his hand. Adam Lockyer followed, then Philip. As John watched, more and more arms rose until even Pandar and Barney Curle stood with their hands in the air. He stood surrounded by a forest of arms which closed about him like a palisade. But through the human barricade, John saw the last member of the Household approach.

Two ragged wings flapped and bounced over the grass of the lawns then advanced through the gate. The Heron Boy strode forward. A broad smile spread across his face. Then he saw the muskets.

His expression changed. He scowled at the Militiamen surrounding John.

'No,' muttered John. He pushed back with his hands, shooing the ragged figure away. But the Heron Boy only aped his movement. John waved and the Heron Boy waved back, grinning amiably at the enjoyable game as a wing caught a soldier's arm. 'Don't touch him!' John called out. But the nearest man jabbed with his musket, catching John in the guts. The Heron Boy's smile faded. He frowned. Then he swung.

The first thwack resounded around the yard as a wing clunked against the nearest helmet. From the Household, a roar of laughter went up. The next man was struck with a thud from behind. Around the yard, the laughter grew louder. Encouraged, the Heron Boy swung with renewed vigour, left then right, a little squad of Militiamen retreating before him. Half-winded, John tried to force a way through. But before he could reach his comrade, he saw Marpot nod to the black-bearded soldier. The man stepped forward and levelled his musket.

'No!' shouted John.

The soldier's eyes never wavered. John watched him step sideways for a clear line of sight. Then a crack sounded in the yard. A puff of smoke shot from the musket.

The Heron Boy stopped in mid-swing. A puzzled expression spread over his face. As the blood bloomed through the front of his shirt, he looked at John as if to ask how, this time, they had lost. But before John could answer, his eyes rolled back. His wings dropped to the ground. The Heron Boy seemed to crumple rather than fall, folding slowly from the waist and toppling sideways to lie on the ground. Then he was still.

Lucretia's voice broke the silence.

'Murderer!'

She pushed her way through the Household, her angry face turned up at Marpot. But as she reached the side of his horse, the man drew back his hand. His gauntlet descended, striking Lucretia in the face. She fell back and the Household let out a gasp. The Militiamen levelled their weapons.

'Lying Jezebel!' Marpot shouted. 'Kneel with me in your chapel, would you? Lie to me before God?'

Blood welled from between Lucretia's fingers. John stepped forward but she waved him back.

'This is the hand,' John shouted at Marpot. 'Come down and take it.'

He waved his fist, standing before the block and glaring up into Marpot's cold blue eyes. He saw Ephraim murmur a few words to his master then Marpot nodded.

'You do not fear the bite of my axe,' he told John. 'Perhaps the bite of your conscience will persuade you better.'

Ephraim murmured again and John saw the mounted man nod. Then Marpot pointed to Philip.

'Take him.'

'No!'

John lunged for the nearest Militiaman. If he could only reach the man's sword. If he could only draw it and drive its length into Marpot's guts, cut him open like poor Phineas. He had only to grasp the hilt and pull it out . . . But a heavy hand fell on his shoulder. A moment later a terrific blow smashed down on the back of his head. The world seemed to spiral up and away. He was falling, down and down into blackness.

The women's voices brushed at his ears, whispering and murmuring then fading away. If he could hold onto one he would wake. But they would not stop. Instead Abel Starling looked down.

'Here we are again.'

John shook his head. 'You're dead. You're my . . .'

'Demon? You knew you wouldn't end up wearing that bracelet, didn't you?'

'No.'

'Wasn't made of sugar, that one, was it?'

John turned away. But wherever he looked, Abel was there.

'First you were sweet on our Cassie. Then Lady Lucy. Quite the ladies' man, John.'

'You don't exist,' John said. 'You died.'

Abel's face had gained a vindictive look. John wanted to get up but a great weight lay on his chest. It was all in his head, he told himself. Or his conscience. Abel pointed a finger.

'That's why you kicked out Clough, wasn't it? You wanted her. And you got what you wanted. Got to raise her skirts, just like Piers said. But it weren't you who paid for the pleasure, was it?'

'No,' groaned John as Abel's face began to fade. In its place, a bright light appeared. A candle-flame. A pair of blue eyes hovered behind it. A face with freckles.

'Know what these are, John?' Cassie touched her cheeks. 'Remember?'

'Sins,' he said.

'That's right.'

She reached towards him with her fingers splayed. Every nail was black. He tried to reply but his head was pounding. A great fist was driving it into the ground. The blackness was rising around him but he fought it, struggling up. Then Cassie's face became Meg's. Ginny appeared beside her.

'Philip,' John managed. 'Where is Philip?'

'Quiet,' said Meg.

'What did they do?' John demanded.

'You should rest,' Ginny said.

'Tell me,' he hissed, trying to pull himself upright.

He saw them exchange glances. Then Meg spoke.

'They cut off his hand.'

The kitchen looked as if a gale had passed through it. Smashed benches and tables were piled against a wall. Broken bowls and jars littered the floor. Hesekey turned from the hearth where he was trying to blow an ember into life. One eye was closed by a purple-black bruise. The other regarded John.

'Where is he?' John asked. 'Where is Philip?'

But there was no need for the youth to answer. A low cry echoed down the passage. Head throbbing, the bile rising in his throat, John hurried past Hesekey, the cries guiding him to the spice room where Gemma, Adam and Alf crouched in the corner. In their midst hunched Philip.

John remembered his mother, crouched on the ground and coughing. Philip rocked back and forth, clutching his wrist and gasping for breath. Wrapped about the stump, a thick clout of rags dripped blood. John felt the heat drain from his limbs. He dropped to his knees.

'Before God I am sorry, Philip.'

Philip shook his head.

'Not you,' he managed. Then a white-faced Gemma grasped John's arm.

'Help him!' she hissed.

John rose to his feet and reeled back. In the passage he found Simeon. Together they hurried to Scovell's chamber.

'Reach up to the shelf,' John told Simeon, pointing into the shadows. 'Pass down the bottles and jars . . .'

He scraped off dust and eased off the corks, sniffing the brimming contents. A few minutes later they were forcing a bitter draught into Philip's mouth. He choked and spluttered. But as the last of the draught disappeared, his struggles lessened and his breathing calmed. As his eyes rolled back, Gemma sank with him to the floor.

'A little at a time,' John told her. 'He will babble. Have strange dreams.'

The young woman cradled Philip's head in her arms. 'I had believed I would never hate another,' she said with a bitterness that John had never heard before. 'But now I have learned.'

The look on her face reduced John to silence. Behind Gemma he saw Adam look up.

Lucretia stood in the doorway. Blood had soaked the front of her dress. A dark purple bruise spread out from her nose, swollen from Marpot's blow. She walked forward and held out a hand, her face beseeching.

'John.'

He looked up at her. But then he glanced at Philip's motionless form. Abel's mocking voice echoed in his memory. *You got what you wanted* . . . Suddenly he could not bear her touch. Rising to his feet, he pushed past her.

'Get away from me,' he told her. 'Get away.'

They buried the Heron Boy beneath the great oak. Alf spoke the words of the service, as many as he could remember. Afterwards they trooped back to the house. The senior men gathered around the table in Firsts.

'They took everything,' Mister Fanshawe reported. 'Ripped up Motte's garden. Drove off the sheep and horses. Even took the hay.'

Ben Martin looked hardly more cheerful, still sporting a bruise on his cheek. 'Quiller sent a man along the Carrboro road,' he said. 'Didn't get further than Callock Marwood. Marpot's camped a troop of his men there. Had to run for his life.'

'If Marpot means us to starve, why didn't he just turn us out and have done with it?' asked Mister Bunce.

No one knew. But then Alf spoke.

'Ask Lady Lucy,' he said. 'He dragged her into the chapel. All the way up the tower. He was hammering away, smashing the walls and cursing. But when he came out he was different. White like he'd seen a ghost. He gathered them up and was gone.'

'It's my fault,' John said, gazing up bleakly. 'My hand for Philip's. But for me laying hands on Clough . . .'

'No one believes that,' Alf interrupted. 'Least of all Philip. We'd have kicked Clough out too. Kicked him harder, wouldn't we?' The others nodded their agreement.

'I should've broke his crown with my shovel,' offered Pandar.

Adam nodded. 'Anyroad, they took the lot this time. They'd have ripped up the trees if they could.'

'Least they left those,' replied Alf, rising to his feet. 'Looks like we'll be finding our supper in the woods.'

Clutching sacks, spades and hoes, they formed forage parties and ventured up into the chestnut groves, fanning out through the glades to grub and root for skirrets and navets, rampions and wild barley. Across the river, in Home Farm's abandoned fields, Adam, Jed and Alf organised teams who hitched themselves to the plough-traces and hauled the heavy share through the loam. Each evening, they tramped home exhausted in mud-caked boots. In the kitchen, Hesekey and Simeon boiled up root-pottage thickened with barley. When the week ended all were footsore and weary. In the bare chapel, Alf led the prayers. Ranked around him, the men and women of the Household repeated the words then sang a psalm. Standing at the back, John watched Lucretia, her face hidden beneath a bonnet.

His hasty words echoed in his head. Their nights in the bedchamber seemed a distant memory now. He felt her absence from his side at night like a cold wind against him, at one with the bleak skies above. But the yard still bore the imprint of the block. The oak rose high over the Heron Boy's grave. The sight of Philip's sling sapped his resolve. He had forfeited her, he thought. He deserved no better. He stole glances at Philip as they ate together until at last he eased the stump from its sling.

'You can look if you like.'

John coloured. 'No, I . . .'

'It was Marpot's act, John,' Philip said. 'He'll answer for it. Not you.'

The work grew harder. John rose before sunrise to beat the cauldron and wake the household. In the woods, those foraging had to venture deeper and deeper to fill their sacks. In the fields the sun beat down, burning the tops of the wheat. By midsummer the green stalks were no more than knee-high.

They formed a human chain, hauling up water from the river in leather buckets and wooden tubs and pouring it down the crooked furrows. The corn began to grow again but by late summer great swathes of the fields were bare. They scythed, winnowed and threshed. They milled the grain in querns. They gathered fruit and picked berries, netted rabbits and plucked pigeons. Falling gratefully onto his cot each night, John had only to close his eyes to sleep.

Still their cheeks grew hollow and their eyes sank deeper into their heads. The roads remained blocked by Marpot's Militia and the yards were empty. That autumn came news of the King's trial. John remembered the sad-eyed man who had beckoned him up, seating him at his side. At Christmas, the Household gathered again in the Great Hall and ate rabbit stew with slabs of coarse cheat bread. As Mrs Gardiner fell asleep and began to snore gently, John glanced down the table to Lucretia.

They had scarcely exchanged a word all year. Her nose had set slightly crooked. It had softened her face, he thought. But at the sight of him she turned away.

The winter deepened. The cold seemed to suck the strength from their limbs. Every morning the Household was slower to muster. When two of Quiller's men fell sick, Meg and Ginny took their places. The pale-faced troop trudged out at dawn and back after dusk, heads drooping, feet dragging, stomachs rumbling with hunger. But there was always more firewood to be dragged down and chopped, more water to be hauled upstairs, more furrows to be dug.

'Half the cabbage is rusted,' Philip told John at Martinmas. 'The kale's worse. The turnips we won't know till we dig them out.' His arm was out of its sling now. 'Some of the men are talking of leaving again. The worst is the meal. Without bread . . .'

John felt the deep weariness in them. Their clothes were ragged and their shoulders slumped. Each morning he faced the same downtrodden faces. New Year came and went. A week later an argument broke out between Jed Scantlebury and Jim Gingell. In a moment they were rolling in the snow under the chestnut trees and landing clumsy blows on each other. The rest gathered around, shouting and yelling. Adam and Peter pulled the combatants apart.

'Go if you want!' Jed shouted. 'You'll get a good welcome from Marpot.'

'It's better than starving,' retorted Jim.

'No one will starve,' said John.

'Won't we?' asked Barney Curle. 'The stores are empty. There ain't much left up here neither.'

'What'll we eat?' asked Peter Pears.

Their pinched red faces turned to him. A few stamped their feet against the cold. John felt their fatigue steal over him.

'He don't know,' declared Jim Gingell. Some began to mutter. One or two turned away.

'Wait,' John said.

They watched him, some curious, others only puzzled as he struggled to order his thoughts.

'This was a garden once,' John said at last. 'Every green thing grew here.'

The snow seemed to swallow up the words. The bare trees stood silent.

'That was Paradise,' Tam Yallop said. 'This ain't Paradise.'

'It was once,' John said.

'He's mocking us,' said Jim Gingell. He turned to those around him. 'Ain't he?'

'Where's it now then?' demanded another voice.

'That garden was ruined,' John said. 'The men and women were left with nothing. Like us. But they survived.'

'How?' asked Jim's brother Jem. 'What they eat? Tree bark?'

John scraped aside the snow at his feet then bent and felt in the mud. He held up a dark brown nut. 'They made bread,' he said. 'They ground up chestnuts and made loaves from the meal.'

He stood before them with Philip beside him. But a discontented murmur spread among the shivering men.

'Is that your Paradise?' asked one of Quiller's men.

'That's pig food,' declared another.

'What'll you and Lady Lucy be eating? Up there on your High Table?' challenged Jim Gingell.

John's face hardened. 'The same as you.'

But the men were shaking their heads. A wave of fatigue rolled over John. He racked his brains for the right words but none came. Perhaps they were right, he wondered. There was no garden. There was no Feast. They were lost long ago. Then a woman's voice sounded.

'Eden had no High Table.'

Hooded and robed in a coarse wool cloak, a figure holding a sack pushed her way through the men then stood before them. She pushed back the hood.

'The first men and women ate together as equals,' declared Lucretia. 'So will we. They were alike in their riches. So are we in our poverty.'

She stood before them, her hands on her hips. John saw their faces soften, curious now.

'We will make this Paradise bread,' she ordered. 'Just as Master Saturnall says.'

'And eat it too, will you?' demanded a sullen voice.

'We shall, Master Gingell,' Lucretia said, picking him out at the back. 'All of us. We shall make it. And we shall eat it.'

With that, she bent and dug her fingers into the snow, picked up a chestnut and dropped it into her sack. Another followed. Then another. The Household stood in disbelieving silence at the sight of Lady Lucretia working. Then John jolted himself from his reverie and bent to join her. A moment later, Philip did too. Next Alf stepped forward.

'Never thought Paradise'd look like this,' he said, bending to pick up the nuts. Adam followed. Shrugging and shaking their heads, the others advanced over the snow, kicking aside the white covering to uncover the wood's harvest.

John shuffled forward, his fingers digging in the snow. But out of the corner of his eye he watched Lucretia. Soon her white hands turned red in the cold. Her cheeks grew flushed. At last she glanced across at him.

'Does it give you pleasure to watch Sir William's daughter labour?'

'Forgive me, your ladyship,' John answered.

'I am not your chaplain, Master Saturnall,' she answered crisply. 'I cannot absolve you.'

'Yet I seek absolution.'

'A strange sentiment from one who shunned his absolver so publicly.' Lucretia scraped a nut from the muddy soil, wiped it on her skirts and tossed it in the sack.

'He shunned all sense,' John said, raking his boot through the snow. 'He shunned the one he held most dear.'

'Did he?'

John felt as if he were venturing out over one of the Heron Boy's icy ponds. One false step and he would fall through. 'He lacked the courage to own his error,' he continued in a whisper. 'He denied his own true feelings . . .'

'Enough.'

He closed his mouth quickly. She bent down again, her reddened hands brushing away the snow. As her fingers dug into the freezing earth, she spoke quietly.

'If you wish to beg for absolution, Master Saturnall, you might have the good grace to do so elsewhere than before the whole Household.'

'Elsewhere, your ladyship?'

But Lucretia had moved away.

'This was our garden! Those were your words!' Her angry face glowed red in the firelight. 'Here we would serve one another as the first men and women did! Here we would "exchange our affections", as you called it. So we did. Until John Saturnall's conscience bade him otherwise.'

'I . . .' John began.

'Be silent.'

The denunciation had begun as John entered the room. It showed no sign of abating.

'How dare you turn from me,' Lucretia continued, jabbing a finger at his chest. 'Scurrying back into your kitchen. No doubt you amused yourself with Ginny down there. I've seen how you look at her.'

'Ginny?' John was baffled.

'Oh!' Her eyebrows flew up in mock-surprise. 'Was it another? What name were you moaning while I bathed your head? Cassie, was it?'

So it was Lucretia who had tended him. Before Marpot had called her up to the tower. As she berated him, John saw that her nails were broken and her fingers chapped. Reaching out, he captured her hands between his palms.

'Forgive me,' he said. He felt her fingers clench within his own.

'How could you, John?' she said quietly, and this time her reproach was worse than any anger. 'How could you turn from me?'

'Never again,' he said. 'I promise.'

He traced her ribs through her pale skin. Her hips jutted sharply from her sides. He ran his finger over the slight bump in her nose. They lay together in the bed and shivered.

'All I could think of was Marpot,' he said as she fitted herself to him. He felt her cheek on his shoulder. Her palm rested flat on his chest. 'What he did to Philip in my place. I could not think of you without his injury. And yet Marpot handled you too. Alf told me he dragged you into the chapel. Before he fled . . .'

'Enough.' She placed a finger over his lips. 'Marpot has gone. We will plant a new garden. You and I.'

They scraped chestnuts out of the snow, roasted them, peeled them and ground them to meal which they mixed with water and set to rise. Tam Yallop and Simeon baked the crumbling flat loaves in the ovens. In the Great Hall, serving men, maids and cooks sat together at the long tables.

'If this is Paradise bread,' declared Philip, biting off a dry crumbling corner, 'then send me to Hell.'

'Philip!' hissed a scandalised Gemma across the table. Adam Lockyer grinned.

'I heard from Bunce there's some dried apple rings left.'

'And dried broom buds,' added Peter Pears.

They chewed.

Spring arrived with a downpour and the news of the King's execution. At the Manor, the Household held a day of silence, remembering the sad-eyed man butchered by Cromwell and his Parliament. As John listened to the rain descend, a drenched Hesekey walked in.

'There's a man in the yard, Master Saturnall,' he whispered. 'He's asking for you.'

A familiar figure stood in the icy rain, a snow-white mule beside him. Josh's hair was almost as white, John noticed.

'I know about Henry,' the driver said before John could speak. 'I knew the moment he marched out of here.'

'I'm sorry, Josh,' John offered. Then he looked up the drive. 'How did you get through?'

'Your Colonel Marpot's been ordered back to Zoyland. They don't like him up in Soughton. The new Lieutenant's secretary's an old friend of yours.'

'Who?' asked John.

'Sir Philemon Armesley.'

John shook his head. 'You're mistaken, Josh. Sir Philemon served the King at Court.'

Josh shrugged. 'Now he holds old Ned's pen. Sits on their Committee too. But that ain't why I'm here.' He gestured back to the string of horses, laden with crates and sacks. 'Got a letter in there. Took it from a fellow who was around by Banbury. He had it from a driver out of Oxford. From Sir William.'

'He will return?' John asked, wondering at Lucretia's reaction. But Josh shook his head.

'Sir William's dead.'

My Daughter, may this Letter reach you in better Health than its Writer who suffers more under the demands of Peace than ever he did on the Battlefield. The Masters of our new Commonwealth are miraculous Men who see deeper into our Consciences than we do ourselves. For they discover loyal Men to be Traitors and those who fought for their Sovereign to be Outlaws. And though they are Thieves they call themselves Judges for whatever escaped their Cannons they would seize now with their Pens.

Some these Commissioners unhouse and drive from their Estates. Upon others they visit barbarous Violence as they threaten against our King. Such is our new Babylonian Captivity.

It pains me as grievously as the Saw that gnawed its Way through my Knee that you must face these Creatures in my place. That they know of those close Conferences which were held here at Buckland is certain for one among our Company serves now upon their Committee. Philemon Armesley presents as many Faces as there are Gentlemen to look upon them. He tells me that he presses our Cause from Within.

All these Woes I bequeath you, and Another. This Day the Surgeons tell me there is a Poison in my Blood. The Apothecaries opine the same. But I have known it long before. Our Legacy has ever been a Poison that creeps about our Veins, mingled with the bright Blood that nourishes us.

Now the Hour is late and you and Buckland are distant. Yet I rest secure, trusting in the Promise that you made to me and knowing now your true Character. For Lady Anne did not give her Life for Naught. In your Hands I know that the Vale will be kept safe. You are my Providence, Lucretia, and hers . . .

John waited for her in the Solar Gallery, composing speeches in his head. But when she came in the early hours, red-eyed with grief, he found himself tongue-tied. She clung to him wordlessly, her body shaking with silent sobs.

In the Great Hall, the black velvet hangings were brought out. The Household conducted its business in silence. Lucretia wore a dark dress and veil. Sitting with John in the bedchamber, she gazed at the doorway.

'He caught me playing here once,' she said. She glanced back at the cradle with its silver bells, the dusty combs and little bottles. 'Gemma and I used to play at Queens and Maids.'

'You must play a different part,' said John. 'You must be Mistress of Buckland.'

Sir Philemon arrived flanked by riders as before, his saddle-bags bulging with commissions. Sitting behind the great walnut table, Lucretia heard out his protestations of loyalty while John, Ben Martin and Mister Fanshawe stood behind her. He would plead their case before the Committee, he promised. He would save the Estate from its worst depredations. But alas, he could not return empty-handed. John watched the man's scar stretch as he offered an apologetic smile, laying out his papers. A composition would have to be paid, he feared . . .

With Marpot banished, the pack-men and carters began to return. Ben Martin and Mister Fanshawe examined the accounts in the steward's rooms, drawing up lists of rents and fees, tallying the arrears and making rounds to collect them. Soon, in the crowded yards, Philip presided over a jostling throng, waving his one good hand at the unruly men. Motte began replanting the kitchen garden. Once again the Buckland Kitchen took its meals downstairs.

Word of the Manor's resurgence spread. Men arrived in search of work. Across the river, a gang of hired hands spread muck under Adam Lockyer's direction. All around the gardens, men and boys dug, cut back, repaired and planted. Only the ponds remained untouched. Beneath the water's dark surface, the fish swam lazily among the weeds.

In the house, the windows in the Great Hall were reglazed and the passages grew crowded. No longer could John and Lucretia exchange glances across the table, nor let their hands brush beneath, let alone embrace in quiet corridors. If John intercepted Lucretia, he hardly had time to take her arm before footsteps approached and she was forced to shake herself free.

'I could not get away!' she hissed after he had again waited in vain for her in the Solar Gallery.

Their encounters grew rarer. A week or two might pass before they kept their assignation. Then they came together in a flurry of desire. The next day, wielding his ladle at the hearth or discussing the next week's dishes with Philip, John wondered if he had dreamed the night's encounter, so abruptly did it wrench him from his life in the kitchen.

But at the end of that year on Old Saint Andrew's Day he laid the table in their chamber and awaited her, holding before him a tray loaded with dishes. She took her seat and, as he bent over her, spoon in hand, she looked up again with a smile.

'If it pleases you, Master Saturnall, perhaps you might sit with me?'

Her hip-bones no longer jutted. He could not count her ribs through her skin. Only Marpot's blow marked her. As they lay together in bed, John ran his finger over the bump.

'Your broke-nosed bride,' she murmured.

'Would that you were.'

That winter, the stores and larders were full. On the Twelfth Night feast John was summoned from the depths by a smiling Mister Fanshawe who led the way up the stairs and past the old buttery, through the passage and into the Great Hall.

Once again the red-liveried cooks, pot-boys, scullions and turn-spits emerged from behind the screen and were beckoned onto the benches. The Household and Estate men shifted up to make room until the Great Hall was a motley of red, green and purple. Philip Elsterstreet contrived a place next to Gemma. Adam Lockyer and Alf leaned over to exchange words with Ginny and Meg. Further down, John saw Mister Bunce and Mister Stone yawn over their cups while Simeon Parfitt hushed three bellowing kitchen boys with an angry wave of his hand. It seemed another life in which Simeon had peered into a blackened pan, his eyes prickling with tears, or Scovell had pressed the ladle into his hand.

Sir Philemon passed their settlement through the Committee, Lucretia told him. The compact would hold, Ben Martin averred, so long as the composition was paid. John looked along the table to Mister Pouncey. He spent his days playing chequers with Mrs Gardiner, Mister Fanshawe had confided. Beyond the housekeeper, Lucretia leaned in and out of view. John nodded to a serving man to refill his cup. Mrs Pole was stifling her laughter next to Mister Fanshawe. As the games and songs grew wilder, the ladies rose to leave. Lucretia paused behind him.

'Come tonight,' she whispered.

It was late before he could slip away from the kitchen. He took the steep stairs two at a time. When he reached the gallery, the door to the chamber was open. Lucretia stood before the fire. She wore the silver-blue silk dress. As he stood in the doorway, she pulled the fabric tighter.

'It almost fits.'

'Perhaps the Queen will call you to Paris.'

'I would not go.'

'Perhaps the Court will return.'

'Not tonight.' She turned to him, smoothing the silk over her body. 'Look, you have fed me up, John Saturnall. You can see the swell of my belly. Imagine if it were to swell in earnest . . .'

He heard the silk rustle over her skin. The faint smell of spiced wine drifted on her breath. She turned her back to him and he saw that she was unlaced. As he reached for her in the candlelight, the dress slid from her shoulders and pooled on the floor.

In the yard Calybute Pardew cried the news of Cromwell's Rump and the Barebones Parliament, of Penruddock's rising and the fall of the Lieutenants. But in the Solar Gallery chamber, the heavy black curtains stayed drawn. Lucretia's belly swelled no more than it had that night. The seasons outside passed unseen, winter quickening into spring, spring bursting into summer, summer waning to autumn until the year turned and the next one began. John breathed in her smell and felt her warmth against him.

'Is this how they were in your garden?' she asked drowsily. 'Did they feast like this?'

John smiled. 'They were hardly so fortunate as we.'

Every year, on Old Saint Andrew's Day, he prepared a feast and served it from a tray. Every year she looked up.

'If you wished, Master Saturnall, you might sit with me . . .'

The dishes grew richer. Barrels and boxes that John had not seen since Lucretia's wedding day began to arrive. Breaking them open he found bitter oranges, Madeira sugar, saffron, long mace and pepper. Once again the kitchen filled with bitter-sweet fugs and clouds of steam, with rich scents and sharp tangs. The posts from Carrboro spoke of the Lord High Protector's absences from his accustomed haunts, then the death of his daughter and at last a sickness that was described by *Mercurius Bucklandicus* as a melancholy humour. Then, a week past Michaelmas, as autumn slipped into winter, a company of red-faced villagers from Callock Marwood advanced up the hill and passed through the Manor's gates. They sang and cheered as they advanced down the drive. They drank from leather flasks. Drawn by the noise, John and Philip hurried out to confront the rowdy crew. Crossing the inner yard, John saw Lucretia accompanied by Mister Fanshawe emerge from the Great Hall and stand at the top of the steps. A frown creased her forehead. At the sight of the Mistress of Buckland, their shouts redoubled. Their leader raised his flask in a mock-salute.

'We're here to toast Lord Ironsides, your ladyship! Our High Protector! The Devil bless his soul!'

John saw Lucretia frown deeper at the raucous behaviour.

'And bless his iron arse too!' shouted another. Then the others joined in.

'Cromwell's dead!' the men shouted. 'Long live the King!'

Around John, the men in the yard downed their tools or put down their burdens and turned to one another. On their faces bewilderment turned to delight.

'It's over, John!' exclaimed Philip as the leather flasks were handed around. The men jostled and shouted.

John nodded and drank. But when he turned and looked back, Lucretia stood motionless on the steps, as silent as himself.

'Our Eden is ended,' he told her that night in the Solar Gallery chamber.

'You would abandon our garden so easily?' She mustered a smile.

'It was never ours,' he answered. 'We only walked within its walls.'

'So did Adam and Eve,' she said.

'They were expelled.'

From *The Book of John Saturnall*: A new-restored *Dish* for a new-restored *King*, being a *Progress* of *Meats* from the base-born to the most noble, called *Wild Boar à la Troyenne*

or every Restoration a Dissolution must be suffered just as every Misfortune does bring a Happiness in its Wake. Eden's breach became the greater Earth's Gain, sending its Fruits far and wide, and, by the contrary Current, Adam's Ease became Sloth, as our tireless Churchmen later called it, and his Wife's Affections were Lust. In these Days the King's Return is a gilded Memory. But that Gold did not glitter so brightly for All.

As a base Beast may conceal a noble One so, contrariwise, the Innards of a surpassing Creature may prove noxious, as the Trojans discovered in that Horse left to them by the Greeks at Troy. So did Many divine when the late King's Son returned, Some being more deserving of their Woe than Others. But All carved the Dish, finding within their Deserts, just or not.

Take these Carcasses, as many as may be gathered and fitted together: a Boar, a Sheep, a Kid, a Lamb, a Goose, a Capon, a Duck, a Pheasant, a Partridge, a Quail, a Sparrow and a Fig-pecker.

Clean and bone the Beasts. Pluck and clean the Fowls, all save the Fig-pecker which should be plucked only. Sew them each inside the last and roast them over Coals or Billets whose Flames have abated. The Ancients lodged Sausages in the place of the Guts and concealed live

Songbirds within a Cavity but our wiser Times eschew such Adornments. Turn the Boar all the Time to cook the Flesh through. Two Days and a Night is an apt Period. Then run the Meats through with a Sword and be certain the Juices run clear . . .

ONE OF CLOUGH'S EYES bulged like a toad. The other was closed by a dark purple bruise. Pressed in the midst of the crowd, John saw Ephraim's split and swollen lips work as he gabbled his prayer. Dressed in tatters with his scabbed scalp bare, the man stood on the scaffold in Carrboro market flanked by two heavy-jowled men, one of whom now reached over and tightened the coarse rope which encircled his neck.

'Pull him up slow!' someone nearer the front shouted to the executioners on the makeshift scaffold. 'Show us his tongue!'

The marketplace had filled slowly that morning but now men and women jostled for space. This was the fifth hanging in as many weeks, a man had told John. He, Philip and Gemma had left the cart and its load at the inn with Adam. At Gemma's insistence, they had taken their places early. Now Philip touched her arm.

'Come, Gemma. Enough.'

The young woman shook her head, her eyes fixed on the platform. A stained block with a manacle nailed to its centre was placed in front of Ephraim. As he finished his prayer the sight of it seemed to strike a new fear into him.

'I never touched no one,' he called out suddenly. But his plea was met by jeers. Below the scaffold, a third man began to sharpen an axe, the whetstone rasping over the noise of the crowd.

'Gemma, come away,' Philip spoke again.

'No.'

At that moment, to cheers from the crowd, the two executioners began to heave on the rope. Slowly, Clough began to rise.

The news of the Lord High Protector's death had prompted celebrations to begin with. But His Majesty's landing at Dover had heralded a more vengeful mood. In Soughton, the Lord Lieutenant and his men had swiftly declared their new allegiance. Only Marpot's Militia had resisted the new order. Now, according to the pages of *Mercurius Bucklandicus*, Marpot's wives were on their way to Virginia while most of his men lay drowned in the rhines on the Levels. Marpot himself had been recognised trying to board a boat at Stollport. 'They choked him to death,' Calybute had told John when word reached the yard. 'Cut his privates off and rammed 'em down his throat with a broom.' Of the Zoyland Militia only Clough remained.

The rope grew taut. Clough's body jerked, struggling against the bonds, his feet straining to touch the floor of the platform. But the men heaved and the noose tightened. Rising with each jerk, Ephraim Clough began to twist and buck. Soon his face turned a dark purple. His mouth opened and a fat tongue protruded.

'There it is!' shouted a woman somewhere in the crowd. 'Now cut him down!'

Clough's struggles were growing more feeble. When they had almost ceased, the two men released the rope. Clough fell onto the planks with a thud. One of the executioners knelt to cut his hands free.

'Lop him!' screamed the woman. 'Give him his master's physic!'

Suddenly Clough revived. He tried to rise only for one of the men to give him a heavy kick. The other grasped an arm and dragged Clough towards the block. They struggled for a moment. Then his hand was in the manacle. The crowd fell silent. This was it, thought John. This was what they had done to Philip. Suddenly he could taste the contents of his stomach. The axeman set himself and swung. The axe fell.

An inhuman scream was wrenched from Ephraim Clough.

'Good God,' murmured Philip.

'Now we can go,' said Gemma.

They shouldered their way out. A second cry reached their ears as they rounded the corner. They heard the crowd give a great cheer.

'Pull his guts out!' shouted voices in the crowd behind them. 'String him up again!'

Clough was shrieking now, long high-pitched screams. They continued almost until the trio reached the inn.

'How'd he go?' Adam asked, tightening a trace.

'Badly,' said John.

'No surprise there.'

Adam pulled at the tack, pronounced himself satisfied, then gestured to the back of the cart where a tarpaulin lay draped over a long rectangular box. John smelled new cedar wood and elm. But underneath these lay another smell, fainter but remembered from the back of a different cart. The wet winding-sheet smell.

'We need to lash it down,' Adam said, nodding to the coffin. 'Can't have Sir William falling off the back.'

The body had been exhumed the day the King landed at Dover yet it had taken three weeks for the coffin to be brought to Carrboro. Now John mounted a bay mare. Philip took a grey, the reins coiled loosely about his good arm. He waited until the cart had rumbled a safe distance ahead. Then he turned to John.

'They will all return,' he told his friend. 'What will you do?'

'Do?' John looked up, engrossed it seemed in contemplation of the dull grey sky. 'Do when?'

'You know well enough.'

John switched his attention from the sky to the verge whose grasses, it appeared, exerted a similar fascination. Ahead, the wheels of the cart bumped in and out of the ruts. Philip regarded him in blunt exasperation.

'When Piers returns.'

'Let us give thanks to God for his Providence that has brought Jericho to ruin. Let us pray he gives us strength to build a new Jerusalem from its fallen stones. We gather on this day to consign to the care of the Lord the soul of Sir William Fremantle, late Lord of the Vale of Buckland. We remember him in our prayers, who fought valiantly for his King and kept faith through the most severe tribulations. Though he be sundered from his daughter, Lucretia, and from his Household, let us take heart that he is reunited with his beloved wife Anne and his fallen comrades. They knew him to be a warrior for his King and his men alike. Now our new-restored King takes his rightful place on the throne and Sir William serves the greatest King of all . . .'

The Bishop of Carrboro's fingers were as thick as before, thought John. His Lordship's amethyst ring sparkled in the gloom of the black-hung chapel, his voice resounding from the newly built pulpit. In the centre, Sir William's coffin rested on its catafalque before the black-clad mourners.

Its arrival at the Manor had seemed to act as a general invitation. Now, behind Lucretia's black bonnet, veil and shawl, sat the Suffords of Mere, the Rowles of Brodenham, Lady Musselbrooke of Charnley, Lord Fell, Lord Firbrough and the Marquis of Hertford. Behind them, beneath the long black banners hanging from the rafters, Sir William's Household filled the wooden benches.

The Bishop signalled that they should pray. John knelt and bent his thoughts to the man, remembering Sir William's entrance into the kitchen on the day of his daughter's wedding. Now that day approached again.

Horses' hooves sounded outside. A minute later the door to the chapel flew open. Five men marched down the aisle, their riding boots slapping on the flagstones, feathered hats flapping in their hands. The foremost, John saw, walked with an odd gait, placing one leg before the other with a strange little shake as if trying to rid his boot of dung. They strode to the front, knelt and crossed themselves before the altar. Then the first turned and bowed extravagantly to Lucretia, throwing back his riding cloak over his shoulder to expose the shiny silk of his tunic and the fine lace of his shirt.

'Lady Lucretia,' Piers announced with a lofty smile to the congregation. 'Pray forgive our tardiness.'

His jowls were a little heavier, John thought. His belly more rounded and his hair dressed differently. But his mouth curled in the same faint sneer as the youth who had left him standing on Naseby Field. From the pews and benches, a murmur arose. But behind her veil, Lucretia offered only the faintest nod.

'My lady,' Piers declared, undeterred. 'I come to claim your hand, as the late King gave leave.' He looked up at the Bishop. 'My lord, I ask that the banns of our union be published at Carrboro and I beg that you proclaim them here . . .'

'Didn't waste any time then,' Philip murmured beside John.

'After filling his face in Paris these dozen or so years,' added Adam on the other side.

John himself was silent.

Upstairs, returning neighbours and courtiers strutted up and down the passages demanding that Quiller's serving men pull off their caps every time they passed or that Motte's gardeners bow when they went strolling in the Rose Garden. Next thing they'd be asking the pigs to curtsy, Mister Fanshawe reported.

Once again, Quiller's serving men lined the length of the staircase, ferrying trays up and down. Once again breakfast shaded into dinner which was hardly over before supper. John welcomed the work, swinging the ladle against the great cauldron, raising the boys from their pallets and summoning the yawning cooks to their tasks. He buried himself in the work of the kitchen, hardly venturing into the servants' yard, let alone the house. But Lucretia stalked his thoughts.

She would not receive Piers, Gemma reported to Philip. A resurgence of her grief was the given cause. She kept to her rooms and saw no one. Meanwhile Piers and his fellows sat up late in the summer parlour offering each other toasts. He had bought a new horse on the Manor's account, Mister Fanshawe reported. And tradesmen from Carrboro and Soughton had begun to arrive, all bearing unpaid bills, according to Ben Martin.

It was another week before John came face to face with his rival. A rare venture took him out to the yard. As John rounded the corner of the stables, a pair of Piers's companions were clapping him on the back.

'Capital, Piers!'

'You horseman!' the other broke in.

'Swordsman!' squawked the first, and all three laughed. But at the sight of John, Piers's smile vanished.

His red nose had taken on a purplish hue, John noticed. The broken veins had spread over his cheeks. He wore a tunic embroidered with the Fremantle coat of arms: a burning torch and axe. For a moment his eyes shifted uneasily but then his demeanour changed.

'Ah, John Saturnall!' he declared jovially. 'I trust you have kept the Household fed in my absence?' Piers turned to the men behind him. 'This fellow appears a mere cook. Yet he is a veteran as brave as myself. Acquitted himself well, let me say. Even did me a service. On Naseby Field, was it not, Master Saturnall?'

'Service, your lordship?' John replied acidly. He could smell last night's wine on Piers's breath. 'Surely you required no service from me. Was not Naseby the scene of the great Callock's Leap?'

There was a short silence.

'I say, Piers. Is he mocking you?' asked one of the companions.

'Give him the flat of your sword,' suggested the other.

'It is but his manner of speaking,' Piers said quickly. 'Leave us while we . . . we recall our old battles.'

The pair retreated. Piers drew John aside.

'We both have our recollections,' he said.

'We both know the truth,' answered John. 'As do Pandar, and Philip, and Adam . . .'

'That was another life,' Piers said. 'We have all gained new masters since then.' A sly smile stole over his face. 'And you too, Master Cook.'

John stared. But now Piers's gaze did not waver.

'Buckland has no master,' John answered. 'Only a mistress.'

'Does it?' As Piers gestured back towards the house, John felt a cold hand grip his guts. She could not, he thought. He had put the notion from him since the day the Callock Marwood villagers had staggered down the drive, waving their bottles. She would not. But behind his denial, this moment had been waiting. Waiting since their first embrace.

'But have you not heard the happy news down there in your kitchen?' Piers went on.

A dread feeling crept over John. He remembered the companions clapping Piers on the back. The talk of horsemen and swordsmen. Piers's smile broadened.

'She has accepted me.'

Barrels of oysters wrapped in seaweed came by boat from Stollport. Fat bream and trout were carried in dripping wooden boxes lined with wet straw. A great conger eel arrived in a crate large enough to hold a cannon and appeared so fearsome Mister Bunce quelled the kitchen boys' mock-screams only by bringing out Mister Stone to take his pick among the screechers. Sacks of raisins, currants, dried prunes and figs piled up in the dry larder. In the wet room, soused brawn, salted ling and gallipots of anchovies crowded the shelves and floor. In the butchery, Colin and Luke marshalled four under-cooks, six men from the Estate armed with saws, a grumbling Barney Curle and his barrow to skin, draw and joint the hogs. Simeon, Tam Yallop and the other bakers lugged in sacks of meal from the Callock Marwood mill while a dray from the ale-house made journeys over the hill, past the gatehouse and into the yard until the buttery and cellar were filled with kegs and barrels. Rhenish wine arrived in a covered wagon, the dark oak tuns resting on a thick bed of bracken. Scents of cinnamon and saffron drifted out of the spice room.

In the kitchen, dressers were opened and vessels counted. Shredding knives and flesh-axes were sent to Mister Bunce for sharpening. Mortars and querns were inspected for cracks. Bread-graters were cleaned and skillets polished. Mister Stone and his scullions scoured frying pans and pots. John supervised.

They would serve dishes to signal the union of the two houses, John told Philip. A subtlety should be constructed from sugar depicting Piers's endeavours and achievements.

'Then we should sew a bag from pig's ears,' snorted Philip. 'And fill it with a quaking pudding.'

'Water and turnips,' offered Adam. 'That's what we ate while he was scoffing in Paris.'

'And Paradise bread,' added Philip. 'Don't deny him that.'

Logs thudded in baskets. Fires roared in the hearths. Under the vaulted ceiling a wave of aromas rolled forward. John slept fitfully, lying on his cot and staring up at the ceiling, thinking only of the feast. A week before the day, there was a knock at his door. One of the new kitchen boys stood holding a rushlight. He looked up nervously.

'There's a lady to see you, Master Saturnall.'

For a moment his heart leaped. But Lucretia would hardly announce her presence down here.

'Escort her here,' he told the boy. A few minutes later, a plump figure advanced down the passage. She entered the chamber with a nod to John and settled herself in the best chair by the fire.

'We all keep our dark corners, Master Saturnall,' said Mrs Gardiner. 'Wouldn't you say?'

John nodded, puzzled.

'Thought I should pay Susan Sandall's boy a visit,' the woman said. 'Now Master Scovell's gone.'

He eyed her in the firelight, trying to divine her purpose.

'It wasn't Richard Scovell she loved,' Mrs Gardiner said abruptly. 'You guessed that, didn't you?'

He nodded, his mind whirling, remembering the conversation he had overheard within these walls. No, it was never Scovell.

'Almery,' he said. 'Charles Almery.'

'That magpie,' Mrs Gardiner said. 'He was a dark one. Even Master Scovell couldn't see into him, any more'n he could know your ma's heart or I could look through that wall.'

Her gaze drifted to the low door that linked his chamber to the one beyond.

'But you said they fought, she and Almery . . .'

'We all have our dark corners,' Mrs Gardiner said. 'Anyone who saw them would have said she hated him. I never guessed otherwise. I never saw into that dark corner. Not till you came.' She looked at John. 'To see you now, it's like looking at him.'

John stared back. 'My father?'

The woman shrugged. 'Almery was well made. And he could speak any tongue under the sun.'

'Couldn't tell the truth in any of them,' murmured John.

'That's right,' Mrs Gardiner agreed. 'Your ma knew it too. But she carried a book with her, took it everywhere. Charles Almery could read it.'

John remembered his mother reciting the words.

'Each had something the other one wanted and neither could resist. But the night Lady Anne died, she caught him down here. Then Scovell found them both . . .'

'Scovell said Sir William threw her out.'

'Oh no. Sir William would never do that. It was almost like he was wary of her. He'd had her fetched from way up the Vale.'

John frowned. 'What would Sir William know of my mother?'

Mrs Gardiner shrugged. 'That I don't know. But I understand this. Your ma got gripped by a passion. And someone's passion gripped her back. And none of them ended where they wanted. You see my meaning, John Sandall?'

She meant Lucretia, he realised. That was why she had come. Mrs Gardiner fixed John with a look.

'I've known her since she was born,' the housekeeper went on. 'She'd go with you in a moment. If she could.'

The housekeeper left her last words hanging. Gripping the arms of the chair she pushed herself upright. 'Now, Master Saturnall, be good enough to show this stranger out . . .'

A hundred questions awaited him in the kitchens the next day, and a hundred more the day after. Yet however many tasks whirled in his mind, he found his thoughts drawn back to Mrs Gardiner's words.

She'd go with you in a moment. Was that encouragement or a warning? *If she could . . .*

'The feast is three days away,' Philip told John the next day. 'You might at least pay attention.'

'The forcemeats,' John said crisply. 'Tell me again.'

Philip shook his head. 'What do you intend, John?' he asked quietly.

'I am her cook,' John said. 'I promised her a wedding feast.'

But that night, Gemma asked for him.

'She has sent me,' the young woman said quietly. 'She would speak with you.'

From the house a muffled hubbub sounded, drifting up on the still evening air. Gemma's boots clopped softly on the path that led past the East Garden wall. John heard a burst of laughter erupt. Piers's companions, he thought. Or merely the end of supper. Ahead the chestnut trees rose. Out of them emerged the chapel, the tower rising like a great stone finger pointing to the sky. Suddenly John was reminded of a different wood.

'She is waiting there,' Gemma said. 'She would not tell me why. She has barely spoken all week.' The young woman hesitated. 'She is not herself, John.'

The chapel door was unlocked. John's footsteps echoed over the floor. Across the nave, the door to the tower stood ajar.

Plaster littered the steps. Marpot's hammer, he remembered. The man had dragged Lucretia up here. Then his mysterious retreat. Above he saw a flickering light.

She'd go with you in a moment . . .

Shattered plaster crunched underfoot. The thought of her waiting swelled in his mind. She could not accept Piers. Not the Lucretia he knew. At last his head rose into the cool night air.

Marpot had not stinted. Even here plaster littered the floor. The tomb resembled a throne. An ancient stone figure sat with its worn face looking out over the Vale. But John's gaze was drawn to the walls, lit by lamps placed on the floor. Mosaics had been set in panels. John glanced at the first in which woods and orchards rose. A familiar river wound its way among them.

It was the Vale. But seen from inside Bellicca's palace. John crouched, his finger tracing the slopes where he had learned his letters. But how was this image here? Who had looked out of the windows of Bellicca's palace? He looked around and caught sight of the worn stone face.

'You know him too, John. You have always known him.'

Lucretia's voice startled him. The young woman stepped forward out of the shadows. Even in the dim light her face looked strange. She had powdered her cheeks, John realised. Her lips were darkened with rouge. A heady perfume wafted from her as she looked at the vista picked out on the wall. Then she spoke in a cold voice.

'He was called Coldcloak. He came here when the Romans went home. He kept the Feast with Bellicca. With all of them. But he betrayed her.'

John stared at her, his mind working furiously. The tomb. The images on the walls. The first of the Fremantles looking out over the Vale.

'Him?' John managed, looking between the young woman and the ancient stone figure. 'Your ancestor was Coldcloak?'

Instead of answering, Lucretia pointed to the next panel in which great terraces climbed in steps to neatly arranged orchards. Bellicca's gardens, realised John. In their midst rose a palace with a great hearth and high arched windows. Men and women thronged about the tables. But a fearsome figure towered over them. He carried an axe in one hand and a torch in the other. He was breaking the tables.

'He swore an oath to God,' Lucretia said. 'Swore it before Jehovah's priests like you told me, John. He would take back the Vale for Christ. So he pulled up her garden and drove out her people. He broke her tables and stole the fires from her hearths.'

In the last panel, Coldcloak fled the scene of destruction. John saw the bitter tears pouring from his eyes. But under his arms he carried trees and bushes. And his hands still held the blazing torch and axe.

'He brought them here,' said Lucretia. 'He stole them. There was no miraculous fire here at Buckland. Or spiced wine . . .'

The ancient stone figure sat before his table. So this was Coldcloak, thought John, staring into the sightless eyes. Then Callock. Then Fremantle. Just as Piers had claimed. As Lucretia stood silently beside her ancestor, he remembered telling her Bellicca's story, how the remote look had come over her.

'You knew,' John said slowly. 'You always knew.'

'Yes.'

'But you kept silent.'

He waited for her to speak. To explain. There would be a reason for her silence. Some compulsion that had sealed her lips as they lay together in the chamber. He could forgive her, he told himself. But she stood in the shadows, as silent as her ancestor. Deep inside him John felt an old ember stir.

'Why?' he demanded.

She watched him through the mask of powder. In the face of her silence, he felt his anger flare.

'You lied to me,' John accused her. 'You lied with your silence. All of you. You stole the Feast from us. You took the whole Vale . . .'

He stared at Lucretia's powdered face and rouged lips. He smelt the heavy sweet scent she wore. This was her true face, he thought bitterly. This powdered mask. But she would answer him, he decided. He would make her answer him. As he reached for her, Lucretia raised her hands. To ward him off, he supposed. But instead she grasped him, her hands cupping his face.

'This is your answer,' she hissed. 'This is what you wanted, isn't it? Take it.'

The whorish scent filled his nostrils. He felt her heat through the thin dress. Her legs splayed. Before he could ask more or protest, her lips silenced him.

From *The Book of John Saturnall*: A *Feast* for the *Union* of *Two Houses* once sundered and at last rejoined, being the *Fremantles* and *Callocks*, served in the Year of Our Kingdom's Restoration

nly those with long Memories will now recall the Union of Piers Callock, Lord of Forham and Artois, to Lady Lucretia Fremantle, in the first Year of the Reign of our second King Charles. Fewer still recall the last Lord of Forham himself. Yet he is daily commemorated in our Speech. When we adjudge a Matter as a heaped-up Extravagance, or a useless Complication over which much Energy is expended to little Purpose or Pleasure, we term it a 'Callock's Subtlety', for that was the Device I caused to be made for that Gentleman's Wedding Feast.

Composed of Paste and glued with Tragacanth, the Theme of this Device was an heroic Feat known as 'Callock's Leap'. A Goat did play the Part of the Lord of Forham's Horse and quaking Puddings and quivering Jellies signalled the Terror that the late Lord of the Vale of Buckland instilled in his Foes. A marchpane Flintlock fired a Forcemeat Ball. A capacious Purse sewn together from the Ears of Pigs and stuffed with Spiced Cabbage resembled, as some remarked at the Time, a great Buttock. It was punctured by a Dagger carved from a Parsnip. Around it was the Lord of Forham's famous War Cry inscribed: 'For God and Queen Mary'.

Of those Tarts and Pies that followed, of the Roasted Meats and Poached Fishes, the Forcemeats piled high and the Kickshaws in the Form of Jewels and Trinkets to catch a Lady's Eye, of these I may say Nothing. At their Service I was already far away . . .

He was running, heart thudding, feet pounding over the East Garden's frosty lawn, past the old glass-house and the back of the dairy, jumping over the low hedges and pushing through the high ones. Approaching the new side-gate, he kept an eye out for old Motte. But it was too early for the ancient gardener. It was too early for anyone except Will Callock.

The sun had yet to climb above the horizon. Frost rimed the grass. Will breathed and felt the crisp cold air sting his nostrils. No one was up except him. No one in the whole wide world. He looked along the East Garden wall and up the path to the chapel. The tower rose before him. Suddenly Will shivered.

He had descended to the crypt that summer, following the coffin that held the body of his father. The corpse had smelt like the man but stronger, the stink of stale liquor seeping out between the cedar-wood planks. Even on this bright winter day, the memory clawed at him. One day, he had thought, he too would have to lie among the cobwebs and tombs. For weeks afterwards he had woken in the night, soaked in sweat and beset by terrors. Then his mother had stroked his thick black hair.

'You miss him, William. Of course you do . . .'

But he did not. His father had spent most of his time at Court. He had returned only to drink and shout. And once to hit Will's

mother. Now the man was dead and his mother spent her days looking through papers with Mister Martin and Master Elsterstreet. The
thought of the one-handed steward reminded Will of his partner in
this morning's escapade.

'Meet me in the yard at dawn,' Bonnie Elsterstreet had told him last
night. Now he looked down towards the deserted space, wondering if
her mother had caught her. Bonnie's mother was famed throughout
the Manor for knowing everything that took place within its walls,
from old Mrs Pole breaking wind to Will himself breaking Master
Parfitt's best china mould or throwing stones at the ancient grave
beside the carp ponds with Bonnie . . .

There she was. Skirts pulled up above her knees, hair streaming out
behind her like a knight's standard, a girl of ten sped past the stables
and across the inner yard. Disdaining the gate, she wriggled through
a crack in the wall.

A minute later they were face to face. Bonnie weighed a stone in
her hand and glanced across at the old well. It had been dug for the
King, old Motte had told him once. The King before this one. Now,
like the coach house and stables and most of the rest of the Manor
according to Mister Martin, it was falling to pieces.

'Reckon you can hit that?' Bonnie challenged him.

They were the same age almost to the day. Conceived on the same
night, Bonnie had confided to Will. She had heard their mothers talking.
Now she pulled back her arm and let fly, her stone speeding in a fast flat
arc to clatter into the well's tumbledown walls. She turned in triumph.

'Ha!'

Will threw and missed. Then missed again. He could wrestle her,
he thought. His arms had thickened over the past year. But if he won
she would sulk. And if he lost . . . The taunts of his friends among the
kitchen boys did not bear thinking about. They both took aim again.

Once again, Bonnie hit. Once again, Will missed. Perhaps he was throwing the wrong stones? He scoured the ground for better ones. Then a man's voice sounded.

'You have to keep your elbow high.'

He stood behind Will, looking down at him. A curiously dressed man, thought Will. For although he wore a fine blue coat and long leather riding boots, in keeping with the fine roan horse that stood patiently by the gate, his headgear was an ancient and battered slouch hat. From beneath its confines, a mass of curly black hair flecked with grey tried to escape.

'You have to throw flat,' the man said. 'Give your wrist a flick at the end.'

With that, the man picked up a stone, eyed the well and threw. The pebble hit with a satisfying crack. The man nodded to him.

'Now you.'

Will raised his elbow and let fly. An instant later he heard the same crack. The man took off his hat and offered a bow.

'And you are?'

'Will Callock,' said Will.

The man nodded gravely.

'And I'm Bonnie Elsterstreet,' said Bonnie, nudging Will.

'I am very pleased to make your acquaintance, Miss Bonnie.' He gave a little bow.

'Why are you here then?' asked Bonnie.

The man raised his eyebrows as if the girl's question only now occurred to him. 'I had hoped for a meal,' he answered at last.

Will watched him glance about. But not to the house. The man's gaze seemed drawn to the chapel and the tower that rose above it. His eyes scanned the high arched openings at the top. Then all three turned at the sound of a strident voice.

'Bonnie! Master Callock! Come away! What are you doing out at this hour?' A bustling woman advanced, an untied bonnet hanging from her hand. Will looked apprehensively at Bonnie. Mrs Elsterstreet's scoldings were not to be taken lightly. But as the woman drew nearer, the man turned to face her. To Will's surprise, Bonnie's mother stopped dead in her tracks. At first it seemed that she might have had a seizure so sudden was her halt. But then an incredulous expression crept over her face.

'John?'

The man offered an apologetic smile.

'Gemma, forgive me. I would have sent word . . .'

But the woman waved his explanation away. Walking up to the man, she gripped him by the arms. Then, to Bonnie and Will's disgust, they embraced.

'Come,' she said, releasing him. 'Philip is up at the house.'

Bonnie's mother seemed to have tears in her eyes.

'Will he see me?' the man called John asked.

'Will he see you? How foolish to ask!'

'And her ladyship?'

'We served the feast as you ordered,' Philip said, the look of amazement not quite faded from his face. He and John sat in the winter parlour. 'Even the pig's ears.'

Gemma shook her head. 'Thank the Lord that Master Piers was too deep in his cups to comprehend. Not to mention that, that monstrosity.'

'A true Callock's Subtlety,' said Philip, grinning at the memory and fingering the silver chain around his neck. 'The very first. What a creation that was. Took Simeon and me the best part of a week. Then, when you left . . .'

'Forgive me,' John said abruptly. He reached across to clasp Philip's good hand. 'I could not stay.'

Philip shrugged as if John's departure belonged to an age too distant to recall. 'All we heard of you was from the news-sheets. The King had tried to engage your services and you had refused. You had sailed for the Barbary Coast. You had travelled among the Turks. The Bishops were calling you a heretic. Then you had joined the Court in France . . .'

John smiled. 'They were restless years.'

'Lucrative ones too, so I heard,' Gemma said approvingly. 'Old Josh said you'd taken the title to half the land around Flitwick without setting eyes on it. And bought him a house in Soughton too. Him and his mule.'

'Not that he's slept a night in it,' John said. 'The land's further up from Flitwick. Good for nothing but chestnut trees.'

They walked down to the kitchens. A tall figure standing at the copper turned at John's greeting then dropped the ladle he was holding.

'You have remained constant in your talents, Simeon,' John said with a smile. He bent to retrieve the implement and handed it back. 'How is the porridge this morning, Master Cook?'

'Master Saturnall?' Simeon exclaimed. Then he turned to the nearest kitchen boy. 'A bowl! A bowl for Master Saturnall.'

The name brought them running. Mister Bunce gripped his arms and asked if he was truly returned. Mister Stone greeted John from the scullery. Asking after Mrs Gardiner, he was told she had passed away two years earlier. Mister Pouncey had followed a scant week later. Adam Lockyer had married Ginny and now ran the Estate.

'What's left of it,' Philip told John grimly when they sat down together. 'Piers seems to have bequeathed most of it to his vintner.'

Alf had taken orders and was priest at Callock Marwood while Peter Pears supervised the old orchards and Hesekey was Clerk of the Yard. The faces swirled before John, old and new jumbled together. As the breakfast service got under way, the familiar noise of the kitchen surged around him. He took his bowl into Firsts and sat with Mister Bunce whose boys sat in tongue-tied silence around them. As he scooped the last of the porridge from his dish he saw that every cook and under-cook was watching.

'A fine dish,' he pronounced. 'A dish any cook would be proud to serve.'

Smiles broke out. Then, as they turned back to their tasks, John saw Gemma waiting in the doorway.

'Her ladyship will see you.'

———————————

The greasy rouge on her lips smelled of pig fat. The heavy scent she wore filled his nostrils. She took hold of him and pushed him back against the wall. He felt her body's heat through her dress. The musky perfume seemed to grow heavier and sweeter. Then his anger was submerged in desire. The same desire he had felt for the whore in the barn. Her hands pulled at his clothes as he grasped her skirts. She urged him on as he closed with her. She seemed to welcome his rough embraces. Then her limbs were battling his own in a wordless struggle.

When it was over, they dressed in silence. John glanced again at the ancient scenes. Marpot must have uncovered them, he realised. Broken the plaster off with his hammer and found his ancient witch-finder waiting for him. No wonder he had fled. Coldcloak had become Callock. Callock became Fremantle, all of them bound by their oath down the generations to Sir William. Of course the Lord of the Vale of Buckland had known where to send when his wife had sickened. And John's mother had come. She had delivered Lucretia. All this passed through his mind as the young woman watched him, inscrutable behind her mask of smeared powder and rouge. Then his baffled rage rose again. He turned away from her. Kicking open the door, he stumbled down the stairs.

Now Gemma's shoes clopped ahead of him once more, leading him through the dilapidated house. As John walked down the passage to Sir William's receiving room, he felt his heart beat faster. The housekeeper knocked and the door swung open.

Lucretia sat at the walnut table, piles of papers and ledgers rising around her. A few lines had appeared on her forehead. A plain dress was buttoned up to her neck. She still wore the mark of Marpot's blow, the line of her nose broken midway along its length. Behind it her dark eyes watched him.

'You have returned, John Saturnall.'

He had thought of this moment a hundred times. But her imagined face had appeared as a mask, impenetrable as it had been that night.

'I have, your ladyship.' Behind him he sensed Gemma shift awkwardly. 'I would ask that we conduct our conversation in private.'

'I have no secrets from my housekeeper, Master Saturnall.'

Very well, thought John. He stood before her in his fine clothes and boots. And yet he felt as he had the first time, with Abel's filthy blue coat draped about his bony shoulders.

'I made the acquaintance of Master William.'

He saw her hesitate.

'He is your son,' Lucretia said simply.

John stared. But Lucretia merely eyed him across the stacks of papers.

'Piers knew?' he asked at last.

'We never spoke of it.'

The boy rose in his thoughts. Suddenly John wanted to be standing over him again, guiding the boy's arm.

'He will inherit the Manor, your ladyship?'

'What remains of it when Piers's creditors have been paid.' She fixed John with a stony gaze. 'Why have you returned?'

John remembered how his heart had jumped at the news of Piers's death. Then the weeks of indecision. Behind it lay her silence that distant night. Why had she not spoken? The question trembled now on the tip of his tongue. But he looked at the woman who sat stiffly behind the walnut table. Now was not the time. He mustered a smile.

'I regret to say, your ladyship, that I must add another name to the list of your creditors. My own.'

She raised an eyebrow. 'What did my late husband owe you, Master Saturnall? Besides a ride on a stolen horse.'

'The debt is not his, your ladyship. It was incurred long before Lord Piers made himself Master of Buckland. Before there was a Manor, when Buckland was still Bellicca's land. Your ancestor took something from mine.'

Her eyes narrowed. 'What is that? What debt do I owe you?'

He watched her across the crowded table.

'Your ladyship owes me a feast.'

Gemma set up a cot in Mister Pouncey's old chambers. There were plenty of rooms, she explained, now the servants were so few. He ate in the kitchen with the cooks.

'What Piers didn't drink he spent on carriages and clothes,' Simeon told John as they scraped their spoons around the pewter plates. 'Now the cellars are all but empty. I haven't seen a lemon since last summer.'

'Just like old times,' said John. 'You'll be baking Paradise bread next.'

'God forbid,' Simeon said with a shudder. Down the table one of the kitchen boys nudged his companion. John heard a short whispered exchange. Then the boy spoke up.

'Is it true you cooked for the old King, Master Saturnall?'

'I did once,' John answered. 'I ate for him too.'

'And did you serve the King of the Turks a feast?'

'Not him. But once I roasted a sheep for a caliph. Very lean, those Barbary sheep. You have to baste the whole day through.'

'And the King of France, Master Saturnall? Is that true?'

'Cream and more cream,' John answered. 'Jellies so stiff they must be cut with Saracen swords. One time the carver became stuck mid-slice . . .'

He told tall tales to the kichen boys and talked with Philip, or Adam, or Mister Bunce or Ben Martin. As the weather grew colder, louring clouds began advancing over the Levels. John walked long circuits of the house, lingering about the old well, wondering if the boy whose elbow he had held might walk up to him again. But Will Callock seemed only ever to appear in the distance, speeding across a garden or racing up a hillside. Returning to the kitchen, John's eyes drifted to the passage that led past the bakehouse and the still room, back into the depths of the kitchens to the chambers where Scovell had lived and his mother had worked. Now, Gemma told him, Lucretia laboured there. If he wants his feast, her mistress had exclaimed after John's demand, then he shall have it. And on Old Saint Andrew's Day too.

'She intends to prepare the dishes herself,' Gemma told him. 'I offered my help but she insisted. Master Simeon too but she refused. Not even a scullion would aid her, she said. She will do all with her own hands, she says. Though in truth . . .' Gemma broke off.

'In truth?' John prompted.

'In truth,' Gemma said, 'she doesn't know one end of a spoon from the other.'

The snows were due, Philip warned him. They would have his horse saddled and ready. Otherwise he would be immured in Buckland until spring. The days passed. On the morning, John washed in a bowl that one of the new maids brought and dressed carefully, tying laces and fastening buckles. Trying to pull a comb through his hair, he felt the ridge left by the musket ball. Philip appeared in the doorway.

'Fit for a king,' he said, looking John over and tugging at his collar. 'Why the long face? Are you not slavering for Lady Lucy's dishes?'

He sat waiting, counting the seconds and minutes, rehearsing what he might say. Her stubborn silence that night. Taking Piers. He believed he understood now. At last the bell sounded for dinner. Then he rose and walked through the house. The serving men he passed touched their caps to him. The maids curtsied. Crossing the knot-garden courtyard he looked up at a gun-metal sky. As he climbed the stairs, his legs felt heavy.

The Solar Gallery was draped with hangings. Glancing out through the windows he saw the hedges of the East Garden. Then a movement caught his eye. A small figure appeared to materialise from inside one of the hedges, a scarf wrapped about his neck against the cold. John watched Will Callock leap the next hedge and run over the lawn. Suddenly an old man emerged. Mister Motte gave a shout and lumbered after the boy.

'Run,' murmured John.

The boy sped away, soon outpacing the aged figure. John smiled, looking after Will until he disappeared then scanning the East Garden. The glass-house still stood, he saw, its frames inviting repair. Pineapples and peaches would grow there, he thought. Fat grapes and persimmons. Above, the clouds appeared to settle more heavily. The outer yard would close the next day, Philip had told him. The stable hands would have his horse ready as promised. He looked along the gallery to the door at the end. Despite himself, he felt his heart begin to thud.

The room was as he remembered it, except the curtains had been drawn and tied back and every object had been dusted and cleaned. A fire burned in the grate and two chairs stood before it. But the little table had been set for one. As he glanced at the bed, he heard the latch to the kitchen stair click. What if he had not fallen through the doorway to sprawl before her in a heap? To look up and see her sharp face peering down . . . Footsteps sounded.

Lucretia entered carrying a tray. She wore her hair in plaits, he saw. But her dress was as plain as before. He made a little bow.

'Good day, Lady Lucretia.'

'Good day, Master Saturnall.'

A flowery scent hung about her. Rose water, he realised. She deposited the tray on the bed and began to arrange the dishes. Picking up a pitcher, she turned to him with a stony expression.

'Sit.'

John sat.

'The Feast began with spiced wine,' she said. 'If I recall it correctly.'

John nodded. 'Flavoured with saffron and cinnamon and mace,' he said. 'And roasted dates, your ladyship.'

'Your recollection is remarkable, Master Saturnall,' she answered as she poured. 'But my own memory differs, when you served this cup to me.'

He drank, and tasted water. Inwardly, he smiled.

'The wine was followed by forcemeats, I believe,' Lucretia continued. 'Of a swan? Then a goose, then a duck . . .'

He remembered the words he had murmured in her ear. The elaborate descriptions for the plain fare he had mustered. Now he would be the one to listen and taste. She spooned out thick gobbets from a little pot. Mashed swedes, John realised. He looked up.

'Eat,' Lucretia commanded.

She served him boiled skirrets, steamed salt-fish, a kind of porridge and dried apple-rings soaked in verjus. He sat stiffly in the chair. He chewed and swallowed while Lucretia stood before him. At last, he put down his spoon.

'Are the dishes not to your liking, Master Saturnall?'

John regarded the platters and salvers. He imagined her clumsy efforts amidst the pots and pans. Boiling and mashing and scrubbing and peeling. How had she imagined this encounter? Suddenly he could maintain his silence no longer.

'You drove me out,' he said. 'That was your purpose.'

Looking up, he saw shock bloom in her face.

'I did not understand it, not for a long time after. The first time I spoke of the Feast you already knew the story. You knew but you kept silent. Why? I asked you and you would not answer. But that silence was a lie, wasn't it? It was meant to deceive me. To provoke my anger. For there was a better question I might have asked you that night.'

She stood before him, silent, her face impassive. Only her dark eyes moved, taking him in.

'Why did you confess? That was the question you feared. Why did you choose that night to tell me what you knew? Almost the eve of your wedding. You could rely on my anger, could you not? On that hot coal I carried inside me. I had told you of it after all. And sure enough my anger blinded me. As you knew it would.' He looked up at her. 'But little by little the mists of my anger cleared. I thought again on what you had told me. He was called Coldcloak, you said. He came here when the Romans went home. He swore an oath to God and he broke Bellicca's tables. He stole the fires from her hearths and fled down the Vale. He came here. That much you said. But there was more, was there not?'

Lucretia's nod was almost imperceptible.

'He swore an oath to destroy her works,' John said. 'But he planted her orchards here. He kept Bellicca's fires burning in his hearths. He remembered the Feast as best he could. And he raised a tower that he might look out over the Vale. Why?'

'To stand sentinel against her,' Lucretia said. 'Because he feared her enchantment . . .'

'Why should he preserve her gardens?' John interrupted. 'Or the fires in her hearths? Why should he seek to keep her Feast? Or build a tower to watch for the glow of her hearth? You know the answer. You knew it that night. Why?'

Lucretia shook her head slowly. But her eyes would not meet his own.

'He loved her,' John said. 'Despite his oath. Despite all he had done. And you always knew it. Because you too loved the one you could not have. Because the same oath bound you.'

Lucretia turned away towards the window. Outside, snowflakes were falling, tumbling down out of the sky. 'I fear you will have to curtail your supper, Master Saturnall,' she said, her face averted. 'The roads are no better than they were before. The least fall will block them . . .'

'You confessed that night to rid yourself of me,' John interrupted. 'You dressed like a whore to drain my desire and drive me away. You denied me. And you denied those sentiments which you declared for me. Just as your ancestor did to Bellicca. You lied to me and you lied to yourself . . .'

But at that she rounded on him, turning from the window, her hand knocking a bowl off the tray.

'I did not lie!' she burst out. 'I could not bear it! Can you not understand? I could not bear to have you close and not to touch you. I could not suffer the sight of you at his beck and call.' She glared down at him, her jaw set, her breath coming fast. 'If I had guessed those humiliations he would devise for me perhaps I would have gone with you. But I did not guess. At first my promise held me here. Later my child did the same. Yours and mine. Yes, I drove you away. I employed a subterfuge and I own to my fault. I whored myself to drive you off. I own that too. Now you reappear after a dozen years and demand that I repay my debt. Now I have sweated in a kitchen, John Saturnall. I have cooked your feast.' She pointed angrily to the half-eaten dish before him. 'Now eat it and go!'

John stared up at her. He had prepared his speech in his head so many times. And he had imagined its end in as many ways. But none of them were this one. Under her angry gaze, he picked up his spoon and dipped it in the nearest dish.

'Well?' she demanded.

Turnip, he thought. Set off with verjus and butter. He swallowed and Lucretia gave a stern nod.

'Does that satisfy you, Master Saturnall?'

'It does, your ladyship.'

'Then eat the remainder and go.'

John scooped another spoonful off the dish. Outside the snow was falling faster. A thin layer had already settled. He chewed slowly, as if savouring the dull mash.

'You will have to hurry,' Lucretia said, and this time John fancied he heard her voice soften. He looked up from the plate.

'And not savour these dishes as they deserve?'

She gave him a sceptical look.

'Do they merit savouring?'

'They do, your ladyship. Most assuredly.'

Did a flicker of pleasure pass across her features? He spooned again and swallowed.

'You are dilatory, Master Saturnall. One might almost think you reluctant to clear your plate.'

'Reluctant? I can eat no faster, your ladyship.' He paused mid-chew as if a thought had just struck him. 'Perhaps if someone were to share this pleasurable task?'

'Share it?'

He rose and pulled out the second chair.

'If it pleases you, Lady Lucretia, might you sit with me?'

He felt as he had when they had gathered chestnuts together, as if he were venturing out over a frozen pond and each step might see the ice crack beneath him. Outside, the snow whirled down, falling thicker and thicker on the broken panes of the glass-house. Lucretia's dark eyes searched his face as they had when he had leaned over her in her chamber, the sweet smells of baked apple and cream mixing with the scent of her skin. This was how she had seen him, he thought. In her chamber.

He waited. Slowly, she sat.

'Are these dishes truly to your liking?' Lucretia asked.

'No dish has ever tasted sweeter,' he said.

'I can hardly credit such flattery, John Saturnall.'

'It is not flattery, your ladyship. It is true.'

Taking up a spoonful, John leaned across the table.

'Taste.'

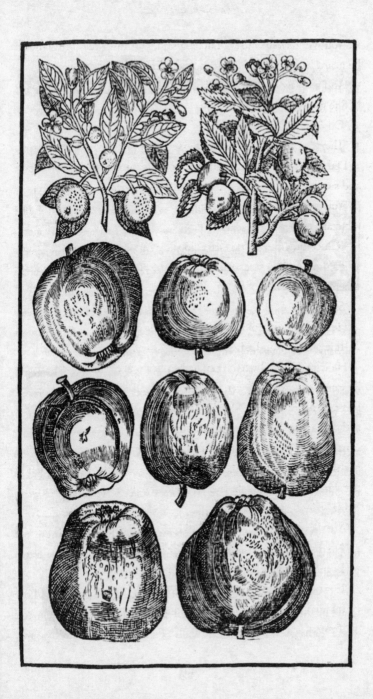

From *The Book of John Saturnall*: A *Last Feast* for those *First Men* and *Women*

aturnus's Gardens were uprooted and his Tables broken. His Feast was lost as I have told. But nothing, the Alchemists tell us, does vanish entire. Every Year, the sweet Waters of the Levels persist beneath the Flood of sour Brine. Each Spring the Tables of Green do rise from beneath the Vale's winter Snows. Each Substance persists, even if it yields to Smoke or Soot; every clumsy Cook knows the Same. For outward Forms may change yet the Essence remain.

These are weighty Matters for a Cook to peruse, who better sweats above a Pot than a Page. But just so does Saturnus's Feast endure, as I will tell.

An Apple was all Eve served to Adam. But that was a Feast all the Same. I have served rich Banquets to Kings and seen a Rabbit on a Stick nourish a Packhorse Driver. I have sensed the rarest Dishes in the Smoke of the meanest Fire, its Flames scarce brave enough to warm the Bones of a Boy and his mother.

A Cook is not apart, as I once was told. And the Feast is not his alone, as I once believed. Now my own Affections advise me better. Now a second Adam pays Court to his Eve.

Now he would serve her as he did once before and, if her Love for Him should suffice, she may sweat above a Pot and serve him too. The Depths of Winter are the Walls of their Garden where they may sit in Amity together. And, if the old God smiles, they may share those Affections that they were wont to do when their World was young, this new-restored Adam and his dark-eyed Eve.

So I have learned, and each Year do that Lesson renew, when she and I together keep the Saturnall Feast.

John Saturnall. Written in the Year of our Lord, Sixteen Hundred and Eighty.

ACKNOWLEDGEMENTS

This book has taken a long and strange route to publication. I would like to offer my thanks to all those who have supported and encouraged me along the way.

Many authors and books opened vistas for me on the seventeenth century and its cooking but my friend Kate Colquhoun's *Taste: The Story of Britain Through its Cooking* was the first. Among the others, I would like to acknowledge *The Closet of Sir Kenelm Digby Opened* (1669), a work of passionate and encyclopedic eccentricity, and Robert May's *The Accomplisht Cook* (1660) which is the Mrs Beeton of the seventeenth century. Hilary Spurling's edition of *Elinor Fettiplace's Receipt Book* (1604 and 1986) is a wonderful practical resource and, in the far culinary background, so is Andrew Dalby's *Siren Feasts* (1996). Interesting salads were found in John Evelyn's *Acetaria* (1699) and almost everything else in Gervase Markham's *The English Housewife* (1615).

More specific thanks are due to many colleagues and friends, in particular to A. S. Byatt (for witchcraft and dolls), to David Mitchell (for synoptic exchanges), to David Moore of Pied-à-Terre (for letting on how kitchens really work), to Doug Seibold (for advice on reductions) and to Emma Soundy (for Elinor Fettiplace). At Bloomsbury, in order of appearance, Alexa von Hirschberg, Alexandra Pringle, Gillian Stern and Mary Tomlinson together transformed my part-baked creation into one fit for the table. My thanks to them for their help and advice; rare and tireless book-cooks all.

My greatest debts go back the longest. My mother, Shirley Blake, not only cooked many meals for me but also taught me to cook. Without her this book could not have been conceived. My agent, Carole Blake, told me to get on with it; her belief, loyalty and encouragement sustained me throughout the writing of these pages. Lastly, to my wife, Vineeta Rayan, who scooped me off the kitchen floor and whose faith restored my own, I would like to offer my heartfelt gratitude and my love. If I write – or cook – for anyone, it is for her.